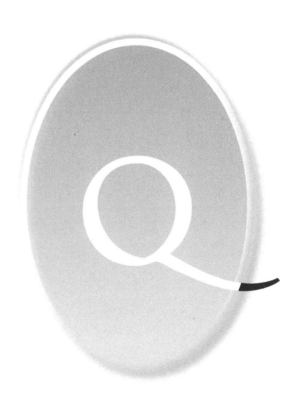

By

BILL HUGHES

In memory of Kathryn Ann Hughes (1922-2009)

HISTORICAL BACKGROUND

The spirituality of multitudes rests between the covers of perhaps the most scrutinized book in history of Western civilization, the New Testament. The Gospels of Mark, Matthew, Luke, and John are our only source of information regarding the life and ministry of Jesus of Nazareth. Biblical scholars believe the Gospel of Mark was written first, in approximately 65 AD, thirty-five years after Jesus's death. The Gospels of Matthew and Luke are dated at 80–85 AD. The similarity in story lines suggests the authors of Matthew and Luke used the Gospel of Mark as a source. In addition, there are verses of Luke and Matthew that do not appear in Mark, in which the wording is identical or nearly identical. A good example is Matthew 7:1, "Do not judge, or you too will be judged," compared with Luke 6:37, "Judge not, and ye shall not be judged." Similarities like this make it a near certainty that these authors plagiarized another written document in addition to Mark. Scholars refer to this document as "Q," short for the German word Quelle, which means source.

Q has been lost to history.

PART 1

CHAPTER ONE

HARVARD UNIVERSITY
Saturday, September 1, 2001, 8:30 p.m.

Julian St. Laurent stopped to savor the moment. Harvard Yard––a warm bath of familiarity––churned with students and revelers two days before the start of classes. Around him high-fives heralded the awkward embraces of old acquaintances renewed. An unintelligible prattle bandied over the crowd.

The thick heat of late summer shrouded the square. Julian's eyes curled over the horde, stopping to watch and assess like a bird-watcher during an early morning stroll. Nearby stood two guys, one whose beverage of choice appeared to be gravy, and another in high khakis, both trying way too hard to have fun. Next to them, three guys with "I'm-trashed" grins above rock band T-shirts coolly assessed the throng. A few others looked as though they'd jumped out of a dumpster, or maybe they were fresh out of detox. All mixed together in a stew of insecurity.

Vibrato guitar riffs echoed off the aged, tradition-encrusted stone edifices and collided with the rising mirth. Julian had no clue about the song. What he remembered was Crosby, Stills, Nash and Young from twenty years before, back when he concerned himself with heavy amounts of alcohol ingestion and way too much pizza, and ended up driving the white porcelain bus till sunrise. A time when a 2 a.m. critique on the musical genius of John Lennon and *The White Album*, played backward, was considered a middle of the day activity and when his life goal was singular in nature––an unencumbered path to a C-cup.

Every year the students grew younger; hell, he had underwear as old as they were. The raucous crowd pretended they were reinventing the wheel, but Julian, always harnessed to his boneyard past, saw himself with his brother, Maxwell, and his best friend, Cooper, doing the same stuff back in the day. He had recollections of forty pounds of Tide being dumped into the Tanner Fountain. He also remembered an assortment of ass-kissing, PBS-spouting fellow students with enough bull to sink a Grateful Dead-stickered VW bus. Fond memories mixed with the bitter ones. In the semi-darkness, he felt a faint flush course through his body like a double shot of finely blended Kentucky bourbon. He still relished the start of a new semester.

Julian startled at the sound of his name, then jerked his head to avoid a dayglow Frisbee. He offered a chin nod to a vaguely familiar last-semester student and proceeded across the yard. Minutes later, he entered University Hall. The marbled steps, worn smooth in the middle and brown with age, led to Dean Wistrom's office.

Julian knew that pivotal moments littered the landscape of every life. He intuited this night was one of those times. For the antiquities professor, things were finally rounding into shape. He had a newly published book and a new love––an amazing young woman, Karlie. But as good as life felt, it was impossible to forget the hardships that had trooped through his life. During his early years, those that define a person, he thought he would never ascend out of his circumstance, a series of squalid addresses at the lower end of Southie. It was fitting that his vindication––full tenure––would occur in such hallowed halls. After a soft knock, he entered and sauntered across a worn but brightly patterned area rug, Tibetan cobblestone, on his way into the main office. The design reminded him of confetti.

"Julian, come in," said Dean Wistrom. A tangle of gray-flecked hair, narrow-set eyes, and a composed mouth bathed in the glow of a computer screen. A surgical gaze met Julian's eyes. "Thank you for coming on such short notice." His voice was an intriguing blend of the Australian outback hiding behind the *R*-deficient dialect from twenty-some years of living in Boston. The dean stood up from behind the rosewood desk, extended his hand in greeting, then motioned him toward a chair.

Caught off guard by his friend's officious demeanor, Julian offered a tentative smile. "No problem, James. Good to see you again." He positioned himself in one of two leather-winged chairs.

The dean pushed the laptop computer aside. "We haven't spoken for what…three months…four months. How have you been, have a good summer?"

"Excellent. Things are good." Julian waited for Wistrom's incisive stare to melt. His fabricated smile was unconvincing.

"Congratulations on your publication. Second book?"

The corners of Julian's mouth moved up in acknowledgement. "Seemed more difficult than the first."

His friend nodded knowingly. The smile disappeared. "We go back a long way, so I'll cut to the chase."

A knot tightened in Julian's chest, like someone was trying to shove a grapefruit down his throat.

"I've always taken a special interest in you, Julian. All you have accomplished, especially after such a rough start in life. I've celebrated your successes." He paused. "I appreciate all you have done for the university."

Julian's brow cooled. He searched the dean's face.

Dean Wistrom continued. "The reputation of Harvard University is paramount, and usurps all else." He chose his words carefully. "A video came across my desk today."

The university magistrate turned the laptop toward Julian. On the computer screen, mesmerizing jade-green eyes, drunk with passion, stared back at him. His eyes jerked from the screen to his friend then back to the screen. He recognized the situation: the conclusion of a candle-light dinner at his house––AUG 24, 2001, was embossed the bottom.

"You need to see this," said Dean Wistrom, not the least bit embarrassed by the visual.

He clicked the mouse. Karlie's head drifted up and then eased down; her forehead glistened faintly though strands of honey-streaked hair. Her lips, engaged in a silent chant, animated a visage that was otherwise exhausted. The camera panned down to her chest, lingered, and then drew back, showing her surrounded by candles, flickering agitated flames, straddling in the intimate act. A bronze thigh, defined and taut, shackled the body beneath. She arched her back like an erotic gymnast on the high beam; her hands crept over her stomach toward her dew-covered breasts. There they

5

remained, but not still. Tiny prisms summoned the surrounding candlelight then danced off her abdomen, stretched tight, synchronous with the carefully choreographed ritual.

No doubt existed about the identity of Karlie's lover.

The clip lasted a minute or so; it seemed like an hour.

Julian's mind raced: a confused matrix of embarrassed arousal, mixed with an awareness of what it would all mean.

The dean sealed the computer, then secured it away in a desk drawer hidden from Julian's view.

"I understand this woman's name is Karlie Reynolds, an undergraduate. Last semester, she was one of your students."

Julian nodded, then wiggled awkwardly in the seat. Blood bounded through the empty shell of his body, then back. "How did you get it?"

"E-mail attachment. Perhaps another suitor. Perhaps someone in the university, jealous of your success. Who knows? It is now in the public domain. That is all that matters."

Res ipsa loquitur. The thing speaks for itself. Julian had no defense.

"You are aware of our mandates," said the dean. "We are entrusted to educate…and protect. You are also aware of our code of conduct. Perception is crucial. How we––the university––respond to situations like these is vital. She's an adult and clearly consenting. Unfortunately, that is immaterial." The dean paused. "I would consider this a significant lapse in judgment, Julian."

Julian listened, but he didn't hear. The ramifications and repercussions stabbed at his brain as if trying to thaw the still frozen visual. He knew what was coming. A bleak contemplation it was with twenty years at Harvard and full tenure so close. He'd be damaged goods in the eyes of the young woman whose love had seemed, just moments before, the thing that made his life complete––the sunrise to his life's cool night. Now what was his future? Bankrupt, gone like a vapor: judged and convicted. And there'd be nary a ripple in the zeitgeist.

Julian's grim reverie was shattered by the quiet. He knew he should say something, but what was there to say? He struggled to move beyond Wistrom's devastating moral judgment, to grasp for some straw of procedure.

"I assume there is a process." His eyes drifted to the window behind his boss, landing on the tangled forest of people in the Yard.

"Of course. Until then, you'll be on a leave of absence. Paid, of course. I should know more by Tuesday. We will take care of your class schedule for the fall semester."

Dean Wistrom stood. The meeting was over.

"I'm sorry, Julian. I won't forget our history." He extended his hand.

Julian left University Hall and was halfway across the Yard before a student's incidental bump jarred him from his stupor. Nameless, faceless bodies, jazzed on Red Bull, jostled about the court. The lick of ZZ Top power chords ricocheted around him loudly, like a cat with its tail caught in a fan. Dazed, he wove his way through a network of reluctant fireflies at the periphery of the square for a few moments of sanctuary in the nearby Appleton Chapel. He paused in the shadow of the church's ghostly pale lights. The glow of his new love and recent successes faded to black. He thought back to his time spent at the children's home with Sister Mary Beth. He searched for her soothing countenance. Julian considered a thousand moments of his life and recalled the times he had saved and remade it with his imagination and his fortitude. He felt incapable of drawing his sword yet again.

Julian reached for the church door handle and hesitated. His gaze settled on a bronze crucifix mounted over the thick oak entry as he thought again of the spiritual succor of his youth and then of Job's tribulations. His hand levitated; its fine tremor was magnified in the stillness. Ten seconds passed, then slowly he drew back.

Cooper. He let his buddy's name percolate for a moment, then retrieved his cell phone and punched in the reverend's number. The phone found the bottom of his pocket before Coop's voice trailed off at the end of the message.

Minutes later, Julian wandered along JFK Street and ended up in front of Doma Liquors. After that, sitting alone in an obscure shadow of the university and looking out over the Charles River, he let loose the Old Kentucky on the back of his throat.

Chapter Two

Saturday, September 1, 2001, 8:30 p.m.

Cooper Saltonstall blinked away his confusion. A bomber's moon stood a hand's width above the horizon. Apparitions stretched out in the distance, shadows cast by celestial light onto the sepia landscape of the rail yard. The atmosphere was dense, humid with the pungent scent of creosote rising from the railroad ties. The iron rails felt cool against his wrists.

"Cooper, it's not complicated," said the Reverend Theodore Phillips. "Just tell me where you hid it."

Blackness softened the three shapes standing over him, making them dark like the reflection off of wet asphalt. The chloroform fog in his head slowly drifted into the sticky night air; he wrestled with the moment.

"Preacher man, your collar is crooked," said Cooper.

The cleric reached toward the fleshy folds of his neck and made a lame attempt to adjust his already straight neckband. "Just plain Teddy P. works for me," he said, the Boston Brahmin evident in his voice.

A year ago at the church Founder's Day celebration was the last time he had seen Teddy P. A more rotund version now stood over him.

"You already know Quincy," said Teddy P. "This is Wee-man. Don't let the fact that he is vertically challenged fool you; he's a scrappy little guy."

A golf tee dangled from Wee-man's lip. Some sort of growth––walnut-sized––drooped from the side of his neck. A snakehead, etched in black ink, branded his left bicep like a netted cantaloupe. He grunted "hello" and picked at his fingernails.

"Hard to imagine your prayers getting more than six feet off the ground," said Cooper.

A smile nipped at the corner of Teddy P.'s mouth. "Just dealing with an ethical issue or two."

"You've got to be exhausted from the struggle…" Cooper paused for a reaction. He squinted through the lingering haze in his mind. "Dexion Society?"

"You've done your homework." The unfinished smile disappeared. His shoulders stiffened, belying the indifference in his voice.

"Part of the Episcopalian hierarchy?"

"No. Nondenominational. A governing body."

"Sounds nice and sterile. And under the smokescreen of piety. Must make you feel good about what you do." Cooper recalled Teddy P.'s propensity for anger; he waited. "And your job is…"

"To keep the secret." Teddy P. waved at a pesky mosquito.

The brim of a black fedora was slung low over Teddy P.'s face. A crooked nose angled from his bloated mug. The image reminded Cooper of a certain aged pugilist at the end of his career; the name wouldn't come to him.

"What happened to you, Teddy P.?"

"Religion is big business. Have to maintain the bottom line."

Cooper gave him a studied look; he hesitated before he spoke. "So you're the nabob of silence."

"Hate to bequeath the unsuspecting masses with more information than they need."

Cooper shot a glance at his bound arms, then scrutinized Teddy P. again. Dread's prickly fingers moved into his shoulders, then his neck. "And you're a killer?"

"Purveyor of accidents."

"Serendipity." Cooper made an effort to wring the fear out of his voice.

"Exactly. Car wrecks, house fires, things like that."

"Getting run over by a train."

"An extremely unfortunate suicide."

"With ropes?"

"Quincy will get rid of those." Teddy P. remained stone-faced, rapt in thought. "The winners write history, Cooper."

A plan stumbled over the turmoil in Cooper's mind. He took his eyes to the next person.

"Quincy, haven't seen you around lately," he said to his former choirboy.

Quincy's eyes were still and watchful. He looked lost, like a child on his first day at a new school.

"Sorry, sir." Quincy was the kind of kid who tacked "sir" onto the end of his sentences.

"Like LL Cool J," said Cooper.

"What?"

"Licking your lips."

"Yes, sir." A lopsided grin filled the face of the taciturn young man.

"I thought I got you straightened out."

"I tried, Reverend Saltonstall…sir."

Cooper surveyed the area from his splayed position on the tracks of the Boston rail yard. The gossamer-tailed mayflies danced circles around a dopey luna moth near a security light fifty feet away. Next to him, the corroded hulk of a boxcar stood sentinel, the sides branded by years of service. Rust feasted on the edges. The "Nichol Plate" logo was barely visible–– from wear and from the dark. The wheels, burnished surfaces pitted with use, served as a billboard for his impending doom. Car headlights flared on the nearby interstate like fireflies on crystal meth. Night was happening everywhere.

"I'm amazed that you stumbled upon the papyrus," said Teddy. "I was sure that proof would never be found. Only conjectures based on rumors."

Cooper ignored Teddy P.'s drivel and his glare. He considered his options. A welcome breeze appeared out of nowhere on its way to someplace else; the smell of diesel tagged along. Crickets scratched communiqués. The hum of his cell phone interrupted their messages and his thoughts. His right arm jerked in response, then relaxed.

Teddy P. smiled and waited for the last ring. "Who else knows about the document?"

"Nobody."

"Surely you told Julian. Had him read it for you."

"He knows nothing. I swear. May God be my witness."

Teddy P. gave Wee-man a chin nod, then received an affirmative dip of the small man's head.

"No, not Julian." He tried to raise his arms. His wrists snapped back to the rails like a magnet to steel.

"Then tell me, where is it?"

A chill coursed through Cooper's body. His resolve choked on doubt. *God give me strength.* After several moments, the sudden fear exhausted itself. He lowered his head to the cinders, confident in his faith and acceptant of his fate. Teddy P. would never find the document. Perhaps someday, in a different time, another poor soul would happen upon it and realize its damning significance, then wrestle with indecision. For the first time in nearly a decade, he no longer felt a weight on his shoulders. *Forgive me, Julian.* The vibrations grew stronger. His time was near.

Teddy P. took a few steps to his right, stooped down face-to-face, and pulled on the ropes. His right eye gave an anxious twitch. "If even a whiff of illegitimacy gets out, a sad morrow will be in reserve for both of us. The bedrock of Christianity cannot be challenged––ever."

"My dilemma for nearly a decade," said Cooper.

"Ambivalence regarding truth versus perception?"

"My priority is the spiritual health of my brethren. It provides an anchor for people's lives. Their bedrock."

"What changed?"

"Didn't want the covenant to die with me." It came out as a scratchy whisper.

"You foresaw this." Teddy P. made a sweeping motion with his hand. "Your own demise."

"Call it a feeling."

Teddy P. stood, turned, and looked down the track. "Coop, the train is coming. Talk. Now."

"And you'll let me go? You'll leave Julian out of this?" He searched the cleric's face for a sign of acquiescence. "I doubt it."

Teddy P. smiled, but didn't answer.

"It's really just a matter of timing anyway. That's the whole point of what we do, isn't it? Redirect the focus from the here and now to the there and then: freedom from the fear of death."

"You've never had doubts about the existence of God?" asked Teddy P.

"Never. Even if I did, it's always better to err on the side of caution, to believe. Remember Pascal's wager."

The reverend nodded a couple of times, his features tightened. "Rest assured, we'll find it."

"Unlikely." Cooper felt the prick of a mosquito on his right forearm, then watched it impregnate itself with blood. "I guess I won't see you in his Kingdom."

Teddy P. hesitated, his defiance replaced by a split-second look of doubt. Then his eyes locked onto Cooper's. "Perhaps not." He paused. "Last chance."

Cooper glared through Teddy P., then let the moment linger. "Go to hell."

Teddy P. hesitated only a moment. "Very well." He touched his right hand to the brim of his hat, turned, and plodded off into the darkness; Quincy and Wee-man fell in close behind.

Cooper's eyes followed them until they became shadows, and then he lifted his head and looked down the track---the beacon of the train drew closer. A funnel of light filled night's canvas. Seconds passed. The stillness grew. Vast, star-speckled darkness stretched before him like a huge black hole. He felt tiny and without consequence. His bravado vanished.

He looked left at the wheels on the fugitive freight car. A nightmare--- wheels crushing his body---nipped at his mind. He felt the squeeze on his chest, the moment of overwhelming pain, the moment of his last breath, and the fleeting moment just before the final moment. Then, with abandon, he flailed for his life. The hemp pulled tight. The burning in his wrists and ankles singed his mind. He prayed and made promises that were impossible to keep.

The vibrations were strong, unmistakable. Another tremor coursed through his body. His arms and legs tensed hard, ready for the blow. He opened his mouth and tightened his jaw, then sucked in the mugginess with deep breaths in and out. *Don't look.* The train's vibrations shot from his wrist to his brain, growing stronger; the train was closer yet. A sticky breeze slipped by and took him back to a summer night on the rooftop of the children's home, with Maxwell and Julian looking at the stars and wondering where their lives would lead them. A sudden surge in the vibrations annihilated the fleeting thought. He felt dizzy, numb. He jerked his legs side to side, his arms up and down, back and forth. His muscles burned. Then, he went limp. With reticence, he prayed.

A soft sound––shoe against gravel––bent through the sultry evening air. A winded Quincy stooped low beside him. Cooper smelled the young man's panic.

"I'm sorry, Reverend Saltonstall, sir."

They swapped nervous glances.

Sweat dotted Quincy's brow. The glint of steel raised overhead, came from a knife held high. Suddenly the image blurred, and the stiletto plunged down. Only a few fibers of the rope parted. Frantically, Quincy worked the knife back and forth. His head twitched up every few seconds. Neither spoke. Panic morphed to terror. Cooper's right leg broke free.

"Quincy, my arms. Free my arms!"

The young man bounced up and assumed a position over Cooper's head, facing the locomotive's urgent approach. The horn sounded. Screeching brakes smothered the noise of the nearby causeway.

"Settle down, Quincy; you're doing fine," Reverend Saltonstall's voice was steady, reassuring.

Right arm free. "Good job, Quincy."

The photons of light shot out of the oncoming train, slicing around the light poles, forming jagged skeletons on the surrounding train cars.

Fifty yards away.

Night was now day. Cooper's heart raced. His mouth was dry, like sawdust had lodged in his throat. His left bicep burned and glistened with sweat. Quincy grunted. The savage assault on the recalcitrant binding continued.

Forty yards.

The death knell from the brakes echoed as loud as thunder. The whistle blared an ominous warning that went unheeded.

Left arm free. Not enough time.

"Quincy! Get out. Save yourself!"

Quincy looked up, his face gripped with indecision. He waited a beat, then jumped left and staggered. Cooper sat up and instinctively rolled to his left.

Twenty yards.

Cooper's right leg flipped over the rail into Quincy's shins, knocking him off balance.

Ten yards.

Quincy teetered forward and sprawled over the rail, his hand on the railroad tie.

Seven yards.

The noise—screeching combined with train's horn—created a bewildering maelstrom. Quincy pushed off the rail with his left hand, with the knife still in his right.

Five yards.

Cooper, lying next to the tracks, hugged the gravel and prayed.

A whoosh––like a giant wave hitting the sand–– preceded the impact by a fraction of a second. The cowcatcher slammed into Quincy's leg at thirty miles per hour. His body did a 360 and landed between Cooper and the dilapidated freight car. The tension on the rope binding Cooper's left leg eased, snapped by the wheel. Astonished by the reprieve, Cooper rolled over and looked up. Supine, Quincy laid next to him, a knife impaled in the middle of his chest at a curious angle.

"Oh my God. No!"

Cooper reached under the shoulders of his Good Samaritan and wrenched him away from the train. He seized the knife handle and pulled. He looked for respirations, checked for a pulse in Quincy's neck, and then stood upright in search for his cell phone. At that moment, a gunshot exploded from the shadows; its report buried in the chaos. The bullet slammed into the back of Cooper's left shoulder with the force of a middle linebacker. He spun forward, with his mouth wide-open and his left arm extended between two of the passing rail cars.

Chapter Three

BOSTON RAIL YARD
Saturday, September 1, 2001, 11:45 p.m.

Maxwell St. Laurent, a homicide detective with the Boston Police Department, surveyed the rail yard scene. Tired gray-green eyes jerked between the two bodies, then to a head six feet away. Bright spotlights stood guard; they grew out of the inky blackness on pedestals like curious giraffes alerted to a ruckus. Yellow tape segregated the bodies and the vagrant boxcar. The medical examiner and his crime-scene minions plucked at the ground like gaggle of under-medicated barnyard chickens.

"Maxwell." Julian approached from the darkness. The gravel broadcasted each step, like a kid on Bubble Wrap.

Maxwell turned the red four-battery Coleman toward the noise. The visual made him wince. Julian's forty-plus years looked sixty. The dark hollows under his eyes and the creases chiseled into Julian's forehead looked like canyons, magnified in the shadows cast by the light beam. A crop of unruly beef-stew-colored hair looked as though it hadn't seen a comb in days. The knot of his tie hung three buttons down his teak-colored shirt; his shirttail hung out on one side.

"You look like crap," Maxwell greeted his brother. "Vodka win?"

"Bourbon," came the terse reply, his voice slurring.

Maxwell stared at his brother, concerned. "Thanks for coming."

"Thought you said suicide," said Julian, his gaze arrested by the sight of the bodies.

"That was the original call-in. Two stiffs." He paused to scan the scene. "I guess not."

* * *

Julian surveyed the area, watching the men at work. A wave of nausea gripped his stomach, followed by a deep gnawing sensation. An incipient headache clawed at his brain. He mumbled, "I figured he would be the last, not the first."

"Max," said the medical examiner, "I'm..." He stopped midsentence and looked at Max, then Julian. The rake-thin redhead made rococo gestures and bounced on the balls of his feet as he spoke. He looked like a pogo stick with red hair.

Max said, "This is––"

"––you," finished Pogo.

"My brother, Julian," said Max.

"Identical," said Pogo.

"Hell, I don't look that bad, do I?" said Max.

Julian extended his hand and nodded.

Pogo shook Julian's hand. "Your brother said you'd be the next of kin."

"After Jesus." Julian hesitated and looked at Maxwell. "He's unavailable."

"I need Julian to look at something," said Max. He glanced at his brother then back to the bodies. "You knew Coop better than anybody. I need you to check out his tattoos, and tell me what you think."

Julian took in a deep breath. Even in his drunken stupor, he could feel the air. He loved the thick part of summer, late in the season, with the hazy humidity and the bugs. Studying his brother, he thought about how little interaction they'd had over the past twenty years. He tried to recall the last time he'd offered Max more than a nod or a simple hello. He couldn't. Prior to that, there were plenty of good times. He remembered back to when he and Max and Cooper had crawled under the fence, at a place not too far from where he was standing, and put cans and other paraphernalia on the track so they could watch the trains smash the stuff. Julian's thoughts shifted back to the events at hand. His friend for life was dead.

"Didn't know priests did body art," said Julian.

"Never mentioned it to you?"

"I talked to him after the ten thirty service on Sunday. Same old Coop." Julian looked at the insects battering themselves into the spotlights. "This wasn't a suicide, Max. Not Cooper. Not now."

Max and Julian swapped weary glances, each searching for solace in the other's eyes.

"His pocket," said Max, pointing to the corpse, "had a bunch of stuff."

Julian's opaque eyes brightened slightly.

"Some roofies, cell phones, computer chips..."

Stymied by the tragedy and the alcohol, Julian had no answer. His thoughts tripped over regret, both for business unfinished and friendship lost. "The only bodies I see are two thousand years old."

"I really need your brain."

"What happened?"

"He was laid out on the track. Train couldn't stop. Engineer's a geezer. And a basket case, not much help." Maxwell's features relaxed in a moment of insight. "No."

"No, what?" Julian was confused and irritated at his brother's monosyllabic communication style.

"It's not related to Billie Ray Roux."

"How'd you know...never mind." Julian shook his head.

"That was a lifetime ago. Has to be something else."

Julian thought back to the episode ten years before––with Maxwell and Cooper and Billy Ray Roux on the boat––then let the notion drop. "What's the deal on the other one?"

"A young punk. No ID. Single stab wound, mid chest."

Julian considered the possibilities. Cooper didn't have an enemy. It couldn't be revenge, but was probably not a random event. "Any money missing?"

"Five hundred dollars in his wallet."

"Hardly chump change." Julian watched Maxwell rotate the band on his left ring finger as his eyes twitched back and forth, body to body.

"There's more," said Maxwell. "Found a picture of a nude boy in his billfold."

Julian's vision blurred; he felt cold. He refocused on the spotlights, then took another deep breath. The air tasted heavy, and felt heavy with the impeding weight of public opinion. "Did it just end up there?" A lilt of hope followed his thought. It didn't make any sense. Someone must have planted the stuff then killed him.

"Checking for prints." Max paused and took his stare out over the interstate. "Julian, we both owe Coop. We're kin."

Julian nodded but didn't move and didn't speak. Confusion replaced the empty feeling. He listened to a can bang hollowly along cinders and then collide against a rail car.

"Did I interrupt something tonight?" said Max.

Julian's head jerked. His thoughts shifted. He recalled how certain the barrier around his life had seemed four hours earlier and how pathetic it proved to be. "Peer review."

Maxwell studied his brother. "It's been twenty years since Livy and I––"

"Twenty-four." The wafer of unease between them congealed into something bigger. The memory of his first love drifted through the alcohol haze. The image of his first date with Livy––a picnic in the Public Garden––popped into his mind. Fogelberg had sung from the tape deck of the couple next to them. It was years ago but seemed like last week.

"It was beyond our control. Never intended," said Max.

"Passion over reason?" Julian's inflection changed. The years had done little to mollify the treasonous act or its heartache. The antipathy would linger.

"Something like that."

"How is Livy?" asked Julian.

"Well. You have her regards, as always."

"And Cam?"

"Doing well. You see him around the Square?"

His nephew had shunned him over the preceding six months, like a beer slinger at a AA meeting. "He avoids me."

"Curious. I'll talk to his mother, see what's up."

Julian nodded thanks.

The crime scene was now barren, except for the bodies. The techs were finished; they huddled nearby. A nomadic cloud covered the moon, creating a black crypt around the carcasses like a cocoon. Maxwell and Julian ducked under the yellow tape. The bodies lay twenty-five feet away. A sheet draped the area above Coop's shoulders.

"They look new," said Julian, scanning his eyes over Cooper's exposed torso.

"That's what I thought."

"Hard to read. Looks like a Q in the center. Random letters. A hangman's noose. Doesn't mean shit to me"

"How about this?" said Max, pointing to the right upper arm.

"Don't know. D-E-X-something."

"I'm seeing D-E-X-I-O-N. Mean anything to you?"

"Not sure," said Julian. He yawned, then rubbed his eyes.

Max pointed to Cooper's left shoulder area.

"Jeez, I don't know. E-C-C-L-E." Julian stooped down to move a hunk of skin and muscle. "Left arm?"

"Gone."

"How about Ecclesiastes, from the Hebrew Bible."

Maxwell brought his hand to his chin. He nodded, apparently appreciative of the suggestion, then held that position momentarily as he thought, and then said, "Julian, priests don't do tattoos."

Chapter Four

One hour later, Julian peered through a breach in Karlie's door. Karlie stood in a Cambridge apartment house in an area of town where a person was only marginally afraid for their life. It had a common entrance, with three apartments downstairs and three upstairs. A sixty-watt bulb covered with a frosted globe lit the hallway. Bug skeletons littered the orb, probably ten years worth. It was something a student could afford to rent, and nothing more than a tax break for its absentee owner.

"Julian!" said Karlie. They swapped confused glances.

"Bad day." Julian could feel Phil Collins's drums in his feet.

"I have friends. They'll find out."

He could see indecision in her eyes. "It's important." His features softened. They stood twelve inches apart; an uneasy space filled the void. "I've been told I look like crap. Sorry."

Karlie's lips relaxed into a smile, the kind that made old men wish they were twenty-four again. "Not your best look."

"Rejected." Julian's dimples creased his face. "You look stunning, as usual."

Karlie was bathed in the hallway light slicing through the doorway. Her hair was a festival of blonde and golden-brown streaks. Her eyes, shaded by long eyelashes but no makeup, exuded a simmering sultriness. A button-up blouse and painted-on jeans finished the ensemble.

"Change in routine," said Karlie.

"We really need to talk." Julian stood in the drab hallway, hands in his pockets, shoulders bent. A subtle sense of urgency tinted his face.

Karlie leaned forward, placing one arm on the molding and her head against the door. Friendly chatter drifted from the room behind her, mixed with someone guaranteeing firm abs in three weeks. She unlatched the door. Julian entered but stopped inches from her, inside her space. A kaleidoscope of thoughts leapfrogged through his mind, shackled only slightly by the liquor. He took her hands in his, then leaned his head against hers.

"Wistrom, my boss, the university, they found out about us––"

From the other room, a voice interrupted the moment. "Hey, Karlie, your turn."

"Chill guys." Softly, to Julian, she said, "Let me get everyone out, and then we can talk." She spun around toward her friends. Julian firmed his grip.

"And Coop's dead."

Karlie did a pirouette. "Oh." She leaned into Julian's chest, tentatively. "What happened?"

"He was run over by a train." The finality of the event stabbed at his heart again.

"We'll talk." Distraction shaded her response. "Give me a sec."

Julian stepped away, with his head bowed to the floor. "I'll probably get fired."

* * *

"Let me speak to them." As Karlie spoke a very restrained smile crept onto her face. She paused––calculated and subtle––so she could assess Julian's declarations and add them to the ongoing construct of her plan. Her first thought: *God, men are so easy.* Then, softly she mouthed, only to herself, she believed, "It worked."

* * *

Julian jerked his gaze up from the floor with a dull, questioning look. "What?"

Karlie startled, then startled again when her cell phone––set on a nuclear level––erupted with "Highway to Hell" and torpedoed the moment. She fumbled at her jeans and then hit the off button. At the same time, Cam St. Laurent whisked around the corner, beer in hand. His shock of curly brown hair and jaunty manner spoke volumes of his carefree college life.

"Karliewhat'sshakin'?" His words slurred into one. "Oh, sorry."

Julian stepped out from behind Karlie; momentary confusion ambushed his response. "Cam." Julian's gaze switched to Karlie then back to his nephew. "I should leave."

"No," said Karlie. "Cam was just leaving. Right, Cam?"

"It's your turn, Karlie," said Cam, as though he hadn't heard. He sucked down a swig of his Samuel Adams. "Nidal scored thirteen points with, G-O-O-G-L-E."

Julian took a couple steps forward and peered around the corner. A Scrabble board filled a small breakfast table, surrounded by four chairs. A Middle Easterner and a willowy redhead, in jeans and a MIT T-shirt, filled two of the chairs.

"Can't use proper nouns," said Julian.

"It's a number," said Cam, cocksure with a not-so-subtle tinge of condescension. "One, with a hundred zeros." Cam sported a sleeveless shirt. A barbwire tattoo gripped his left bicep.

"Learn something every day," said Julian. His nephew stood six feet tall, one hundred and ninety pounds. Julian's size, different distribution. Cam's body announced the narcissism of too much time in the gym. "You don't seem the least bit surprised to see me."

"I'm not," said Cam. "That's two things you've learned today."

Julian stepped halfway and extended his hand. "You look well."

Cam ignored the offer and took a long gulp of his fermented brew. "You don't."

Julian felt a wave of awkwardness. He considered the abruptness, the attitude. All jacked-up on himself. A kumquat would be more charming. "Just the business of life. Don't have the ability to live in the Zen moment like you apparently do."

"Dude, that sucks for you. Tribulations of the bourgeois."

"Cam," said Karlie.

"Oh, forgive my manners." Cam turned and opened the refrigerator. He stared at last week's Chinese carryout. "Can I interest you in a beer?" Each strained syllable came out with barroom clarity.

Julian looked at Karlie, then to Cam. "Whatever."

"You two see each other much?" asked Karlie, unsure how to handle the impromptu pissing match.

"Not as much as I––" started Julian.

"Too much."

The words lanced across the room and forced Julian to mentally bite his tongue. He tried to orient himself, thinking back twenty-three years. Disco was nearly in the dumpster, President Carter was…well, the second most famous Carter, and self-pity from Livy's hasty departure had rendered him moribund and really pissed off. He'd been there; maybe he needed to cut Cam some slack. Or, maybe not.

"Aren't you going to introduce me to your friends?"

"Sorry," said Cam. "Not sure what happened to my manners."

"Perhaps forgotten, along with your spelling."

"Say what?"

"One, with a hundred zeros is g-o-o-g-o-l, not a proper noun."

Cam sloughed off the mild rebuke. "Nidal, Gretchen, this is Julian St. Laurent, my uncle and an antiquities professor. Harvard. This is Nidal Ahmed and Gretchen Sachs."

Julian nodded greetings and assessed the Middle Easterner. He appeared to have been raised on a cloud of money and inherited privilege.

"Harvard? Computers?" said Julian to Nidal as he extended his hand.

"No, MIT, structural engineering," Nidal said without further pleasantries.

"Don't believe everything Cam tells you. I'm not that bad."

"He rarely mentions you."

An uneasy silence settled over the group.

Julian took a pull on his Sam Adams and tried to evoke a pleasant Cam-memory. He could count on two hands the number of times they had been together. A camping trip to the Berkshires with Maxwell from ten years before popped into his mind. Another outing to Fenway, again with Maxwell, from five years earlier. A handful of family events. Not much else. The body ink and muscle must have been recent additions. He barely knew his nephew. Julian searched his mind for the alleged crime and came up empty. Whatever it was couldn't be an act of commission. Perhaps omission.

"Karlie," said Nidal, "it's late. I think it is best if Gretchen and I leave."

Karlie made no attempt to dissuade them.

"Could I leave my documents here tonight?" asked Nidal, pointing to a two-foot-by-three-foot folio lying on the end table. "Pick them up in the morning. You'll be here?" It was a question and a statement.

She nodded. "Here, let me put them in the closet, top shelf."

As Nidal and Gretchen worked their way toward the door, Julian studied a montage of pictures on the wall: Mark Twain, Stephen Crane, Edgar Allen Poe, and F. Scott Fitzgerald. Stephen Crane's eyes challenged him to leave while he still had a chance, saying that courage is merely a state of mind, oft alcohol enhanced and oft a precursor to acts of foolishness. But Cam's smugness bordered on arrogance. Julian needed to leave, but he had to know.

He spun around to face his nephew. "Why the attitude, Cam?"

Caught off guard, Cam hesitated and took another pull on his beer. "I guess I don't like being lied to. By Mom, Dad…you."

"What are you talking about?"

"You should know. You tell me!"

Julian mentally retreated into a transient wave of melancholy as he quickly sorted through the detritus of his past. The words of Kurt Cobain popped into his mind––something about missing the comfort of being sad. He thought about all that wasn't when he was a child, the forgotten birthdays, the after-thought Christmases. Somehow he and Maxwell had survived in an imaginary safe place they'd created in their squalor and neglect. Then, after being abandoned by their mother, there were vivid memories of a month trapped in a dreadful warehouse. He could still remember the fat man's speech impediment––'sh' for s. By necessity, he and Max had stayed close for twenty-two years. The music finally disappeared that wintry day at the church in 1977. He missed not having a brother.

"Cam, it was a different time, different agenda. Things happened. Things you don't need to know."

"Let me decide!" Cam raised his chin ever so slightly.

Phil Collins had finished his song. The silence was filled with a TV man promising buns of steel. Anger and resentment, sequestered for many years, slowly oozed out into the synapses of Julian's brain. Now was the time to walk away, before he said something he'd regret. He turned toward the door, took a half-dozen steps, then stopped. *I can't leave it like this.* Still staring at the door, he spoke.

"Your paternal grandfather could have been anybody who could get it up for a Scollay Square hooker forty-six years ago. Your grandmother? A heroin addict." Julian paused then slowly turned the door handle.

"Keep going." The attitude was gone. The air of malevolent hatred was not.

Julian released the knob and continued. "She could only tolerate one of us, so she picked me. A random, cruel choice, but one your father has never gotten over. He had to sleep in the garage. It was dreadfully hot in the summer and frigid in the winter. In the cold months, he'd sleep leaning up against the wall to keep warm. In the house, I got to hear Mom do her tricks. Sometimes they'd beat her up, and then I'd have to patch her up." Julian looked at Cam with the faraway eyes of a man reliving hell.

Softly, Cam said, "Keep going. I need to hear it. Say it."

Julian didn't reply.

Cam held his empty beer can chest high, then let go. An impatient, hollow clang echoed floor to ceiling.

Julian's hand settled once again on the doorknob.

"Don't leave!"

Julian turned the knob.

Without warning, Cam charged down the diminutive hallway into his uncle's back. Julian bounced into the door, then recovered from the surprise enough to turn and land an uppercut to Cam's gut. He backed a retreat to the kitchen. Cam followed.

"Cam! What?" Julian shrugged his shoulders and upturned his hands.

Cam, glossy-eyed, ignored the plea and charged, shoulder first. Julian's fist landed on Cam's jaw, then cascaded against the bridge of his nose. Blood erupted. Cam followed with some stuttered shots to Julian's head. Julian then twisted his body and fired his elbow into Cam's exposed ribs. Cam retaliated with the same and propelled Julian backward into the refrigerator. Magnets and carryout menus tumbled over Julian's head and shoulders like leaves on a blustery October day. Cam hesitated a moment, then started toward Julian, who was sitting defenseless on the kitchen floor.

Karlie, simply acting on instinct, launched from her position onto Cam's back. "Stop! Now! Both of you."

Cam, without taking his eyes off of his uncle, flung his right arm back, sending Karlie in a downward arc into the corner of the kitchen countertop. From there she dropped like a limp doll onto the floor, out cold.

The fight lasted no more than sixty seconds.

Cam glanced back, distracted by the noise of Karlie's smash, but then rotated his head toward Julian. "We're not finished."

Julian ignored the declaration and scooted the eight feet to Karlie's side. He checked for a pulse, then checked her eyes. Without looking back, he said, "Cam, get your head out of your ass and call 911!"

CHAPTER FIVE

The next morning pregnant clouds, the color of car soot, had moved in and laid an oppressive blanket over the city. Julian made a quick stop at the Cambridge Hospital and the Commercial Avenue Funeral Home before heading to the Boston Police Department. Karlie had escaped with only a concussion but had been kept for observation. At the funeral home, Julian had wrestled with the question of why anyone would need a ten-thousand-dollar casket. The funeral director, with his plastic smile and spray-on tan, had mustered a look of fabricated concern, like someone might get seeing a motorist stranded on the highway next to their $250,000 Bentley Continental. Cooper was not about pretense. The thousand-dollar box would work just fine.

By the time Julian arrived at Boston Police Department, located at the corner of Ruggles and Tremont, the windshield wipers were working full-time to spank away jumbo-sized late-summer raindrops. The sheet-lime-stone walls of the BPD building looked out of place in its suburban setting, like a new pearl-white Cadillac in a parking lot full of storm-gray Buicks. Soon, Julian was attempting to clear a place to sit in his brother's fourth-floor cubicle.

31

"What in the hell happened last night?" said Maxwell, before Julian had a chance to excavate an uncluttered spot.

"What didn't happen," said Julian. A groan accompanied the deployment of his buttock onto the chair.

"With Cam. I heard from Livy that Karlie spent the night in the hospital. Said you'd know something about it."

Julian explained the particulars to his brother, Cam's father. "Cam asked some questions. Claims he's been lied to his whole life."

"About what?" asked Maxwell.

"Family stuff. I still haven't figured out the alleged deception. Told him about us."

"About Mom?"

"Yep." Julian noticed the fugitive speck of a cruller on Maxwell's shirt.

"Julian, we promised each other. Silence, remember?"

"Sorry. My mind was frazzled. Booze, Cooper's death."

"I apologize on Cam's behalf, and I'll make damn sure he does so himself."

"No problem. We were both drunk. Unfortunately Karlie got caught in the middle." Julian reached over and grabbed what looked like a reasonably fresh Dunkin' Donut from a box on the desk. "Any idea what happened at the rail yard?"

"Is Karlie OK?" asked Maxwell, answering a question with an unrelated question.

Julian could only nod a yes since his mouth was doughnut filled.

Max picked up a file and rooted through it. He looked back at his brother, started to say something, stopped, then thumbed through the folder again. "Still not sure. The lab found Cooper's prints on everything--picture, knife--everything."

Julian's head jerked up. "There's no way Cooper killed that kid."

"And probably no way to find out what he--they--were doing there."

"Maxwell, you've got to clear his name."

Maxwell stopped halfway through the folder to consider a page. He read it then looked up at his brother. "Maybe his nightmares caught up with him, and he went bonkers."

"No way."

"Everyone has a private side."

Julian could hardly refute a universal truth. His mind worked to make sense of what he had seen the previous night and what he was hearing. He felt hungover; little people in his head played squash.

Maxwell closed the file and tossed it on the table. An empty Pepsi can clanged to the floor. Julian grimaced.

"You see Cooper much, away from Trinity?" asked Maxwell.

"Occasional beer at Bukowski's."

"Any close friends?"

"Jessie, the bartender."

"You know him?"

"Yeah. Just barroom talk, though. Changes with the season. Sox. Celtics. Patriots."

Maxwell nodded then walked around his desk and crafted a seat at its edge. He hesitated before he spoke. "Um, maybe we should grab a brew sometime. Been awhile."

Julian took another bite of the pastry. His gaze shifted to the wall behind Maxwell's desk, taking in a diploma for a liberal arts degree from Boston University, a police academy graduation photo, and a picture of himself and Maxwell standing on either side of Carl Yastrzemski, 1967. The Sox beat the Orioles four to two that day. Sister Mary Beth had somehow scored ten tickets. Orphans day or something. He recalled that Cooper had been standing on the other side of Maxwell, out of the picture. "Sounds good. Maybe hoist a tall one for Coop. Next week?"

Maxwell smiled in agreement. He retrieved the folder he had thumbed through previously. "When you saw Cooper on Sunday, did he complain about anything or mention not feeling well?"

Julian thought for a moment as he finished his donut, then shook his head. "No. Why?"

"I spoke to the pathologist about thirty minutes ago." Max locked onto Julian's eyes. "Cooper was dying."

"What?"

"Lung cancer."

"Shit. He know?"

"Don't know. Plan on calling his family doc tomorrow."

Julian reconsidered everything he had seen at the crime scene. The details remained the same, but the picture changed dramatically. He knew that Coop knew about his disease--no need to ask anyone. He admired Coop even more, something he didn't think was possible.

33

Max put the finishing touches on the doughnut he had been working on. The two brothers sat for a moment. The gloom clung stubbornly to the clouds outside. Only the splatter of raindrops against the window broke the silence.

"Need to find that arm," said Julian to disrupt the quiet. "Ecclesiastes has a shitload of verses. Be nice to narrow it down a little."

"We're trying. Any thoughts about Dexion?"

"I don't recall any connection to the here and now. Twenty-five hundred years ago, Dexion was a society founded by the Greeks to honor Sophocles, the playwright, after his death. I doubt if that's a time, or subject, any Episcopalian priest would be particularly interested in. It was almost five hundred years before Jesus."

Julian picked up the Sunday *Boston Globe*. On the bottom of the front page was a story about the French Bishop Pierre Pican's conviction on the rape and molestation of an untold number of boys from 1996 to 1998. "The other night we thought…" he hesitated and threw the paper on the floor. "The name Billy Ray Roux popped into our heads."

"That was twelve years ago."

"But––"

"He was slimeball. A douche bag. We were exonerated. Forget it."

"We killed him."

"Stage 20 Films, Ltd. died that day, along with its CEO and director. Just think of all the kids we saved from his hellhole."

Julian nodded, then acquiesced his spot on the chair to Maxwell's paperwork morass and headed for the minifridge. He pilfered a Pepsi, threw a large gulp into the back of his throat, and then walked to the window. Ruggles Street had turned into a parking lot.

"Librium," Julian said.

"What?"

"Librium. We used Librium to help kill Roux."

"So?"

"You said Cooper had Rohypnols in his pocket."

"You think that's what Coop's death is about? A vigilante in over his head?"

"Just thinking out loud," said Julian.

"What about the tattoos?"

"May not have anything to do with anything." The gloom outside chased Julian back to his seat. "Had time to check out Cooper's office yet?"

""Dropped by the parish house this morning."

"And?"

"I met Agnes Vandenbosch, the rectory housekeeper. A major nutcase. Wouldn't let me in until she felt the bumps on my head."

Julian's eyes brightened slightly as he recalled Coop's stories about Miss Agnes, as he called her. He had never met her; he hadn't known her last name until now. "Your bumps OK?"

"Yep, but apparently my tarot spread sucked."

"What?"

"She's into tarot cards, too. Didn't like what she saw. Wouldn't talk after that. Got to take some pictures. Saw candles and shit everywhere. Even a frickin' hissing snake for crying out loud."

Julian laughed. "Looks like she has you by the balls."

"A frightening visual. Maybe you could give me an assist."

"How? Lost my Dick Tracy decoder ring years ago. Plus, we should have the same bumps, same spread."

"She thinks Dick Tracy is a pussy."

"Just get a search warrant. Or call the SWAT team and bash the door down. Simple."

"That's plan B. Trying to keep it friendly. You know, good cop, good cop. Between the church and the parish house, the place is chock-full of nooks and crannies. A million places to hide stuff."

"What're you looking for?"

"Anything that will tie together computer chips, a picture of a naked boy, and possibly Old Testament scripture."

"Mysterious non sequiturs." Julian stood up again and stretched; he was ready to leave. "I don't know, Maxwell. I've got a saloon full of issues to deal with. I'm not a cop."

"We're kin, remember?"

Julian said nothing.

"I agree with you," said Maxwell. "He didn't kill himself."

"What do you want me to do?"

"Just stop by and let her check out your bumps."

"On my head?"

Max gave his brother half a grin, just for effort. "If you pass the sniff test, maybe you can get into the inner sanctum. Or find out where it is. Or find out if there even is one."

"She pretty upset about Cooper's death?"

Max didn't answer directly. He turned to retrieve a Diet Pepsi from the minifridge.

"I hadn't thought about it, but no, not in the least."

CHAPTER SIX

NIDAL'S APARTMENT, CAMBRIDGE
Sunday, September 2, 2001, 10:00 a.m.

The urgent text message from Karlie came minutes after Julian left the police station. *Gretchen called. Terrified. Please take Nidal's papers to his condo. Pronto.* She finished with the address. Street closings and streetlights delayed Julian's trek.

Julian knocked on the door of Nidal's condo for the third time. No response. He called Karlie. No answer, so he left a quick text. Indecision nipped at his mind. He looked both directions down the corridor of the Memorial Drive residence. The silence within reared against Julian's senses. It didn't compute.

Julian glanced at his watch, then at the door again. As he turned to leave, he spied a faint half shoe print on the blue hallway rug. It looked fresh, like ink or paint. Julian did a half-pirouette and knocked on the door a fourth time. The door opened a few inches with a twist of the handle. *Not locked.*

"Nidal? Gretchen? Anybody?"

The lights were on as was the TV--the volume muted. The silence buzzed in his ears. Julian could see NFL game films. He pushed the door open the rest of the way and took a few hesitant steps into the foyer. The security chain hung impotently, ripped from the molding. Julian wrapped his hand around his car keys, fist tight, knuckles white.

"Anybody home?"

Julian waited. He was struck by the incongruity of the room. It was spotlessly groomed, almost to the point of being sterile. The room was a large space with very little furniture. Traditional Muslim artifacts mixed with signs of Western decadence were scattered here and there. On one side of the living area was a plush beige sofa, on the other side a simple, worn prayer rug. On the counter, an open box of strawberry Pop-Tarts jutted up against a pack of pork-free chewing gum. A Jakarta shirt hung over a simple chair, with a pair of black Regino shoes sitting on the rug nearby. Julian's eyes were drawn back to a Jacksonville Jaguars' football player running across a giant Hitachi plasma-screen TV, mounted next to a wall hanging of gilded Arabic script with five suras and a relief of the Prophet's Mosque.

Julian took ten steps toward a finely polished mahogany table. A water pipe stood tall over a kiblah compass, a copy of the Koran, and a book by Syed Qutb entitled, *Milestones*--a jihadist militant handbook. Underneath that, he found a quarter-inch thick bundle of printer paper, clipped together. The front page read:

PROJECT FOR THE
NEW AMERICAN CENTURY
P.N.A.C

REBUILDING AMERICA'S DEFENSES

Julian glanced away, looking around. He walked to the breakfast counter. A half-filled cup of tea was still warm. Partially eaten flatbread, rice, and lamb meat littered a plate nearby. He spied three more shoe prints, more obvious than the one in the hallway, leading away from a spiral staircase ascending to a loft. Black. Julian stooped down to touch one of the prints; it was wet and red. Julian stood and scanned the room for a weapon. Nearby was an ornate table lamp--metal, solid. He popped off the lampshade, removed the bulb, and yanked the plug.

The spiral staircase extended six feet above his head. He started up with a tentative step. Halfway up, the sour smell he'd noticed earlier turn fetid. Taking another step, he heard it, an insistent whisper. *A gurgling sound.* He finished two steps at a time and arrived in a sadist hell––two bodies, nude and sliced nearly beyond recognition. The one on the bed had red hair. *Gretchen!* She was lying on a dark red sheet, white at the edges, and a tortured grimace was frozen on her ghostly pale face. With her throat filleted open, her head hung to the left at an unnatural angle. Her tortured eyes were in a death stare. On the floor lay Nidal. His earlobes were missing. His throat had been filleted open like Gretchen's; blood continued to ooze out of a deep, grotesque wound onto the Persian throw rug. A deep, red stain circled his bloodied left hand.

An involuntary shiver of revulsion snaked through Julian's body. He yanked his cell phone from his pocket and dialed 911. He waited. In the silence, a gurgle erupted from Nidal's throat.

"Nidal!"

Julian dropped down and extracted earlobes from the Middle Easterner's mouth. A worm of maroon blood trailed. He grabbed a pillow, yanked off the pillowcase, and wrapped it around Nidal's neck. Two fingers were missing from the left hand. Julian pulled his belt off and wrapped it around Nidal's left arm. As he reached for another pillow, he felt a hand on his arm. Julian startled and looked at Nidal. His eyes were open, listless, glazed. *911!* Julian picked up the phone again.

"It's a massacre. Hurry. Ambulance. 214 Memorial Drive. Number 326. I won't hang up." He dropped the phone onto the rug.

"Nidal."

Nidal's lips moved, but no noise came out. Julian pushed down on the sodden pillowcase to put pressure over the tracheal gash.

The voice was now a whisper, no more.

"Kar…danger…go."

Julian adjusted his fingers over the front of Nidal's neck. Nidal's eyes closed.

"What? Say again, Nidal."

"New Yor…Man…Washing…"

"I don't understand."

"Pa…per."

"You want paper to write on?"

Nidal blinked his eyes. His respirations were labored, his face tortured, sallow.

"Hang on, Nidal. I hear an ambulance."

Julian popped up and turned. He scanned the room once, twice, then ran over to a nightstand. He ripped the drawer open. Nothing. Julian twirled around again. No desk. No paper. He ran over to the stairway, then took the stairs four at a time. Julian made a beeline for table in the foyer and found a BIC pen and a pad of paper in the first drawer he tried. The sirens drew closer. In six seconds, he was back at Nidal's side. Julian's eyes met another death stare. The gurgling had ceased. Julian looked for a pulse, but felt only his own. He lifted Nidal's chin, opened the mouth, and blew in a large breath. A curious sound, like a squeak from a toy mouse, leaked from the pillowcase wrapped around Nidal's neck.

"Damn."

Julian snatched up the BIC pen, cracked it in two, removed the cartridge, and snaked the tube under the pillowcase, through the open neck wound, and into what he thought might be the airway. Julian bunched the cloth around the pen base and offered three prolonged breaths though the plastic cylinder. Nidal's chest wall rose only slightly. The sirens drew closer. He waited a long moment and tried again. Holding the clear pipe secure with his right hand, he pushed five times on Nidal's chest with his left palm. Blood shot out of the pen barrel over Julian's face and chest. It felt strangely cool. He heard commotion at the condo door.

"Up here."

Julian blew five more times though the tube, then looked toward the stairway. Alarm registered on the faces of the first responders. They hesitated only a moment as they tried to comprehend the craven acts of depravity. By the time Julian had offered one more breath, the equipment case was open, IV and airway supplies out, tourniquet applied, and CPR initiated.

Julian backed away and leaned up against the bed. The odor of blood and death slammed into his nose. He let loose the vomitus that had settled in the back of his throat. Julian felt disconnected; the voices and commotion around him seemed distant. He scanned the room and noticed things he hadn't before. A whirlpool of chaos––furniture overturned, holes in the wall, drawers emptied onto the floor. Near one hole he noticed a wall safe, closed, but pockmarked with divots. He felt something hard under his left palm. A finger, Nidal's. He withdrew in revulsion and jerked from his trance.

Kar…danger…go.

Julian snatched up his cell phone and another one strewn on the floor. In a moment, he was across the room and down the stairs. By the time he got to the door, he heard people getting off the elevator at the end of the hall, around the corner. *Police.* Police procedure meant questions––wasted time. Julian turned right, opposite the direction of the elevators, and headed for the stairwell. The door on the ground floor read, "EMERGENCY EXIT ONLY, ALARM." Julian burst through at a dead run.

CHAPTER SEVEN

MEMORIAL DRIVE, CAMBRIDGE
Sunday, September 2, 2001, 10:43 a.m.

"Maxwell, get someone––anyone––the hell over to Cambridge Hospital. Now. Lights and sirens. Room 411."

Julian dissected the car-cluttered causeway at forty-five miles per hour as he spoke into his cell phone. Dried blood caked his face and clothes.

"What's going on?" said Maxwell, still in his office at the BPD headquarters.

"Do it. Just left a blood bath. Karlie is in deep shit."

"What in the heck are you talking about?"

"In two-shakes-of-a-stick you are going to hear about a slaughter. Two MIT students. Tortured. Carved-up. Memorial Drive condo. I was there, Maxwell. Spoke to one before he died. Warned me."

Like a silent movie, a vision of the carnage played out in his head. Julian swallowed hard to force the image from his mind.

"About what?"

"About Karlie. She's in trouble."

"Why were you even there?"

Julian swerved to avoid a slow-moving Taurus. "I got a text message from Karlie after I left your office. The victims were friends of hers. They were at her apartment last night. The guy left a folder of papers, and asked Karlie to keep an eye on it. Maxwell, it was butchery. Sick." Julian laid on the horn of his blue Volvo. "Butt-wipe."

"Julian, hold on." Muffled conversation filtered through from the other end. "OK, I've dispatched a unit. Cambridge Police. They're closer. You said two people?"

"Yes. MIT students. A Middle Eastern guy and a Caucasian female."

"Still alive?"

"Which piece?"

"Wouldn't be Gretchen Sachs and Nidal Ahmed, would it?"

"Don't know their last names. But Gretchen and Nidal. That's it." There was a break in the conversation as Julian wrestled with the car at a stoplight. "How'd you know?"

"They were questioned late last night about what happened at Karlie's apartment."

"That's bullshit!" The signal faded. "You still there?"

"Can hear you fine."

Another horn blared in the background.

Julian continued. "Karlie will clear it up. Just get someone the hell over there, now."

Julian showed up at the hospital nine minutes later. Two Cambridge Police Department vehicles were parked cockeyed at the entrance, lights flashing. Julian climbed the steps two at a time. He approached the nurses' station, a sea of Formica bathed in fluorescent lights. Everyone in the area stopped talking. Julian looked road weary and broken. His curly hair was in disarray. Dried blood caked his face and hands; maroon patches speckled his T-shirt and jeans. A Cambridge policeman––cherub-faced and small in stature––broke away from his interrogation and met Julian. His hand hovered over his service revolver.

"Excuse me, sir," said the officer. He held his other hand up to stop Julian.

Julian, for the first time, noticed the stares and became uncharacteristically self-conscious. "I need to see Karlie Reynolds."

"Who are you?"

"Julian St. Laurent, Maxwell's brother. The guy who requested you guys."

"Are you related?"

Julian hesitated. His eyes narrowed. "I'm a friend, one of her professors." Julian leaned into the policeman's hand.

44

"I'm sorry. I don't think that will be possible."

"Why not?" Julian's voice was taut.

"She's missing."

Julian flailed at the policeman's arm, bashed into his partner's shoulder, then raced down the hall toward his worst nightmare. He turned the corner, expectant.

"Oh no! Oh my God, no!"

Julian leaned up against the wall, his veneer of toughness spent. The pathos of the last twenty-four hours came crashing down. He staggered forward then knelt at the edge of her bed. He was in a Kafkaesque world--a shadowy nightmare where the flotsam that hovered near the fringes of society made the rules. He laid his head on the bed. After several minutes, Julian regained his composure and turned to find two police officers behind him. He stood up. He was in no mood for procedural bullshit.

"You have no idea where she is, do you?" The vehemence in his voice was not subtle.

"Sir," said the short officer, "we have put out an all-points bulletin. They won't get far."

Julian now stood tall with a stony expression. Miró-like patterns in the dried blood covered his cheeks.

The policeman continued. "Mr. St. Laurent, we need to know where you've been and what you have done."

Julian didn't speak.

"Sir, we need an explanation, now."

"I know you are both just doing your job, but you have no idea what you're up against. You won't--we won't--ever see Karlie alive again." There was a sudden intensity in his eyes, a new level of urgency in his voice. "I've seen first-hand..." Julian stopped talking and looked at his blood-covered hands. "I've seen first-hand, the depravity..." The visual of what Karlie faced was too much.

"Mr. St. Laurent..."

"Julian. My name is Julian."

"Julian, a warrant has been issued to bring you in for questioning, regarding the assault on Karlie Reynolds last night."

"You've got about thirty seconds, and then I'm out of here."

"Julian, if you don't come voluntarily, we will have to arrest you."

"Call my brother, Detective Maxwell St. Laurent. Boston PD. Know him? I promise I'll come in as soon as I find Karlie."

"We'll locate her. Rest assured."

"Officer…" Julian paused to look at the policeman's name tag. "…Baker, I don't think you understand what I am saying. Go to 214 Memorial Drive and see what we are up against. Tortured. Sliced and diced. The clock is ticking. We have minutes, not hours, not days. Unless we locate Karlie soon, her body will be in pieces…and, even worse, she'll still be alive. After a while, if God is merciful, she will die."

"We have our orders."

"Change them, goddamn it. Did Karlie file a complaint? Hell no. I didn't do anything. It was an accident."

"Not according to witnesses."

Julian thought of Gretchen and Nidal. "It's just my nephew, Maxwell St. Laurent's son, blowing smoke up your ass. Right?"

"I'm not at liberty to tell you. We just need to ask some questions."

"And I need you to call your buddies at the 214 crime scene. See how many of them are tossing their cookies. Find out what they are dealing with. I'm not the bad guy here."

Julian could see indecision in the eyes of Officer Baker. Julian looked at his watch. His mind raced to find a plan.

Finally Officer Baker said to his partner, "Jason, call Simon over at 214, and see what's shakin'." He looked at Julian.

"Thank you," said Julian. "While you are doing that, send a unit to the apartment of Cam St. Laurent. He's a Harvard student. He's next. Don't know his address. Call Maxwell. I'll be next, after that. They won't stop until they find what they are looking for."

"What are they looking for, Julian?"

"I wish I knew."

CHAPTER EIGHT

CAMBRIDGE POLICE CAR, CAMBRIDGE
Sunday, September 2, 2001, 12:30 p.m.

Julian knew. The papers were in the trunk of his Volvo. He sat in the back of the Cambridge Police patrol car. Julian studied the screen of the cell phone that he'd snatched off the condo carpet. He scrolled down the call log to figure out whose phone he'd picked up. It didn't take long. *Has to be Nidal's.*

> ALL CALLS
>
> Gretchen
> September 2, 9:34 a.m.
>
> Unknown caller
> September 2 9:32 a.m.
>
> Karlie
> September 1 8:21 p.m.
>
> Gretchen
> September 1 8:04 p.m.

Shah
September 1 4:52 p.m.

Unknown caller
September 1 3:43 p.m.

Gretchen
September 1 10:05 a.m.

Julian pushed the down button once to access the second call on the list, then pressed OK.

Unknown Caller
9:32 a.m.
Sunday, September 2, 2001

It had to be them calling Nidal. It fit the time frame. Nidal panicked, and then called Gretchen immediately after--9:34. Maybe they threatened Gretchen. Or maybe they held Gretchen hostage and Nidal didn't know it. Or maybe he asked Gretchen to go to Karlie's apartment. Gretchen came up empty then was forced to call Karlie. Julian committed the number to memory.

Five minutes later, the duty officer at the Cambridge Police Department offered Julian a cup a coffee while he waited in the interrogation room. A few minutes after that, Maxwell walked in.

"Hey, thanks for coming," said Julian.

Maxwell offered a nod.

"Do I get to make a phone call?" Julian spoke to the tabletop.

"I'm sorry about Karlie."

Julian looked expectantly at his brother, but said nothing.

"We'll find her," added Max.

Julian nodded and moved his despondent stare to the floor.

Detective Frank Nedry entered the room with a manila folder in hand. Frank was a blustery guy with a serious gut that was not much smaller than Rhode Island. He had a mean look, like a guy who could push Humpty off the wall, and appeared slightly more miserable than happy. He wore a blue sports coat over a green shirt; the colors wrestled with each other.

"Long time, Frank," said Max. "Appreciate you letting me sit in. This is my brother. Julian, this is Frank Nedry." Maxwell looked at his brother. "Frank understands most monosyllabic words."

Frank smiled. They exchanged pleasantries and shook hands.

Max continued. "Julian says he needs to make a call. I thought since he isn't under arrest…"

"No problem," said Detective Nedry.

Minutes later, Julian stood in the back parking lot. Sunlight escaped through gaps in the cumuli that boiled across the sky. A stout breeze coiled around his ankles and ruffled the leaves. He mentally prepared himself for the worst and then added an ecclesiastical appeal in the way of a small prayer. Julian opened the phone, scrolled down to the number, then pushed redial.

"Yes," came a voice after four rings.

Julian startled. Then analyzed. *Cheerless.* "I want to talk to Karlie." He held his breath.

"Who is calling?"

A wave of relief worked through his neck and shoulders. "The guy who has what you are looking for." He made a conscious effort to stifle the hope that crept into his voice.

"How is it that you know I am seeking something?"

Foreign. "I saw your handiwork."

"What am I looking for?"

"Papers. A folio."

"Concerning what?"

Strange, he sounds nervous. "Don't know. Don't care."

There was silence on the other end. Julian hesitated. He knew he had one chance. "May I speak with her?"

"She has not been harmed. We are considering our next step."

"I must be it––your next step." Julian made a mental note to keep his promise to God.

Once again there was silence, longer than the previous. A hand went over the mouthpiece, muffling conversation in the background. "Perhaps we can agree to an arrangement."

"Does it involve the removal of any of my body parts? I'm fond of most of them." A feeling of dread swept over Julian as he spoke. His mind flashed back to the carnage. His flippant words sounded foreign and inappropriate, even to himself. *What are the rules of discourse with a fanatic?*

"Do you have a choice?"

"Of body parts?"

"No, about whether to deal with me or not."

"I told you I haven't looked at the documents. Neither did Karlie."

"Oh, but I have to assume both of you have seen them."

Dread shrouded the optimism he felt only seconds before. "Why should I give you the documents if you're going to kill us anyway?"

"Like I said, an arrangement. I have something you want. You have something I want."

"Not at all convincing."

"Your only choice. Otherwise, death is certain––for both of you."

"So it is for everyone––eventually."

"Sooner than you might like."

A brief chill reminded Julian he was getting in way over his head. This visceral response was silenced by a vision of a psycho slicing his way through Karlie. In his mind, he tried to work the police into the puzzle. He couldn't find a fit. "An exchange?"

"Exactly."

"Go on," said Julian.

His foe was silent. Again, Julian heard muffled conversation. Sounded foreign, like Arabic or Farsi. No reason to cover the phone.

"Now," said the foreigner

Strange. Panic in his voice. "In a public place," said Julian.

"Only you," said the voice. "There will be no law-enforcement officers. Your friend can be killed very quickly, or very slowly."

"No cops," said Julian.

After a moment of silence, the voice on the other end said, "Prudential Center."

"Hancock Building." There was no hesitation in Julian's response.

"Copley Square," said the voice immediately.

"I like that. What time?"

"One hour."

Julian glanced at the nearby policeman again then looked at his watch. *One o'clock.*

"I'm still covered in blood, need a shower. Five hours."

"Six o'clock, then."

"I'll wear a Yankees cap, so you can find me," said Julian.

"You are a brave soul."

Has been in the city for a while. "If you harm Karlie, I'll make sure you're wearing the hat before I remove your eyeballs. Then the Red Sox Nation will finish you off."

"I hardly think you're in any position to make threats."

"Oh, but I am. From what I saw of your cutlery skills, you're very interested in what I have. If your boss sees that I have it, perhaps on the evening news, you won't live long enough to see which of your body parts he's most fond of."

"I am the boss, as you put it."

"Doubt it. This is way bigger than you or me. What I saw was the work of zealots with a very large agenda and a very intolerant chief."

There was a moment of silence, and then the voice said, "Six o'clock."

Julian pushed the disconnect button. Middle Easterners killing each other didn't make sense. He considered his plan. Not good. No choice. He looked at his watch again then walked over to the patrolman.

"I'm ready." Without stopping, he continued toward the back door. "Game at Fenway today?"

"Doubleheader," said the policeman.

"Start the second yet?"

The patrolman looked at his watch. "Soon."

"Which way is the wind blowing?"

"Blowin' in."

Minutes later, Julian was back in the interrogation room. He worked his way around the faux-wood Formica table and into a slat-backed chair. Detective Nedry turned a chair around, sat down, and rested his forearms on the back. Fat hung through the slats. Years of horrendous hours and worse food hung on his face.

"OK, what went down last night at Karlie's apartment?"

Over the next five minutes, Julian gave Frank an account of the events.

"You claim Gretchen and Nidal were not even there when the incident happened."

"Correct. But it wasn't an incident. It was an accident, like I said."

"I guess it's your word against Cam's, your nephew—who would have no reason to lie—Gretchen's, and Nidal's."

"Will Karlie's statement mean anything?"

"Victims of abuse tend not to say anything against their abusers. They fear retribution in a system they don't think can protect them."

"Guilty until proven innocent?'

The detective showed no expression. The give and take lasted another ten minutes. Then Detective Nedry jumped to the events of Sunday morning.

"What happened at the condo this morning?"

Julian stared at the remnants of a chili dog on Frank's green shirt as he reviewed the events. The detective sucked in slugs of java through his coffee-stained teeth as he listened. Julian answered questions. The detective countered. Julian nodded a lot.

"So, they are after the folio of papers?" said Detective Nedry.

"That's the only thing that makes sense."

"Where is it?" The detective shared a glance with Julian and Maxwell, visually inviting Max to chip in anytime he wanted.

"Don't know."

"I thought you picked it up at her apartment."

"It wasn't there."

"I see." The detective pulled a pack of Marlboros out of his shirt pocket, bashed the bottom of the pack on his left palm, then lit one. "Any indication of illegal entry?" A haze appeared over the desk.

Julian peeked at the mirror and watched the cloud advance across the table. "Don't know; I'm not a cop."

In the mirror, he watched the detective glare--a cop sizing up the perp. Looking for nervous ticks, uncertainty, sweat--the tip-offs that make or break a case. Julian knew what was going on. He decided the detective was definitely someone you wouldn't want to poke with a stick. He also noticed the accused looked unruffled.

Julian shifted around toward his brother.

"One more thing," said the detective.

Julian's weary eyes rolled back; his response was silent, irritated.

"Do the initials P.N.A.C. mean anything to you?"

He looked at his brother then back to the detective. "No. Should they?"

Their eyes locked. The detective's look was indifferent, like the yellow walls of the room. Maxwell finally broke the silence.

"Julian, do you need anything? "

"Shower and a change of clothes?"

"I've got a clean set of sweats in the car. Frank, can you show him a shower?"

"Downstairs. Basement. Next to the workout room."

The detective gathered his folders then mashed the smoldering butt of his cigarette into the ashtray.

"Are you done with me?"

Frank wrestled the sports coat around his paunch. The tie did a satisfactory job of hiding the lunch stain. He nodded at Julian then headed for the door. "Max, I'll call you later. Julian, don't leave town."

Julian waited for the door to close then spoke softly. "Could you drop me at my car?"

Max scrutinized his brother.

Julian took his eyes back to the tabletop.

"Remember, you lost your decoder ring." Maxwell paused, started to say something else, then stopped.

"What?"

"What you going to do with it?" Maxwell's face lit up with a smug-cop grin.

Julian returned the smile.

"Hey, I'm no idiot," said Maxwell.

"Is Frank?" His smile disappeared as abruptly as it appeared. The task at hand weighed heavy.

"Doubt it. Think he is cutting you some slack."

"Just give me five hours. Then I'll spill the beans."

"I assume no cops?"

"Yep. Part of the deal. Can't risk it. Any slip up and Karlie is in pieces."

Maxwell reached over and put his hand on his brother's shoulder.

"I need you to do something for me," said Julian. "You'll probably need to call in some favors––maybe a lot of favors. And I need it done within the hour."

"Shoot."

"John Hancock Building. A door on the Saint James Avenue side needs to be unlocked and marked with a small piece of tape. The middle elevator should be open and ready to go. Disable all the other elevators. They can lock up at eight o'clock."

"Anything else?"

"Anybody around here have a Yankees cap?"

Max's face sagged like he had just been told to make his final arrangements. "You're joking, right?"

Julian waited a beat for Max to relax. "Just thought I'd ask."

A grin inched onto Maxwell's face. He turned to leave. "We're identical. They'd never know."

"Maxwell, I won't ever forget what I saw today. I have to do it myself."

CHAPTER NINE

BACK BAY, BOSTON
Sunday, September 2, 2001, 5:25 p.m.

Julian sat in his Volvo on a side street in the Back Bay. Sticky perspiration dotted his forehead. There were tourists everywhere, going this way and that frenetically, like a one-legged cat trying to bury a turd. Many, with cameras slung around their necks like dog tags, drifted in and out of the open shops and restaurants. An amphibious sightseeing vehicle rumbled by with more people and more cameras. The tall buildings echoed a flurry of impatient honks, adding to the chaos. The sunlight played off the windows of the high-rises. In the sapphire reflection of the Hancock Building, he could see eerily perfect facsimiles of Copley Square and Trinity Church. Above that, clouds piled high over a red sunset. *Red sky at night…must be nice weather tomorrow.*

Julian contemplated the bundle of humanity around him, on the street and in the passing cars. Well-coiffed, air-kissing personages of the upper end, involved in their gratuitous hobnobbing, mingled with the street people and their dead-end expressions––people trying to live out their lives with minimal heartbreak and hassle. Others, young people, who were aggressively underdressed, solicited for something—perhaps an end to world hunger—and were evidently more concerned about the human condition than their attire. On the street sat a gnarled man with an empty sleeve, a nearby crutch, and a sign, "Homeless." Julian wondered about the pathos that dwelt inside the sleeve. He scanned the street for a menacing stare, a lingering gait, or an ephemeral look reflecting off a storefront window--something just not right. Julian rechecked his gun, a Walther P99, a loaner from Maxwell. A rheostat of doubt ratcheted in his mind. The ringing of his cell phone silenced the worry. He checked the caller ID.

"Not going to change my mind," said Julian.

"Not my intention," said Maxwell on the other end.

"What then?"

"The CIA called."

"It was just a goddamn accident, not an international intrigue."

"One of their undercover operatives was killed, slaughtered."

"Nidal?"

"Righto. They're upset, to say the least. Want their federal mitts on that folio. There's supposed to be a dead drop today."

"Makes a little more sense now. The guy I spoke with on the phone sounded Middle Eastern. I couldn't understand why they would be killing each other."

"Apparently it was Nidal's job to keep an eye on the Muslim elements at the university."

"Something going on?" asked Julian.

"Ever heard of Osama bin Laden?"

"Not sure. A terrorist?"

"Powerful, rich terrorist. He's a Saudi and a friend of the Taliban. Head dude for a group called al-Qaeda. Responsible for the '93 bombing of the World Trade Center and the bombing of the USS Cole, among other things."

"What does that have to do with MIT?"

"The bin Laden clan donated a shit-ton of money to the university in the early '90's, when two of the bin Laden cousins attended law school in Boston. They gave a million to the School of Architecture and Planning for Islamic architecture and another mil to Harvard for Islamic law. Now yet another bin Laden cousin lives in the same building as Nidal."

"Wonder why he left the contraband at Karlie's?"

"Safe haven, I guess." He paused. "Julian, you have to hand the papers over."

"How do they know I have them?"

"They don't. I stonewalled 'em. But it's just a matter of time before they find out about your call."

"Copied all the stuff," said Julian. "Hid it at home."

"What if I come out tonight and pick it up? Have some stuff about Cooper to show you anyway."

"Sounds good. Karlie and I could be there by nine or so. Find the arm yet?"

"Nope. You look at the papers when you copied them?"

"Couldn't make too much out of it."

"Well?"

"Not sure. Architectural drawings of a building or parts of a building. A high-rise. Stuff about height-to-weight ratios, wind loads, gravity loads. Lots and lots of numbers. Something was scribbled in the margins about maximum flame temperatures and diffuse flame temperatures. Did you know that steel melts at fifteen hundred degrees centigrade? Hell, I don't know. Didn't mean too much to me."

"Names or dates?"

"No."

Silence filled Maxwell's end of the phone line as he added the info to his construct. "Don't want to hold you up anymore. Where did you hide it?"

"A table by my La-Z-Boy. Front room. There's a false space behind the drawer. It's rolled up and stashed in there."

"Thanks, see you at nine. Julian, for God's sake, your sake, Karlie's sake, and my sake, be careful."

"No problem."

Five thirty, time to rock 'n' roll. Julian pushed disconnect then exited the car. He took a circuitous route to the Stuart Street side of the Hancock Building. He passed Stanhope Street, Trinity Place, and an alley or two. There were more cameras and more empty stares from people who wished they had a mailbox. Everywhere were nameless faces in the crowd, average in every way imaginable. He didn't spot any suspicious behavior. I.M. Pei's blue-glass behemoth extended sixty stories above him. He entered the building to check the elevator one more time, exited, and then worked his way, again in a circuitous manner, to the Saint James Avenue side.

Five forty. Julian removed the Yankees cap from his back pocket and plopped it on his head. Now he was certain he was being watched. His stickiness had long since turned to sweat, dripping from his armpits to his belt. Every nameless face was now a conspirator; every car was an insurgent vehicle. He stood at a forty-five-degree angle, facing northwest to give himself a lucid view of Copley Square. He was seeing clearly, but flying blind. Doubt gnawed at his brain. He felt for his Walther and clicked the safety off.

Julian spied a fellow, with his beard frosted gray, peeking out from underneath a bedroll on the south side of the rectory. The neglected man belted back a brew from a bag-covered bottle. He seemed indifferent. He couldn't be the police. Julian checked the building tops––no snipers. Then he checked the sidewalks, no fast shadows. Finally after eighteen minutes, out of the corner of his eye and two blocks east, he spotted three cars moving together. Their cohesion was out of sync with the randomness of the street. An Audi, a Toyota truck, and a Durango SUV––all black. Julian straightened up then walked to the curb. His sweaty right hand found the Walther. A single drop of sweat rolled down his jaw, like condensation on a cold bottle of beer on a warm day. His fingertips felt like a porcupine had left its mark. The Durango stopped fifty yards away, just this side of the intersection. The other two vehicles continued. The occupants came into view. All wore ski masks. It looked like there were two people per car. *Six to one. Not good.* From inside the Audi, something winked faintly in the sunlight, something shiny––a weapon. *No chance.* The Toyota sped up, pulled a U-turn at the end of the block, and stopped, facing east. The Audi stopped midblock, directly across the street. Karlie sat in the back, still in her hospital gown. Her big, round eyes told the story. Julian directed his gaze to the front seat.

"You found me," said Julian.

"What happened to Copley Square?" asked the mask-covered zealot.

"Better view from over here. How's this going to work?" He didn't have to yell to be heard.

"Give me the papers."

"Karlie first."

"In case you haven't noticed, Mr. St. Laurent––Julian––you're outnumbered."

Julian hesitated, surprised. "Thought we had an agreement."

"We do. Did you look at the papers?"

"Meant nothing to me. Doesn't matter. You're assuming the same, anyway. I know your reach. I won't do anything to risk Karlie's safety."

"The folder. Now."

Julian scanned the street then the building tops. "Which one?"

His foe hesitated, caught off guard. "There is more than one?"

"I took the liberty of cutting your documents like a jigsaw puzzle. Then I mixed them up and put them into three different folders. I hope you don't mind."

"What do you expect to achieve by doing this?"

"I'm giving you a chance to show good faith."

"How?"

"You put Karlie, standing by herself, next to the car, and I'll tell you where to find the first one. Have your minion retrieve it."

"How do I know you're going to give me all the pieces?"

"You don't. I have nothing to gain by cheating you." He studied his foe's eyes. "You won't kill me here now, until you're sure you have all the pieces."

The masked felon didn't answer immediately. Julian surveyed the area again. Still clear. No cops. The traffic was still relatively light.

"Ahmed," the zealot finally said, "let her out. Have her stand by the curb."

"In the trash bin, there." Julian pointed.

The felon had his minion secure the folio, and then he quickly checked the contents. "Have her stand on the other side of the car. Woman, you run, you die."

Quick study. "The opposite side of the sign, there," said Julian, pointing to a covered information center at the edge of Copley Square.

The foe carried out the same routine. While he examined the contents, a police car stopped at a light one block east, in the lane close to the curb, with its right turn signal on. The felon noticed. Neither said a word. They waited. Each scrutinized the other. The deal—a capricious arrangement at best-- hung in the balance. Julian wanted so badly to transcend the moment, run over, grab Karlie, and steal away into the night. *Certain death.* The masked foe and Julian waited for the light to turn green. *Why didn't he turn right on red?* Horns honked. Julian startled.

CHAPTER TEN

COPLEY SQUARE, BACK BAY
Sunday, September 2, 2001, 6:15 p.m.

The landscape darkened as soon as the strobes on the police car flashed on. At the worst possible moment, Einstein's time-space continuum was thrown into disarray; each event played out in slow motion, one cell at a time. Julian lurched forward, through moving traffic, his arm extended toward the Audi and toward Karlie. With his other hand, he reached for his Walther. The Audi driver fired two quick shots. The first slammed into Julian's right upper chest, going 1,140 meters per second. His body jerked backward, flat out in the middle of the eastbound lane of Saint James Street. They yanked Karlie back into the car like she was attached to a bungee cord. The Durango stationed east on Saint James burst from its parked position, cutting off the police car's advance, and headed directly for Julian's prostrate body––going in for the kill. Those pedestrians not already watching turned at the noise and then instinctively dove to the hot sidewalk. The Durango exploded head-on into an eastbound cab. A transient flame shot from the underbody of the taxi. Glass spewed from curb to curb.

Julian, dazed, rose off the pavement in time to see the Audi accelerate west on Saint James, through a yellow light—gone. He spun around. Two of the masked felons emerged from the wrecked Durango. One stopped, turned, and bracketed a spray of eight shots into the advancing police vehicle. The officer slumped over; the car continued full speed into the smashed Durango. More glass and chrome carpeted the street. Unfazed, the foes made a beeline toward the antiquities professor. Julian swiveled and headed for the Hancock Building. As he reached for the door, the huge plate-glass window to his left exploded from the burst of a machine pistol––fifteen bullets in less than a second. The noise from the Steyr was barely perceptible to the human ear. One of the bullets blasted into Julian's right scapula and bulldozed him to the ground again. This time, with his adrenaline amped, he was up in a second. Julian streaked toward the open elevator, jumped into the cubicle, and pushed sixty. Another round of lead ricocheted off the doors. The elevator headed up, slowly at first, then fast. An inescapable feeling of dread––an uninvited specter––crept into the elevator. *They still have Karlie.* He arrived at the sixtieth floor. All the other elevators registered *G*, except elevator number one. The indicator overhead read fourteen. *Shit.* He spun around and ran toward the exit.

Outside the door, two complete paragliding packs were opened, ready to go. Julian's heart sunk when he thought about what could have been. He thought of his last paragliding adventure with Karlie in the Berkshires. *Bed and breakfast.* Julian jerked his head around in search of an implement to block the door. *Nothing.* He grabbed the closest pack and headed for the west end of the building, probably forty yards away. Noise echoed from the stairwell behind him. He ducked behind a ten-foot-high structure, possibly an air conditioning unit. Ten seconds later, with straps attached and sail ready, he glanced around the unit. His pursuers, now dressed like Boston cops, walked in an expanding circle from the stairwell door. One was heading toward him; one went the opposite way. They were cautious. Deliberate. Concern branded Julian's brow when he turned and spied a wall four or five feet high at the south end of the roof. He hadn't noticed it earlier. In high school, it wouldn't have been a problem; twenty-five years out of high school, it represented a major problem. He wondered if there was a straight drop or ledge on the other side of the wall. He glanced one more time from his area of concealment. A gust of wind tickled his sideburns. *Now or never.* Julian jerked around and headed in a dead sprint for the building's edge. Five seconds later, gunshots pinged off the air conditioner. *Low.* Ten yards after that, more shots. *High.* Julian felt like he was running on a treadmill; his legs were thick with fatigue. The bulletproof vest Maxwell had given him was bulky, and the sail was cumbersome. His chest wall spit fire from where the bullets had smacked the Kevlar. The sound of feet intensified behind him. At the wall, Julian threw the sail ahead of him, planted his foot into one of the decorative squares in the barrier, slapped his hands on top of the wall, and then catapulted over into the netherworld, sixty stories over the asphalt. *No ledge.*

Shackles of fear enveloped Julian as he plummeted the first ten floors in a free fall. His stomach lodged in his throat. The ground charged at him. His face warped into a grotesque mask; his clothes mashed into a second skin. *Too close to the building.* He waited for the end.

Somewhere around the fortieth floor, the sail caught a random breeze and yanked him up and away from the high-rise, like he had been shot out of a cannon. The landscape took on a whole new look. The streets that seconds before were corridors of death, now looked like shimmering ribbons of asphalt; the streetlights sparkled like yuletide adornments. The nip of the September evening air penetrated his thin summer clothes; it never felt better. The reaper had nearly won. It was like the first sip of a fine wine.

Julian yanked the guidelines to gain altitude. Dusk was gathering, and the breeze blew steadily at his back––blowing "in" like the policeman said. Off to his right, a patchwork quilt of clouds puffed up around the setting sun, a communion of reds and oranges and yellows. Rays of sunlight danced with the scullers on the Charles River. Directly below, the madcap evanescence of Beantown played out in its full regalia. The Massachusetts Turnpike was a kid' s delight––bumper-to-bumper Matchbox cars. The Hynes Convention Center was a dark slab, like a huge tombstone. The world looked strangely clean and manageable. The only other unmistakable landmarks were the omnipresent Dunkin' Donuts and random McDonald's franchises that littered the metropolis below; the Green Monster of Fenway loomed dead ahead. If numbers meant safety, Julian would be quite safe; Red Sox Nation would protect him. Julian remembered the Yankees hat and jettisoned the offensive accoutrement. A minute later, he was close enough to read the name on the back of the Ranger's right fielder: Ledee.

CHAPTER ELEVEN

NEAR HARVARD UNIVERSITY
Sunday, September 2, 2001, 8:42 p.m.

axwell cruised down Trowbridge Street. Not slow. Not fast. Old Victorians, Colonials, and remodeled hybrids lined the way. *Very Andy Griffith.* Harvard Square was less than a mile away. He passed Julian's house. A fundamental stillness that defied logic pervaded the area. It was Labor Day weekend. *Students should be everywhere, moving in.* After another twenty feet, he passed a Cambridge police officer, Seth somebody, camped out in his Taurus. He was second-shift surveillance. Maxwell slowed up a bit, held up his shield, exchanged nods, and then preceded slower than before. Cars lined both sides of the street. He found his parking spot forty yards away.

Maxwell disabled the interior lights then slid out into the night. It was dark––inky dark. And quiet. The moon––one of those fall moons that take your breath away––looked dramatic just above the horizon. It was orange, like a basketball, and covered with patches that looked like black mold. And it was too low in the sky to help. He stood still to let his eyes adjust to the night. The quiet and the dark could play high jinks. Maxwell held three thick folders in his right hand. Second thoughts prompted him to pop the trunk and hide them among some refuse. He checked his gun then headed for the side of the street opposite from Julian's house.

Shoulder-high hedges lined the sidewalk, thick and gnarly, probably decades old. Lots of places to hide. It smelled like fall––football weather–– with a slight nip in the air. One block over, a dog barked and then another. Then it was quiet again. He stopped, scanning the area ahead and behind. It was too dark for shadows. After another twenty yards, he spotted Seth. Max got his attention then advanced low on the shotgun side. He spoke in a near whisper through the open window.

"Hey, Seth. Max St. Laurent, Boston PD."

"Hey, Max. I remember. Police benefit last year."

"Yep. My brother's house. Anything?"

"No. Too quiet."

"Thinkin' the same thing. How long you been here?"

"Better part of an hour."

"Listen, I'm going in. Julian's supposed to get back soon. Hopefully with his girlfriend. Let me give you my cell number. Anything at all, call me."

"No problem."

The men exchanged numbers.

"Julian stashed some shit in the house. High priority. CIA wants it."

"Didn't know."

"Nobody knows. There's keen interest from foreigners to get it back. Presumed Middle Easterners, although not confirmed. Nasty dudes. Same guys who sliced up the MIT students today. Don't hesitate to shoot the sons o' bitches in the balls if you see them."

"They have balls?"

Maxwell offered a half smile then backed away and continued up the street, away from Seth and away from the house. He arrived at a thick maple and ducked in behind it. This put him thirty yards from the house a variation of a Gothic Revival. It was dark yellow, with two chimneys, and a steep-pitched, cross-gabled roof. *Nice house.* Maxwell crossed the street, casually. The houses were pinched together. All the houses had small yards and lots of mature trees. Maples, oaks, sycamores. The smaller crab-apple trees were already discarding their leaves. In eight weeks, they would all be skeletons.

Maxwell walked by the house, easily, like a neighbor out for a walk. At the driveway, he took a sharp left, crouched low, and then scooted past an alcove off the front room toward the freestanding garage in the back. The moon gave only faint illumination to a small backyard enclosed by a four-foot-high fence. He turned on his flashlight, a short blip. No footprints. After drawing his gun, he scooted from the back gate to the back door. Locks, OK. Door, OK. No broken windows. Max removed the key from his pocket then made his way through the back door.

The warped entrance popped open then creaked. Maxwell cringed, stopped, and listened for a full two minutes. Old houses tended to breathe; he listened for a hiccup. *Eight fifty.* Over the next fifteen minutes, Maxwell cleared one room at a time, first, the main floor, then the upstairs, and then the basement. Satisfied, he made a call to Seth. He stashed his piece and then headed for the La-Z-Boy in the front room. A seventies-era ceiling light hung down near the chair. It looked like a Japanese pillow of some sort. *Ugly.* Maxwell stooped down in front of the table and removed the drawer. He found the hiding space in the back and extracted the papers, rolled up nice and tidy. Max circled around the recliner, took a seat, and then yanked on the light chain.

There was an initial flash, like the light had just burned out; a delay, measuring tenths of a second; and then a fiery explosion. The gasoline-filled light bulb evaporated in tongues of flame that shot out in all directions. Within seconds, the incendiary device grew fat with oxygen and filled an eight-foot-wide area around the chair. No human could react in that short span of time.

Seth was out of his car immediately. He would say later the scream lasted for no more than ten seconds. By the time he reached the front porch, he had his phone out and had speed-dialed the dispatcher. The burly cop charged through the old front door and slid across a slick wood floor on a layer of glass. Thick, noxious smoke filled the room, along with the inferno's dirge. Flames feasted on the century-old cherry and oak, devouring in seconds what had probably taken an artisan months to mold together. Seth couldn't see Maxwell. There was no human motion. The La-Z-Boy chair was engulfed in fire. The heat and smoke were overwhelming; Seth was no match for the conflagration. He surrendered his spot and moved to the street. People had already gathered. The fingers of fire danced out the windows on the first floor; smoke poured from windows on the second. Sirens echoed in the distance. The house moaned and creaked as tendrils of flame worked their way high into the night sky.

CHAPTER TWELVE

BOSTON POLICE DEPARTMENT
Sunday, September 2, 2001, 9:20 p.m.

For Julian, the game was called in the bottom of the 7th––on account of jail. He tried to explain his way out of having a bulletproof vest and a loaded gun while standing in right field at Fenway Park. It's hard though, like trying to explain erectile dysfunction to a child. Fortunately, Ricky Ledee, the Ranger's right fielder, was friendly enough; unfortunately, the authorities were not.

This time Julian was cuffed. Twenty minutes later, he walked into the Boston PD headquarters. The clock behind the desk said nine twenty. Julian considered the possibilities. The Middle Easterner would initially assume he was killed and then receive word of his attempted flight to safety, or death. The zealot wouldn't know for sure. *Advantage, St. Laurent*. The felon would realize after looking through the folders that one-third of the papers––the most important parts––were missing. *Advantage, St. Laurent. The Middle Easterner wouldn't kill Karlie right away*. Julian's rumination was thwarted by the sharp edge of the third folder burrowing into his armpit. The police would confiscate it. He'd have to use his stashed copy to fabricate a new folder. Once he had Karlie back, they could get themselves arrested—protective custody with less paperwork. He needed to make some calls, first to Maxwell, then to his foe. Time was wasting.

Nine thirty. Julian sat in an interrogation room very similar to the one in the Cambridge Police Department. He wondered if the architects of the two police stations watched the same cop movies. There was a desk, two chairs, surveillance cameras in the corners, and a big mirror on the wall, presumably made of one-way glass with cops sitting on the other side. Julian looked long and hard at himself. In his mind, he was twenty years old, but he hardly recognized the mug in the mirror. There were creases on the previously smooth jaw, dark caverns under his eyes, and patches of gray peppering his brown, curly hair. Julian took an inventory on his life––*no parents, no children, no wife, and probably no job*. His only family was Cooper and Maxwell, and Cooper was dead. He remembered that the funeral was tomorrow. He pondered Coop's legacy. He had much to be proud of. He would be missed. The totality of his own legacy was a bunch of scholarly articles, a couple of books on the Hellenistic period, and a battered pair of Adidas.

Nine forty-five. *Why the delay?* More thoughts bandied through his head. If they found the folder, it would mean waiting for the CIA or FBI or someone else to show up. More time would be lost. He needed to talk with Maxwell. He needed to get moving. He needed to get Karlie back. As soon as the police got involved, she was as good as dead.

The minimalist decorative approach of the room caught Julian's attention again. The BPD needed to arrest Martha Stewart. He thought about how he might have to concoct a third folder. Julian attempted to reconstruct the pictures in his mind, each line, each number. The mental geometry lasted for seven minutes.

Nine fifty-two. Detective Ian Foster entered the room with two associates. The smell of Old Spice followed them in. Detective Foster looked round and slightly confused, like one of those guys who used a nightly six-pack to resolve the affairs of the day.

Introductions were made. Beverages were offered. The mood was somber; their faces were grim.

"We're sorry to keep you waiting, Julian," said Detective Foster, his voice a gravel-coated rasp.

Cop must have died. "Did your patrolman die? Outside the Hancock building."

"Yes, he was a good man. I received the reports from the scene and from Fenway. We need some details, Mr. St Laurent. But…"

"I'm sorry. I can—"

"But," continued Ian, "there is something else."

"You need to know, the guys chasing me on the roof were dressed like Boston cops. One had a machine pistol."

The three detectives shared a look. Detective Foster, apparently the senior officer, gave a nod to his junior partner, who turned and left the room.

Too late. They'll disappear into the night.

The detective twisted and directed his attention back to Julian. "Like I said, there is something else. I'm afraid I have some very bad news."

Julian searched one detective then the other for an indication. His heart sank.

"Oh no, not Karlie! They didn't kill Karlie."

"I don't know anything about Karlie."

"What then?"

Detective Foster shared a look with his partner and then Julian. "It's your brother, Julian. Maxwell is dead."

Julian again looked at one policeman and then the other. "No, you are mistaken. He's waiting for me at my house." Julian waited for acknowledgement of their error. He was confident. They said nothing. "No, it can't be."

"I'm so sorry for your loss, Julian."

"Not Maxwell. Please God, not Maxwell." The words tumbled out of Julian's mouth. Every dark night in his soul, every moment of personal suffering, suddenly lost all meaning. The demons had once again found a voice.

Initially, there were no tears. The stress and fatigue of the previous two days had paralyzed his senses. He leaned over, arms on his knees, mute as a rock. After a moment, he said in a soft voice, "Eli, Eli, la'ma sabach-tha'-ni?"

"What, Julian?"

His haunted, empty eyes looked up. "My God, my God, why hast thou forsaken me? It's what Jesus said when he was on the cross."

Detective Foster looked at his partner again. "Can we do anything for you? Get you anything?"

The long hand of Maxwell's past reached out and grabbed Julian, suddenly, like a light bursting into a dark void. His pain intensified all the more as he recalled how Maxwell suffered in the garage, then later. It was much worse later. All those horrible days and nights at the warehouse. Violated. *And Santa, only a heartache.*

71

Julian looked up at Detective Foster. "Do you have pastoral services available?" He wiped a tear on his sleeve.

Ian looked at his partner and gave another nod. The partner excused himself to summon the priest. Then silence fell.

Julian said, "What happened?"

"Seth Jamison, a Cambridge PD patrolman, was an hour into his surveillance shift at your residence when Max showed up. He and Max spoke. Then your brother went in to make sure everything was OK. He saw Max check out each room, one at a time. Real careful. Max finally ended up in the front room. About a minute later, the room exploded in flames. Some sort of incendiary device. Possibly gasoline. Seth called dispatch immediately then entered. The house was consumed within minutes."

"It should have been me. It should have been me." Julian spoke to the floor, his voice disconnected, soft. "No one knew he was there."

The room was quiet for nearly a full minute. Detective Foster stood patiently as Julian worked through his grief. Finally, he looked at the detective. "I need to talk to the CIA."

CHAPTER THIRTEEN

"You killed him!" Julian yelled into his cell phone at the Middle Easterner. It was two in the morning. Julian sat ensconced in a bunk room at the Boston Police Department. It was the captain's private room. He had nowhere else to go. "Thought we had a goddamn agreement," continued Julian.

"I know not of what you speak," answered the zealot.

"My house is gone, burned to the ground. My brother is dead."

"I know nothing of a fire. I know not of your brother. I did not harm him. May Allah be my witness."

Julian hesitated. He was emotionally spent. His mind was frayed *No one knew Max would be there.*

The felon continued, "I'm a holy warrior. My acts of jihad are acts of worship."

"No one else could possibly want me dead."

"Are you sure, Mr. St. Laurent?"

Julian sorted through the debris in his mind. *Cam? No way. The university? It made no sense.*

"I need the third folder," said the Middle Easterner. "Have you informed the police?"

"I won't do anything to risk Karlie's life. Let me speak to her."

"She is sleeping. Unharmed."

"How do I know?"

"Mr. St. Laurent, trust me, you must."

"Trust you? You tried to kill me twice. You killed my brother."

"A most worthy foe are you. Most infidels are weak, without spiritual strength. You are strong. I sense you will find your brother's killer."

Julian listened carefully to each word, the nuance of every syllable. His brain was all he had to work with. He did not have the equipment to triangulate a cell phone call or compare signature scratches on a shell casing.

"We still have an agreement?" asked Julian.

"I need the folder; you want your Karlie."

The line fell silent as Julian considered his options. The police were still not on the list.

"There is a funeral today. One o'clock. Cooper, my dearest friend, nearly a brother. You do not profane your Allah. I would do nothing to defile my friend."

"Yes. Go on."

"Saint Joseph's Cemetery, West Roxbury. There is a creek that flows through the back of the property. A service road crosses it twice. Near the southernmost bridge is a dense pine forest. The service road leads out of the cemetery to Denham Street, which feeds directly into the VFW Parkway. It's the perfect escape route. Remember, I wouldn't use my dear friend's funeral to find you. I'll do that later. All I want is Karlie––safe."

"What do you propose?"

"Have one of your soldiers observe the funeral unnoticed from the pines. After the service, I'll walk to the bridge. It's only a hundred yards. I'll place the folder under the bridge, on the cement ledge of the culvert. Then, I'll walk back to the grave site. No tricks. When I turn around five minutes later, I expect to see Karlie."

"Five minutes?"

"To check the folder. Certainly you know which pieces of the puzzle are missing?"

"It will be done. You know our reach."

"I do."

Exhaustion took hold. Nightmares of the worst kind followed. Julian woke up in the early morning confused and tired, a poor start for the day of Cooper's funeral. The weather, as predicted by the clouds the night before, was pleasant enough; it was sunny with a few scattered cumuli.

The sunlight arched through the trees leading up to Livy St. Laurent's front door. Sun-dappled clumps of purple mums lined the path. The house was a nondescript split-level with bricks on the bottom and white aluminum up top. Julian paused midway and turned. The policeman waited in his Crown Vic. Julian puzzled at his hesitation, and realized he was nervous. A tragic time, a strange emotion. He had seen Livy on only a handful of occasions over the previous twenty years, each time only briefly. Never alone.

Julian knocked on the door, although he probably could have simply walked in. Moments later Cam answered. His eyes were red, sleep deprived. He looked sharp in his three button Brooks Brothers. The confederate-gray tie hung from a bulky Windsor. Another St. Laurent generation, spooky in his resemblance to Maxwell. They made brief eye contact, but neither spoke. Both looked at the floor, hoping to find instructions on what to do next. Neither wanted to spoil the day. Julian finally extended his hand. Cam offered a single firm handshake in return.

"I'm sorry for your loss, Cam." Not original, but heartfelt.

"Come in, Uncle Julian. Mom's upstairs." He backed away and made a quarter turn, then stopped. "Sorry."

Julian pressed his lips together in a hint of a smile then bobbed his chin once.

Cam echoed the nod, then disappeared into the kitchen. The house smelled of fresh-brewed coffee. Livy appeared at the top of the staircase a moment later. Julian had prepared for this moment, but found himself unprepared. A prism of sunbeams slanted through the window and cast Livy in a spotlight as she descended the staircase. Only Renoir could have done justice to the moment. She looked radiant in her simple black knee-length silk dress. Julian's stomach tightened. Livy's cobalt-blue eyes narrowed in an attempt of warmth; they were unsullied by the years and held a mixture of despondency and bravado, as false as it might be.

A shattered smile accentuated a few early forties wrinkles. The smile, as it was, he remembered; it felt good. A strand of auburn hair hung down over her left eye; the rest was clipped up behind her ears.

"Hello, Julian." Her luscious voice carried the lilt of sorrow. Underneath the sadness, it hadn't changed.

In an instant, emotions and feelings totally foreign to each other fused together in odd, new ways. Julian's mind was being ambushed at the worst possible time, in a situation beyond his control.

"Livy, I'm so sorry for your loss."

Livy lowered her eyes deferentially as she approached and finally stopped three feet away. Their eyes met again; only their history spoke.

They studied one another. Between them passed years of random thoughts, never spoken.

She reached out and took his hands. "I'm sorry."

Julian waited a beat then took the next step and embraced his sister-in-law. Time was supposed to take care of feelings. The faint smell of Shalimar, musty and feminine, took him back to the steps of the church. The long-forgotten feeling of her arms around him quickly produced a montage of images. Julian experienced the blurred sensations of the joys and the heartbreak of his unrequited love. After a moment, he realized the insanity of his sentiment. Common sense returned to banish the long-buried emotional luggage. Julian backed away.

"Julian, we can help each other."

Livy's expression of muted resilience quickly faded to quiet acceptance.

"They were after me. It should have been me," said Julian.

"When I saw Captain Childers at the door…I knew the day I had dreaded for twenty years had finally arrived." She followed with a weary sigh. "What is going on, Julian?"

"I don't know."

Silence filled the space, but there was no discomfort.

"Maxwell told me you've found someone. I'm happy for you."

The reference to Karlie prompted Julian to look at Cam then back at Livy. He wondered if Maxwell would still be alive if Karlie hadn't been thrown against the kitchen counter. *She would have been home, not at the hospital, when Gretchen showed up Sunday morning.*

"Her name is Karlie."

"Will I meet her today?"

"I'm not sure." Uncertainty shrouded his deep-seated fear. He tried hard to imagine a positive outcome to the post-funeral collaboration.

"Do you still have that old Volkswagen?"

Livy's attempt to lighten the mood seemed curious; first, she'd mentioned Karlie and then referenced a long-lost joy they had once shared.

"Unfortunately not. Ran out of duct tape. That old clunker held a ton of memories, didn't it?"

They shared a brief smile.

"Do you care which suit I wear?" asked Julian.

"No. You're thinner than Max." She hesitated a moment, as if unsure whether to continue. "You need to take care of yourself, Julian." Concern etched the corners of her mouth.

"I'm sure whatever is in the closet will work fine. Give me twenty minutes. Then we can go."

Julian turned toward Cam, who was standing in the foyer.

"I want you to stay close to your police escort. Twenty-four seven. No extra trips. Just classes and home. Got it?"

"Uncle Julian, I'll be OK."

"No, you won't. I saw what they did to Nidal and Gretchen. It's beyond anything you can imagine. Until the police figure this out, for your mother's sake, for my sake, you cool it for a while. Trust me. You wouldn't have a chance in hell against these guys."

Cam stood tall, didn't respond immediately, and then finally nodded agreement.

Chapter Fourteen

An hour later, they drove through the front gate of Saint Joseph's Cemetery. Numerous gravestones sprouted up like earthly incisors, many festooned with diminutive flower groups. Julian estimated well over a hundred people at the grave site, most of whom he did not know. Julian was certain Cooper had affected all their lives for the better.

The memorial service was reverent. Julian had requested that the proceedings be kept brief; duration was not a criterion for quality. He glanced several times over his right shoulder at the pine forest. He saw no one.

The end of the service could not come soon enough. He offered a final eulogy for his buddy. After that, he spoke with those well-wishers who needed to be spoken to. He made sure Livy and Cam had protective surveillance, then excused himself for a quiet moment at Cooper's grave. It was then that the finality of the moment hit him—hard.

Julian assured his police guard he was quite safe and then headed for the spot where the two service roads came together. It was a lonely place, the road that ran behind the pine forest. The cicadas' grating banter provided a background soundtrack. The pines saturated the air and threw harsh shadows over the needle-slick trail. Julian looked up at a thousand black birds heading south. As he neared the bend, the ground sloped off to his right toward a creek that meandered parallel to the road. It was really no more than a thread of water in a trench. Julian rounded the bend where a path veered off to his right. A small building––maybe a maintenance shack––was nestled in an area at the end of the path, thirty yards away. The building was nondescript. It had weathered wood, double-sliding doors, and shingles missing from the roof.

The bridge––a simple cement culvert––lay straight ahead. Julian ducked underneath and placed the folder in an obvious spot. He looked at his watch; three minutes had passed. On the way back, he stopped at the path and then veered left toward the hut. Within thirty feet of the door, Julian heard noises––primal noises. The pine needles leading up to the shack were scattered, and the overgrowth was bent. He crouched down and worked his way to the corner of the building, out of direct sight of the doorway. The noises were muted. He heard a man's voice speaking a foreign language in a one-sided conversation. Julian found a board––solid, maybe oak from an old fence––under the weeds that choked the edges of the building. Julian took off his suit coat and tie and then rolled up his sleeves. The points of his black Oxford wing-tip shoes reflected in the sun. He advanced toward the door. The grasshoppers scattered, and the foreign tongue grew louder. The wood felt rough in his sweaty hand. At the door's edge, the reality of what was going on inside rattled his brain. A ripple of nausea preceded a tidal wave of rage.

Julian's hard, spare body tightened in response to the emotion. The bands in his shoulders grew taut. He banished thoughts of surveillance. Jacked up on hate and a wave of adrenaline, he barreled through the door. The hot, putrid smell of moldy grass and stale oil filled his nose. An olive-colored ass bobbed up and down. Another Middle Easterner straddled the victim, holding her down.

"Motherfucker!"

With the venom of pure hatred pulsing through his veins, and a million striated muscle cells playing in concert, Julian swung the board through a wide arc and into the side of the felon's head with full extension. It was a walk-off home run. The splintering skull sounded like a ripe watermelon striking the ground from a two-story fall. The foreigner simply leaned to his left and melted into the dirt floor of the shed. Julian had failed to notice the two-inch spike that protruded from the end of the board. It was now part of the zealot's brain.

Julian let go of the board and spun around. The other Middle Easterner had his gun nearly horizontal. A grimace filled the foe's face, and his perfect white teeth provided a prime target. The wing-tip shoe reached the bull's-eye at the same time the gun discharged. The crunch of facial bones and the sensation of teeth moving into the middle of the man's head added fuel to the frenzy.

Julian glanced over at Karlie, who now cowered behind a Dixie Chopper lawn mower. Her jade-green eyes––big and round––wandered in a daze. Waif-like, naked, and shaking, her normal olive complexion looked pale. Tears mixed with sweat. Her mouth was pulled taut with a gag wrapped tightly around her head. Blood swathed her stomach and the insides of her legs.

Julian's second kick, which caught the foe as he was falling back, landed directly under his chin. It should have taken the guy's head off. The third shot hit midsternum, sending shards of bone into the felon's miserable heart. The man slumped to the ground.

Julian's need for vengeance coursed though his body. The essence of his life had been eviscerated over the previous forty-eight hours. He had been impotent to do anything about it, until now. Sweat flowed off his forehead into his angst-filled eyes. His heart pounded. He staggered backward as he readied for his next attack. His abdominal muscles tightened again as he sent a flurry of kicks into the head of the toothless felon. Sanity was breached in Julian's frantic attempt to regain his old life. In the end, the Middle Easterners were reduced to lumps on the dirt floor, only their clothes labeled them as human. Julian's life still sucked.

The policeman, alerted by the discharge of the gun, finally pulled Julian away. Julian stood with his feet three feet apart and then slumped backward, panting, sweating. Blood littered his white shirt. He looked at the policeman, but said nothing.

"Self-defense," said the policeman, who returned his stare. "Don't remember the number for 911."

Julian took the suit coat offered by policeman, nodded "thanks," and then walked to Karlie. The floor was slick with blood. He bent down; their eyes met. No words were said. He covered her with the coat, removed the gag, and then picked her up and walked silently by the policeman, down the long pine-tree shaded lane toward the cemetery.

PART 2

Faith is the assurance of things hoped for, the conviction of things not seen.

Hebrews 11:1

CHAPTER FIFTEEN

Julian's fingers rolled across the keyboard of the baby grand. It was Saturday morning, three days after Maxwell's funeral and five days after Cooper's: five days of quiet conversation and reflection. The events had changed all of them, especially Cam. Karlie remained in the hospital.

A somber G-chord of "Same Old Lang Syne" echoed off the hand-hewn beams above him. Julian looked at the ceiling as he played; he found no answers. His gaze shifted to the stairway. Livy made her way to the main living area carrying a carrot-sized plastic Kool-Aid container filled with cherry Kool-Aid, a favorite since her sophomore year in college. She wore plain jeans, a white T-shirt, and Birkenstocks; her face was devoid of makeup.

"Fogelberg." Her voice was modulated, non-committal.

Julian dipped his chin once and continued to play. Livy took a seat on the bench next to him. They looked straight ahead, like they were riding in a car. Safe.

"Remember, 'Part of the Plan,'" said Livy.

Julian stopped playing and looked at her. A shy smile interrupted her sadness.

"Our song," said Livy.

"Says who? I don't recall voting." A hint of a smile creased Julian's face and absorbed a small portion of the unease that sat between the remotely acquainted old friends.

"You remember." A statement. "1974. Or was it '75?"

"Nixon's resignation. '74." Julian returned his attention to the keyboard. He played a few more notes, but then stopped abruptly; his fingers balked over the ivory slips. "Why didn't you show up…" Julian hesitated.

"…on our wedding day." Livy finished then recoiled, caught off guard. Shards of early-morning sunlight stabbed through the venetian blinds, casting a fence onto the walls; she was surrounded. She studied the tattered cuffs of her jeans. "I don't know. It was an emotional decision."

"That's it!" His words lanced across the void. Disappointment framed his mouth. "Twenty-four years I've waited to ask that question." He studied her eyes, looking for the real reason; they flickered an apology. Then he relented, ambushed by her smell, which merged with his memories.

"All relationships are full of nuances," she said in a monotone voice. "Hurt feelings. Poor communications. Trivial slights." She redirected her gaze from Julian to the floor. "Maybe the perpetual fear of being dumped prevents complete honesty. Or the landscape was not quite as you remember. Maybe you should look again." She paused. "I recall another student."

Julian's disapproving look said they weren't going there. And if it was an issue at the time, it was only imagined. He considered her smokescreen of words and then thought back to what was and all that happened since, all those years he'd spent under the emotional poverty line. "I never got my Woodstock album back."

Livy tried to smile. Nervous hands rolled the unopened Kool-Aid back and forth. "Maybe I couldn't see the relationship as it was."

"In its perfection?" Julian's attempt at sarcasm was met with silence. His eyebrows slid together. "I guess there is always a better way––"

"––to love?"

"––to say something. But I guess relationships are more about what is not said." Julian's attention drifted to the wall, landing on an artist's rendition of an onion. He couldn't imagine Maxwell bringing it home. Then it came to him; they'd never had that last beer. He hated unfinished business––things not said.

"You'd think our joking and frivolity would have fulfilled the communications requirement," said Livy.

He heard her but didn't say anything. His mind wandered.

"I never apologized," she continued.

Julian thought for a moment before he responded. "I've never understood apologies. Are they supposed to make right something that was wrong?"

The sunlight filtered through the trees and into the room. Barbed wire now rested on the shadowy fence.

Julian continued, "Afterward, I almost left. Thought I could hide out with some Aboriginal tribe…tie a gourd around my johnson…get herky-jerky by a campfire."

A real smile fought its way onto her face, the first one in days. "Silly, it wouldn't have ever worked."

"What, gourds not big enough?"

They shared the joke, a welcome respite from the melancholy that had commandeered their lives. Julian played a few more lines of "Same Old Lang Syne." They both sang softly to themselves, trance-like. Emotions toyed with the words.

"We tried to reach beyond the emptiness, but neither one knew how."

Only near the song's end did they consider the lyrics. Both felt a wave of awkwardness. Julian stopped playing and looked at her. Her features softened. She twisted the top of the Kool-Aid and then watched a worm of cherry squirt onto the carpet. Livy studied the scarlet blotch for ten seconds and then tears began to eke down her cheeks.

"Why in the hell do they have to fill these things to the top?"

She placed the container on the desk and then buried her face into her hands. Julian reached around and pulled her close. The tears continued for several minutes. Finally, Livy raised her head and nestled into his shoulder. Her opaque eyes stared vacantly out the window.

"I miss him so much," said Livy.

The hum of the washing machine in the utility room filled the background.

She drew away and looked at him, face blotched, eyes red. "How do you do it?"

"What?"

"This. You've lost your best friend and your brother."

Julian thought back to the tragedies of his life, the deaths of close acquaintances and his college mentor and father figure.

"Just get up every day. The soundtrack lingers for a long time. A smell, a gesture, reminders are always there." A vacuous stare greeted Julian's glance. "All you can do is put in the requisite time. One day you've gone an hour without thinking about it. Then you can see there might be a way out. I know that's cliché…but it's true."

Another tear returned, and another, then worked their way over Livy's cheeks and dropped abruptly to her chin.

"For the first time in my life, I feel lost," said Livy.

That was an emotion Julian was far too familiar with. "I think we tend to take for granted the people around us––friends, family. Like they're always going to be there. When we can't ever see them again, for whatever reason, their memories turn to phantasms that haunt us."

Livy again buried her face in her hands, this time wiping the tears from her eyes one at a time.

"It's a huge void to fill," said Julian. "You have to learn to deal with your own life, again."

Julian placed his hands on the keyboard. He searched for a clever note but couldn't find one. Livy rose from the bench and headed toward the kitchen. He finally happened upon "Run for the Roses" then wove his way through the song. As he finished, he turned to find Livy plodding across the parquet floor.

A cell phone ring bumped him from his thoughts. He looked at Livy. She looked back, then at his pocket. Julian hesitated, unsure, then removed the phone and flipped it open.

"The police watch you, but they cannot protect you."

The foreigner who had held Karlie. Julian turned away from Livy. "You got your papers."

"My men never returned. I had to send more."

Julian was back in the shed; dead felons were lumps on the floor. His heart skipped a beat, slowed, and then raced to make up for the miss. A current of unease slogged through his mind as he glanced back at Livy. He crossed the room and stole a look through the blinds. The police surveillance car filled a spot on the street. "I think our business is done."

"I think you are mistaken."

The connection went quiet. Julian released the blinds and shoved the phone back into his front pocket. His mind darted here and there, from one thought to another. He maintained his position near the window, vigilant, and then took another anxious peek toward the blinds. But instead of looking through the blinds, he looked at them. And he fixated upon them, his mind locked with indecision. A memory sparked of the Wistrom video. He hadn't really thought about it until now, but he realized the video that got him fired––of he and Karlie making love––had been filmed through blinds very much like the ones he stared at. Karlie's open bedroom blinds. They'd been left open that night. He remembered wanting to close them. *What did she say the night of Coop's death? "It worked."*

There is a universal "oh-no" feeling a person experiences at the first inkling of a grievous error. It is a feeling of not wanting to be privy to it and hoping it can be wished away but knowing that it can't. It's a visceral thing. Suddenly, that "oh no" feeling busted out of a synapse in Julian's brain and sent a cold chill through his body. *Damn.*

"What?" asked Livy when Julian failed to offer an explanation about the preceding phone call.

Julian, bumped from his reverie, said, "Nothing."

CHAPTER SIXTEEN

LIVY ST. LAURENT'S HOUSE
Saturday, September 8, 2001, 9:15 a.m.

Another few minutes passed, filled with house clatter and awkward glances.

"If I have to get up every morning, I need some answers," Livy finally said.

Julian startled. "I told you, absolutely nobody knew Maxwell would be there. Nobody. They were after me."

"Who's after you?" Her plea was tentative and urgent at the same time, as if she wasn't sure if she really wanted to know the answer to the question she had to ask.

The creases in Julian's forehead deepened. "Maybe Middle Easterners looking for papers left at Karlie's. Maybe somebody else from a long time ago. Something I did with Cooper and Maxwell." He leaned back against the wall, his hands on a ledge; he took in a deep breath then let it out slowly. "Hell, I don't know."

"Not an enemy in the world, then all of a sudden people are lining up to kill you?"

"Bad week."

Livy crossed the room and stopped in front of Julian. She touched him high on his neck, at the base of his skull. Her fingers kneaded his taut muscles. "Fred Lewis––Max's boss––brought Max's car back yesterday." She waited for him to acknowledge her. "I found some files buried in the trunk."

"Maxwell was bringing them to my house the night of the fire. That's what he was doing there. Waiting for me."

Livy moved her hand to the back of Julian's. "You need to figure out what happened."

"Get the files back to Fred. He'll figure it out." There was no hesitation in his response. Julian crossed the room to the aquarium that was juxtaposed to a slate entryway. The yellow tangs glided past, one after the other. Their skin looked rock hard and impenetrable to the outside world. He did a half-turn and looked at Livy. "The cases I look at are two thousand years old. The police will figure it out. We just have to be patient."

"Someone killed Cooper. Someone is trying to kill you."

She made a visual plea. He said nothing.

"It can't be a coincidence."

He still said nothing.

"Just look at the files. I know I have no right to ask any favors of you. But I can ask that you do it for Max, for Cooper."

Julian's eyes settled back into the serene depths of the aquarium. He watched a stoic tang slip through the kelp, then nibble on a piece of romaine lettuce. "Where are the files?"

A moment later, Livy appeared with a box. He met her at the mahogany dining-room table, moved aside flowery remembrances of Maxwell's funeral, and then asked Livy to empty the carton. Three thick files slid out. Livy sat down. Julian did the same then picked up the first folder. He shuffled through the stack of papers, trying to figure out how it was organized—it wasn't. He stopped at Cooper's autopsy report.

2 September 01

Dictated: Dr. Julio Aberrato
Copies to: Detective Maxwell St. Laurent
          Detective Brandon Douglass
          Dr. Julio Aberrato

Clinical: Blunt-force trauma, train
Primary cause of death: Decapitation
Secondary findings:

    1.) Amputation, left arm
    2.) Bullet fragments, glenoid fossa, left shoulder
    3.) Fractures, left ribs, 2-7
    4.) Fracture, clavicle, left
    5.) Rupture, spleen
    6.) Perforation, duodenum
    7.) Laceration, liver, grade 2
    8.) Bronchiogenic carcinoma, lung, with metastasis to hilar nodes, bone

"Huh," said Julian.

"What?"

"They found bullet fragments in Cooper's left shoulder. He never got shot in the time that I knew him."

"So he was shot recently? Is that what killed him?"

"Not sure. Maybe someone shot him before the train got him. Or the cancer."

"Cancer?" Her eyes widened.

"Lung cancer. Cooper never said anything to either one of us."

"So he didn't know?" She took the sheet from Julian.

"Don't know. In my mind, he did. Maxwell was going to call Cooper's doctor to find out what Cooper knew. Not sure he got a chance."

Livy let go of the report then slumped back into the chair. "You've got to figure out what happened." There was frustration in her voice.

Julian said nothing in response. He continued to sift through the papers. Most meant nothing to him. "Curious."

"What?"

"Sunday morning, when Maxwell told me about the cancer, he didn't say anything about the bullet fragments."

Livy gave Julian a questioning look then said, "He was forgetful like that."

Julian zipped through the second folder as if he was looking for the two of clubs in a deck of cards. Forty or fifty digital photos fell out of the third file when he picked it up. On top was the bloody crime scene at the rail yard.

"Livy, I don't think you want to see these."

"But, I––"

"Cooper was decapitated, remember?"

Livy agreed with her eyes, got up, walked to the end table to retrieve her Kool-Aid, and then retreated to the kitchen.

Julian reconsidered the photos. He moved the photo of Cooper's headless torso to the bottom. The next was of the other body. Then came close-ups of the tattoos covering Cooper's chest. The letter *Q* was inked in Gothic script over the sternum, surrounded by seven letters––*C, H, K, P, S* and two *W*'s––one each at the points of a pentacle, two on the arms of the surrounding pentagon. The word DEXION was embossed on the right shoulder, and ECCLE was on the macerated skin of the left. A one-inch-high hangman's noose was positioned over his left chest. The next three images were close-ups of trace evidence. Then, a photo of an arm. Unfortunately, it was mangled, making it impossible to decipher the ink. Julian set this picture off to the side. Next was a picture of an old lady. Her skin was porcelain; her hair was white. Then came a cluttered desktop. *Cooper's desk?* The next photo was a countertop with various knickknacks and candles. *Hell!* Julian flipped back to the picture of the old lady. She stood in what appeared to be a study and wore a simple black sweater with a red shawl wrapped around her shoulders. A circular brooch gathered it together on her upper chest. The adornment looked dusky-gold, ancient, and worn. *An heirloom of some sort.* Markings etched the metal.

"Livy!" She was still close, in the kitchen.

She rushed in expectant and concerned.

"Do you have a magnifying glass?"

"I think so." The tightness in her face eased noticeably. She turned and started up the stairs.

Julian scanned the rest of the photos, looking for more taken inside the parish house. Footsteps in the kitchen disrupted his concentration.

"Find it?" Julian asked without looking up.

"You're still here," said Cam, car keys in his hand.

Julian's head jerked up. "Oh, I thought you were Livy."

Cam struck an unnatural pose, like a statue. Julian did the same. An awkward silence filled the space. The pause lingered longer than it should have.

"I thought you'd be gone," said Cam.

"The police thought surveillance would be easier if I stayed."

Cam nodded. "Stay as long as you like." He moved stiffly toward the stairs and then made a hesitant turn. "It helps Mom…not being alone." Cam maintained his eye contact.

Livy met him at the bottom, carrying a magnifying glass. "You're back."

"Got the trip down to a science."

"Cam," said Livy to Julian, "has been doing some chauffeuring for some computer big shots. He's been going to Logan all summer. "

"Cab company out of business?" asked Julian. He added a grin, hoping it might represent a baby step.

"Just trying keep my foot in Google's door." Cam turned and ascended the stairs.

Livy handed the magnifying glass to Julian. "Find something?"

Julian held up the picture he was studying. "This, I presume, is a picture of Agnes, the housekeeper who lives in the parish house at Trinity Church." Julian paused. "I just realized that in all the years Coop and I knew each other, I never once went into the parish house. We played on the same soft-ball team, had beers at Bukowski's, went fishing, and went to Sox games." He looked at the picture again. "Maybe he wanted to keep pleasure from business."

"And this is interesting, why?"

"Give me a second."

Julian, with pencil in hand, studied the magnified photo then wrote various letters on a piece of scrape paper. He substituted one, then another, trying different combinations.

"I assume this is Greek," said Livy.

Julian nodded. "I apparently don't know shit-from-Shinola when it comes to interpersonal relationships, but I do know Greek, modern and ancient."

Livy smiled. Julian continued to sort letters.

"Have you been back to your house…since…?" asked Livy.

"No." Julian's lips pursed together.

"Do you think it's too early?"

"I don't know." Julian paused and studied Livy. "Today? Together?"

"I think so."

After another minute, Julian wrote out a row of Greek letters, then, next to it, the English translation: B-U-C-E-P-H-A-L-U-S. He turned the paper around and showed it to Livy. "Unbelievable."

"What is it?"

"The name of a horse, a very famous horse. Actually the not-so-famous horse of a very famous person."

She looked at the paper then returned a blank stare.

"I guess you don't recognize the horse's name, Bucephalus. Hopefully, you've heard of his owner: Alexander the Third of Macedon."

Livy still looked perplexed.

"Alexander the Great!"

Livy looked at the picture then back at Julian. "What is it?"

"I thought it was a brooch at first, but I think it's a horse buckle, something used by the ancients to attach blankets and other stuff to their horses."

"What would she be doing with something like that?"

"It's probably a fake––thrift-store refuse."

"But if it isn't, it would have to be two or three thousand years old."

"Two thousand, three hundred and thirty-seven."

CHAPTER SEVENTEEN

TRINITY CHURCH, BACK BAY
Saturday, September 8, 2001, 11:20 a.m.

Julian and Livy strolled through Copley Square, west to east. The late-morning sun had finally burned off the chill from the previous night. A glorious day it was. To their left, bobble-headed pigeons wandered near a gaggle of hornets contesting a peach carcass. The breeze delivered mouth-watering aromas from a nearby restaurant. The sun painted shadows onto the square and Boylston Street as taxis rattled past.

Julian stopped and directed his gaze up. There was nothing subtle about Trinity Church. Embedded on Back Bay landfill and forty-five hundred wooden pilings, the Copley Square location bestowed the grandeur of a cathedral to the fortress-like edifice. The westwork was typical Romanesque architecture––thick walls and rounded arches. The portico was executed with three brownstone arches bordered by columns topped with foliate capitals. Arched, mullioned windows highlighted by ashlar stonework layered the next level. An imposing high-shouldered tower with a square-shaped lantern rose high above.

"It's certainly not Madame Tinkertoys' House of Blue Lights is it?" said Julian, looking up at an ornamented pinnacle.

The mention of the establishment of carnal pleasures, made famous in their favorite movie, *Easy Rider*, brought a rare moment of joy to Livy's face.

"It's supposed to put people in the mood for salvation, not sex," said Livy, her smile still playing around her lips.

Julian and Livy headed left toward the back of the church. Once in Trinity's shadow, they could see two homeless fellows settled in the portico, leaning up against the granite. A thick, soiled sleeping blanket covered their legs; despair covered their faces. Beard stubble filled in their sunken cheeks, taut under grizzled heads. Julian threw a nod in their general direction then walked over and dropped a couple of twenties into their cup. Vacant stares acknowledged the gesture. Two crumpled, bottled-shaped bags appeared from under the sleeping bag. The younger gestured to Julian to take a nip; Julian smiled, and mouthed "What about the lady?" The man tipped his bag toward Livy and then offered a gappy grin. Livy winked; Julian laughed and waved, and they proceeded around the transept to the back.

On the east side of the church, they entered an L-shaped cloister that connected the place of worship to the parish house. A broad, semicircular brownstone apse jutted up against the south edge of the covered walkway. A small courtyard was ablaze with ranks of mums. They turned right toward the rectory. Twenty feet later, they found a sign near the thick main-entrance door--"Deliveries Downstairs." Julian and Livy took the steps. The musty smell of decay permeated the dank stairwell. Water seeped from crevices in the bricks. The mortar was green and black and missing in spots. Intricate spiderwebs filled the shadowed corners. At the bottom of the stairway was a five-foot square entrance area, bordered on two sides by musty bricks and on the third by a four-hinge door---carved oak, at least three inches thick. There were four bolts per hinge, sixteen rusted bolts dotted the left side of the door. A peephole was positioned just above a tarnished brass knocker, which was shaped like a wild boar with a quoit hanging from its nose. A security camera spied from the ceiling. The inked sticker plastered on the side looked pristine.

Julian knocked. After a moment, the peephole darkened. He smiled and looked up at the camera.

"What are you, nine-parts mush?" The voice from behind the door sounded wrinkled, like an Opal or a Mabel. Or maybe a Fern.

"Excuse me?" Julian was slightly bewildered.

"I know your kind, you highfalutin shyster. Told you not to come back. Now get your behind out of here."

Julian and Livy looked at each other with bemusement. Livy whispered, "She thinks you're Maxwell."

"Maxwell was nine-parts mush?" He turned his head toward the door. "Ma'am, excuse the interruption. I'm a friend of the reverend. I wanted to ask you some questions."

The lady didn't respond. The peephole turned white. He looked at Livy. "I think she left. Maxwell warned me. Any ideas?"

"Doesn't sound like she's from around here."

"Not from the South either. Must have escaped from the mother ship."

"You goofball, be nice. She's just old. We'll be there someday."

"Feel like I'm there already." He added a sigh. "Beam me up, Scotty."

Livy offered an affectionate tap on the shoulder. "Maybe she's one of those crotchety old ladies who likes things that guys like."

"Breasts?"

"No, silly. Monster trucks. Football. My aunt Esther was like that. An ornery as hell Celtics fan. Red Auerbach was God, Bill Russell, Jesus."

"So?" Julian made a quarter turn to face Livy.

"Sweet talk her, but not with girly stuff."

Julian faced the wooden planks and offered a single knock. The peephole darkened again.

"You still here?" There was a surprising gritty quality to the weathered voice.

"Yep. Hey, I was wondering. How's your team lookin' this year?"

A hoarse chuckle drifted from the other side of the door. "Can't get any worse. One and fifteen last year. Finally got rid of that pansy, Leaf."

Julian looked at Livy, smiled, and said "thanks" with his eyes. "I guess San Diego should have drafted Manning instead."

"You got that right. Boy, they got a good one this year."

"Quarterback?"

"No, you idiot. Draft pick. Tomlinson. Running back."

"No offensive line," said Julian.

"No problem, they got Flutie from those damn Patriots."

The peephole lightened again. Julian looked at Livy. They heard a clunk from the door.

"You sure know how to sweet talk a girl," said Livy.

Julian returned a skeptical look.

Three more distinct bolts clinked over a period of fifteen seconds.

"I guess she's security conscious," said Livy.

"You think?"

The door sucked open to the length of a security chain.

"So what you want?" said the old lady. The shadows darkened her face.

"I was Cooper's best friend growing up. I just wanted to talk with you. Ask some questions."

"About what? Don't know nothin'. He's dead's all I know."

Julian softened his expression and smiled at the old lady. He purposely let the pause linger. "Think you're right about Tomlinson. Texas Christian. Great prospect."

The granny hesitated and then unlatched the door. "Don't try nothin' funny, or I'll knock the both of you from here to next Wednesday. Have you pissin' scarlet for a month." She raised her cane and added a shake, apparently to indicate the mode of transmission.

Julian and Livy entered into a combination utility room, storage area, and kitchen. Foodstuffs and knickknacks overflowed from the shelves, floor to ceiling. They stood on a frayed yellow-striped throw rug on a worn wooden floor. He extended his hand.

"My name is Jul––"

"You can skip the bull crap. You're that cop."

Julian realized Maxwell was dead-on about the lady. She looked as old as the church. Her face was slack and gray with deep-set eyes. She had pinched lips, veiny skin––especially her cheeks––and wispy white hair. She couldn't have weighed over a hundred pounds dripping wet. A four-foot-long snake, tan with large, dark brown blotches, stretched across her diminutive shoulders with its head resting on her gnarled left thumb.

Julian kept his hand extended, undeterred. "Actually, you're referring to my brother, Maxwell. My name is Julian."

The lady eyed Julian up and down. "You ain't afraid of my snake. That other fella was. Must be tellin' the truth."

"Just a gopher snake. Does it have a name?"

"Bob."

She put the snake back in its tank, then extended her hand to Julian, then to Livy. "Name's Agnes."

"My name is Livy."

"You're not from around these parts," Agnes said.

"Indiana originally," said Livy.

"Which coast is that on?" The old lady offered a yellow smile. She turned and tottered into the main part of the kitchen. Julian and Livy followed.

"I guess visitors…not so much," said Julian.

"Don't fret. Same way I feel about Doc Ferguson, my gynecologist. So, you want some coffee? I hate coffee. Damn them Columbians and damn their siestas and damn their tacos, and how come they go and get all important about finding this damn country."

Julian and Livy looked at each other. *Damn!*

"Ugh…no thanks." Julian ran his hand through his hair a couple times to tame the curls. He waited for the lady to drag out her Tarot cards. The paused lingered.

"Get on with it, boy."

It appeared that there would be no divination of his karma today. Surprised, Julian scrambled to find the picture of the heirloom and handed it to Agnes. "What can you tell me about this brooch?"

"I thought you said you had questions about the reverend?" The lady eyed him then offered a suspicious sneer. She looked at the picture. "Just found it…sittin' around."

"Where?"

"Why you so interested?"

Julian looked at Livy, unsure, then back at Agnes. "I would like to see it. I'm at Harvard. Professor of antiquities."

"Found it on the reverend's desk. Sometime back. In his study down here." She pointed at a door at the end of the hallway leading off the kitchen. "Think he used it as a paperweight."

"Anything with it?"

"Nope." Agnes paused. She looked perplexed. "Didn't go into his study. Private place." Agnes rose from the seat, then shuffled over to the counter to retrieve a package of cookies. "Want some?"

Livy checked with Julian. "Thank you, no. May I help you with that?"

Agnes shook her head no. A minute later, she returned with her Oreos and a half gallon of milk

"Could I see the brooch?" He paused. "It might be valuable, very valuable."

Agnes hesitated a moment, opened an Oreo, and, with care, licked the icing out of the middle. She held up another, twisted it apart, and showed them the inside layer.

"This is the entertainment section." She added a crotchety grin.

Both Julian and Livy reconsidered and took a few cookies out of the bag and joined Agnes in the time-honored custom of eating the center first. After Agnes finished, she rose from her chair then returned with the brooch in one hand and two cups in the other. Julian received the faded ring and peg as if he were handling a delicate piece of china. He placed them on the table, produced a magnifying glass out of his pocket, and lowered his head over the artifacts, studying first the ring, then the peg. The ring was five inches in diameter, about an inch wide, an eighth of an inch thick. It was dusky gold in color and streaked black. There was no mistaking the Bucephalus inscription. The back was blank, worn smooth.

Agnes broke the silence. "Count your eggs before the chicks, pretty boy?"

Julian made eye contact, said a silent "thank you," smiled, and then said, "Guilty as charged." He studied the relic closely.

"Are you married?" asked Livy, to break the silence. Sympathy laced her voice.

"Nope. He up 'n died."

"I'm sorry. How long were you married?"

"Until he keeled over. It was a Saturday." Agnes looked up at Livy; the scowl was back. "Then my sex life went all to hell."

An embarrassed moment passed between Julian and Livy, and then he spoke, "Do you have any idea where the reverend might have gotten this?"

"Nope."

Julian thought back. He remembered Cooper had celebrated his ninth anniversary at Trinity earlier in the year. "I can't recall. Who was the minister before Cooper?"

"Reverend Toulukian."

"I remember…thick white hair, bushy white mustache. Could always tell what he had for breakfast on Sunday mornings." The corners of Julian's mouth turned up at the recollection. "Tell me, is he still alive?"

"He died. Suddenly one day."

"Oh." Julian looked at Livy. Livy indicated that it might be best if they left.

"I've spoken to him," Agnes continued, looking blankly at the checkerboard linoleum floor. "He's not well."

Julian and Livy exchanged confused glances. "I thought you said he died," said Julian.

"Oh, he did. But, his spirit lives…here." Agnes raised her arm and made a slow sweeping gesture.

Julian, at a loss for words, looked for help.

"Ah…" said Livy. "Do you have frequent…encounters?"

"Every month or so. At night…usually after the news, before Leno."

"Uh huh," said Julian. "What does he say?"

"It's only a feeling. He is restless."

"So you can't ask him questions?"

Agnes abruptly jerked her head in Julian's direction. "Hey, I said it's a feeling, not AT and T."

"I'm sorry. Do you see anything?"

Agnes didn't answer. She reached for another cookie. It appeared the time for talk was over, and time again for her liturgical exercise. Agnes placed the cookie between the edges of her bent index fingers and twisted. Julian, his inspection complete, placed the artifact on the table and slid it toward Agnes.

"It's the real deal, isn't it," said Livy.

Julian was certain his expression said it all, but he answered anyway. "Yes."

CHAPTER EIGHTEEN

MEMORIAL DRIVE, CAMBRIDGE
Saturday, September 8, 2001, 12:30 p.m.

Julian and Livy drove across the Charles River on their way from Cooper's private place to Maxwell's last place. They were in no particular hurry. Protective police surveillance tagged along behind. Various books and papers collected from Cooper's office rested on the backseat.

"Something's not right," said Livy.

"About what?"

"Agnes."

Julian glanced over at Livy. His look of astonishment ambushed her look of puzzlement. "Ms. Obvious!"

"I know she's a crazy old coot--"

"And a ribald fossil" interrupted Julian. "And a pack rat. There was a 1985 *Consumer Reports Buying Guide* in the pantry."

"It's more than that."

"Hey, we can start with her brain." Julian's gaze drifted left to the rowers in shells and kayaks on the Charles. For just a moment, memories were sparked of an earlier time. He looked at Livy then back over the river. Livy's eyes also brightened.

"Did you see any pictures?" asked Livy.

Julian thought back and realized he hadn't--not one.

"What grandma doesn't have pictures," said Livy as a statement and not a question.

"Maybe she didn't have any children?"

"What about Bob, the husband?"

"You didn't find him in the closet, did you?"

"Pictures!" Livy rolled her eyes, exasperated with Julian's flippancy.

"We didn't go into her bedroom."

"That counter over the sink--the empty counter--was covered in dust, except for five clear areas. Looked like something--maybe picture frames--had been there for a long while."

"Well, aren't we Nancy Drew."

"No woman is going to keep a snake home on her kitchen counter," continued Livy as though she hadn't heard him. "And her refrigerator. There was nothing on it. No magnets, notes…nothing."

"Livy, she's a weird old lady. They do weird things."

"OK, how about this: in the bathroom, there's a closet with a mini washer and dryer tandem stacked on one another. Behind that I found a cat litter box--on its side. Where's the cat?"

"Maybe Princess was lunch…for the snake."

Undeterred, she continued. "In the bathroom I found three pill bottles."

"She's a very senior AARP member, for crying out loud."

"Diabetic medication. For a hundred-pound Oreo-inhaling old lady?"

Julian glanced over at Livy; the smile was gone from his face. "Whose name was on the bottles?"

"Agnes Serrault."

"What were they doing in his bathroom?"

"Shared bathroom. Her bedroom was on the other side."

Julian nodded but didn't reply. They went from one stoplight to the next without speaking. "Hard to imagine. She is really old." Julian drummed his fingers on the steering wheel then stopped and looked at Livy. "Sorry." He ran his hand over his gnarled scalp. "She did know a few things about Cooper."

"Maybe she was well coached."

They finally reached Harvard Square. After a right on DeWolfe Street, they took a left and then another right onto Julian's street. As the charred remains of his house came into view, Julian slowed then stopped. A blackened chimney stood sentinel over the hedgerow. The crime-scene tape draped around the property fluttered in the breeze. The air in the car thickened; he rolled down his window. The landscape was chaotic, a matrix of painful memories and sorrow jumbled together in one big black mess. Julian's trance was interrupted by Livy's sniffles.

"We don't have to do this," said Julian.

A honk from behind made them jump. He pulled to the curb and turned off the engine. The beautiful day did nothing to mollify their souls, each bruised with its own sorrows.

"Just stay in the car," said Julian. "I'll only be a few minutes."

Julian opened the door and put his left leg on the ground. He felt her hand against his arm.

"Wait. I need to see."

Tentative steps brought them closer to the ruins. The sun was hot against their faces. Their feet crunched on charred refuse. Black pools of water filled low areas of the driveway. Parts of scorched furniture littered the yard—skeletal graffiti telling of the tragedy. A soot-covered bathtub laid half buried in the cinders. Leafless trees surrounded the remains like cachectic mourners at a funeral. The lingering stench of burnt wood clogged their nostrils. It was a hard slap of reality for both and confirmation of what they saw and felt.

They ducked under the yellow tape. Livy stood bolt upright, trying to take control over her sinking heart. The fingers of the madness around them grabbed at their minds and distorted their reality.

"I hope…and pray…he didn't suffer," said Livy.

"Seth Jamison said it was immediate and overwhelming. No time for pain or thought."

Silence fell between them. Questions bandied in their heads, but answers remained hidden in their melancholy.

"Julian, I need to know." Their eyes locked. "Who did this?"

Julian didn't answer. A breeze plucked at his ankles, creating a tiny whirlwind of ash and grit. A solitary locust started a grating dirge. They headed toward where the front door had been. At the porch, Livy stooped down and laid a simple bouquet of flowers on the ash-covered bricks, and on top of it, she placed an old hunting knife.

Both sorted through a snarl of memories. They bowed their heads and said a prayer.

After that, there was nothing left to say. They turned around in unison and navigated their way over the killing field of charred furniture to the sidewalk. Neither looked back. Both were lost in recollections, sobered by the residue of Maxwell's final seconds. Halfway to the car, Julian's eyes were drawn to a random piece of litter laying an inch or so off the sidewalk, next to the trunk of an old, thick maple. The roots of the tree had disgorged the sidewalk up a couple inches, creating a crevice. A white golf tee––a long one, the kind used for jumbo drivers––had settled into it. Julian kneeled down to pick it up. Imprinted on the side was, "pride prolength+plus>360cc." It looked moth-eaten. He glanced up.

"Do you have a Kleenex?"

"What?" asked Livy.

"I've seen this before.

CHAPTER NINETEEN

Julian sat alone in the guest bedroom of Livy's house surrounded by crime-scene folders and memories. An hour before, they had shared a simple dinner of cold sandwiches with Samuel Adams. Livy appeared at the doorway with two cups in her hand.

"Coffee?" said Livy.

"Honey?"

"Of course."

"You remembered."

Livy smiled. "Find anything?"

Julian took a sip then thumbed through the photos from Maxwell's folder. Fifteen deep in the pile, he found the one he wanted and placed it on the table. Livy, in a terra-cotta cotton robe and Birkenstocks, took the picture and settled into a chair. After a moment, she picked up the baggy-encased golf tee––the one they found earlier––and held it under the desk lamp.

"Identical," said Livy. "The same nervous person gnawed on both."

"That's what I thought." A memory of what the Middle Easterner had said over the phone flashed through his mind––*I sense you will find your brother's killer.* "The tee in the picture was found near Cooper. In the rail yard."

Livy held up the baggy then looked at the picture again. "Could be our Rosetta Stone."

Impressed, Julian smiled. "It connects Cooper with Maxwell. Well, Cooper with me. It means Maxwell's death is probably not related to Nidal's papers." He took the tee from her and peered at it through a magnifying glass. "This has to be more than chance."

Livy's face visibly relaxed with the conjecture.

"Hardly proof, but..." Julian let the thought linger, then continued. "Maxwell apparently applied the screws to the lab folks. I found a DNA report of the saliva on the rail-yard tee." Julian waited for Livy to look up. "I think they can get this guy."

Livy looked at the tee again then dropped it back on the desk; trouble creased her face. "Chain of evidence. We should've had the surveillance cop take the tee."

"I realized the same thing after I looked at the picture. It's probably worthless now."

Livy inched back in the chair as she drew up her knees. She peered through strands of golden wheat-colored hair that had shifted over her eyes.

"Hey, we'll be OK. The pathologist found some weird DNA. Cam's helping me figure out what it means."

Livy's look brightened again, a mood ring for the info bit of the moment. "You find anything in Cooper's stuff?"

"Not sure. Still looking. We definitely need to go back the parish house."

"We have lunch––"

"Tomorrow, sometime. I have to pick up Karlie from the hospital in the a.m. Maybe in the afternoon"

"How's she doing?"

"Well, as of an hour ago."

Livy acknowledged the good news. "Please don't take the horse ring." Concern added more lines to the worry already etched into Livy's forehead. She wrapped her arms around her legs and put her chin on her knees.

"I need some of the other books." A smile appeared on Julian's face for no apparent reason.

"What?" said Livy self-consciously. She tugged her hair behind her ears.

"The way you're sitting. Same as twenty-five years ago."

Livy's smile raised just the corners of her mouth. "I wouldn't talk, Mr. Honey-in-my-coffee."

Julian reached over and picked up Cooper's Bible and handed it to Livy. "Look at Gospels of Matthew and Luke."

Livy propped the tome in her lap, opened it near the end of the Old Testament, and then thumbed her way to Matthew. The paper was thin, delicate; a musty smell floated off the pages. In the margins, neat block letters in red ink spelled a single word, written many times. "Amphilochus?"

"Sixty-five times. In Luke and Matthew––mostly Matthew. One in the Gospel of John. No other notes in the entire book. Nothing underlined."

"What is it?" Livy skimmed through the rest of the New Testament.

"Who. In Greek mythology Amphilochus was the son of Eriphyle, his mother, and Amphiaraus, his father."

Livy looked at Julian, confused, then back at Cooper's Bible. "What could that possibly have to do with the New Testament?"

"Nothing. Greek mythology never happened. The Bible is history. The only thing that makes it interesting is this." Julian handed Livy another picture, a postmortem close-up of Cooper's right shoulder tattoo.

"Dexion?"

"Maxwell asked me about the tattoo a week ago. It made no sense. Now it makes perfect sense." He took a few sips of coffee.

"What?"

"The Dexion Society was formed after the death of Greek tragedian, Sophocles. To honor his legacy."

Livy's eyes brightened as though she had remembered a name long forgotten. "*Oedipus the King?*"

"Right-o. I guess you didn't skip high-school English class."

"Got to sit next to Eddie Johnson, our quarterback. A cutie. Looked great in those tight football pants." Livy sat back and crossed one leg over the other.

"Did the teacher let him use the pointy scissors?" Julian remained stoic until he got a smile out of his sister-in-law, then continued. "Scholars have papyrus fragments of what is thought to be a poem, "Amphilochus," attributed to––"

"Sophocles."

"You got it."

The reflections of Julian's voice were uplifting. For the first time in days, he was back on the job. He finally had a distraction, something to divert his attention from matters of death to matters of the mind.

"There absolutely has to be a connection between the two. Has to. The tattoos looked new to me. There is nothing else in that Bible––Cooper's personal Bible––only the word, 'Amphilochus.'"

"And Cooper is dead."

Julian's elation dissipated as quickly as it rose, like Christmas lights on a rheostat. "And Cooper is dead."

The declaration brought them back to their grief.

Julian sighed, pushed the top of his laptop down, and leaned way back in his chair. Livy looked at the wall. The inertia created by the melancholy was paralyzing. The battery-powered alarm clock announced time's passage.

"When Cam gets home, could you send him up here?" Julian finally said. Livy nodded.

"Another question…" Julian put his hands behind his head. "Did Maxwell have a file cabinet where he kept papers—maybe private papers?"

Her eyes widened. "In regard to what?"

"I found a curious combination of phone numbers on a page in Cooper's address book. Maxwell's is on the list. Possibly something about the 'Project for The New Democracy'…or 'New American Democracy'…something like that."

"Oh, that." Livy's face suggested awareness, and her tone indicated disapproval.

Julian waited. "And…"

Livy sat up, leaned forward, and put her arms on her knees. Her head dipped; she stared at the oval throw rug covering the pecan-colored wood floor.

"You don't have to say anything. It's none of my business."

"No, it's OK." Livy leaned back and looked up. "Remember back in college…Tuesday nights our junior and senior years?"

Julian guffawed. "Hell, I barely remember what I had for breakfast today."

"That was my study group night…remember? Every Tuesday, I disappeared and met with my study group."

Livy waited for a glimmer of recognition to register on Julian's face.

"Oh, you mean poker night."

"I didn't play poker."

Livy drew her legs up again. Julian smiled.

"Ah, that's why you never said anything," said Livy. "You sneak." She picked up the closest thing available, which happened to be a mouse pad, and tossed it at him like a Frisbee.

"Hey, how do you think I paid for all those pizzas?"

"Actually, there wasn't a study group."

"Sneak!" Julian hurled the mouse pad back at her. "Tupperware parties?"

"Hardly. John Birch Society meetings."

There was a moment delay, and then the light went on in Julian's head. "You and Maxwell."

"I went once, on a whim, with a friend. Remember, back then everything was black or white. There were no grays. We couldn't talk politics. Hell, you wore George McGovern underwear."

"Bad haircuts."

"What?"

"Those were the guys with the haircuts."

"They got 'em; you didn't. Anyway, Maxwell was there. We got to talking."

Julian's look said it all.

"Hey, it was just one of many things. I told you before, it was just an emotional decision. When I got to the church that day, I just froze…couldn't do it." She hesitated. "Maxwell followed me home. I was confused. He was familiar."

She stood up and walked over to him. She placed her hand on his neck, caressed him a few times, and then bent over and kissed him on the cheek. "I am so, so sorry." She stopped talking; the silence between them was unsettling. "I should never have put myself in that position." Livy didn't return to her seat but stayed with her right hand on Julian's shoulder. "It was never romantic, until…" She stopped when she realized she was only making it worse. "Maxwell continued going to the meetings. About the time of Clinton's impeachment proceedings, I was pretty much fed up with politics. Maxwell was obsessed, worse than ever. The Lewinsky thing stole the Bircher thunder. He continued to read *The New American*, the Bircher newspaper. Then in 1998 or '99, he got involved with the Project for the New American Century. A Conservative think tank." Livy turned and sat down in the chair again. "The Birchers were more against communism than for anything in particular. The PNAC is a spend-gobs-of-money, make-the-USA-super-cop-of-the-world group."

Julian waited then spoke. "So how was Maxwell involved?"

"Not sure. Just meetings, I guess. With his schedule, there was no way to keep track of his comings and goings."

"So how do you know––"

"By all the papers on his desk. Letters to editors. Recruitment material. Much more recent…"

"Like…" He stood up and began to pace from one end of the throw rug to the other.

"Just more stuff. I didn't look. It's in the closet, if you want to take a peek." Livy raised her eyelids to offer a visual olive branch. "That help?"

Julian picked up one of Cooper's address books, opened it to the fourth page, and then passed it over to Livy. "Recognize any of those numbers?"

Livy scanned the list then looked up. "Just Maxwell's cell."

"The fourth number is the cell phone number of Karlie's friend…the one that got sliced and diced…Nidal."

Livy's neck muscles tensed. "Maxwell wasn't involved. No way."

"Not implied. Just saying that Cooper and Maxwell might have known Nidal; maybe they all had PNAC interests. Nidal was carved up so that some-one could get the papers he had."

Livy sat down in the desk chair. She whirled around and leaned forward. "How do you know they were after the papers?"

"Trust me, I know. They were desperate. That's why Karlie was kidnapped."

"Where'd the papers go?"

Julian relayed the relevant parts of the story.

"So it was a schematic of a building––"

"High-rise."

"Which one?" Livy rocked back and forth, the motion interrupted occa-sionally by the staccato movement of her right foot. Her Birkenstock fell off and made a clunking sound as it landed on the floor slats. She jumped.

"The CIA guys couldn't get enough from the third of the document that I gave them to ID it. At least not as of a few days ago."

"Maxwell couldn't be involved…ever."

"Maxwell said Nidal had contacts with the CIA. He was supposed to do a dead drop…"

"So Nidal was a CIA agent?"

"I don't know. I don't think so. Maybe an operative of some sort. Maxwell just said the CIA was very interested in what he had."

Livy sat straight in the chair and stretched. She picked up her mug, blew over the top, and then took a sip. "So why the CIA? Why not FBI?"

"Don't know. Maxwell said only CIA."

Julian lay back on the bed, placing his feet on the ground and looking at the ceiling. He concentrated on the globe of the ceiling light. A minute passed. Livy stood.

"I'll let you work," said Livy. "There's a shelf in the back of the closet. It used to hold sweaters. I filled it with papers, old and new. There's a two-drawer file cabinet next to that. Knock yourself out. I'll send Cam up when he gets home."

CHAPTER TWENTY

LIVY'S HOUSE
Saturday, September 8, 2001, 6:45 p.m.

Minutes later, Julian sat in the closet sorting through boxes and folders. One entire shelf, one and a half feet high, was filled with PNAC stuff. He found a statement of principles, an article on rebuilding America's defenses, and notices of meetings. Below that was another shelf with insurance papers, a copy of a will, and police-department policy manuals. On the bottom shelf, near the back, he happened upon a yellowed folder, labeled "MEDICAL." Inside he found old medical records, like lipid profiles, chemistry profiles, and echocardiograms. Ready to move on to an "Old Receipts" folder, he happened upon a pathology report, faded gray and curled at the edges, with the date 1982. At the bottom, it said, "Impression: Azoospermia." Underneath was an equally old yellow envelope bulging with papers with a return address of "Meridian Obstetrical and Gynecology Associates." Julian hesitated a moment and then opened it. On top was a dictated summary of Livy's hospitalization for Cam's birth: October 11, 1977. The third page was an operative report, "Hysteroscopy, June 3, 1983: Normal." He thumbed through the rest and then returned the papers to the envelope, the envelope to the folder, and the folder to the shelf.

He thought back to February 2, 1977, walking down the church aisle into the lobby and then running out to the street in search of Livy. His thoughts morphed onto what happened afterward. The lost, melancholy-filled months. The months of self-pity and heartache. What did Livy just say—*it never got romantic until...* He realized now he had never actually thought about the events after that day; he had merely existed in an inanimate survival mode, trying to handle another serving of life's crap. Months turned into years. He simply had lost track of time.

"Uncle Julian?"

Cam's voice knocked Julian from his trance. He quickly straightened the folders and walked out to the bedroom.

They greeted each other with nods and what had become the usual—awkward silence. Mixed-up thoughts choked Julian's voice. Cam carried several loose papers; he dropped them on the table.

"The stuff you wanted," said Cam.

Julian wasn't sure what to do or what to say. The events in Karlie's apartment with Cam and Nidal flashed into his mind. *I guess I don't like being lied to. By you, Mom, Dad.* "What did you find?" Julian added a smile, perhaps to disguise what he suspected or his embarrassment of not having the supposition until now.

"You can read it. It's all there." Cam's curled hair looked mussed and way too familiar. Cam turned and headed out the door.

"Cam?"

Cam turned and looked back.

"You in a hurry?" Julian took special care to keep his voice measured and calm.

"No. Sam Jenkins is comin' over."

"Going out?"

"Nope. Just chillin'."

Is the edge gone or is it just my imagination? Julian picked up the papers and quickly scanned down the first page. It concerned the DNA found on the crime-scene golf tee. "You do good work." Julian studied the last line, then looked up. "So the guy is a midget?"

"Dwarf. Achondroplastic dwarf. Midgets are symmetrical, just height challenged Not enough growth hormone. Dwarfs have short legs. A cartilage going to bone problem."

"So we're lookin' for a dwarf." He continued to scan the sheet.

"For what?" Cam let go of the door handle and took a few steps into the room.

Julian showed Cam the tee and then explained the circumstances.

"So you think the guy who chewed on this tee killed Dad?" Cam swung the chair around and sat down. He draped his arms over the back, casual like.

"Your mom thinks it may be our Rosetta Stone."

Cam nodded and gave a chin nod toward the papers Julian was holding. "Keep reading."

Julian scanned the sheet again. "Neurofibromatosis?"

Cam nodded. "A dwarf with neurofibromatosis." He smiled.

Julian returned the look. "Is this a good thing?"

"Could be."

Julian kept looking at Cam, waiting for an explanation.

Cam finally smiled back. "Neurofibromatosis is a disease that gives people lumps and bumps––neurofibromas––all over their body. Some have only a few bumps. Some have a lot. Remember the Elephant Man? Some also get brown spots."

"A midget with bumps and spots. I'd say that narrows it down quite a bit." Julian began to pace.

"Dwarf."

"Sorry, dwarf." Julian scanned the third sheet. "So you found ten different James Toulukians?"

"Yep." Cam reached over and flipped to the last page. "Six that fit our parameters. Filed tax returns sometime between 1970 and 1992. Checked each one."

"Which one of these is the Reverend Toulukian? When did he die?" Julian looked up at Cam and made eye contact, maintaining it.

Cam smiled again, smug. "Unless someone has a scam going, he didn't. He's still collecting social security. Medicare is paying for some sort of rehab."

Julian's eyes brightened. "Like I said before, you do good work. You didn't crack into government systems, did you?"

"Thanks, but hey, I'm not that good. Not yet. Blue Cross of Massachusetts, plan B, pays Medicare co-pays."

Julian put the paper down, then sat down on the bed directly across from Cam. "Where are the physical therapy bills going?"

"You'll like this. The Somerville Home."

"Our Somerville?"

"Yep."

Julian stood up and grabbed his car keys from the desktop. "See any health records?"

"Just ICD-9 codes. I checked a few of them. Chronic obstructive lung disease. Hypothyroidism. Hypertension. Osteoporosis."

"Any mention of dementia or Alzheimer's disease, strokes, anything like that?"

"Didn't check all the numbers."

"You pretty sure about all this?

"Hey."

Julian tried to think back to age twenty-four. He couldn't remember being so cocksure about everything.

Cam looked at his watch then back at Julian. "You going out there now?"

Julian nodded. Cam turned to go.

"Cam." He stopped and turned. "A couple of questions before you go. Different topic. Do you remember the first time you met Karlie?"

Cam's look blanked. He hesitated. "I don't know, I guess, why?"

Julian sat down on the bed. Cam remained by the door. "Did you approach her, or did she come up to you?"

Cam took a step back into the room. "Hey, I have no interest in Karlie. We're just friends."

"Hey, no harm. It's about something else."

Cam thought for a moment. "She came up to me. Outside Andover Hall. Asked for directions. We ended up goin' for a Coke."

Julian nodded and then checked to make sure he had his wallet and car keys. "One more thing. She pretty handy with computers?"

"Like a hacker or getting e-mail?"

"Hacking."

"She taught me a few things."

"You think she'd be able to hack through a firewall?"

"Maybe. Not government, but private. Probably private."

"Hospital?"

"Don't know. Maybe."

CHAPTER TWENTY-ONE

MEDFORD STREET, SOMERVILLE
Saturday, September 8, 2001, 9:10 p.m.

Julian was serious about making the trip to the nursing home, despite the hour. Livy ditched her robe but kept her Birkenstocks. She wore a simple white T-shirt tucked into her 501's. The traffic was light; the car was dark. Julian felt uneasy sitting next to her. An occasional streetlight projected a carousel of oblique shadows through the car; these quickly receded only to be replaced by similar bizarre, but different-shaped, shadows from the next streetlight. The road wandered this way and that. On occasion, the tire noise from a patch of broken blacktop drowned out the radio. An oldies station played a Gloria Gaynor song––something about surviving. The breath of fall touched the air. On nights like these, the world looked almost manageable to Julian. He thought back on the events of the day.

"What's the story on the knife—the one you left on my porch?" Julian asked the question to exorcise his unease.

"It was our knife." Livy spoke softly, almost in a whisper. "Maxwell's fishing knife and my camping knife. We joked about who would lose it first."

"I don't remember him being much of a Rambo."

"He wasn't. At first we did the simple things…family campsites in the Berkshires…Pittsfield…Lenox…occasionally a side excursion to

Tanglewood, to the music festival. Then later, we started doing our own thing. He liked the fishing part."

"The only sport that requires beer."

"My thoughts exactly." She paused, and then added, "Rocky."

Julian gave her a questioned look.

"Girls like Stallone as Rocky. Not Rambo."

"Ahh, so that's the difference between men and women." He bashed the heel of his hand against his forehead.

Livy offered a raised brow and then reached over and flipped through a few stations before returning to the oldies. They went through a couple stoplights, processing music-generated memories.

"Cooper told me you're doing survivalist stuff." Julian nudged his window down a couple inches.

"It's all your fault; you got me started. Remember our Appalachian Trail trip? And the paragliders." They shared the memories. "One thing led to another. At first I used the usual stuff like tents and food. Sleeping bags. Then I started going out two or three days with only a knife––that knife."

"No food or water?"

"We––the group I go with––live off the land. Find what we need. Make fire. Find fresh water. I love it."

"That's your happy place?"

"Not really. Just something I need to do. But less so now. A reaffirmation of sorts."

Julian ran his hand through his curls, then tapped on the steering wheel a few beats. "Perhaps some sort of existential tantrum?"

"Not that complicated. Just cheaper than Prozac."

"How about guilt…self-flagellation."

"For what? The wedding? That's ancient history." Livy folded her arms over her chest and looked straight ahead.

Julian glanced toward Livy. "No," he said in a soft but definitive tone. "For not telling Cam." He wrapped his lips carefully around each syllable.

Livy jerked her head toward Julian. "For not telling him what?"

Julian stared through her.

In an instant, realization swept over Livy's face. Her past had finally slithered back into her life. The allegation seemed to suck the oxygen out of the car; the well-conceived delusion, years in making, disintegrated in the vacuum. Livy's features hardened in a flash of anger. Then her contour went limp in a wave of resignation––or maybe relief. A life interrupted. She buried her head into her hands.

"You couldn't have expected to hide the truth forever."

Livy sat up and tried to inch closer to the door; she was out of inches. Julian pulled the car over to the side of the road and then turned off the engine. The car shivered into silence. He rolled down his window the rest of the way. The faint puff of city noises drifted through the opening.

"Damn it, Livy!" Julian gave the steering wheel a two-handed bash then lowered his head onto his forearms. The reality of being a father grabbed him, hard. Ethereal notions did nothing to summon the emotions, not like reality. He remembered a welter of events in his life. He contemplated all he had lost out on and how hopeless it was to try to get it back. Not knowing his father made it worse. He took in two deep breaths, slowly exhaling each. Dogs barked nearby. Horns honked. People slept and dreamed. Nobody cared.

"It was a such an emotional time," Livy finally said. "I compounded one bad decision with another, on top of another." She turned her legs toward him and looked up. Her fingers remained knitted together in her lap. "I kept waiting for you to show up or call or write––to do something. I was prepared to deal with the confrontation, not precipitate it. But days passed, months passed, years passed…nothing…you never showed up. Then it was too late."

Julian leaned his head out the window. There was a nip in the evening air; it felt good. "Maxwell knew." He said it as a statement.

Livy nodded yes.

Julian raised his eyebrows to acknowledge the response and then turned his gaze toward the window. "You got married so soon afterward; I assumed you two had been seeing each other for a while." He relaxed and considered her confession––letting the idea that he was a father settle in. Actually, it felt good. "I was just getting out of bed each morning."

Livy dabbed her tears with the back of her hands. "When did you figure it out?"

"Tonight."

"How?"

It was never romantic, until… "The right words going in the wrong ear."

Livy looked at Julian, confused.

"That, and the old medical records in the closet." Julian reached out and placed his hand on the back of Livy's. He felt a fine tremor.

"Did you tell Cam?" Trepidation was suggested by her tone, by the way she said "Cam."

"No. But I suspect he knows. Probably found out six months ago."

"How?"

"I'm working on that."

Livy was catatonic. She spoke in a whispered tone, nearly imperceptible. "How do I make it right?"

"Fess up. Start the healing."

Livy stared at her hands and said nothing.

"You need to sit down and explain everything to him." Julian struggled to establish eye contact with her. "He blames me. He thinks I knew all along and never took responsibility and was part of a cover-up. I suspect he thinks you were in a jam and Maxwell was your white knight."

Livy nodded her head once.

The fresh September air, mixed with a trace of Livy's Shalimar, wafted through the car. Livy took in another deep breath; her breasts strained against the thin T-shirt. For an instant, Julian tried to remember back to the time of Cam's conception—a time when he had finally learned to trust people, a time when he actually believed in the fantasy called love. But he couldn't find it. The vicissitudes in his life––event after event––had created a barricade that he had been unable to dent in the past twenty years. He gave Livy's hand a gentle squeeze and then started the car. Neither spoke until they reached their destination.

CHAPTER TWENTY-TWO

They pulled up on a side street facing the Somerville Home. The three-story block-C-shaped brick building loomed over a brightly lit courtyard. A flagpole stood tall in the center; taps had already played. The entrance lights cast tilted shadows on the quad. The windows were lonely black holes between stark white shutters. The front door was locked.

The charge nurse accepted Julian's story about a family tragedy. Their passage to the second floor was without sound. The noise of their steps was swallowed up by the carpeted hallway.

"Why do old people smell old?" Livy posed the question as they searched for room 268. "When I was a kid, I was always afraid of my grandpa. He smelled so old."

Light escaped from the door's edge when they happened upon the room, so they knocked once and cracked the door open. An elderly man reclined in bed, reading. Under a nest of white hair, his brown eyes, still and watchful, peered up at them over reading glasses. A bulbous nose floated on a bushy gray mustache. A nasal cannula, nestled in the prodigious crop of whiskers, delivered oxygen. The dark circles under his eyes consumed his cheeks. Folds of skin weighed heavy on his jaw. His initial look was one of startle and then fear. He dropped his book and reached for his carved oak walking stick. He fumbled with it and then watched it cascade out of reach. His ill-fitting pajama top imprisoned his search for something else.

"Reverend? Reverend Toulukinopolis?"

The old man stopped thrashing and looked up at Livy and Julian, his angst replaced by resignation.

"You finally found me," he said in a voice that reminded Julian of Mr. Howell on *Gilligan's Island*.

Confused, Julian and Livy looked at each other then back at the cleric. "We're not here to harm you." Julian extended his hand. "My name is Julian St. Laurent. This is Livy St. Laurent. I want to ask you some questions."

The old man extended a hesitant, arthritic hand. "How'd you get in here?"

"Under false pretenses, I'm afraid. You don't remember me, I'm sure. I attended, on occasion, your services at Trinity years ago. I was a childhood friend of Cooper Saltonstall."

They shook hands, but clearly the suspicion lingered. "You are no longer friends?"

"Oh." Julian looked at Livy and then back to the reverend. "He died last week. Killed."

"Killed?"

"Yes."

The cleric sat up in bed and tugged the sheets up to his neck. A bag, half-filled with urine, hung on the lower bed railing; the connecting tube snaked under the bed covers.

"Who killed him?"

"I don't know." Julian leaned over and helped him with the sheets. "You're not surprised."

The old man nodded thanks, then put his hands at his side. "How did you find me?"

"The Internet and a very smart nephew...son." Julian shared a knowing glance with Livy. She added a heartfelt smile. "Dead people don't file taxes."

For the first time, the old man offered a bittersweet smile. "I'm surprised the ruse worked for so long. What is it, ten years now?" He coughed, coughed again, and then again; it was unremitting for thirty seconds. He reached for a nearby tissue, then deposited a glob of yellowish phlegm. He abandoned the used tissue on the nightstand for safekeeping, next to several others. An empty pill cup and an extra set of glasses stood at the corner. "Sorry, my lungs. I'm afraid they're about all used up."

"May I get you anything?" said Livy, picking up a nearby wastebasket and nudging away the deposit of used tissues. "Besides a new set of lungs."

"Thank you, no." His mouth hinted at a smile. "I'm sorry. I've forgotten my manners." The old man motioned to the seats next to his bed. "I've observed that dead people don't receive many visitors." As they pulled two chairs to the edge of the bed, he continued, "You're a very handsome couple. Are you husband and wife?"

Livy, taken aback, looked at Julian, a blush clearly stamped on her checks. "Why, no. In-laws."

An uncomfortable silence settled over them for a moment. Then Julian spoke. "You assumed your original surname after your death?"

"Not very imaginative I'm afraid. Short notice."

Julian nodded as he tried to piece together the scenario that ended with the reverend in the Somerville Home. "Did you come from the old country?"

"Yes. Long ago. I met Rita, my wife, God rest her soul, in the fifties. Nineteen fifty-two to be exact. July fourteenth. She was vacationing in Greece with her family. I followed her to the states. We married. It was during those unsettling postwar years. McCarthy dominated the news. I changed my name. It seemed the right thing at the time."

"Mrs. Vandenbosch thinks you are dead," said Julian.

"Who?"

"The housekeeper in the parish house."

"I'm sorry, I don't know her. Agnes Serrault was my housekeeper."

Julian and Livy shared a look, recognizing the name from the medication vials. "Was Mrs. Serrault there when you left…ah, died?"

"Yes. She made calls to the appropriate people. Helped Reverend Saltonstall settle in. I never got the chance to meet him."

The old man gazed across the room, perhaps recollecting times past. Julian followed his eyes and allowed the moment to linger. Julian noticed a fine tremor, something he hadn't seen before, slow, like a goose taking flight. The cleric looked like a shivering scrawny cat in a cold drizzle. He felt lonely for the old man.

"What can you tell me about a gold ring and peg? A horse-blanket buckle. Very old."

Reverend Toulukinopolis's head jerked, surprise filling his eyes. He hesitated. "I'm sorry, I don't know anything…" He stopped talking and then looked at Livy and Julian, his gaze long and deliberate. "I guess I could easily deny everything. But my time is near." The old man lowered the bed and then rearranged his pillow. "How do you know of this buckle? Hearsay?"

"I've seen it, held it. I––"

There was a knock at the door followed by a nurse bending her head into the room. "How are you doing, Reverend? May I get anything for you?" She hesitated, waiting for an answer. "Pastoral care?"

Confusion registered on his face, followed by a look of understanding. "Oh no, Joyce. I'm fine. Julian and Livy are here for me. Thank you for your concern."

"I'm sorry," said Julian. "I suggested some ill wind had visited your son." He hesitated. "You do have a son, don't you?"

"Sons and grandsons and granddaughters. You were saying?"

"I'm a professor of antiquities at Harvard. I recognized it immediately."

The reverend shook his head up and down, deliberately, in a gesture of approval. He removed his reading glasses. "I'm sorry."

Julian and Livy shared a questioning look.

The reverend failed to notice. "The last time I saw it was in 1992."

"Your last year at Trinity?"

He nodded. "I stashed the artifacts in a wall, which was subsequently bricked over. Away from human view, I thought, forever. We were undergoing renovations at the time."

"Artifacts?" said Julian. "More than one!"

"Six things."

"You buried them all?" Julian hitched forward in his chair and rested his forearms on his knees.

The old man nodded.

"I absolutely need to know what you had, what you buried. Lives are at stake."

Certainty returned to the reverend's face, then defiance. He gripped his sheets and didn't speak.

"Do you know the significance of the buckle?" asked Julian.

He nodded again. "That of Bucephalus, a horse. His owner, Alexander of Macedon, the son of Philip II." The old man spoke slowly, like a distinguished teacher. "Professor Minton at the university identified it."

Julian's eyes widened. "When was that?"

The urgent tone in Julian's voice was obvious to the old man.

"Early1992. January or February. I don't recall for sure. Definitely after the holy season."

Julian spoke softly to himself, "It makes sense now."

"What do you mean?"

"Dr. Minton was my mentor, nearly a father. He died in 1992. I was told carbon monoxide from a leaky water heater." Julian stood up and walked a few random steps, his hands in his pockets. He stopped and turned toward the bed. "Why would you have something like that—the gold ring?"

The reverend cleared his throat. "Serendipity or act of God. One can never know for sure. I'm convinced it was an act of God. A father protecting his son."

Julian and Livy again swapped questioning glances. "You, protecting your son?"

The old man smiled and shook his head. "No, no, much bigger than that. God protecting the legacy of his son."

"Jesus!"

"Exactly." The reverend and Julian shared a knowing look. "My grandson brought it to me. Contraband. 1990. He was a Special Forces soldier casing caves in Pakistan at eleven thousand feet and just happened upon it. He found it in a crevasse sealed with molded mud bricks. It was bone dry. The items were in a wax-sealed container—a silver ossuary chest—in a time-hardened, white substance that turned out to be natron. They used it to—"

"—mummify pharaohs in Egypt," finished Julian.

"Exactly."

Julian sat down and scooted even closer, his eyes wide, his look animated. "Incredible. Alexander spent a year in Egypt. Thereafter, his troops referred to him as *pai dios*, son of Zeus. He left Egypt with the equivalent of five hundred pounds of natron, enough to mummify one person—himself, should he die in battle. He fought his way to what is now Pakistan, the endpoint of his thirteen-year campaign. It took him three years to subdue the Pashtuns of Afghanistan and the Hindu Kush mountains. Bucephalus was killed at the Battle of Hydaspes in 326 BC, on the eastern slopes of the Hindu Kush, after which he founded the city Bucephala. Alexander wanted to continue his quest into India. It was 323 BC. His troops refused. He headed home, caught the fever, and died in Babylon. Undefeated in battle, he died one month short of his thirty-third birthday." Julian realized he was droning and stopped his discourse. "You didn't answer my question. Why did the stash end up in your hands?"

"Rita was fluent in Greek when I met her. We raised our three sons to read and speak my language. One son, Alantos, then carried on the tradition and taught his sons Greek. Anthony, my grandson, found the artifacts and read them."

"Them!"

"Two." The reverend smiled, clearly enjoying the give and take. "A papyrus and a vellum codex."

"A vellum! From 340 B.C. Very unusual for that period."

"Yes, the leather cover was etched and bound. Only one page was in poor condition."

"Please tell me, Reverend Toulukinopolis, what were they? I have to know."

"Only one. The papyrus...*The Iliad*, was in very distressed condition, especially the outer most rolls."

"Alexander's copy of *The Iliad*! The Greek Bible. He slept with it under his pillow. He thought himself the new Achilles." Elation registered in Julian's eyes. He looked at Livy in an attempt to share the moment and then back at the old man. "Why did he bring them to you?"

"The vellum codex. Special Forces soldiers work with a great deal of autonomy, often in small groups of four called bricks. The day Anthony found it, he was with his brick near Khyber Pass, two miles inside the Pakistani border. They weren't supposed to be there. He read it as well as he could. The ancient Greek text gave him trouble. But he had time, especially at night. His fellow soldiers soon forgot about it. He realized its significance and realized no one could ever see it." The reverend stopped talking.

Julian waited for an explanation. With none forthcoming, he said, "Amphilochus."

The old man looked up, surprised. "I thought you..."

"In Cooper's––Reverend Saltonstall's––personal Bible, I found a rubric in the Gospels of Matthew and Luke. A single word, Amphilochus."

"And nothing else?"

Julian nodded.

"And Reverend Saltonstall was killed, you say?" He paused. "That is why no one can know."

"People are dying *not* knowing. You need to tell me what is so important about a Sophocles poem written four-hundred years before the birth of Christ." Exasperation and fatigue registered in his voice.

"A poem? You're mistaken. *Amphilochus* is a tragedy…a play."

"A play! In a vellum codex!" Julian was lost in the moment. "Alexander must have considered it very important." He stopped and thought. "But how can it be that two thousand years later, an Episcopalian minister was killed to keep it quiet." He made a visual plea to the old man.

"Julian, I like you. And you too, Livy. I warn both of you—let it go. Forget it. Just go away for a while and let it blow over."

Julian draped his fingers on the edge of the bed. He lowered his head, then began tapping his thumbs against the railing. Fifteen seconds passed.

"Don't bother looking for my grandson or Sergeant Walker, Sergeant Lattimore, or Captain Edwards."

A confused look filled Julian's face.

"The four men in the brick. All dead, mysterious circumstances."

"Oh, I'm sorry. Together, in battle?"

"No, nary a noble death in the entire group. Accidents. One by friendly fire. Then a car accident, a house fire, and a drowning. Imagine a Special Forces soldier drowning." The old man shook his head.

"A house fire?" Julian and Livy looked at each other.

"All within six months. The last half of 1991. I was seventy-two. Rita had died in '86. Cancer. It was obvious what I had to do. I sealed the artifacts in the church and then arranged for my death." He paused again, possibly to reflect. "That was the last I heard of the artifacts until now—although, I've often tried to grasp the significance of *Amphilochus*. It eludes me still."

Julian leaned over and put his hand over the reverend's hand. "What can I do to gain your confidence?"

The old man looked at Julian, eye to eye. "If you are who you say––the Reverend Saltonstall's best friend and a Greek scholar––I find it curious that he never showed you the document and never even mentioned it to you. I suspect he had nine years to do so." He paused and considered the conundrum. "You must be a spiritual person."

Livy spoke up. "More than you can ever know."

"What makes you think he had it for nine years?" asked Julian, somewhat tortured by the fact that his friend never told him about any of this. "You never met him, right? Never spoke to him."

"Late in 1992, shortly after I left, I read in the newspaper how Trinity shifted off its foundation and ruined our renovations."

"I remember that," said Julian. "Something about hydrostatic pressure from the Hancock Building next door."

"Trinity Church, along with entire Back Bay area, was built on landfill. The engineering required to build the church was amazing, for the Hancock building, more extraordinary still. It was finished in '76, I think. They conjectured the weight of the sixty-story building right next door to the church, literally pushed it off its foundation––moved it two feet. At the time, I wondered if the stash was exposed. But I was dead. I couldn't do anything."

"Nine years. I can't believe he didn't say anything."

"I have a question for you," said the reverend.

"Of course, anything."

He looked first at Livy and then slowly shifted his age-worn gaze toward Julian. "Have either of you come into danger recently?"

Immediately, Julian realized his concern. "Oh, Reverend, I'm so sorry."

"What?" asked Livy.

"The Dexion Society," Julian said, looking at her.

"They have a name?" the old man said. "A secret society or some such nonsense. I should've known."

"I have been threatened. Livy's husband––my brother––was killed. They were after me. I thought it was regarding something else."

"My, my. You have two people wanting you dead. I suspect you'll need God's help more than I." A tone of resignation registered in his voice.

"We have police protection. My brother was a Boston cop. I'll get you protection."

"This is bigger than you and me. I suspect this has been going on for some time."

"Centuries, I suspect. That's why you need to tell me what your grandson gave you."

"To stop it would be to expose it to the world." He hesitated and looked at his hands as he considered what he should say next. "It is hard for me to fathom the ramifications on Western civilization if *Amphilochus* were ever brought to light. Quite possibly, nothing would happen. But maybe, just maybe, it would lead to the downfall of our society. Julian, I'm not given to hyperbole." The minister took his gaze to Julian's. "You can't expose it since you don't have it or know of its whereabouts. So anything I say would only bring harm to you. If you should happen upon it, the decision will be yours...and yours alone. Then..." He raised a gnarled index finger. "...you'll need to summon your entire life experience in order to decide what to do. Remember, it ended the life that I knew."

"What about the other three things that Alexander buried?"

The reverend picked up his book, checked that his place was marked, and placed it neatly on the nightstand. He reached for the light switch on his TV controller and turned off the overhead light. Livy and Julian stood up, ready to leave. Apparently, they were finished.

"I want to thank you––" started Julian.

"Perhaps," said the reverend, "considering your vocation, it wouldn't hurt to tell you about the other artifacts." He paused, then coughed and cleared his throat again. "Four other ancient artifacts, one you've seen." He held up his gnarled right hand, his thumb and index finger spread two inches apart. "There was an exquisite––"

From the hallway came an alarm. Continuous. Unmistakable.

CHAPTER TWENTY-THREE

SOMERVILLE HOME, SOMERVILLE
Saturday, September 8, 2001, 10:15 p.m.

Julian looked at Livy, then said, "Curious time for a fire drill. Check the hallway for traffic, then grab a wheelchair and an oxygen tank. The good reverend goes with us."

Livy spun around and jogged toward the door then disappeared into the hallway. Julian reached over, put his arm under the old man's back, and pulled him upright.

"Do you need oxygen all the--"

Livy smashed the door open, winded. "Plan B. I smelled smoke. It's the real deal." Neither moved. "Close by."

"Hell! Reverend, can you go without your oxygen?"

A face addled with fear and a nod was his answer. His mustache quivered like it was maggot infested.

"OK." Julian spoke loudly to the old man. "I'm going to put you over my shoulder and carry you down. You'll hold your urine bag. Can you do that?"

Another nod.

Julian prepared himself. He looked at Livy. "As soon as we get outside, get our police escort, and grab the first responders. Reverend Toulukinopolis goes in that van."

Julian bent over, draped the preacher over his shoulder, then heaved himself to an upright position. The senior was light, and the hall was misty with smoke. Staff personnel ran door-to-door, rousing the guests. Wheelchairs appeared here and there. Some patients waited at the elevator, guided by the less-infirm residents. Aids backed other wheelchairs down the stairwell. Progress proceeded at a snail's pace as patients on the stairs advanced one deliberate step at a time. Crying was heard. Nurses barked orders.

"Empty the second floor first," came an urgent voice. "The fire started in the second-floor kitchen. Then get up to three."

The seconds wasted away. There were no wet heads in the crowd; the sprinklers weren't working. Coughing and loud breathing battled fright and agitated voices. All ambient noise was drowned out when a door opened on an upper floor and allowed the shrillness of the intermittent alarm to enter the space. Livy led the way, and Julian followed; his breath came with effort. Breathing the smoke gave him a sensation of vertigo. He nearly fell. On the first floor, two security men, who themselves could have been residents, directed the patients toward the front parking area.

By the time Livy, Julian, and the minister reached the lot, the first fire unit pulled in, lights flashing. A symphony of sirens filled the cool night air. Julian dipped down and placed the minister on the cement flagpole base. As he turned, he saw a tendril of fire shoot out of a second-floor window. Four windows away, on the part of the C stretching toward the street, a window exploded, chased by more flames. Then, on the opposite parallel section, a third-story window exploded. Three separate fires. Livy looked at Julian, uncertain what to do.

"Guard him until the paramedics arrive. Then grab one. Stay close to the police."

Their police escort approached on the run, walkie-talkie to his mouth.

"Where are you going?" Livy couldn't disguise the fear in her voice.

"This is a tragedy in the making," said Julian.

Livy nodded, touched her fingers to her lips and then touched Julian's cheek. "Go. Be careful. We'll be OK."

Julian bent down and patted the old man on the shoulder, got a reassuring smile, and then headed back into the building. Confusion reigned. The enfeebled elderly shuffled here and there. Grim terror filled the faces of those not demented beyond help. Bewilderment filled the faces of the rest.

Some stood alone, afraid to move. Others rambled about, perhaps in search of a parent long departed. Still others huddled together like sheep, unsure what to do or where to go, waiting for the slaughter. IV poles on wheels clashed with wheelchairs. Only the hint of smoke wafted through the lobby. He found four ladies clogging the portal, so he led them out two at a time. The next trip in, the smoke had increased from a trace to a haze. A skeletal old man sat near the exit gasping for breath. Julian put his arm around his back, planted his fist in the man's armpit, and then literally dragged him from the building.

The smoke was thicker yet, the next time in. First responders were bringing order to chaos. Julian remembered the earlier admonition about the third floor, so he made his way to the stairwell and then threaded his way up to the top floor. Those patients seemed more robust than those on the second: more mobile, less infirm. Those frail by stature, gait, or health seemed to have a better half, literally, to help them. The smoke came from the west wing. Tears dripped down Julian' cheeks; his eyes burned. He yanked off his shirt and tied it around his mouth and nose and then ran down the hall, banging on and opening doors. Some of the units were apartments with several rooms; many were already empty. He reached the end of the main hall, but skipped the last four doors, so he could look around the corner, where the C in the building extended out toward the street. He felt a rush of heat against his face like he had just opened a blast furnace. At the hallway's end, gray smoke hid the ravages of the devouring blaze. Tongues of prancing flames––a communion of marmalade, yellow, and white––jumped out of several doorways and from the ceiling in a frantic search for more oxygen. A body lay ten feet in front of the closest flame, twisted in an unnatural position and still. Julian hesitated, started forward, and then turned back to help those that he could. He quickly checked the first of the four rooms he had passed; surprisingly, he found a couple in bed, with a room air cleaner nearby set at a high-speed whine. The room smelled smoky, but the air was breathable. He got them up. Fred and Alice assured him they could make it and that he should help the others. He headed to the next unit. Empty. The next room was locked on the outside and curiously empty. It was probably home for sundowners, elderly people who succumb to confusion during the night and are kept safe with secured windows and doors. He passed another open door, a unit he'd previously thought empty. Julian heard a voice––the unmistakable hissing sibilance of an *s*. He went cold and stopped; it was an autonomic response. Then, he heard another hissing *s*: his deep-rooted demons had found a voice.

"Schweetness, we have to leave. Schoon!"

An undecipherable response followed. Julian looked in––a voyeur to his past life. In the dimness of the room, half-turned and looking out the window, an old man stood, shorter, balder, and fatter than he remembered. Thick lips glistened with spittle. For an instant, Julian remembered those lips close to his. For a tiny, infinitesimal moment, he was a boy, cold and shaking and standing in front of the brightest of lights. Julian was ripped from his reverie when the man spoke again.

"Marsona, schweetness! Hurry, we have to go. Now!"

Julian jerked his head left, and in a doorway leading to another room or the bathroom, stood a pitiful old lady: a wicked, evil thing. The awful ugly answer to the question that had haunted him his entire life. Skeletal and frail, like a dried-up junkie would look, she stood, stooped over a walker. Nearly bald, a few wispy strands of gray hair went this way and that. Her robe hung open. The skin that used to be her breasts drooped pathetically over a protuberant abdomen; a feeding tube poked out from the middle. She had no teeth. Her skin hung in folds on her face and neck. She had a sallow, sickly complexion. Julian was drawn to her eyes. He had always been fearful that he wouldn't recognize his mother, should she be an anonymous passerby on the street. But her eyes hadn't changed. Those haunting eyes that held hate and provoked only fear were the same. They were a requiem of his buried hopes and forgotten birthdays, a time when the future was only a vicious joke. The chaos––the smoke in the hallway and the flashing police lights that drifted in through the window behind them—blended away to nothingness, so focused was Julian on her eyes. He became strangely conscious of the sound of his own breathing, so he took a step back to better conceal his presence. His mind raced. *She knew all along.* His whole life he had wondered about this moment––what he would say, what he would do. For the past twenty years, his thoughts of death rays for his mother had intertwined with a longing to hear penitence from her mouth and see remorse in her eyes. The moment was at hand. The question and answer stood before him.

She was in the main room now; they spoke words Julian couldn't hear. The pervert fastened the robe for her. The corpulent lips moved again; spittle spewed out. Disgust riled Julian's stomach. The crackle of the flames from around the corner, fifty feet away, prompted him to check for his safety. When Julian looked back into the room, they peered back. He sensed, in their feeble, drug-racked brains an inkling of recognition. Perhaps no certainty as to who he was, but a vague notion that they had seen him sometime in the past, recent or long ago. Maybe it was the way he looked at them that evoked the response or the way he stood or his eyes.

He pulled the shirt from his mouth to give them a clear view. Strangely their look—whatever it was––morphed into some form of curious loathing. Was he mistaken? He looked again. It was certainly not a look of sympathy or reconciliation. Disembodied specters of Cooper and Maxwell flashed through his mind. He wondered why they should die when scum of the earth, perpetrators of crimes of every hue, should be allowed to live. *What kind of God would allow this? Why would he not keep better score?*

Like a hard slap, it struck him. His whole life he had attributed his escape from the vacuum of depravity that was his childhood to his faith in Jesus. Sister Mary Beth had assured him; he had believed her. But maybe it was just dumb luck that he and Maxwell and Cooper made it out. Maybe life was navigated by twists of fate, nothing more. It scared him to think the flotsam standing in front of him may never have to answer to anyone––perhaps after death, but maybe not. There had to be moral accountability at some point in life's cycle. A scale to measure things good and bad and then make things right. If not, what of morality? Could he rely on God for anything, or nothing? He thought of all the dark nights etched into his soul and the time spent trying to untangle himself from his childhood and bandage the frayed pieces of his life. *Mom, are you proud of who I am? And God, how about you?* Julian glanced down at the doorknob. The pedophile opened his mouth to speak, the bulbous lips parted. *This is for you, Maxwell, and all those frightful nights spent in the garage…and for me. And for everything that happened thereafter.* Julian bade adieu to his past. He closed the door, turned the lock, and walked away.

CHAPTER TWENTY-FOUR

LIVY'S HOUSE, BOSTON
Sunday, September 9, 2001, 7:20 a.m.

It was a short night. Julian woke early, unable to sleep. Sleepy fingers of light peeked through the blinds throwing horizontal black bars on the wall. He thought back to hours before and the cerebral gymnastics he had been through. It took only a moment to exorcise the spirit of unease. He was emotionally spent, but in his early morning mental haze, he felt right, at least by Maxwell. For years he had carried the guilt of getting to sleep in the warm house. The burden had finally been lifted--the debt repaid. His mind drifted back to the smoky hallway on the third floor of the Somerville Home. *She knew all along.* Drug addiction was no excuse for absolute failure as a human being. He felt no remorse. He also thought back to the day he, Maxwell, and Cooper had pushed Billy Ray Roux off the boat into the deep Atlantic. A wrinkle worked through his brain: the moral scales applied to everyone. But the buoyancy of fatherhood helped him block these thoughts as he navigated the hallway, walking down the stairs and into the kitchen. Half-asleep, he startled as he entered.

Cam sat at the table, reading the back of his Cheerios box; he also jumped. "Dude!"

Both offered the other a half smile.

"You scared the heck out of me," said Julian. He turned to fetch a cup. "What's so interesting about Cheerios?"

"Riboflavin."

"Right." Julian loaded the Keurig machine, pushed a button, and positioned the cup, bearing a Red Sox logo, underneath the spigot.

"What's it for?"

"Hell if I know." The coffeemaker hummed and churned, but nothing came out. Julian bent down to peek up into the mechanism, always the best way to fix something. "I remember now. It's another name for saltpeter."

Cam smiled, scooped up another spoonful of O's, then looked up. "I thought you were Dad."

Julian let the thought brew. "Sorry. I'll comb my hair next time."

Cam resumed his analysis of the Cheerio box. Julian shifted his eyes from the coffeemaker to Cam. He realized how little he knew about his son. "You're up early."

Cam looked up again. "Yeah, I like to get up and get––"

"Stuff done. I'm like that."

The Keurig light turned green, and the Red Sox logo warmed up as the fresh brew finally poured in. "Coffee?"

Cam declined. Julian joined him at the table. He grabbed the front section and took a sip. "Plans for the day?"

"A few." Cam wouldn't take his eyes off the box.

"Maybe after you get that riboflavin thing figured out, you could work on world hunger."

"That's easy." Cam poured himself another half-bowl of cereal.

Julian scanned the first page of the *Globe*. At the bottom was a story about two young men found dead in the same Harcourt Street apartment. The deaths were considered suspicious for a new strain of smallpox. Julian switched to the sports section. "Did you see the Patriots the other day? Brady looked pretty good. Eleven of nineteen, one TD."

"He'll never play in the regular season. Kraft gave Bledsoe a hundred and three million dollar contract in March."

"You're probably right."

Idle chat was a tough sell early in the morning. Achieving oneness with a special vitamin or the sports section was not.

After page four of the sports section, Julian looked up. "How'd you like to break into a computer today?"

Cam, surprise in his eyes, studied his uncle. He didn't answer right away. Julian continued. "A personal computer. Laptop. Dell."

"What do ya hope to find?"

"Twenty-dollar ATM withdrawals and Myspace nonsense."

"What do you think you'll find?"

"Not that."

"Sounds fun."

"You want to know whose?"

"Nope. But Mom said something about going out today. Something she wants to talk about."

Julian hesitated, caught unprepared by a wave of apprehension. "Sounds more important. We can do it later."

Livy walked into the kitchen, robed and radiant. Her hair was fashioned in an early morning jumble, her eyes sleep-filled. "You guys look like you're having way too much fun." She headed for the coffeemaker.

They swapped small talk for a while. Cam shuffled the fifth page of the *Globe*'s Section *C* in front of Livy. It showed a picture of Julian hauling a geriatric patient out of the nursing home. A Somerville fire truck filled the background. Livy and Cam decided he was their hero. Cam mentioned something about getting him on Oprah. Livy wanted to feel his muscles. Julian enjoyed the ribbing but had trouble with the fuss. He suggested escorting a helpless, demented senior out of a burning building was simply the right thing to do.

Urged on by Livy's insistence, Julian and Cam headed to Karlie's apartment. Before departing, Julian asked Livy to find out which nursing facility Reverend Toulukinopolis had been transferred.

Julian was simply following Karlie's instructions to get her some clothes prior to picking her up at the hospital. He found the key in the hiding spot. They didn't need it. The superintendent had not yet fixed the lock from the previous break-in. Together they found the mess left by the Middle Easterners and the police only days before––chairs overturned, drawers emptied, wall hangings discarded on the floor.

"The computer is in her bedroom," said Julian. "I'll grab some clothes."

"So, what am I looking for?"

"Stuff that a college coed wouldn't normally have on her computer."

Cam disappeared around a corner at the end of the hallway. Julian repeated what he and Livy had done at the parish house. The fact he was the second one through the apartment actually made it a lot easier. The problem was he didn't know what he was looking for. And he really didn't want to find anything.

The minutes passed. He found a diamond pendant in a box, buried in the flour jar. It looked old, but he wasn't sure, maybe an heirloom. The couch yielded three quarters and four pennies and two very old Cheetos. He decided the Cheetos were probably not family heirlooms. Behind the poster of the four American authors was another, a movie poster for some B-movie––*Big Problems*. A large-chested blonde filled the advertisement. In the bathroom, in an empty bath-powder container resting on the back of the toilet, was a prescription bottle: Seroquel, filled August 7, sixty were dispensed, thirty-five remained.

She had turned the extra bedroom into a study. He checked every book but found nothing. There were several art books and an array of old English and American authors. All looked well-read. Back in the kitchen, he emptied a mayonnaise jar and found nothing. In the freezer, he discovered two frost-covered Tupperware containers buried at the bottom of the ice container. One contained a baggy with fifteen brown pills embossed with the word "love," along with a coke pipe. The content of the other was not only bizarre, but also disgusting––four used condoms. He found out everything he needed to know about the surrounding food emporiums' takeout capabilities by reading her refrigerator door. He found a couple of fireproof, combination-locked boxes in the closet. One was heavy, and both were refractory to his efforts to guess the combinations. Another metal file cabinet had a keylock that he couldn't penetrate. He made a mental note to watch sleuth movies more closely. Curiously, he found no family pictures. No old letters. No high-school crap. Failure drove him from the closet to Cam's side.

"Find anything?" asked Cam.

"Yes and no," said Julian. "Yourself?"

"Yes and no." Cam typed steadily as he spoke, stopping periodically for the high-speed Internet connection to change. "She's got a primo unit. Plus a whole D-drive locked safely away behind a password. If I had time, I might be able to sneak into it. I assume we can't keep her waiting."

"What's the 'yes' part?"

Cam stopped what he was doing and peered up at his uncle. For the first time, Julian saw the look of a normal, inquisitive college student––no attitude, no agenda.

"Did she talk about money much?" asked Cam.

"Not really. Just the usual poor-college-student routine."

Cam continued. "Expensive gifts? Fancy trips?"

"Nope. Complained a few weeks ago about having to pay fifty dollars to change her class schedule. Why?"

"She's loaded." Cam spun around and tapped the keyboard a few times. Quicken 98 filled the screen. After a few more keystrokes, her checkbook ledger popped onto the screen.

Julian took control of the mouse and scrolled down the list. "Hardly twenty-dollar ATM withdrawals." He studied the entries. "Amazing."

Cam grabbed the mouse and scrolled to the bottom. "Not many coeds have a checking balance of $79,432.24." He glanced up at Julian. "She's received a $10,000 wire deposit the first of every month since she has had the account."

"Where is it coming from?"

"The Santa Barbara branch of Chase."

Cam looked up at Julian; they shared a what-the-hell look.

"This surprises you, too," said Julian.

"I had no clue. Curious that she would get her panties in a twist over fifty bucks."

"Anything else? Saved letters to friends? Letters home?"

"Nope. What's the deal on her parents? Must be loaded."

Julian turned and paced the room. "She said her dad died. Never said how. I don't know shit about her mom. I brought it up once. She clammed-up. I dropped it."

"Maybe Dad left her an inheritance. A trust of some sort, with regular payouts."

"Possible." Julian sat down on the bed. He thought back to the first time they made love on it. "What have you tried in the way of passwords?"

Cam went through a list of four. "These damn things are often set with a limit. She put it at--"

"Five, right?"

"Yep."

Julian rose from the bed and walked over to look behind the laptop. A gray box sat juxtaposed to the computer. "That's what we're trying to get into?" Julian offered a chin nod toward the box.

Cam nodded. Julian paced. Neither spoke.

"Can you Google something for me real quick…Seroquel. It's a medication of some sort."

Cam made a few clicks. "Seroquel. Ah…antipsychotic...used for bipolar disorder, obsessive-compulsive disorder, Tourette's syndrome, schizophrenia…ah…sounds like good shit." Cam laughed.

Julian didn't. He felt like he needed some.

"That's enough." Julian's tone was definitive. "You know, this isn't a very feminine room is it? Never noticed before. I always assumed she didn't fix it up because she didn't have any money. A Wal-Mart bedspread. No matching window treatments. No frills. No doilies. None of the usual girlie bull crap they pack into their rooms."

"It's like a hotel room."

Julian finished the thought. "Like she wasn't planning on staying." They looked at each other, not sure what it meant. "So, we have one more try at the password."

"We can rip off the hard drive. Give me enough time and I'll––"

"Not sure we want to announce our efforts." Julian paced a few more laps and then sat back down on the bed again.

"Any ideas?" asked Cam. "Just want me to take a shot?"

"No. Let me think." He paused. "What was the name on the money transfer?"

Cam shifted back to the Quicken folder. "No name, just a number and an FBO designation. Initials: KAR."

"Karlie Ann Reynolds." Julian looked at his watch. "We need to scoot. Let me think while I take her clothes to the car. Keep looking. Try to hack into her old e-mails."

Julian grabbed a grocery sack from the kitchen, rifled through her lingerie drawer, and then rummaged through the closet. Halfway out of the room, he dropped the sack and turned to Cam. "Damn!"

Startled, Cam looked up. "What?"

"One second." Julian jogged out to the mess littering the living room, grabbed the overturned picture frame, pulled the *Big Problems* poster from underneath the American authors picture, then jogged back to the bedroom. His face flushed with anger, he handed the poster to Cam. "Look at the bottom, the tall font, the actors in the movie."

It took Cam a moment to orient himself, and then he started reading them off. "Hogan Black. Tark Shelby. Hell, I can't read this."

"Keep going."

"Lobsang Merino. What in the hell kind of name is that? No wonder I've never heard of the damn flick."

"Keep going."

"Robin Fox. And…" he stopped and looked up at Julian. "And Karlie Reynolds."

"An alias for our Karlie Roux," said Julian.

"Who's that?"

"I suspect the daughter of Billy Ray Roux."

"Thanks."

Julian took his hand off the poster and resumed his pacing. On the second trip back, he unloaded his anger into the sack holding Karlie's clothes. "Damn it!" Her underwear ended up somewhere in the living room.

"Want to fill me in?"

"Look at the bottom of the poster. See where it says Stage 20 Films? Try that. Type in: S-T-A-G-E-2-0, all large caps."

Cam hesitated.

"Do it." Cam did as he was told, then pushed enter. The turning-wheel icon assumed a small position in the middle; five seconds later, the hard drive opened onto the screen––two rows of folder icons. "Bingo."

Julian stooped over Cam's shoulder. He corralled the mouse and clicked through the files. Cam commented periodically.

"Name change finalized June of last year. Same first name. Borrowed the vixen's last name. Clever." Another folder. "Shit, a forty-million-dollar trust fund dated 1989. Must have been when her dad died. Forty million." Another folder. "A year in France. Studied abroad. Then, back to Stanford last year." Another Quicken folder. "Curious. A three-hundred-thousand-dollar donation to Harvard, in May 2000. Ended up transferring from Stanford in August. Let me guess, not the best student in the world."

They spent the next five minutes scanning through the documents and files. Finally, Julian had enough and said, "Let's go."

Chapter Twenty-Five

CAMBRIDGE HOSPITAL, CAMBRIDGE
Sunday, September 9, 2001, 10:20 a.m.

Julian offered to take Cam home. Cam declined, so they headed to the hospital. Julian was grateful for the company, but now, with his suspicions confirmed, he felt pissed off and embarrassed, so chat was scant. He offered very little in the way of an explanation.

They pulled into the Cambridge Hospital parking lot. A week before, he had dodged flashing patrol cars on his way to find Karlie. He decided when he got done kicking himself, he would dredge through the depths of his 2001 romantic escapade. *The eternal sap.*

Minutes later, he stood outside Karlie's room. It was a confusing matrix, the situation. To shed light on its entirety might involve rehashing the details of the boat ride from twelve years before. Plus, he was not an actor. He didn't know if he could convince her that he didn't know. He usually was not one to avoid confrontation, but for now, a two-step around the problem was the goal. The game plan was to get out of the hospital with a minimum of muss and fuss.

"Hey Karlie," said Julian. His voice wavered as he walked across the room. "Ready to go?"

Karlie smiled and extended her arms. "Hey, Julian. Cam! This is a surprise." Julian offered a perfunctory hug. "Talk about awkward."

Cam held his hands out to his side. "You're safe."

Julian detected a nanosecond of disappointment in Karlie's expression.

They exchanged banter for a couple more minutes. Karlie changed out of her hospital gown; the wheelchair appeared at the door, and they were on their way.

On the ride home, they established that Karlie was glad to be out of the hospital, and the antibiotic pills tasted bitter, but the pain pills were great. The chill between them remained.

"It's such a beautiful day," said Karlie. "The best part of fall. Let's go out on your boat. Now. It would be fun. Help me forget about all that happened."

Julian was taken aback. She was inside his space. He needed to extract himself for a few hours and figure out what to do. His smile was obligatory. "Not sure she's ready," was all he could offer.

Karlie stuck her arm out the window. "The sun feels luscious. We don't have to go far." She batted her long lashes and leaned over to expose the breast she intended him to see. Julian glanced at Cam in the backseat—guys talking with their eyes. Julian thought he detected a yes.

"Cam," said Julian, "you in a hurry?"

"I'm cool."

Confirmed.

"There you have it," said Karlie. "Two to one."

Julian mulled over the possibilities. Since he didn't have his head up his ass anymore, he decided he needed to be proactive and precipitate the confrontation this time, maybe on the boat. Or maybe not. He wondered if she would be repentant. After all, he literally had saved her life. They could call it even, go their separate ways—lesson learned. But would she simply drop it, something perhaps years in the making? It was a tough call, hard to know how to handle—elusive, like trying to find the cool side of a pillow on a warm, humid night. He shook his head, thinking how close he had been to dying for the bitch.

Karlie noticed. "What? You're shaking your head."

"Oh, no, I was just thinking. A small trip might be OK. You need to stop by your place?"

"Definitely. Need my boating gear."

The early afternoon sun danced off the white-cap-laced sea. Karlie, Julian, and Cam stood on the dock and looked at a symphony of crafts bobbing up and down––the sound of serious money. The *Sister Mary Beth*, white, sleek, and thirty-four feet, was moored at the far end, in steerage.

The wind gusts ruffled Karlie's luminescent streaks as she boarded. Her legs went on forever, glistening with a fine layer of perspiration, slender succulent poles extending from the barely visible slant of her buttock. Over her yellow bikini top she wore a sheer white T-shirt. She carried a large white tote bag and looked as though she had packed for a week, not a one-hour cruise. Even before they got underway, she stripped away the skirt and the shirt. The dearth of swimming-suit material underneath was dazzling. It bothered Julian a lot that she struck such a stunning pose and that he even noticed. He steeled himself to tread very carefully.

Karlie leaned over in front of them to stow clothes in her bag. The afternoon performance had evidently started. Julian and Cam eyed each other; Cam raised his eyebrows, and Julian shook his head. *A poster child for the narcissistic.*

"Karlie, you certainly don't look any worse for the wear," said Cam. "I'm overdressed."

Karlie laughed. "This is what we wear in California. That's a country on the Pacific." She leaned over again to get her sunglasses and then put them on top of her head.

"I'd avoid the big waves."

"Or maybe not." Karlie winked.

Julian sat down in the captain's seat, twirled around, and pushed the starter. The Crusader 425 horsepower inboard rumbled to life––with a deep-throated growl that hinted of raw power. Cam tapped Julian on the shoulder and gave him an approving thumbs-up, possibly acknowledging that men over forty can actually do something cool. Julian stood and motioned for Cam to take the wheel. On the loud avenues of the ocean's highways, communication was often done by hand gestures and facial expressions. Cam smiled a yes and sat down. Julian pointed toward the gas gauge and then to the marina gas depot a quarter mile away. Cam nodded, and they headed northeast.

The marina matron tried to sell them a half-dozen cheese dogs along with the gas. She was the antithesis of Karlie at maybe just a couple of M & M's shy of two hundred fifty pounds. But she was a fun gal, and, in the grand scheme of life, light-years ahead of Karlie. Julian mused that he should learn to recognize high-maintenance when it was staring him in the eye.

They settled in. Cam took it up to thirty knots; he was a quick study. He aimed for a little spit of land off the port bow––the Deer Island lighthouse. Jets arrived and departed from Logan International on their starboard side. Karlie, suffering from some degree of seasonal affective disorder after being cooped up in the hospital, drank a beer while reclining on the cushions along the stern. Julian stood close by Cam, his arm draped over the back of the captain's chair. Cam munched on some Cheetos and drank a grape soda.

"Should have gone with the gas lady's cheese dogs," said Cam, glancing over his left shoulder. "Cheetos just aren't workin' for me."

"I was going to suggest the roast duck with the mango salsa." They yelled at each other to be heard. "The gas lady has a limited wiener skill set."

Cam looked up at Julian. "That's a scary thought."

Julian made a quick trip to the galley to grab himself a grape soda. He came back with his shirt off. A chained silver crucifix dangled from his neck. In the background, the sun cast a glow on the Boston skyline. Sunlight reflected off the windows like a thousand jewels. The city center rose up like a magnificent crown; the surrounding weather-stained and time-tarnished low-rise structures of the metropolitan area formed the curly flaxen locks of the king. Diesel permeated the air; a salty mist rose from the engine churn. Julian turned and rested his arm on the captain's chair again, his feet spread wide to contest the hull cracking into the tumultuous surf. It was exhilarating, and exactly what he needed—time to figure out what to do with Karlie.

His thoughts were splintered minutes later when a light twelve inches to his left, the one located over the galley stairway, shattered, sending glass into his neck and onto Cam's hands. Julian instinctively ducked and turned. Cam did the same as his right arm shot out, jamming the throttle to the idle position. The bow of the boat bobbed down deep toward ocean's bottom and then shot-up like a rocket and finally settled into an ocean swell. The sudden quiet was not as unsettling as the gun Karlie held aimed at the center of his chest.

CHAPTER TWENTY-SIX

ATLANTIC OCEAN, BOSTON
Sunday, September 9, 2001, 1:00 p.m.

Julian's initial confusion was pushed aside by a surge of fear. A shiver eclipsed his body followed by an overwhelming sense of panic. Nobody spoke. An empty beer bottle rolled to and fro on the deck to the cadence of the waves. Karlie smiled, a lazy Sunday-afternoon smile. The salty air licked at her shoulder-length hair. Her eyes looked familiar, yet totally foreign.

"I feel fucking great." Her lips relaxed in a wide-open smile, advertising the alliance of drugs and alcohol.

Julian nodded toward the gun. *Get her talking.* "Your idea of safe sex?"

"You got it."

"Foreplay?"

The capricious stranger laughed a yes—a seductress's laugh, ripe with possibilities.

He nodded with a half smile; his mind regrouped. "You can go ahead without me."

"Think I just might do that." She inched the index and middle fingers of her left hand toward her suit bottom then stopped and smiled.

Julian watched but didn't respond. A kaleidoscope of thoughts cascaded through his mind. The charade of counterfeit closeness stirred fire in his stomach. The sun felt like a flamethrower on his shoulders, but the breeze felt cool. If she wanted him dead, he'd already be dead.

"Been ages since I've been trashed," she said.

Julian looked down at the bottle.

"The chaser. Seroquel, Percocet, and Ecstasy. It's great when the drugs are workin' for you." She looked down at her chest, aware of the stares.

"The girls are nice, aren't they? Especially when I dress them up…or down." She laughed, a curious, high-pitched laugh. Amused contortions distorted her mouth. "Not the double-D's like my mom." She paused. "The poster…*Big Problems*. That was my mom, so I'm told." She paused again. "You know, Julian, we really have a lot in common, you and me. Only thing I really remember about Mom is being told, 'she's in rehab.' Over and over. Must have been in rehab a goddamn thousand times. Hell, I never saw the bitch. A fuckin' crack whore just like yours, until she OD'd. Then, it was just Dad and me and his latest girlfriend. You knew my dad, Billy Ray Roux. Funny thing, he died when I was thirteen. You don't happen to know anything about that, do you?" She rambled and slurred her words. "God, I'm horny. Must be the drugs. What, the cat's got your tongue?" Karlie fired the gun again, this time into the panel next to the throttle. Cam's hand jumped off the steering wheel.

She reached up and pulled a few strands of hair from her eyes. "Now that I think of it, maybe we aren't so much alike. After Daddy was killed, I had nothin'. But you had your make-believe world. Damn, you've got God bad."

"You don't––"

"Cam, turn the fuckin' engine off. I can't hear shit." She waited a moment. "Thanks. As you were saying…"

"You don't want to do this." Julian checked his immediate area, looking for weapons, for escape. He needed to keep her talking.

"Oh, but I do. I've been waiting a long time. Revenge, pure and simple."

"I didn't––"

"Cut the crap! And there wasn't even a damn trial—insufficient evidence. No body. It was dark. He'd been drinkin'. Fell overboard and drowned. *Right*." She took her stare to her other target––Cam. "Your daddy, the cop, and a priest and a Harvard professor. They'd never tell a lie. Especially a goddamn preacher. Bullshit!" Her eyes shifted back to Julian. "The night you came to my apartment and told me Cooper was dead, I couldn't believe my luck. He would've been the tough one."

"Karlie, do you know what your dear father did to make money?" Julian spoke softly, his manner purposely subdued.

"He made motion pictures, directed, produced…was damn good." She dipped her head to her arm to wipe the sweat off her brow.

"Yeah, he made pictures. Porn. Kiddy porn. Maxwell, Cooper, and I were a just a few of his stars. The worst kind of scum."

Karlie raised the gun and fired again. He heard the *sphit*, and then the plastic window behind him splintered. His head jerked.

"Bullshit. He was legit. Not Academy Award stuff, but not bad for an indie."

Julian caught her gaze and wouldn't let go. "Those are the most heinous crimes, crimes against children. Worse than murder."

"Oh, the defiant one. Cut the crap. Don't think I can do it, do you?"

"If you were sober, no." A wave hit the boat and knocked Julian into Cam. He regained his balance. "This is a bad decision."

Karlie ignored the rebuke. "Know where you screwed up today? The goddamn mayonnaise jar. I was in a hurry and expected a mess. I noticed the empty mayonnaise jar and thought, what in the hell would those Middle-Eastern assholes be looking for in my goddamn mayonnaise jar. Then it struck me. Checked my freezer…computer…looked at the poster. Strong work on the password. Cam, you figure that out?"

Cam hesitated, unsure. "Uncle Julian did." His voice cracked as he spoke.

"You can cut the crap too." Her expression was haunted. "Julian's your dad. You know it. I wasn't sure you'd take the bait about the hospital records. Thought the brain in your dick would mess with your real brain." Karlie smiled. "Saw you screwin' me in your mind. All you bastards do. By the way, I was scammin' you. Julian doesn't know. I suspect you and Mommy need to have a heart to heart. She's got the goods and probably has had 'em since you were an 'Oh no!' in her monthly."

She laughed at her own joke, the same high-pitched laugh as before. "But hey, Julian, I suspect that's something you might've figured out." Her eyes tried to crumple up in a pale imitation of warmth. "Your life's so Frank Capra."

She was manic now. Sweating. Agitated. Like a cat in heat, she mashed her butt into the cushion. "Man, this shit is great." She adjusted her suit, rubbing her sweaty right breast. After a few moments, she calmed down. Her gaze steadied.

Julian and Cam shared an uncertain look.

Karlie continued her rant. "Julian, your life was screwed from the start. Then you got lucky. Sister Mary Beth pulled you and Maxwell out of that hellhole. News flash: Jesus had nothing to do with it. He died, and then the spin doctors took over. Made him bigger in death…just like Elvis, but not as big as Elvis." She laughed at her own joke, again. "And the Bible…gibberish…a fairy tale—ancient bullshit passed down like it's primal truth. All religions are crap. Muslim mothers convincing their children to make suicide bombing a career choice. How can any fucking ancient text justify that kind of bullshit?" She stopped and studied the St. Laurents, maybe to get a reaction, maybe not. "Julian, you've always wanted to be closer to your god. Well, here's your chance."

Karlie stroked the gun barrel with her left index finger. The movement was slow and deliberate. She steadied it with two hands and spied down sleek steel cylinder.

Thoughts and fear––mostly fear––bandied about in Julian's head. He fought to hold her gaze, willing her to lower the gun. For the first time he saw inside, viewing the insanity behind the charm. She hesitated. He shot a glance to the left at Cam's fear-addled face. The brashness had dissolved, replaced by a look only someone who thought they were going to live forever can muster just before they die. Julian wrestled with the moment, then took two steps to his left and placed himself between the gun and Cam. He spread his legs and crossed his arms over his chest.

Karlie lowered the weapon; disbelief registered on her face.

Julian spoke, "'We've got to live no matter how many skies have fallen.'"

"*Lady Chatterley's Lover.*" She displayed her perfect water-picked teeth. "Impressive, quoting D.H. Lawrence just before you die." She stifled the smile; her forehead creased. "Why in the hell did you kill my daddy?"

Julian's mouth was parched, his brow wet. Fingers of dread clouded his mind. She was out of control. "The matrons over in Framingham will love to fondle the girls…stick broom handles in various…trust me; it's no fun."

"Won't get caught."

"There are two of us. You aren't that good of a shot."

The corners of her mouth eased up. "Oh, but I am."

"How does that work?" He exaggerated a consternated look. *Keep her talking.*

"This has been an improvisation from the start. The fact that you three scumbags were free and my daddy was dead ate away at me for years. Like all those jerks obsessed over OJ walkin', I couldn't get on with my life. I turned twenty-one, got control my trust, and then went to work. Learned a shit load about computers. Found out all you bastards still lived in Boston. Then, you said 'hi' to me at Elsie's Sandwich Shop." She stopped speaking. Her eyes moved out to the horizon. "You were drinking a chocolate frappe that day." Her eyes bounced back to Julian's. "I hit the jackpot when Cooper got run over and Maxwell was turned to toast. The time table got moved up. After I almost got myself killed by those goddamn rag heads, I figured I needed to finish up and blow this pop stand." She taunted him with the gun. "Guess you couldn't get the lock box open."

"One gun, two people," Julian repeated.

"Oh, but I'm getting to the good part."

The rapacious stranger reached down, not taking her eyes off the St. Laurents, and pulled a Tupperware container out of her tote. She placed it on the cushion then stood up.

"Oh, officer," she cried in anguish, raising her left forearm to her brow as a thespian might do in a middle-school stage production. "It was horrible. I told him to stop. He was out of his mind."

Karlie grabbed her bikini top and gave the string a quick yank and then dug her fingernails into an area above her right breast, hard enough to draw blood, and then finally drew her fingers down very slowly, creating four parallel tracks. "Rape, pure and simple."

Julian couldn't believe what he was seeing or hearing. "You've forgotten. You just got out of the hospital. No proof."

She picked up the container and shook it. "Remember what you saw in here."

Her bittersweet smile was frightening.

Karlie continued. "Viable sperm. That's rape. My word against…oh, that's right, you were dismissed from the university for inappropriate relations with an undergraduate. Shame on you: a serial sexual predator. Love it."

Julian nodded his head like he was thinking. He grabbed Cam's leg to get his attention. He waited a moment and then used sign language. Cam responded by grabbing Julian's fingers. Julian then fished his cell phone out of his back pocket and blindly zipped through a three-button entry.

"What about Cam?" He chin nodded toward the condom-containing canister.

"No problem." She looked around, inside the boat and out. "Don't see him."

She raised her gun again, steadied it with both hands, pursed her lips, and then smiled.

"Say high to God and Jesus and all your other imaginary friends for me…after I obliterate that goddamn crucifix."

Julian inched his right foot a half step closer to the control console, and then he waited for the muzzle flash or a sound. The moment stretched to two. The nose of the weapon gave a nervous jerk, once then twice. *She can't do it.* At that moment, "Highway to Hell" erupted from the cell phone in her tote bag. Karlie's eyes drifted down for only a moment. AC/DC never sounded so good. Julian's bulky thigh muscles tightened, his knee flexed and jerked ramrod straight. He shot forward, his body extended, arms outstretched over the chasm, eyes focused on the pistol.

Cam grabbed the chrome-covered edge of the windshield and pirouetted over the side of the boat.

Julian saw the flash, heard the *sphit*, and then felt the pain.

CHAPTER TWENTY-SEVEN

ATLANTIC OCEAN, BOSTON
Sunday, September 9, 2001, 1:20 p.m.

Karlie looked up a split second before Julian's outstretched hand touched the gun. He felt the warmth of the barrel and watched in slow motion as her eyes widened then scrunched down into a grimace. He curled his right shoulder and crashed cross body into her. Karlie's shooting hand jerked up, and her body jacked back into the cushion. A whoop gushed from her mouth as she melted under Julian's weight. Another shot flashed from the cylinder. Julian clamped down on her wrist, his adrenalin-amped muscle squeezing bone against bone. She yelped in pain. The next sound was the thud of the gun on the floorboard. Julian relaxed against her velvet moistness and musty, feminine scent. A moment later, another fiery shock assaulted his brain as he felt the sensation of teeth against his ribs. An impulse raced into his right triceps, drawing his elbow down full force, like a pneumatic jackhammer, into the side of Karlie's head. Her long body went limp under his sweaty torso. Julian's attention was drawn to streaks of blood smeared over her taunt abdomen. He pushed himself off her upper body in search of a source. No holes. No active bleeding. Pain from the backside of his right arm jolted his brain again. Blood snaked down his arm into his palm.

Julian stood and steadied himself against the syncopated sway of the boat. Karlie looked lifeless, straddling the cushioned bench with her suit bottom balled up underneath her. Her chest made shallow repetitions up and down. He grabbed the gun from off the deck, secured the safety, and stashed it in his back waistband. He checked the tote for weapons and found a rolled towel, a tube of suntan oil, her passport, and a wad of cash. In the towel was a pair of jeans and a tiny string garment. Her cell phone hung halfway out of a jean pocket. One of the zippered tote compartments contained a makeup pouch and a pill container with what looked like Seroquel and Ecstasy and another white tablet that he presumed was Percocet.

Julian spun around and took a half-dozen steps toward the edge of the boat.

"Cam, it's OK." He yelled to be heard over the waves and the wind.

There was no response. He dropped the bag and peered over. Waves tickled the side of the boat––he saw black water all around and nothing else.

"Shit! Cam! Cam!"

He stretched to his limit over the railing to look aft and then toward the stern.

"Cam!"

Julian twirled around to check Karlie. He yanked the gun from his waistband, pried out the magazine, and cast it into the sea. He removed the chambered bullet, tossed the gun toward the tote, and then snatched the key out of the ignition switch and crammed it in his pocket. He kicked the tote bag into the galley, and then in one swoop threw one hand on the railing and flipped his legs over, landing feet first in the surf. The salt water felt like acid gnawing on his arm and chest wounds. The cold staggered his body. His wet jeans felt like lead weights; the powerful jet undercurrent boiled around him and put a stranglehold on his feet. He flipped over and headed down. The seawater nipped at his eyes. He corkscrewed his way aft, about eight feet under the water, through the icy current. His last breath struggled somewhere between his lips and his lungs. Julian broke the frosty grip, launched himself up, took a breath, and then headed under again, circumnavigating the bow then down the port side. Six feet ahead, two pant legs dangled from the surface. Julian kicked hard three times to escape the vacuum and gasped for air as his head shattered the surface. Cam clung to a towline attached to the railing. His blue lips quivered, and his eyes were tentative; a smile replaced his panic.

"Cam! You scared the hell out of me. What happened?"

Julian reached his son and gave him a one-armed embrace. They both shivered.

"I heard the first shot before I hit the water. I got to the surface and heard another. It was quiet. I waited about ten seconds and then headed under the boat. Thought I could sneak up behind her." He waited a moment. "God, this water is colder than shit."

"Let me give you a shove," said Julian.

The fizz of the moment gave way to silence. Karlie, either from the head smash or the drugs, snoozed on the cushions. They covered her up and then ignored her. The boat rocked about aimlessly. Julian rummaged around in a first-aid kit. With a little goo and some gauze, he was good to go, at least for the trip home. The bullet had torn skin and fat off of his upper right arm, but the muscle and bone seemed fine. The bite wound on his chest was superficial.

Cam sat down on the cushions next to their captive. "Thanks."

Julian looked up from his chest wound. He started to speak, but nothing came out. They were isolated on a boat in the Atlantic. There was no Livy or Karlie or anyone else to act as a buffer. He swiveled in the chair and faced his son.

"No problem." Julian nodded and offered a reserved smile.

"No, it is a problem. I turned on you—turned on family. I insulted you and disrespected you, your beliefs, all your accomplishments, all you've been through. I--"

"Don't worry…"

"No, let me finish. I would have given up long ago. But, you didn't…you don't. Then, after all my bullshit, you stepped up, ready to take a bullet. I am truly humbled and grateful. I don't deserve it. Not at all."

Julian rose and walked over to Cam. He stuck out his hand. Cam reciprocated. "Let's start over. You're an adult; you don't need bedtime stories." He paused. "I'll give you attaboys when you need them. Help show you what the ride looks like."

Julian and Cam maintained eye contact. For Julian, it was like looking in a mirror.

"Why?" asked Cam.

"Why what?"

"Why did you step in front of me?"

Julian thought for a moment. "I don't know. Instinct I guess. It's what parents do."

Cam nodded as he seemed to mull over the answer "How did you do it…make it on your own?"

Julian pushed Karlie's legs out of the way and sat. He leaned forward, put his forearms on his thighs, and looked out on the Boston skyline. The sun felt good against his face. "Practice, I guess." He paused. "You put a kid in any situation and they adapt." He leaned back and let the sun massage his body. "My whole life has been about improvisation and serrated edges. I just do what I have to do to dull them a bit."

Julian reached over and picked up a stray bobber lodged under a board on the deck. He worked it in his hands. "Maybe I gained from not having parents." He shifted his gaze to Cam. "You know Winston Churchill was ignored by his parents. His mother was an American, not that different from Karlie's or mine. His father told him he was a wastrel, that he wouldn't accomplish anything in his life. In his memoirs, Winston said that if a solitary tree grows at all, it grows to be sturdy. I like to think that I'm a solitary tree."

Cam considered the words. He looked hard through Julian, as though he was trying to visually dissect him. "How about God? "

Julian looked at his son with a hint of surprise in his eyes. "Don't know. Not anymore. When I was at the home with Sister Mary Beth, I believed. I really believed. Life can be a Class-Five shit storm sometimes. When it blows in, it's easier to tolerate if you can convince yourself it's not random. You know…'everything happens for a reason: God has a plan.' Euphemisms to help understand all the crap we can't begin to fathom." Julian took his eyes from Cam to the Boston skyline. "But now, when I see all the shit that happens everywhere, every day, day after day, I wonder if the ancient Greeks had it right. For them, life's crap was just the price of admission." He searched for a glint of understanding from his son. "There have been dark days." He paused then stared again at the slats on the floor. "Lots of brain noise."

"Stern days."

"What?" Julian looked up.

"Stern days. Churchill always referred to them as stern days, not dark days."

Julian gave Cam a distracted nod. Despite what he had just said, he knew a lot of his life had been decapitated––no way to get it back. But maybe now he could dump the cargo, the pathos of his old life. For the first time, he saw a future. "Listen Cam, go easy on your mom. That's what she was going to talk to you about today. She was young and made some bad decisions. We all do."

"What happened?"

"Talk to your mom first. Then, if you want, I'll give you my version."

"Sounds good. What are we going to do with her?" He nodded toward Karlie, who was sprawled on the cushion.

Julian laughed and shook his head. "We were both flummoxed, weren't we?"

"Never saw it coming," said Cam.

"Same thing with love––a capricious little lady." Julian tested his paternal look on Cam.

"So, what do we do with her?" said Cam again.

Julian thought back on Karlie's hideous charade. "Not sure. Should be a slam dunk; let her entertain herself in the slammer for the next five years. Put a mirror in her cell, and she'll do just fine. But I hate to open that can of worms. Your dad…Maxwell…" Julian fumbled his words, dropped the bobber, and then offered a self-deprecating smile. "…and I dodged a bullet ten years ago. Everyone knew Billy Ray Roux was a slimeball, but we were headed for a very long time-out anyway. Cooper made the difference. There was never a trial, and there's no statute of limitations on murder. If she gets me on that, she wins––I lose."

"But she's a few cards short. Bad witness."

"From the trauma of losing her dad. Prosecuting attorneys would make her look like a poster child for the parent deprived."

"If we don't say anything now, the opportunity is lost. And we end up in cement shoes."

They shared questioning looks.

"Let's head back. You drive."

Cam took the controls. Thirty minutes later, they were met by a gaggle of cops and a paramedic van. Chain of evidence procedures were followed. Statements were made. Then Karlie took the perp walk to the patrol car. Julian allowed the police to photograph his wounds and then had the paramedics work their magic but declined a trip to the hospital.

CHAPTER TWENTY-EIGHT

LIVY'S HOUSE
Sunday, September 9, 2001, 2:50 P.M.

"Peaceful trip?" Livy made the inquiry after Julian explained they had taken a short cruise.

Cam and Julian looked at each other, at a loss for words. "A storm chased us to shore," said Julian.

"That's funny, I missed it."

"So did we."

"What?"

"Nothing. Hey listen, I need to pay Agnes another visit. Cam, why don't you and your mom have some mother-son time? Be back soon."

Livy nodded OK. "What happened to your arm?"

Julian looked at the wrap on his right bicep. "Cut myself shaving, no problem."

Cam clasped Julian's hand and gave him a hug. "I owe you one, man. Thanks."

"*De nada.*" Julian received a perplexed look from Livy and then headed for the door. "Where did the good reverend end up?"

Livy's face stiffened, along with her posture. "I was on the phone for an hour. Nobody knows. He's officially listed as missing, lost in the fire."

Julian stopped his trek toward the door. "What? No way."

"Exactly what I said." Livy's eyes turned down. She folded her arms across her chest.

"You put him in a paramedic van last night, right?"

"I did. A policeman helped me."

"Which ambulance service? County or private?"

"Don't know. Looked like all the others."

Dread crept into Julian's thoughts. "What did the paramedics look like?"

"I don't know. Two guys. One was real short, really short."

Julian and Cam jerked their heads toward each other. Their stares met halfway.

"Shit," they both said at the same time.

"What?" asked Livy.

"I killed him," said Julian. He sunk into a nearby chair, placing his elbows on his knees and his face in his hands. "Damn, damn, damn."

"What?" asked Livy, again.

Cam described the golf-tee DNA and its connection to the dwarf––her Rosetta Stone. Julian considered their next step.

Livy beat him to the punch. "We've got to tell the police."

"Too late. I gift wrapped him. The reverend was off their radar. He tells them he doesn't know where the vellum is. They say fine…and kill him."

Julian ran both hands through his hair and then paced in baby steps around the table with his hands jammed in his pockets.

"Heck," said Livy. "This just became a no-brainer. We stop looking." Livy walked over to Julian and stood directly in front of him, with her hands on her hips. "Tell me you'll stop looking."

Julian didn't answer directly but retreated to the sink, standing in front of a window. Outside the sunlight played off the wind-blown leaves like green-and-yellow confetti. He thought back to what the cleric had said. *To protect the legacy of his son.* "Tell me how something written four hundred and twenty-five years before Jesus's life could denigrate him. Religion back then was a totally different game. Greeks had thousands of gods. There was no sacred text. Hell, they didn't even have to believe any of it. It makes no sense."

"Maybe I can help," said Cam.

"Stop!" said Livy. Her eyebrows furrowed into one another; determination creased her lips. "This is absolutely crazy. People are dying. This isn't some stupid guy movie where the good guys win and the world is saved. These people evidently have the means to kill when and where they want. Four Special Forces soldiers, Professor Minton, Cooper, Maxwell, maybe Reverend Toulukinopolis." Livy paused to wait for a response or a reaction. "We can't win."

Julian considered what she said before responding. "Remember what the preacher said, 'to stop it would be to expose it to the world.' Our way out."

"He also said that its exposure might lead to the unraveling of Western civilization—"

"—Or have no effect at all," Julian finished.

"It's a lose-lose situation," continued Livy, not willing to back down.

Julian stood, leaning up against the sink with Livy in front of him. Cam sat at the dining table. No one spoke.

"Julian," said Cam, "give me a synopsis. What's going on? I can help."

Julian obliged his son. It took thirty minutes. When he finished, the room was again quiet. The voice of Jim Nance on the TV was making introductions––opening day in the NFL, a late game.

"There can't be that many vertically challenged people in this city," said Livy. "Just give the police everything we have. They'll find him."

"That won't accomplish anything," said Cam.

"Why not?"

"Money," said Cam.

"What?" said Livy.

"Follow the money. If Cooper really did find a Dexion Society linking back to King Constantine and if Reverend Toulukinopolis thinks that what he knows would destroy the legacy of Jesus, it's clear that *Amphilochus* must bring into question a basic tenet of Christianity. Who would be the biggest loser? It's not a tough question. Religion is big business. Huge. The Catholics alone are worth many billions, and that's just one piece of the pie. Arresting a dwarf wouldn't mean diddly-squat. There have to be hundreds more ready to take his place. There is a huge stash of cash to protect."

"Julian," said Livy, figuratively and literally standing her ground, "take your man shoes off and drop it. Let the police take care of it."

Julian glanced at Cam and then directly into Livy's anxious eyes. "I need to get some more books from Cooper's study. I think he's made a pretty good case for a two-thousand-year cover-up. I'd like to see it. Clearly the only way to stop this is to find the vellum codex."

"Julian, stop it!" said Livy. "You have no chance of finding it. There's no Cooper. No clues. No map. It's worse than a needle in a haystack. Hell, we don't even have a haystack. We've got the entire Trinity Church complex or, even worse, the whole city of Boston."

Julian hadn't ever been married, but he still recognized her look. Maybe he should back off. He hesitated. "The cops aren't going to waste their time looking for some damn book. They could solve every one of these murders, but it won't mean shit."

This was more than a line in the sand. Like a meteorological-cloud-filled Rorschach test, she saw dragons, and he saw parchment.

"Let's say you find it," said Livy. "Might as well paint a big sign on your back—'kill me.' Why don't we make your funeral arrangements now."

CHAPTER TWENTY-NINE

TRINITY CHURCH
Sunday, September 9, 2001, 4:00 p.m.

Julian stood alone in front of the thick, four-hinged door of the parish house. Cam had agreed to stay with Livy for some mother-son time. Julian assured her that he'd be perfectly safe with Granny.

"What do ya' want?" said Agnes, as Julian stepped through the door.

"A thigh master." He grabbed the cuff of his pants and yanked it as high as he could. "Isn't that one of the sorriest-looking thighs you've ever seen?" This crinkled her face only a smidgen. He dropped the cuff and stood up. "Hope I'm not bothering you."

"You are. Was trollin' the online personals. It's a damn pisser. They're either post-op or dead." She gave Julian a dismissive glare that declared damnation to all men.

"So no takers."

"Invited a guy over for margaritas. Went rogue on me. Said his bowels were locked up."

"Ms. Vandenbosch, I just wanted to make sure you were doing OK." Julian's most charming smile did nothing to soften the crust.

"Hogwash. Should've warned me you were comin'. Would've put on my Vera Wang."

He followed her hobble through the cluttered entry into the kitchen. Her pants––corduroy with a floral print––bagged out in the back and dragged on the floor. Her threadbare taupe sweater was tattered at the sleeves. Used tissues bulged from one of her pockets. Curiously, there were now four photos on the counter over the sink. The remnants of a half-eaten Oreo littered a paper plate resting on the kitchen table next to an open laptop. The TV graphic said the Patriots were only behind by seven. She had the volume turned down, and classical music was playing from a radio or CD. She sat down and took a swig out of a large canister.

"Game day. I've got my mojo workin'." She tipped her mug toward him. "Want some?"

Julian nodded yes and ended up with a crucible full of purple stuff. She shoved some Oreos his way.

"Is that Mozart?"

She smiled a gray smile. "Heck, I wouldn't know Mozart from a chainsaw. Just like the way it sounds. Where's your pretty friend?"

"Stayed home." Julian picked a magazine off the table. *Ethan Allen Furniture*, August 1993. He raised his eyebrows. She noticed.

"Been meanin' to read it."

Julian smiled. "Hey, you up for some questions? We're still trying to figure out what happened to the good reverend."

"Get a hitch in your giddyap?" She nodded toward his arm as she twisted her Oreo apart, dissected the middle, and then tossed a good-sized gulp into the back of her throat.

"Just a scratch. Did you say you worked for the Reverend Toulukian before the Reverend Saltonstall?" Julian took a sip. It tasted like vintage grocery-store, possibly Boone's Farm, wine.

"Yep. Early nineties."

"What can you tell me about him?" Julian noticed liver spots on her face and neck that he hadn't noticed before. She looked older, frailer.

"Had the personality of a paper cup."

Julian nodded. "Had any more spiritual encounters?"

"Nope. Been as quiet as church mouse." She added a rare smile, minus a few teeth, thinking she had come up with a good one.

He gave her a look that assured her that she had. He decided to shift gears. "Were you here when the church shifted in '92?"

Her eyes opened wide, like it happened only yesterday, then jerked around, the motion short and agitated. "Scared the bejabbers out of me. All week it had rained harder than a cow pissin' on a flat rock. Was a Tuesday. Was gettin' ready for the elders' dinner. Thought it was an frickin' earthquake."

"Afterward, do you remember seeing any old papers?

"Heck no. Just remember gettin' all gussied up for nothin'. Hell of a mess. Ruined my dinner." She took another sip of her fermented brew. "How's the wine?"

"Good."

"Poppycock. It sucks. If ya like it, you probably need to go to man camp. But hey, put some hundred-fifty proof rum in it, and that'll put hair on your tush."

Julian couldn't help but smile, but the visual made him wince. "Have there been any major renovations since then?"

"Nope. Just small stuff."

"Could you show me where the foundation cracked?"

"Was gettin' ready to rearrange my underwear drawer." She offered a you're-out-of-luck shrug of her shoulders. "Hell, yes. Let me get a flashlight."

Agnes grabbed an Oreo on the way toward the hallway.

"You don't happen to know where Cooper got his tattoos, do you?"

"You think he's going to ask a dinosaur like me where to get his body-work done? Didn't know he even had 'em." She shook her head back and forth then teetered around and headed forward. "You've been in one too many tractor accidents, sonny."

He guessed that was a no. Agnes opened a door, which looked little used, leading to a dank, dark basement. A moldy smell blasted Julian's nose. The light from the hallway cast itself into the inky darkness. The skeletal shadow of an upside down plunger appeared on an overhang. The steps disappeared into oblivion. She pulled the chain of an overhead light. Rats scratched in the darkness as Agnes's feet creaked an announcement of intrusion. Julian ducked. The stairway was low and narrow. Agnes stopped and swatted away a curtain of spider webs at the bottom of the stairs. It was ten degrees cooler. She yanked on another chain––sixty watts and not nearly enough.

The décor in the forty-five-foot room was cluttered; a shadow lingered behind every bric-a-brac. The near wall was decorated with three filing cabinets; rust feasted at the bottom of each and loose papers stood high on top. Next to those was a metal four-shelf case. A water-stained fertilizer bag, an old car battery, hedge clippers, work gloves, and carburetor cleaner filled the bottom shelf. Bike gloves and a bicycle tire pump rested under a yellow bike helmet on the shelf above that. A new Paketa racing bicycle hung from the ceiling; a yellow insignia embossed the seat, and yellow stripes lined the rims.

Agnes coughed and waved her gnarled hand in front of her nose. "Forget your Odor-Eaters?"

Julian hesitated and then, after his eyes adjusted, scanned the room. What looked like new brick formed a wall on the far end.

"I thought you said there hadn't been any recent work done?"

Agnes followed his eyes. "Hell, I forgot about that."

"What was it?"

"A door."

"To what?" Julian headed toward the fresh brickwork. Spider webs tickled his face. Clots of fresh dirt jammed the soles of his shoes. The cement grout had rough edges, definitely new. A rancid smell flirted with his nose.

"Down."

"There's a layer below this?"

"So I'm told. Legend has it, a hundred years ago, this church smuggled people in and out of Boston. Hear tell that a certain Theophilis O'Grandy, who ran a boarding house and bar across the street, was a crimp. Used to drug ne'er-do-wells, haul them through the tunnels to the Charles River, and then load 'em on ships bound for ports unknown."

"The church was involved in illegal activities?"

"Things were tight for years after the big fire in '72--1872."

Agnes shuffled along a floor that was suffocating under a thick layer of old insulation, empty jelly jars, and newspapers. Two hinges of a thick plank door winked at them from behind a workbench. A rusted circular saw and a big-jawed vise rested on the table.

"That's where we need to go," said Agnes.

"I guess you come down here all the time."

"You're a freakin' laugh a minute. You're the one who wants to see it."

Julian struggled but finally nudged the workbench aside. A dead-bolt latch secured the door. A nearby can of WD-40 and a hammer took care of the warped entry.

"You're pretty handy with that hammer."

Julian looked at the old lady. "That sounds suspiciously like a compliment."

"Don't get used to it, sonny boy."

They were met by a thick, fetid stench; the air was pungent with the smell of rotting flesh. Julian clicked the button on the yellow flashlight and found a place lost to time. They tugged their shirts up over their noses. Two dead rats, half-decayed, sprawled before them. Open sores spilled out onto the cropped fur. He scanned the ground; the blackness softened and shapes formed. Their feet treaded carefully, hesitantly. Near the far wall, packed piles of dirt rose next to four shadowy voids, like someone had been looking for something or trying to hide something. Julian took small steps toward the first pile and peered inside. Nothing. Same with the next two. The last hole, located at the far end, looked six feet long. A tattered shirt lay half buried under the dirt pile next to the hole.

He looked back at Agnes. "Know anything about these? Hear anything?"

"Heck, my hearing ain't worth beans."

Julian searched her expression for truth and then stepped forward and peered in, certain he would see Reverend Toulukinopolis's inquisitive eyes looking back. His shoulders assumed their normal position. It was empty.

Cracked walls lined the passageway. Black moldy hunks of cement littered the tunnel. At shoulder level, the cement blocks jutted out six inches from the ones below. The tunnel angled up at a twenty-degree angle, and the overlapping block work continued beyond the end of the light beam. Dust particles danced in the light stream. The ceiling consisted of eight inch by eight inch rough-hewn planks,. Water seeped from the splintered mortar. Agnes progressed at a snail's pace up the incline. Spent by the trek, she spoke in winded fragments.

"Takes us…under the…the church. Comes in…the chancel behind the altar. Mr. O'Grady…the story goes…would pay busty…crucifix-wearing bimbos…to lure horny guests…to the church. One prayer…and an opium-doctored glass of wine later…they'd wake up in…wherever."

A moth-eaten wooden ladder leaned up against the crumbling-stone end of the tunnel. Twenty feet overhead, the light beam settled on a three-foot-by-two-foot marble slab.

Julian pushed on the heavy stone door and raised himself up through the hole. Agnes was right. He lay in the chancel, looking up at the underneath edge of the alabaster-and-onyx marble alter. Directly above, a huge wooden cross, decorated in gold leaf and polychrome, dangled from long bronze chains attached to a high-domed ceiling. The rear of the altar consisted of elaborately carved shimmering marble panels with inlaid mosaics, and Alps-green marble boarders. One inscription read, "One Lord, One Faith, One Baptism, One Goal, One God, and Father of All."

Julian lowered himself back into the tunnel.

CHAPTER THIRTY

LIVY'S HOUSE
Sunday, September 9, 2001, 5:45 p.m.

Julian returned to Livy's house with a box full of Cooper's books. He stole away in the guest bedroom for the better part of two hours, studying what Cooper had spent nine years dissecting. Spread on the desk in front of him was a Latin edition of Erasmus's *In Praise of Folly*. Julian scribbled notes, referred to Cooper's notes, and talked to himself. "Absolutely brilliant!" He counted out the numbers––one, two, three, five, eight, thirteen, twenty-one, and on, so that the preceding two numbers summed the third. The Fibonacci sequence. In neat, block font, he printed the letter corresponding to each number, then read it:

IN THE SHADOW OF DEXION, CHRISTUS PALLIDUS.

A tap on the door suspended his effort.

"Dinner." Livy stood in the doorway.

Julian jumped and then smiled. "Sorry. You surprised me."

"I come unarmed." Livy held her hands waist high. Her expression suggested displeasure.

It took Julian a moment to recall that he'd nearly died earlier in the day. "Hey, I would have said something, but I figured Cam would fill you in."

Livy entered the room, sat down on the bed, and then reached over and took his hand.

Without looking up, she said in hardly a whisper, "Cam told me what you did for him on the boat." Livy brought his hand to her lips and then angled her head. "Please don't die."

She arose from the bed, patted Julian's shoulder, and then left the room.

Conversation at the dinner table was sparse. Discussion of the weather led to a discussion of Cam's classes, and then to nothing. Cam inquired whether he could move back to his apartment.

"Honey, we can talk to the police," suggested Livy.

"No!" said Julian.

Cam looked up, surprised.

Chagrined, Julian dragged a fork through his mashed potatoes and then offered, "Sorry."

Livy smiled. "We'll cut you some slack."

"I'm serious though. I spoke with the police today. They arrested three guys for Nidal and Gretchen's murders. Middle Easterners. Saudis."

"So?" said Cam.

"No more police protection."

Livy looked at Cam. "We stay together, dear."

"Plus," said Julian, much louder than he should have, "this Dexion thing is way, way bigger than I thought. Not exactly sure how to get us out."

Livy put down her fork and wiped her mouth. Concern etched her face.

"I've been going through Cooper's books and papers. It's unbelievable."

Cam put down his fork, looked at Livy, and then back at Julian. "And…"

Julian pushed his plate back and draped his elbows over the table. "OK. Like I mentioned before, this thing--Dexion Society--goes back to King Constantine."

"The Council of Nicaea, 325 AD," said Cam.

"Right. Two of the bishops couldn't agree to the Nicene Creed. They believed instead, in the opinion—considered heresy—of a guy named Arius. They were both exiled. An order was given to destroy the writings of Arius regarding *Christus pallidus*--the pallid Christ. This included a directive to destroy the other significant document--singular--the thing of Dexion.

The penalty for those failing to comply was death. The amazing thing is, Cooper actually found specific references in papyri excavated from an ancient Alexandria, Egypt, dump heap in 1978. They were deciphered years ago, but nobody realized their significance then. Now we do. Archeological proof of the start of a two-thousand-year cover-up."

"So Dexion was born," said Cam.

"Exactly." Julian straightened up in the chair. "King Constantine sent Hosius of Cordova, his right-hand man, to the library in Alexandria to locate and destroy all known copies of an important document just days after the Council met. The Alexandrian library was the think tank of the Greek world. Every ship entering the city's port was searched for scrolls. Those found were copied; the originals were kept at the library. Seven hundred thousand scrolls were stored there. The index of the library's contents filled one hundred and twenty scrolls. Copies of *Amphilochus,* found at the library and destroyed, most likely represented a significant percent of the total. The average guy was illiterate and didn't own scrolls. Over the years, the rest just disappeared."

Julian took a swig of his Coke and then continued. He described what he had, minutes before, discovered in Cooper's notes about the writings of Erasmus of Rotterdam, the sixteenth-century ordained minister. Julian explained how Cooper searched the seminal manuscript, *In Praise of Folly,* for coded text utilizing all the usual cipher techniques—letter substitutions, transpositions, Caesar cipher, and the rail-fence cipher used by the ancient Greeks on the battlefield. He finally happened upon the references to Dexion and *Christus pallidus* using the Fibonacci sequence. He next outlined Cooper's evaluation of Voltaire, who essentially took Erasmus's baton two hundred years later in his compendium of *Philosophical Letters.* There he found references to Dexion Society, *Amphilochus,* and a pallid Christ.

Julian looked around the table; skepticism peered back.

"You have to remember," said Julian, "it was a different time. They couldn't just spit it out. People were put to death for the wrong beliefs. Voltaire spent a major portion of his life on the run, exiled from France."

Julian went on to explain how Voltaire, during his exile, struck up a friendship with John Churchill, the first Duke of Marlborough. He told them how in the 1720s, after the duke's death, Voltaire and Benjamin Franklin developed an acquaintance at Blenheim when both were in their late seventies. Julian reminded them of Franklin's opinion of religion: a necessary support for the morality and basic maintenance of society.

A question or a statement flickered around Livy's lips but was left unsaid. She moved her chair back as though she was ready to get up.

Julian wasn't sure if this indicated displeasure or disinterest or disbelief; he continued anyway.

"Later Voltaire lived with Frederick the Great. I couldn't find any of Cooper's notes on the Prussian king, but the king's opinion of Christianity is well known––metaphysical fiction stuffed with absurdities that some imbeciles actually believe…his words. Frederick Nietzsche was easy. Cooper found the Fibonacci-coded reference to Dexion in *Human, All Too Human*, *The Twilight of the Idols*, and *The Anti-Christ*. And he found a pallid Christ reference in *The Anti-Christ*. Interestingly, neither were referenced in *The Gay Science*, best known for the line, 'God is dead.'"

Julian then related how Cooper indirectly traced Dexion to America through Ralph Waldo Emerson, a Unitarian minister. Julian pointed out how Cooper found, in a William James notebook entry, a reference to a conversation he'd had with Emerson, his godfather. This notation was dated 1873, during James's years at Harvard—a time when he sparred, philosophically, with Oliver Wendell Holmes, among others, in an informal group they called "The Metaphysical Club."

"That's the thing," said Cam. "It is incredibly unlikely that any of these guys ever had proof of anything. Just rumors of some flaw in Jesus's persona. Gossip of a clandestine society dedicated to a secret—whatever it was. Can't imagine it changed their minds. Just fortified their suspicion, and put a pejorative spin on all things Jesus. Erasmus and Voltaire were born with a bent for skepticism. Both were men of religion who looked for reasons to be provocateurs. Dexion just gave them another reason to attack the sacred cows of Christianity: ritual and dogma."

Julian acknowledged the point but then continued. "Emerson was a mentor to Emma Lazarus, who happened to hang around Henry James, William's father. She was Jewish, so all bets are off, but her poem 'Tannhauser' has the line, 'A pallid Christ, unnatural, perfect, and a Virgin cold…A creed of suffering and despair.' Cooper scrutinized Emma's poem 'The New Colossus,' on the Statue of Liberty, long and hard but couldn't find anything. There is a whole ream of people Cooper could have looked at in the Concord area. Emerson let Thoreau live rent-free on his property.

Emerson found houses for Nathaniel Hawthorne and Bronson Alcott, Louisa May's eccentric father. Feminist author Margaret Fuller edited a magazine called *The Dial*, financed by Emerson. An absolute plethora of material to be studied--but Cooper didn't and I'm not. So, as far I can tell, Cooper and Reverend T. are the only two people, both in recent times and both men of the cloth, who have actually seen *Amphilochus*. They couldn't bring themselves to reveal the contents. We have a chance to do that."

"'Action with the scholar subordinate.' You're a scholar--an idea man," said Cam.

"Impressive. Emerson. Must be giving your studies due diligence. But you left off the end of that quote, 'But yet essential.'"

"Let me play devil's advocate," said Cam. "Let's say you...we...find whatever it is that Reverend Saltonstall may have hidden—if he did indeed hide something. What are you going to do? It's not worth dying, just to be a footnote in history." He paused a beat. "Not sure I could handle having two dads die in the same week."

Julian said a thank you with his eyes and then switched his gaze to Livy and then back to Cam. "I don't know what to do. I've spent pretty much my whole life in survival mode. I've never been accountable to anybody."

"But...?" said Cam.

"But I keep asking myself what could scare off two modern-day preachers and warrant a death penalty two thousand years ago?"

"What if a critical plank of Christianity is pulled?" asked Cam. "Look at what Christians are already expected to believe. Life after death, heaven, hell, God... A huge leap of faith is required. It defies logic. It defies any kind of inquiry. Take anything away from that, and then the leap gets even bigger...huge...impossible."

"That could be what Cooper and Reverend T. were thinking," said Julian.

"And what Dexion is looking at now. Less believers, less churches, less money."

Cam and Julian studied each other. Neither spoke for a moment.

Then Cam continued, "Maybe we shouldn't go there. To undo something two thousand years in the making, so well entrenched in our daily life. It means nothing to me; I'm an atheist. But there are so many people who find consolation in prayer, taking the leap, going through the rituals, and reading the text. Maybe we should leave well enough alone."

"I don't think I can. My life is academia. As trivial as it may seem, I need to know what Alexander the Great put under his pillow between his *Iliad* and his dagger. Unfortunately, I've drawn you both, unwittingly, into this mess." He paused to get a reaction, waiting for some sort of feedback. None was forthcoming. "I'll stop looking if you want me to. If so, we need to get out of town. Now. We do not pass GO."

CHAPTER THIRTY-ONE

LIVY'S HOUSE
Sunday, September 9, 2001, 6:20 p.m.

N o immediate decision was made. Julian, Cam, and Livy quietly finished their meal. The conversation was small talk mostly. Julian added honey to his coffee. Cam took his black.

Livy said, "You never finished the part about the Churchills. Left us hanging." Her declaration hinted at sarcasm.

Julian smiled, feeling self-conscious and slightly embarrassed. "I think Cooper was trying to link Princess Di's death to Dexion."

"You're kidding," said Cam. He laughed, nearly choking on his coffee.

Julian handed him a napkin. "Remember, Voltaire spent several years at Blenheim Palace hanging out with John Churchill, the first Duke of Marlborough. Winston Churchill, the duke's grandson, was a very accomplished writer. In fact, he won a Nobel Prize and wrote an extensive biography of his famous relative in an attempt to revive the reputation of England's great war hero. The duke's daughter––Ann––married a Spencer. Winston was born at Blenheim. He lived there for years and retired there. Princess Di––a Spencer and a distant relative––visited the palace on occasion. It was thought she learned something while rummaging through the archives. I'm not sure what she did to warrant suspicion. Cooper conjectured someone with Dexion drugged the chauffeur, Henri Paul. Cooper discovered the alleged alcohol intoxication was a fabrication by persons unknown. He even visited Lady Di's island grave and then went on to Blenheim Palace. Unfortunately, Churchill was a prolific writer. Cooper was still sifting through the volumes when he was killed. It sounds like a stretch to me, but stranger things have happened."

Cam was laughing out loud by the time Julian finished. "Jeez-laweeze! Dexion killed Kennedy, right?"

"Hey, I'm just the messenger."

The table grew quiet; the affairs of the day were finally taking their toll.

"Something else for you to gnaw on," said Julian. "Mysterious circumstances, maybe chronic arsenic poisoning, surrounded Emma Lazarus's death in her mid-thirties." He paused for a reaction. "So, what's the verdict?"

"Sounds like we're stuck," said Cam. "Dexion will assume we know something, especially after your rendezvous with the good preacher at the nursing home. Heck, if they're killing Princess Di, we've got to be on their A-list. Our only chance would be to stay close to the police, keep looking, find what Cooper hid, and then get it to the *New York Times*––quickly. But only a short-term search, maybe a few days. If we don't find it, I think we need to skedaddle for awhile."

Julian took his gaze to Livy.

"This is a mess," said Livy. "I think we should dump it all in the lap of the police now. We definitely need to let them know everything we know. But I can agree with a short-term search. A day or two, max. I doubt if Dexion is patient."

Thirty minutes later, they had dealt out all the relevant material onto the kitchen table, including the contents of Maxwell's folders and the material gathered at Cooper's office.

"The key has to be the tattoos," said Cam, after scrutinizing the pictures, reading the files, and thumbing through Cooper's Bible. "That's a lot of trouble to go through. It probably took a couple visits. He knew he was dying. He probably knew he was being watched and didn't want to tell you for whatever reason—probably didn't want to get you killed." He picked up the photo of a raw, bloody arm. "It would be dandy to know what was on this."

"I asked Agnes about the tattoos. She had no clue Cooper had them, and I didn't see any receipts." Julian reached over and pulled up Cam's shirtsleeve. "Where did you get yours?"

"ReGeneration over on Western, in Cambridge. Sligo Taft, good guy. Why don't we head over there tomorrow? A priest filling his chest with print might have started some tongues wagging."

Julian wrinkled his eyes with a smile. "Sligo?"

"Yeah. Guess his mom was a major Yeats fan. Apparently Yeats lived in County Sligo, Ireland."

"What do you think about this stuff?" Julian laid the photos of the objects found in Cooper's pockets out on the table.

Cam picked up the picture of the computer chips, then grabbed the magnifying glass. He looked at it for about two seconds.

"They're RFID chips." He backhanded the photo to the table.

Julian waited for the rest of the answer. "And they do what?"

"Not much. RFID stands for radio frequency identification. Basically, it's a bar code on steroids. It has a very small chip whose sole purpose is to store a number; that's it. It's attached to an equally small antenna. When the chip hears a particular radio signal, it responds by broadcasting the number back."

"How far can they transmit?" asked Julian, picking up the photo.

"Depends. A few centimeters to miles. Depends on the size."

"Why would a cleric have three of these in his pocket?"

"Beats me. The British used a variation of this to identify friendly craft during World War II. Now they're used by companies for inventory control. Vets use them to ID pets. They're used in passports. Lots of things."

"People?"

"Sure. You could implant one in someone or just sew it into a piece of clothing or hide one in a shoe."

"Cross country?"

"Something this small––no. Unless you combined it with a cell phone or a computer."

Julian thumbed through the pictures and handed a photo of three cell phones to Cam. "How about these?"

"Those would work."

Julian dropped the photos on the table and paced the room. He ended up at the piano, sat down, and played a few random chords. Cam picked up the stack of pictures and looked through them again. He stopped at one and held it up for Julian to see.

"Cooper had these in his pocket?"

Julian stopped playing and nodded.

"Rohypnols," said Cam.

"That's what Maxwell said."

"What does that have to do with Dexion?"

"Don't know. Maybe nothing. Did you look at Coop's Monopoly board? The numbers…GPS coordinates?"

"That's what I thought," said Cam.

"I checked the seven marked properties with street names in Cambridge, Boston, and the surrounding area. I found an Indiana Avenue and a Pennsylvania Avenue, a Saint Charles Street, but not a Saint Charles Place. No Boardwalk. No Park Place. The GPS coordinates didn't correlate with any of the street locations."

"Code?"

"I think so," said Julian.

"For the vellum?"

"Maybe. Need to check 'em out."

"Might take a while." Cam grabbed the Monopoly board and sat down at the computer on Livy's desk. He punched in a few keystrokes for Google Earth, waited, and then punched in a few more. An aerial view of Boston popped onto the screen. He worked the mouse over to one of the GPS coordinates. An aerial shot focused on a house. Cam turned and looked at Julian. "This is Saint James Place." Julian got up from the piano bench to look over Cam's shoulder.

"Run-down. Hardly worthy of its saintly dispensation." There was surprise in Julian's voice.

"This particular crib happens to be on…" Cam moved the mouse. "…Plympton Street."

Julian glanced at the game board. "Six properties are marked, plus the one in the middle. Why don't you check those and then print 'em."

Minutes later, Julian shuffled through the photos of the GPS-marked properties. He held up a picture of a gas station. "Which one is this?"

"Center of the board."

Julian dropped the prints and picked up the crime-scene photos. He pulled one out and showed it to Cam.

"Sturbridge Isle truck-stop matches," Cam said to himself. "Cooper's pocket?" He received a nod. "You don't think Cooper would hide the vellum at a truck stop, do you?"

"It's probably the last place I'd look," said Livy. "Maybe that makes it a good spot. Maybe he hid it in a long-term locker. The GPS street addresses…" Livy nodded toward Cam's aerial pictures. "…maybe they're the combination."

Julian walked to the refrigerator. "Pie anyone?" He got a couple yesses and made the appropriate cuts. Halfway through his piece, he looked up at Cam. "I can't recall…where's Sturbridge?

"About a hour west. I-95."

"What do you think, road trip?"

"Sunday night," said Cam, "nothing else going on."

CHAPTER THIRTY-TWO

STURBRIDGE ISLE TRUCK STOP
Sunday, September 9, 2001, 9:45 p.m.

Julian, Cam, and Livy arrived at the Sturbridge Isle truck stop an hour and a half later. Paranoia collared them. Since they no longer had police surveillance, they used every cinematographic auto-evasion maneuver they could recall. At Livy's insistence, Julian carried one of Maxwell's old revolvers, tucked neatly under his long shirttail.

A huge four-bay service area was located next to a truck wash, which was juxtaposed to the truck stop. Lights in the service area were on, and a couple of mechanics were at work. The football-field-sized lot was packed, wheel to wheel, truck after truck––possibly sixty trucks. The snowball-yellow-and-red lights of the rigs gave the place a festive ambiance, like a huge outdoor Christmas display. Puddles of light from the cabs offered the only interruption to the straight lines and neat squares of red and yellow. On the other side of the lot, tall argon torches scattered light over the elevated awnings like huge martian tripods.

Julian, Cam, and Livy wove a path into the restaurant. A layer of smoke hovered near the ceiling. Four tables were occupied. They chose an empty one near the front window. Moments later, a waitress was tableside.

Her nametag said "Brenda." She had the big hair working for her with a rear-facing pompadour-like thing that probably had its own zip code.

"Brenda," said Julian, "before we order, have a couple questions for you."

She instructed them where the lockers were located and indicated she'd never seen Cooper. Brenda took their order––coffee for all and more pie for Julian and Cam. Julian sent Cam into the men's room to look for lockers. Then he and Livy made nervous conversation. Both watched the lot as they spoke. Cam returned with the report of a dozen lockers, all with keylocks. He handed Julian a piece of paper with locker numbers. Julian checked them. Their food and drinks arrived. While they ate, each tossed out ideas regarding the contents and whereabouts of *Amphilochus*.

"Has to be in the church. It has lots of nooks and crannies," said Livy. "It's safe. He wouldn't risk being outside the church with it."

Julian thought of the rat-infested pits in the basement of the parish house. He made a mental note to secure a shovel.

"I'll get online and check Back Bay building permits for the last ten years," said Cam. "I'll check where they remodeled. Narrow it down."

Julian made a mental note to bust through the new brick wall. He rubbed his eyes. The magnitude of their search was unsettling. Thoughts of sleep made it seem a whole lot less important. The thought of holding something Alexander the Great had once stashed under his pillow made him want to keep going.

"Cooper did funerals, didn't he?" asked Livy.

Cam looked at his mom, slack-jawed. "Coffins?" He groaned. "Ten funerals a year for nine years. That's a shit load of diggin'."

"Maybe those tattooed letters are somebody's initials," said Livy.

"Grave robbing is probably a felony," said Cam. "Call me silly, but I don't want to be anybody's prison bitch."

As they waited for their check, an older sedan, possibly a Buick, pulled into a poorly lit area west of the restaurant. The headlights blinked off and on. Sixty seconds later, headlights from a nearby powder-blue Kenworth, stationed on the edge of the pack, went on and off three times in succession. Julian sat up in his seat. A lady in jeans, a light jacket, and tennis shoes eased out of her car. She looked out of place, but strangely comfortable, like she had been in the lot before. She folded her arms across her chest. A man, older and heavyset, eased out of the truck cab and made a beeline toward her. They exchanged pleasantries. She handed him a large envelope and then opened the back door. He reached in, pulled out a child—looked like a boy, hard to tell the age—that was sleeping and lifted him up, resting the child's head on his shoulder like a dad might do. He headed for his truck. Julian gave a chin nod toward the lady to get Livy and Cam's attention. The lady stood uneasily until a female traveling companion emerged from the truck. Together they got things situated inside the cab and then pulled off the lot. The lady ambled toward the restaurant, hands in her pockets, head down, weary, not vigilant, and not looking around. For Julian, there was something familiar in the way she walked and the way she held her head. Livy made a furtive move to get her cell phone out. He mouthed to her, "please wait."

The lady entered.

Now there was no doubt in his mind. It was the angle of her nose and the gentle, slightly down-turned eyes. He tried to imagine her in entirely different garb. She gave a practiced nod to the cashier then found a seat and took off her jacket. Julian noticed a beautiful complexion but a general plainness to her appearance; she wore no makeup. Her face had more experience than someone in her twenties, but lacked the telltale eye creases of someone in her forties. She looked confident but without pretense. Julian rose and walked to her table. His stomach knotted up, butterflies took flight.

"Excuse me. My name is Julian St. Laurent. May I sit down?"

Her startled look changed to suspicion. She reached inside her purse. "Have we met?"

"I knew your mother." He fought to hold her gaze. He kept his hands where she could see them.

"I think you've mistaken me for someone else." She pulled her phone out of her purse and flipped it open.

"There is no need to call anyone. I saw a state cop in the parking lot when I came in. I'll go get him, if you like." He took a step back and then hesitated, unsure how to proceed. He considered everything and then decided to take a chance. "Is Sister Mary Beth still alive?"

The lady's eyes widened; her brow wrinkled in confusion. She looked over at Livy and Cam then back at Julian. She didn't speak.

Her silence was confirmation. "You look just like her. When you walked in, I thought you were Sister Mary Beth. But I knew it couldn't be. You are her daughter."

"I think you are mistaken." She fussed with her purse and then looked around––for help or a familiar face, he wasn't sure. She scooted toward the seat edge, ready to leave.

"I don't think so." Julian stood tall, but not threatening. Faces, he never forgot. "May I sit?"

She hesitated at the seat's edge and looked again at Livy and Cam. She nodded surrender and stowed her phone.

"I'm so sorry to alarm you. I couldn't help myself." He placed his hands palm down on the table, extended toward her. "I owe your mother my life."

The lady extended her hand. "My name is Mary." They exchanged introductions and studied one another. "Then you lived in the home."

Julian nodded. "Do you know your mother?"

Mary's mouth turned down, and her eyes drew a blank, apparently confused by the question. "I was eleven years old when Sister Mary Beth took leave," said Julian. "In 1966. No explanation was offered."

Mary's shoulder relaxed. The pleats in her forehead faded. Her lips remained perfectly still, parted only slightly, with the faintest of creases at the corners. She remained mute.

"Toward the end of the year, she returned. I had two Christmases that year." Julian smiled at the recollection. He paused. "That would make you thirty-six. Your birthday, maybe August or September."

"August fourteenth."

"I loved your mother more than anything in the world. Is she still alive?"
"Yes."

"I've tried to find her." He looked for a hint in Mary's expression. "You work with her, don't you?"

"I used to. She's no longer able."

"And Reverend Saltonstall?"

Her eyes opened wide in surprise, followed by her first smile. "What a wonderful man."

There was a moment of silence. Julian thought of his friend. "I don't recall Sister Mary Beth leaving again, after she came back."

Mary looked at her hands resting on the table. "She placed me with foster parents. Wonderful people. When I was fifteen, I got to meet her."

Julian studied Mary's eyes. "Then, not again for a while?"

"She chose the Catholic church and Jesus over me. I thought I would never forgive her."

"What happened?"

"I graduated from Boston College and went to work for the state––Child Protective Services. She showed up one day with a child. A thirteen-year-old girl."

"Serendipity?"

"She said so. But I wonder."

Julian said nothing. He could see she wanted to talk.

"Reverend Saltonstall had approached her with this child—the child of one his parishioners. The mother, who claimed the girl was being sexually abused by the father, had brought her to him at the church. The mother wanted her daughter safe and her husband home, rather than in prison. The mother convinced the father the child had run away. He didn't care. He was a drunk."

She stopped talking and took a sip of her coffee. She glanced at Livy and Cam.

"And?"

"Not much else to say. I'd been spinning my wheels in the agency for a few years. I was way too familiar with the bureaucratic mumbo jumbo. I placed the child with a family. Problem solved."

"I assume there were more."

"There were. Six months later, another child came from Reverend Saltonstall. It was another convoluted situation , another discrete placement." She looked at Julian with renewed conviction. "There are lots of couples starved for children, any age."

"And you kept doing it, getting kids off the street."

"Each encounter was more heartrending than the previous." Her voice trailed off in a way that suggested there was another reason. "And I missed not having a mother."

"Did you see Cooper frequently?"

"At first, yes, then not so much. The risk grew. We communicated through e-mails mostly. Developed codes." She paused for another sip. "He became an aggressive advocate. Mother said he told her that's why God had saved him...to save the children."

"Were you expecting a child the day Cooper died?" Julian thought back to the rail-yard crime scene and the picture of the boy in Cooper's wallet. "Nine- or ten-year-old boy. Park Place, perhaps?"

Mary smiled for the second time. "I guess you found his silly Monopoly board. Mother told me about it." She sighed and looked at Julian. "Such a dear, dear man. A saint." She went on to relate to Julian how they used the Monopoly board property names as code for safe zones and meeting places.

They shared the moment. Julian felt proud to have been a part of Cooper's life.

"Did Cooper ever say he was in danger? I think the person who killed him also killed my twin brother, that lady's husband." Julian continued, pointing at Livy. "We're trying to figure out what it's all about. Cooper's personal effects led us here. Anything you know might help."

Mary studied Livy with different eyes. "Only in the last year or so, I think. Suggested, but not stated, in his e-mails. He became frustrated with the system and the never-ending stream of lost souls masquerading as children. He became more aggressive. He actually hired two ex-military guys part time to help pull the kids out of the muck of their lives. He'd get a whiff of abuse situations, a kiddy-porn producer, a guy selling teenage girls to a man in Malaysia, things like that. He'd involve the police." She looked at her hands, then sighed. "The criminals would be back on the street within the week."

Julian leaned forward. "Any names you can remember? The military personnel? People who might have a score to settle with Cooper?"

"I'll see what I have."

Julian nodded thanks and then gestured to the parking lot. "Why the truck driver?"

"About five years ago, we had a situation regarding a child from Chicago, a runaway. His rich dad checked out as legit and not abusive. The reverend always insisted that I check; I have contacts in every big city. The kid arrived with some juvie offenses. Dad wanted to keep things quiet. The kid's cousin was a teamster. We returned him home. The word spread. All we work with are volunteers. Most were foster kids or abused as children themselves."

"What about the computer chips, phones, and Rohypnols?"

"Every child is...was...so important to Cooper. He'd use the chips and phones to keep tabs on them. Always kept in contact with the parents. Sometimes he would arrange for counseling or social services. Often he paid for it himself, through church funds or his own. Sometimes the kids, especially the younger ones, had to be sedated, so traumatic were their experiences. The medication would help them forget what they had been through. The ones who didn't want to go home or were in abusive situations, I'd handle in the traditional manner. But the runaways with second thoughts, those are the ones we helped the most."

"Mary, I'm concerned for your safety. And for your mother's."

Mary showed her warm smile for the third time. "I appreciate your concern. I'm OK, and Mother is quite safe."

"You sure?"

"Very. She is a resident in Stockbridge, at the hospital for the psychiatrically impaired. She's been there about three years now. Just lost touch with the real world. Guilt, I think. She was way beyond words of absolution."

Julian gave her a questioning look.

"I don't think she ever got over her fall from grace––me."

CHAPTER THIRTY-THREE

LIVY'S HOUSE
Monday, September 10, 2001, 2:34 a.m.

Julian was dead tired, but restlessness ruled. He watched each hour come and go while performing the nocturnal gymnastics of an insomniac. Exhaustion finally won. He dreamed.

Julian woke when he hit the floor––sweat covered, his heart racing. Deep, rhythmic, pulsating arrows of pain shot from the right-arm wound. He twisted his feet free of the sheet. Something wet worked its way past his right eye to his cheek. Julian reached for the nightlight, then saw blood on his hand. He glanced at the corner of the nightstand and back at his hand and then stumbled his way into the bathroom.

Later, the morning sun beamed into the kitchen. Livy entered as she had the previous day, sleep in her eyes, hair in disarray, but elegant in her long white robe. Julian, already up, worked the front section of the *Globe*. They acknowledged each other with a nod and said good morning with their eyes. Livy fussed around with the Keurig machine then sat across from Julian. She dragged the sports section to her side.

"It's amazing you ran into Mary last night," said Livy, without looking up.

Julian nodded.

"Makes me wonder if that's why Cooper died," said Livy. "He must have royally pissed off someone. An abusive father perhaps."

"Remember your Rosetta Stone, the golf tees. I still think it's about the vellum codex." Julian took another sip in an attempt to shuffle the strands of sleep out of his brain.

She paused and looked at him. "What in the hell happened to your face?"

He reached up to the small cut in his eyebrow. "Rough night. Tried to kill myself on the nightstand."

Livy stifled a smile.

Julian pushed the paper away. "Hey, listen." Julian paused to select his words carefully. "You're right. We need to leave town as soon as poss--"

Just then, Cam strolled into the kitchen. With his robe on and a good start to a bad hair day, he grunted hello and headed for the cereal cabinet. After grabbing a bowl and the carton of milk, he aimed for the table.

"More riboflavin today?" asked Julian.

Cam smiled. "I'm thinking about goin' with the cyanocobalamin. Game-time decision."

"Right." Julian studied Cam for a moment then opened section one again.

They made small talk. Cam finished his cereal in minutes, then asked, "We hittin' the tattoo shop later?"

"Don't think so," said Julian.

Both Livy and Cam gave him a surprised look.

"Change of plans. I need to talk with your mom."

Cam nodded OK then headed to the shower. Julian stood, grabbed his coffee cup, and headed for the sink.

Livy pushed her section of the paper away and placed both hands on her cup of coffee. "So, what's up?"

"Not worth the risk." Julian rinsed out his cup and then glanced back at Livy. "Let's get out of town."

Livy waited a beat. "Why the change of heart?"

Through the kitchen window, cardinals and sparrows sparred over seed in a feeder twenty yards away. A pesky squirrel hung down in an attempt to access the grain. Beyond, a few mature maples separated Livy's house from the neighbors. The maples gave way to big oaks and then pines.

"It came to me last night…in a dream.," said Julian as he studied the battle over the seed.

Livy waited, then spoke, "What?"

"What's in the vellum, what *Amphilochus* represents."

"And?"

"If I'm right, I would have to agree with Reverend Toulukinopolis. Hard to tell how much the church or Western civilization would suffer. In this day and age, possibly nothing, maybe a lot. Tough call."

Livy walked over to him. She put her arm on his shoulder and laid her head up against his arm.

Julian turned toward Livy. He took her hands in his. "I need to keep you safe. If anything happens to you…"

"Don't worry. We'll be fine."

Unease settled onto Julian's face. "How are you financially?"

"Julian, we'll be fine."

He waited for the real answer.

"No problems, really. Maxwell saved. Insurance payout. City benefits. We're OK."

"Good. We need to take care of business today then disappear for a while. No credit cards. No jobs. I have a friend in Idaho––"

"Hold on."

"I'm serious. Our only chance would be to find *Amphilochus* and make it public. Too many things will have to go right for that to happen."

"What was it, the dream?"

"Cooper's Bible. The very first thing I looked at. It's all right there: the rubrics in the margins. Mostly in Luke and Matthew, but there's that one in John. That's what threw me off. John has a totally different style, different story. Coop marked the account of the adulteress. You know…'those of you who have not sinned, cast the first stone…' that one. Last night I remembered it was originally––in fifth-century Bibles––part of Luke. A scribe somewhere along the way moved it."

"How'd that help?"

"It unified everything into the Synoptic Gospels. Then I knew there had to be a common thread."

"So what's in the vellum?" Livy added the question to her confused look.

Julian took his gaze from the bird feeder to Livy. "How much do you know about the Bible?"

"Never pay much attention in church. Just sing the songs."

"OK." Julian took a deep breath as he organized his thoughts. "Without the four Gospels of the New Testament," he explained, "Jesus would have died an obscure Jew executed for sedition against the state. The very first mention of Jesus of Nazareth in any of the hundreds of thousands of non-Christian first- and second- century sources came in a letter from Pliny the Younger, a local official, to Roman Emperor Trajan in 112 AD."

Livy did some quick math. "That's eighty years after his death!"

"Yep. And that was only a single line mentioning that the Christians worshiped someone who called himself Jesus. Other than that, there is virtually no mention of Jesus anywhere. Nothing. Zilch."

Julian went on to explain how scholars determined the Gospel of Mark was probably written first, maybe 60 or 70 AD, possibly thirty years after his death.

"Matthew and Luke were written some ten to twenty years after that," he continued.

Incredulity remained pasted on Livy's face. "I never realized."

Julian continued by explaining how similarities between the Gospels of Matthew and Luke suggested the authors of each used Mark as a source and that nearly identical wording in Matthew and Luke, not found in Mark, suggested another source was also used.

"Over the years," said Julian, "that other source has come to be known as 'Q,' from the German word *Quelle*, or source."

"The Q on Cooper's chest," Livy said as a statement, as she evidently recalled the photo. "So what happened to Q?"

"Lost to history somewhere in the first century. But––"

The doorbell chimed loud and long in the front hallway, interrupting Julian. He looked at Livy and then toward the front door. "Expecting anyone?"

"Nope. I'll get it. Probably for Cam," said Livy.

Julian held out a flat palm. "Stay here."

"I thought you said we'd be safe for a while."

"I'll get it," he repeated.

Julian took a quick detour to the bedroom for Maxwell's gun. At the door, he checked the peephole. A Boston cop stood tall in a freshly starched uniform. A radio earpiece rested on his ear next to a short sideburn from a trim cut. A cord snaked into a pinecone-sized microphone clamped to his collar.

Julian turned and yelled back toward the kitchen. "It's the police. You call them?"

"Nope. Be sure to check their badges," came the matter-of-fact reply.

Julian turned toward the door. "Hold your badge up to the peephole."

The officer complied. Julian unlocked the door and then the deadbolt.

"What may I do for you, officer?" Julian checked the driveway then the street. He didn't see a patrol vehicle, only an unmarked car.

"Sorry to bother you, sir. My shift, surveillance. I found something I thought you should see."

The policeman stood two inches taller than Julian's six feet. The trace of a tattoo peeked below his short-sleeve shirt.

"I thought it was stopped. Yesterday, I got a call from Detective Foster."

"Didn't get the memo. I can leave if you want."

"No, no, it's good you're here. We definitely need another day." He looked at the officer's hand. "What's that?"

The policeman held up a six-inch-long piece of black rubber tube, about a quarter inch in diameter. "Noticed it in the grass near the driveway. Checked it out. I think it's part of the brake-fluid line to that car right there. Found some suspicious fluid underneath the vehicle."

Concern worked its way across Julian's face. He reached back to secure the lock on the door, shut it firmly, and then moved quickly toward Cam's '98 Nissan Sentra. Down on his knees, he could see a puddle under the car.

"Hell." Julian stood up and looked around. "Good work, Officer…" He looked at the cop's nameplate. "…Timmonds. Appreciate it."

"Sir, we're trained to look for things that aren't quite right."

"Appreciate it," Julian repeated. He mind was on fast-forward, making a list of what they needed to do before they left town.

"So, should I stick around? Could use the overtime money."

Julian's eyes jerked, startled by the patrolman's voice. "Yes, please do. We're going out in a little bit. Running some errands. Think you could follow us?"

"Be happy to. Your brother was a mentor. It's a shame. He was a good man."

Julian nodded thanks and then turned to go back into the house. Five feet later, the officer spoke up.

"Excuse me."

Julian turned. "Yes."

"Do you have a license to carry the gun?"

Julian had forgotten about Maxwell's pistol stashed in his jeans. "Ah, no. It's one of Maxwell's." Julian stopped and turned toward the officer.

"Not a problem for me, but it might be for others. Massachusetts has strict handgun laws. Mandatory jail time."

Julian gave an irritated nod. "I'm worried about a bigger can of crap than that."

"Trust me, I hear ya."

Julian turned to go in. Once again, the officer spoke up.

"Excuse me."

With a hint of impatience, Julian turned again. "Yes."

The officer stood, his shoes about two feet apart, his thumbs hooked into his belt. "You ready to use it?" The officer paused. "Don't carry it unless you're ready to pull the trigger. You'll only get yourself killed."

"I'll remember--"

The officer's portable lit up. The officer showed his palm to Julian while he listened into his earpiece. After five seconds, he dipped his chin and then spoke. "Ten-four. I'll check it out."

Julian spoke expectantly. "What?"

"Nothing. Everything is fine. Another situation."

Julian turned to go, then spun around one more time. "I thought you were off duty, overtime."

The patrolman hesitated. "Uh, I am. Not unusual to get calls. Have a good day." The officer drew his left index finger to his forehead, then headed back to his car.

Julian tried the doorknob and then remembered he'd locked it. He tapped the doorbell. Then waited. Thirty seconds passed before he realized he was still waiting. He turned to wave to the officer. The car was gone.

"No!"

He mashed the doorbell four times, then slammed his fist against the door. Panicked, he shimmied his way around a Norfolk pine and cupped his hand against the window. Cam approached, a towel wrapped around his waist. The lock clicked. Julian barged through the entry before it was opened.

"Where's your mom!"

"Don't know. Bathroom, maybe."

Julian was eight steps closer to the second floor before Cam finished. He bolted down the hallway, checking each room as he went.

"Livy!"

The master bedroom was empty. He crashed through a closed bathroom door, expectantly.

"Livy."

Empty. No steam on the mirror. No towels on the floor. He pirouetted and ran head-on into Cam. Cam tumbled to the carpet, his towel falling to his side. Julian hardly noticed.

"Livy!"

Julian ducked into the kitchen and then descended the basement stairs four at a time. Three rooms and a bathroom were empty. The walkout sliding-glass door was unlocked. Julian pulled the gun, released the safety, then took off in a sprint through the backyard. He hurdled a short row of hedges, dodged a swing set in the neighbors' yard, nearly got his head removed by a low-lying limb, and then arrived at an empty neighborhood lane. Winded, he looked up and down the street. All he saw were for open garage doors. No neighbors milling about. No school children waiting for their buses. Nothing. A gray SUV he'd seen while gazing out of the kitchen window only thirty minutes earlier, was gone.

CHAPTER THIRTY-FOUR

LIVY'S HOUSE, BOSTON
Monday, September 10, 2001, 9:10 a.m.

Minutes later, Julian bolted up from the basement. In the kitchen, Cam sat with military stiffness, tight fisting a gold disk. He studied an eight-by-eleven-inch piece of paper laid out on the table. Cam glanced up, locked onto Julian's eyes, and then nodded toward the missive.

TO: Julian St. Laurent

RE: Livy St. Laurent

You have twenty-four hours to find papyrus. You fail, she dies. You call the police, she dies. 555-3425 to exchange. ONE CALL is all you get. You already know we have people on the inside.

"I should've known. A damn lawyer," said Julian.
Cam said nothing. His expression spoke for him.
"Sons of bitches live in memorandum."

Julian leaned over the table and scrutinized the note—–the paper, the font, the syntax. Distracted by an object in Cam's hands, he reached out and placed his hands over his son's. Cam cupped them open then looked up.

Boston Police Department No. 865. Julian eyed the gold badge.

"Where did you get this?"

"Front yard." Cam's voice was measured.

"Maxwell's?"

Cam nodded.

Julian took a deep breath and let it out slowly and then played the table with his thumbs. A look settled over his face, the faraway stare of a man burned by life way too many times. Ten seconds later, he straightened, walking to the sink and then back. "Get dressed." Julian spoke softly, but without equivocation.

Cam looked up, incredulously. Neither spoke. After a five second delay, Cam slammed the side of his fist onto the table, dislodging a glass of orange juice onto the tile floor. Shards sprayed out on impact. "How the fuck can this happen." Cam's voice was not loud but firm and full of quiet anger.

Julian startled then trudged back to the table. He cleared a place, moving a near-empty cereal bowl and two sections of the morning paper. With his index finger, he traced out a one-foot-by-two-foot rectangle.

"What do you see?"

Cam looked at Julian, then at the table, and then at his father again. "Nothing."

"Exactly. *A blank canvas.*" Julian waited to make sure he had his son's attention. "That's the rest of your life." He tapped inside the rectangle. "That's what counts, how you fill it."

"Why in the hell didn't Cooper just tell you? Nine years ago."

"Listen to me. Worrying about what-ifs…is just wasted time."

"I can't do this." Cam looked overwhelmed.

Julian knew the feeling all too well. "I can't do this on my own." He put his arm around his son. "It numbs the mind—–fear. Sucks people of reason." They both stared at the blank canvas. "You're in my world now. When you're served a shit sandwich, you eat it or—–"

"Find the son of a bitch who made it?"

Julian nodded. "Cooper kept this to himself, maybe out of respect for my beliefs. But when his time came—–when his doctor told him to make plans—–he realized he couldn't take it to his grave. He had no family. He chose me. But he allowed me to decide on my own terms." Julian paused. "We can do this for your mom––and Maxwell."

"So let's say we find it. They'll kill us anyway!'

Julian thought back to all that had happened. Nidal's apartment. The Hancock Building. Maxwell's death. "Maybe. You can't stop what's coming."

Julian walked over to Cam and put his hands on his shoulders. They stood eye to eye.

"Stern days," said Julian. "Churchill's life was a study in perseverance."

"But only twenty-four hours."

"I guess that makes it a damn-important day then, doesn't it?" Julian stepped away. "Get dressed!"

Cam, taken aback, hesitated a moment and then turned to leave. He stopped. "You believe the part about having people inside the police department?"

"No doubt. It was a curious situation, the day after Cooper's murder. And just now, they knew our police surveillance had been stopped. It all makes sense now."

Minutes later, they wove their way through rush-hour traffic on their way to the tattoo parlor. Both belted back two-fisted gulps of coffee. Months of refuse littered the floor of Julian's Volvo. There was goo in the cup holders that deserved the attention of the Environmental Protection Agency. In the backseat lay a large tote with the files and photos, Cooper's Bible, Cam's laptop, two flashlights, and a couple of shovels.

Julian spoke. "When we get a chance, get online and check Back Bay building permits."

Cam nodded. He studied the photos of Cooper's tattooed chest.

Julian continued. "We have to go to Trinity today. We need to get into Coop's office and see if he buried anybody with the last name of Eccles."

Cam looked up. "You said Ecclesiastes, Old Testament."

"Hopefully, Sligo will know something. Then we can knock that name off our to-do list."

"The key is the ink." Cam held up the picture of Cooper's torso.

"I agree, but it doesn't mean much to me. Except for the Q." Julian slowed for a light. He reached for a CD in his map case, then popped it into the player. Frank Sinatra's voice streamed through the car. He looked over at Cam, who gave him a strained look. "Helps me relax."

"The *Q*?" Cam looked at his father expectantly.

Julian continued. "I think that's what this is all about––*Q*."

Cam eyes opened wide, his mouth opened halfway. "As in the New Testament?"

"Yes."

"Cooper found *Q*!"

"Think so."

"Impossible." Cam again glanced down at the post-mortem picture of Cooper's chest tattoos. "I thought we were looking for the vellum––*Amphilochus*."

"If you look at Cooper's Bible––and I checked it again––everything he marked is material from *Q*. The Sermon on the Mount, the beatitudes, the Lord's Prayer, the parable of the mustard seed, everything." Julian stopped at another light. He looked at his son.

"*Amphilochus* is *Q*!"

Julian nodded a yes. "A twenty-five-hundred-year-old tragedy. Fiction."

Cam's face brightened. "Karlie is right after all. Rabble-rousers, Jesus and Elvis. Both just trying to change things a bit." Cam got Julian's attention and then raised his eyebrows. "First-century Jewish Christians––spin-doctors––doing work to legitimize a new religion."

They rode silently for an entire block, processing the possibilities.

Cam finally spoke. "The Pope is totally screwed if this gets out."

"It would indeed challenge the credibility of a rather elaborate story."

Cam paused for a moment. "You remember the Shabaka Stone?"

"*The Philosophy of a Memphite Priest*?"

"Yep. From the ancient Egyptians. Remember what it said about creation? 'Ptah thought it, then said it on his tongue, and it became real.' That sounds a whole lot like Genesis to me. So I guess if *Amphilochus* is *Q*, then New Testament authors just carried on the plagiaristic tradition of the Old Testament."

Julian and Cam chewed on that thought for a long while. Midway down Western Avenue, ReGeneration popped into view. Julian pulled over seventy-five yards north.

"How's it goin' down?" asked Cam.

"Sligo cool?"

"He's an OK guy. A little shy…an artist."

"We don't have much time. Why don't you go in first. See if you can get him to talk. Focus on the left arm. Then I'll mosey in. Five minutes?"

"Sounds good."

Julian extended his fist. "Be careful."

Cam reached into the glove compartment for the gun.

"Why don't you leave the gun? We should have carte blanche for twenty-three more hours. They want us to find it. They won't kill us just yet."

Cam nodded then headed out. He needed to cross four lanes of city traffic and was forced to pause.

Julian waited and watched. The ReGeneration sign was hand painted on plywood, red on black. Matching red letters in the windows advertised their services. Stationary-sized poster board showed sample tattoos, art of loss, love, and rites of passage––external markers, the meanings of which were inaccessible to those who saw them. A city bus stopped across the street and diverted his attention to the surrounding area. A takeout Thai spot, a Laundromat, a chiropractor's office, a liquor store, and a small market advertising fresh produce, filled the block. Two-wheeled shadows of passing vehicles reflected off the windows. A T-shirted student with a Nike backpack narrated his every step into a cell phone. An old lady, a bowling ball of a woman, with a ratty-looking red stocking cap pulled a small cart filled with a single grocery sack. To Julian, she looked like one those people who dressed their dogs with a Santa hat during the holiday. She stopped briefly at a midblock alleyway and then proceeded, maintaining her gaze on the bus. The bus pulled away. She would have to wait, which meant her yippy white poodle would be forced to yip impatiently at home. He noticed Cam had finally made it safely though the morass of cars. Julian's eyes went back to the granny then to the alley.

No!

Julian was out of the car in less than an instant. He headed across the thoroughfare, dodging forty-mile-per-hour killing machines. Once he reached the other side, he jerked his gaze down the block. A dwarf stood ensconced in the shadow of the alley, phone in hand, finger poised over the screen.

"Cam!"

Cam walked briskly, sixty yards ahead, oblivious to Julian's voice. It had been years since Julian needed his top speed; time had abducted it somewhere along the way. He opened his mouth at the same time another bus rumbled by. Its fusion with the random city noises created a cacophony of sound. His warning again went unheeded. Fifty yards ahead, the old lady shuffled by the front of ReGeneration. Cam reached for the door handle. The dwarf's shape disappeared in the shadows.

"Cam! Stop!"

Cam hesitated and looked west. He took a step back, nearly colliding with the woman. Another bus and a twelve-wheeled service truck rumbled past and blew a wall of grit into Julian's face. When he was fifty feet away, the street noise finally died.

"Get away! Get down!"

Cam stood paralyzed and confused.

Julian went horizontal the last five feet and crashed full force into his son. An "Umph" escaped from Cam's mouth as he jerked backward toward the ground. Julian draped his body over Cam and then covered his own head. The old lady startled, stopped, and inexplicably turned toward the shop.

She took the full explosive force face-first. Shards of glass blasted from the storefront, instantly violating the old lady's thin skin with thousands of tiny razor-sharp lances. Her body was sucked into the billowing plume and onto the first lane of Western Avenue, where it was minced, along with her Pepperidge Farm bread, chicken, and lettuce, by the grill of a passing plumber's truck. The sickening thud was lost in the reverberating concussion of the blast. A whirlpool of debris rained down over a fifty-yard area. Flames reached out toward the late-morning sun. Shattering windshields and crumpling steel followed the sound of car and truck tires screeching trails of rubber. Then it was quiet. Twenty seconds later, distant sirens filled the air.

Julian did a five-second assessment of his body and then rolled off Cam, who sat up immediately and performed a similar survey. Cam's ashen face registered fear, but other than that, he was fine.

"You're OK." Julian yelled over the chaos. A statement. A wish. Both.

The blast had singed the back of Julian's head. Licks of flame got both of them off the ground. Julian snatched Cam by his shirt, pulling him to his feet and into the thoroughfare.

"Help these people. Stay alert."

Julian got another nod and then turned around and headed toward the alley. He reached for his gun as he rounded the corner. Rusty, overflowing dumpsters, angled in odd directions, lined the entire block. Shadow-shrouded entryways loomed in between. A section of gnarly, corroded chain-linked fence enclosed a courtyard; a lame attempt at a garden and two moth-eaten lawn chairs filled the area. He stopped after twenty yards to listen––for breathing, movement, dogs barking. He heard sirens mixed with the ambient city noises of the city. At the end of the alley, River Street bustled with traffic, totally oblivious to the mayhem only one block away.

CHAPTER THIRTY-FIVE

BOSTON
Monday, September 10, 2001, 11:00 a.m.

Thirty precious minutes ticked away before Julian and Cam extracted their car and themselves from the chaos.

"What in the hell was that?" asked Cam.

"Someone didn't get the memo. Plan B: use us, then kill us."

"Fuckin' lawyers don't screw up memos. Maybe it was those prayer-rug assholes."

"I saw that little-shit dwarf in the alley." Julian spoke in a monotone voice. "You know, I don't like fat people, especially happy fat people. I'm getting pretty damn close to not liking small people."

Cam picked a piece of glass out of his hand. "You calling 'em?"

"Only get one."

"Won't be able to use it if we're dead."

"Like I said, we can't stop what's coming. I suspect that diminutive piece of shit is probably getting a brand-new asshole as we speak."

The near-death experience silenced them until the next stoplight.

"Thanks again," Cam said. He reached over and put his hand on Julian's shoulder. Julian acknowledged the gesture, and Cam continued, "I must have been a cat in a previous life. Or you're my guardian angel."

Julian smiled. "One of those two."

They rode in silence again. Julian unexpectedly aimed the car onto Boston University Bridge.

"I thought you said Trinity," said Cam.

"I did. But if we had parked in front of the tattoo shop, we'd still be stuck there or in a cab. We need another car just in case. Plus, some extra clothes."

Cam reached into his pocket for his keys.

"Your brake line is history."

"How––"

"Doesn't matter. Get your mom's keys. Change your shirt. Put on something bright. Sick, nasty bright."

"What for?"

"I'm sure they're watching. We may need to use it to their disadvantage. Also, grab some clothes for your mom. Plus a couple of dark hoodies for us. We may be grave digging tonight. While you're doing that, I'll get the stuff out of the garage that I need. Make sure your phone is working. I'll follow you to the church. Put your mom's car on Boylston near Trinity if you can, but don't spend all day looking. I'll park on Clarendon across from the parish house. I'll meet you in Copley Square, in front of the church."

Forty minutes later, they stood before the four-hinged parish house door. Their first four knocks went unheeded.

"Must be sorting her underwear," muttered Julian.

"What?"

"Nothing."

"What's so important?"

"I want a explanation."

They had been talking to the door. Cam turned and looked at his dad. "For...?"

"They couldn't have known about Cooper's ink. Agnes didn't have a clue until I mentioned it."

"How'd Dexion know which shop?"

"They couldn't. But there can't be many. Probably should let the police know."

Julian looked at his watch and then turned and bounded up the muck-covered steps two at a time. Minutes later, they walked through the front door of Trinity. Two ladies at the door directed them to the downstairs bookstore for an entry ticket. Five dollars.

Even God is on pay-per-view. "Funny, didn't see a dish outside," Julian mumbled to himself.

"For collections?"

"Nothing."

Julian and Cam slowed as they entered the bookstore. They looked at each other, knowing what the other was thinking. Julian nodded. He took one side, Cam the other. They checked each book. They checked behind each book.

"Are you looking for anything in particular? Maybe I can help you."

Julian turned and met a pleasant smile. A short lady––five foot noth-ing–– stood behind the cash register. He stopped his search and approached the counter. She spoke again. The smile stayed. Nothing wrinkled. Nothing moved. It looked like Botox gone bad. He began with small talk. After dis-cussing the weather, they started in about homeopathic remedies for her corns. Way too much information.

"I'm looking for something leather bound, maybe twenty-five hundred years old." Julian hoped for a reaction. He got it. She wouldn't be of any assistance.

They finished their search, got their tickets, and then headed upstairs. In the narthex, they encountered the most famous stained glass in the build-ing––John La Farge's *Christ in Majesty.*

Salvation, not sex. Julian thought back to Livy's offhanded comment. He had been in Trinity hundreds of times and never thought about it before, the act of walking into a church. Today he did. He detected a slight sub-mission of will. He imagined low, earnest voices and whispered prayers. Shimmering marble panels with gilded spiritual inscriptions surrounded the altar; an enormous cross hung overhead. Huge prophets and evange-lists peered down through crystal eyes from the glass above. The sunlight streaming through these magnificent stained windows gave birth to a kaleidoscope of patterns, delivered onto the interior mosaics below. He felt humbled, even still.

"Not many people here," said Cam.

"It's a chapel."

They split up. Each ambled about, searching and formulating a men-tal catalogue of potential hiding places. The clue would be subtle. They checked under pews and looked for cracks in the wood, incongruities in the friezes, ripples in the grout. After thirty minutes, they met in the front pew.

"Waste of time," said Julian. He sat down with a sigh, his voice heavy.

"No kidding. We could spend months in here. We need to figure out the body art."

Julian scanned the church then turned toward the altar. A braided rope denied public entry. "Do you have a T-shirt on under that?" He nodded at Cam's teal-and-fire-engine-red polo.

Cam looked around the church and then at his father. He nodded.

"Take it off, and hold it until I tell you. In about one minute, when those people leave the church..." Julian gave a chin nod to an Asian-American family of four posing for pictures in front of the stained-glass rendition of *Jesus' Ascension* in the south tower. "...I want you to tie it around your nose and mouth."

"We robbin' the bookstore?"

Julian watched the family closely, waiting for the right moment. "Yeah, robbing the bookstore." He edged toward the altar. "Just follow me." He looked at Cam to make sure he got the message, and then glanced back at the family.

A minute later, he said, "Now."

They were over the rope and hunkered down behind the altar in five seconds. Julian waited and then peered around the edge. Cam draped his nose and mouth. Julian splayed his knees on either side of the marble slab. Only with close inspection could a person see the fine line of missing grout. He slipped his four fingers into a well-concealed lip and heaved up. The tight rubber seal made a *slup* sound. A stench chased the opened door.

"When we get to the bottom of the ladder, wait for me. Then we hustle. It's dark. It's nasty. It stinks like hell, and this is something you don't need to breathe."

Julian handed Cam a flashlight. Cam headed down carefully; Julian followed and secured the hatch. The wood from the ladder crumbled in his hands. It moaned from the weight of two men. At the bottom, rats looked up at the intruders. Their noses and whiskers twitched with transient interest; then they quickly returned to their scavenging. Julian checked out the pits again. They worked their way into the basement proper without problems. Agnes, fortunately, hadn't locked the basement door.

The apartment was strangely quiet. No Mozart. No chainsaws. They walked warily down the hallway, into the kitchen. An open package of Oreos littered the kitchen table, next to an open laptop.

"Agnes."

Julian checked the computer. Dead battery.

They stood still, listening.

"What's the story on those rats? Nasty," said Cam.

"Not sure. There was an article in the paper the other day about two stiffs found in an apartment about four blocks from here. I guess they're worried about smallpox. It's been extinct in the US for fifty years. I've been vaccinated––you haven't."

"Can rats get smallpox?"

"I Googled it the other night. It said no. I'm not convinced."

Julian thought it curious that if a new smallpox epidemic had popped up in US, it had started in Boston. He reminded Cam of Zabdiel Boylston, the Boston physician of the 1770s who introduced smallpox inoculation into the American colonies with the inoculation of his son. A smashing success it was, by luck or by design.

They finally found themselves in the entryway. Cam pointed to a computer-sized device on the top shelf.

"Probably for the surveillance camera," said Julian. "Not sure what happened to Agnes."

Julian unlocked all four latches on the front door then returned to the kitchen.

"You need to get your computer. Check building permits, death notices for 2001. Eccles."

"Is there anyone who could have put the vellum in Coop's coffin?" Cam said, thinking out loud. "That's the last place I'd look."

Julian stopped and thought. "You remember the letters on his chest?"

"Let's see…two W's, K, C, H, S, and…a…P. Seven."

Julian said nothing for a few seconds. "Don't see the connection. We may need to check though. I hope not. Long drive to the cemetery." Julian looked at Cam. "We have to hope like hell he didn't put it in any casket. Would take hours to dig up one of those damn things."

Cam turned toward the door to retrieve his computer from the car.

"Where you going?"

"To get my computer."

"Not that way. They saw us walk in the church."

Cam looked at his watch. Julian pointed toward the back. When they reached the end of the hall, he peeked into the bedroom. The bed was unmade; clothes littered the floor. Julian checked the closet. A quick search revealed no secret compartments or false walls.

"Julian! Problem."

Julian turned. Cam stood one step into the dark bathroom; the light wouldn't turn on.

"What?"

Agnes lay naked and blue below the surface of a bath, full to the top. A plugged-in radio lay next to her at the bottom.

They quickly removed the radio and checked the body. "Too bad, cool lady. Charger's fan," said Julian.

"Mom dies if we report this to the police."

Julian took a couple phone pics then turned. "Let's go."

CHAPTER THIRTY-SIX

PARISH HOUSE, TRINITY CHURCH
Monday, September 10, 2001, 12:40 p.m.

Fifteen minutes later, Cam worked on his computer at the kitchen table. In the study, Julian rifled through Cooper's old receipts for the second time. After he found what he wanted, he turned his attention to a cup of keys in the desk drawer. Indecision prompted him to stash the whole bunch in his pocket. He rechecked every inch of the office and found no hidden compartments, no coded messages, and no fake walls. He looked in and behind every wall covering. He checked the ceiling. He checked the mattress again and then underneath the chessboard. He even sliced the chessboard open and then rushed into the bathroom and took the toilet apart. He checked all the pipes under the sink. Nothing. He looked at his watch. One o'clock. *Time is wasting.*

In the kitchen, Julian found Cam with his chin on his hands, his distraught face eight inches from his laptop screen. An image of Maxwell standing outside the door of the apartment filled the screen. Julian watched silently.

"Surveillance-camera footage?"

Cam nodded. "Downloaded it with my FireWire. It's an event recorder. It only turns on when someone shows up at the front door or leaves."

Julian noted the time and date at the bottom. *Sept 2, 2001, 0714.* He thought back to the rainy Sunday morning, eight days previous. Maxwell's hair looked wet. He disappeared into the apartment then left a short time later. The picture went blank for a moment then another body filled the screen, head to toe, with an angle shot of the face. "Pause that."

Cam tagged the keyboard with his finger. "What?"

Julian ducked his head down to Cam's level. "He looks familiar. Hard to see his face with that hat on." Julian pointed to the white-banded collar just below the man's chin. Julian noted the date/time stamp. *Sept 2, 2001, 1032.*

"How far back does it go?" asked Julian.

"June. The machine was installed in February. It's a continuous loop. Here, let me help you."

Cam grabbed the mouse and clicked the first frame. *June 8, 2001, 0823.* It showed an elderly, heavyset lady, with a purse dangling from her right forearm, her left hand closing the door. She disappeared up the stairs.

"Who's that?" asked Julian.

"Just watch."

Cam zipped through frame after frame. Neither spoke. The progression was obvious. The same old lady came and went. Cooper showed up periodically, mostly at night––a few times very late, with dark clothes and a hooded sweatshirt; it was the middle of summer. They saw a grocery deliveryman, a pizza man, a repairman, and maybe a plumber. On and on it went until *Sept 1, 2001, 2331*, the night of Cooper's murder. On the screen was the same large cleric, wearing his broad-brimmed fedora, standing next to a child–– no, a dwarf! Both carried a suitcase. Behind them stood a sleepy-looking Agnes. They entered. Twenty minutes later, the cleric and the dwarf left. The dwarf returned with Bob's tank. A lump of some sort protruded from the dwarf's neck. The next footage was of Maxwell, the one they'd just watched. Next were multiple frames of workmen coming and going. Then, more grocery deliverymen. *Sept 4, 2001, 1343.* The cleric appeared again, staying for a ten-minute visit. Julian leaned over and pushed pause and then advanced one frame at a time. Then he reversed the process several times. The shot of the cleric entering showed him tipping his head thirty degrees toward the camera. It showed his right cheek, nose, and a partial view of his right eye. Julian went back and forth several more times.

"I do know that man." The frame stayed frozen on the man's right cheek. Julian racked his mind and studied the frame. Finally it came to him. "The

Reverend Theodore Phillips!" He rolled the picture back and forth a few more times. "I saw him at old South Church a few times, several years ago. A very distinctive voice. Good speaker. And a piss-poor memo writer." Julian checked one final time to make sure. "God's hired gun."

"'A preacher with a pecker too big,'" said Cam in nearly a whisper.

Julian's eyebrows rose, and his jaw sank. "What!"

"Steinbeck. *Grapes of Wrath*. Always liked that line."

Julian shook his head, offered a half-smile, and then turned his eyes back to the computer screen.

"And Dexion," said Cam.

"And Dexion," Julian repeated. Julian reached over and pulled a chair to the table. "It's curious they didn't get rid of the camera."

"Maybe they were using it to keep tabs on the hired help."

"And forgot about it? Hard to imagine."

"He's not suspicious. A preacher."

Neither spoke for thirty seconds as they put the info into their ongoing construct.

"Think it's time to call the police? We have a name…and time…and a body," said Cam. "Bodies," he corrected himself. "Agnes's predecessor has to be here somewhere. I sure as hell didn't see them carry out a body."

Julian looked at his son. "You don't think we can find the vellum?

"You had the same feeling in the church. Unless we figure out the seven letters, we have no chance. Even then, it's a small chance at best."

"If we tell the cops…" Julian paused. "I can't imagine the cleric thought too long about what he did to Agnes." Julian rubbed his eyes, then lowered his head onto his forearms, which rested on the table. After a moment, he reached over and restarted the footage.

Sept 9, 2001, 2301. Thirteen hours ago. The cleric and the midget were at the door again. This time it took them longer to get in. Evidently Agnes was asleep. *Sept 9, 2001, 2356.* They left, both with gloves on.

Sept 10, 2001, 1154. Julian and Cam stood at the door, impatiently. The next shot was of the old lady—Agnes's predecessor, dated June eighth, the beginning of the reel.

Cam pushed rewind, bringing it back to them waiting at the door. Julian pulled the files over and then extracted the photo of Cooper's chest.

"Would the FBI be the same as the cops?" asked Cam.

"Hard to know."

"With FBI capabilities, how long do you think it would take to them to find the cleric…find Mom?"

"Not long on the cleric. I doubt he's gone into hiding." Julian chose not to answer the other part.

Cam didn't respond.

"There's no control group," said Julian. "We'll never know if we did the right thing. Shit sandwich." Julian paused. "Maybe we could do both at the same time. Call the FBI and keep looking."

"What happens if we do and we get the call––'you blew it, sorry.'" Cam looked at Julian. "I couldn't live with that."

They both stared at themselves on the computer screen, going through the door. An omnipresent view of the world. *How nice it would be.*

"If we can't find it, she dies because of something we couldn't do, *not* something we did."

"Why are we having this conversation?" asked Cam.

"Because we're totally screwed. He knows we won't find it. I suspect he's been snooping around for years."

Cam turned off his laptop and stashed it away. The enormity of their task weighed heavy.

"How about this?" said Julian. "We give ourselves till eight o'clock. If we're still sitting here with our heads up our asses, we call the FBI, not Boston City."

CHAPTER THIRTY-SEVEN

TRINITY CHURCH
Monday, September 10, 2001, 12:50 p.m.

C am packed the surveillance equipment in with his computer. They left the door of the apartment unlocked. Agnes would be a random death to anybody else.

The fifth key Julian plucked out of his pocket fit the rector's office door. Julian manned the filing cabinet.

"OK," said Cam, looking at his computer screen. "Four Eccles have died this year in the immediate Boston area. Frank J., Preston S., Alma Q, and Dansforth L. I found fifteen going back to '92. Bad time to be an Eccles."

Julian handed a receipt to Cam before he dug into the files.

"Roc Gear Inc., two hundred and thirty-nine dollars," Cam read. "So?"

"A waterproof case that also protects against chemical corrosion and impact. Nineteen inches by fifteen inches by seven inches. Big enough. Look at the date."

"February 14, 2001," said Cam.

"What's it mean to you?"

"He kept the vellum in the church until this year and then bought a case that is waterproof and corrosion resistant. I'm thinking now it's subterranean somewhere in Boston."

"My thoughts exactly. We have to start making suppositions––"

"To have any chance. I hear you."

"Remember the pits in the basement? Thought at first Dexion had gone on a scavenger hunt. But…another supposition…I don't think they know about the tunnel. Hope like hell they don't."

"So, red herring?"

"Probably, but if Coop used them, he would have avoided taking the vellum out of the church. There's scripture on the marble walls behind the altar. The letters may match the tattoo. If so, I'll dig deep. If not, then not so deep."

"It'll go faster with two. I'm younger."

"And unvaccinated. I'll do it."

Julian had been sorting as he spoke. "Here…Alma Q. Eccles died July 24. Cooper did the service at the Forest Hills cemetery. Close by. I don't see any other Eccles."

Julian stood up. "Check all the funeral billings. Look at the initials. See if they match the letters. Be creative. I'm going down to the dungeon."

"Question." Cam held the chest-tattoo photo in front of him. "What do you think of the pentagram around the Q?"

"Not much. It's actually a dual pentagram. A pentagram circumscribed by a pentagon. You might be thinking about an upside-down pentagram representing the devil. His is upright; it represents goodness and health. Ancient Greeks used it as a talisman. They put it on their coins. Pythagoras attached fire, wind, water, things like that to the points of the star."

"This isn't another one of those damn Freemason things is it?"

"Freemasons used the pentagram, but nothing in Coop's research points to them."

"What about the distribution of the letters? And what's the deal on that damn hangman's noose?"

"Get online and check. See where Pythagoras put his *elements*. See if they correlate with the letters. Google hangman's nooses. See what comes up. We may be doing some serious digging tonight. We'll have to be selective. I can't imagine we could do more than two graves." He turned to grab his shovel. "Anything on the building permits?"

"Nothing," said Cam. "The church was finished in the 1880s. They rebuilt the altar in '38. Repairs in '91. The place shifted in '92, and they fixed it. Remodeled the basement bookstore in '98. Sounds as though Cooper maintained access to the vellum until February of this year. No major work this year."

"Except the new brick wall in the basement."

"On our list. We'll need a sledge hammer."

"I'll be back within the hour, hopefully by two. Then we need to rock 'n' roll. Keep doing what you do best."

Julian's smell heralded his return an hour or so later. Sweat dripped from his brow and soaked his shirt.

"You need to join Agnes for a bath," said Cam.

"She'd love that."

"Anything?"

"A hundred-year-old rum bottle, empty unfortunately. You find anything?"

"While you were scoopin' dirt, I found some of my own."

Julian's eyebrows jumped with interest.

"Agnes Vandenbosch is really Martha Vandenbosch, wife of Robert. He used to be a church elder here at Trinity. Some sort of intrigue developed between Robert Vandenbosch and Reverend Toulukinopolis. Possibly something involving Robert and another parishioner, a female. Reverend T. canned his ass. Maybe Martha, our Agnes, didn't know the details and carried on the feud."

Julian considered the information. "Anything else?"

"Probably not. The Pythagorean pentacle is probably a no go. I worked it every which way. I found seven Cooper funerals since March where the deceased had initials that would include our seven letters. I Googled them all for their occupations, associations with Cooper, hobbies, or affiliations. Found a few things." Cam handed his notes to Julian. "Not sure any of it would warrant inclusion in a sixteen-hour search. Maybe if we had weeks. I'd check Coop's coffin before I'd check any of these. Finding it in the good reverend's eternal crib would add a certain symmetry, don't you think?"

"He should have just put a big *X* on his chest and skipped all the drama."

"Maybe we should be looking for a live body who could have put a waterproof case in a casket," said Cam. "Close friends?"

Julian leaned back in his chair, placed his hands behind his head, and closed his eyes. He was tired. After thirty seconds, he opened his eyes and sat up in the chair. "Jessie."

Cam readied his fingers over the keyboard. "Last name?"

"Can't remember. Won't be in Google anyway."

"If you're born, you can be Googled."

"Bartender."

"And a priest. Strange."

"They played on the same softball team. Bukowski's."

"Dead Authors Club, over on Dalton, near the turnpike?"

"Yep." Julian removed his shirt and placed it in the trash. "So our best leads so far are Eccles's coffin and Coop's coffin?"

"Yep," said Cam. "And the brick wall."

Twenty minutes later, they walked into Bukowski's, a curious establishment. It resembled the inside of a train car. It was probably no more than twenty feet wide but at least forty yards long. It was cramped and smelled of stale beer and pickles. Pictures in the entry served up the general ambience of the place. One showed a mix of males and females, possibly a coed softball team, all with large grade-A carrots jutting from their zippers. In the next picture, the same group, sans carrots, proudly displayed the middle-finger salute. It looked like the type of place made famous on *Cheers*, where everyone knows everyone else. A chalkboard next to the door highlighted the specials of the day, more beer specials than food specials. The words "croissant" and "salad" jumped off the board. Julian wondered if they had food for men. A moderate lunch crowd filled the booths on the right, snaking all the way to the back. The bar on the left extended halfway back, with a multitude of glasses and liquor bottles above and in front of the patrons. Those at the bar clutched their drinks and spoke in whispered tones––life in the twenty-first century. A spatter of laughter blew by from somewhere in the back. Cam and Julian chose an isolated spot at the bar.

The bartender approached. His face's leathery lines crinkled up in a patronizing smile. A big guy, Julian remembered he was ex-military. The tattoo on his left bicep suggested the same. He slapped a couple napkins on the counter.

"Dudes," he said without really looking at them.

Julian offered a smile.

"Jessie, long time." Julian extended his fist.

After a moment's delay, Jessie showed his real smile. "Julian! Good to see ya. You on injured reserve, man?"

"Retired. Hey, this is my son, Cam. Cam, Jessie. Cooper, Jessie, and I played on the same softball team many years ago."

Cam and Jessie bumped fists. "My pleasure," said Jessie.

"You were at Cooper's funeral," said Cam. It was a statement.

Jessie looked surprised. "Right. Good memory."

Julian and Jessie made small talk for another minute. Julian and Cam begged off the beer special and went with coffee. Jessie disappeared to the back and came back with a plastic tube of honey and the fresh brew.

"I can't believe you remembered."

"My job. Hey Cam, your dad is a pretty good ballplayer. You need to coax him out of retirement. Our shortstop went down last week. Just started the tournament."

"Maybe we can swing a deal," said Julian. "We need some information."

"Also my job. Shoot."

"We're checking into Cooper's death."

"Thought they said suicide."

"Don't think so. In fact, I'm sure it wasn't." Julian picked up the bear-shaped honey container as he spoke. "You two were pretty close?"

"Yep."

Jessie excused himself to attend to a customer. He stashed a tip into a canister on his way back and offered the remote device for the TV to another patron. Then he returned.

"You know Sister Mary Beth?" asked Julian.

"Yep. Came through the home about five years after you guys. Usually spent Christmas with Coop. He said only good things about you. Good man. Too bad."

"When did you last see him?"

"See him or talk with him? I saw him at Trinity three Sundays ago."

"Talk to him."

"Maybe a month ago. Not at softball. He didn't play this year."

"Where?"

"Here."

"He come in often?"

"Occasionally."

"By himself?"

"Occasionally."

"How about the last time?"

"With a group. Maybe eight guys. They left a nice tip. Maxwell was with him."
Julian eyes brightened. "Maxwell?"

Jessie nodded. "Sorry about your brother. Fine as they come."

Julian smiled thanks.

"None of them drank much. Seemed like business, not pleasure."

"Remember any other faces? Names?"

"Nope. Mostly midforties. One young guy. A Middle Easterner who did a lot of the talking."

Julian sat up and then looked at Cam. "Middle Easterner, huh? Hear what they talking about?"

"Bits. Pieces. This 'n' that."

"Anything you can share?"

Jessie looked down the bar and then toward the front door. He leaned into them. "Probably heard more than I was supposed to. The Middle Easterner was excited, making lots of gestures. He wouldn't stop talkin'." Jessie looked down the bar again. "Sorry." He scooted away toward a customer, who apparently had his heart set on a longneck.

Cam looked at Julian, expectantly.

"Nidal's cell phone number was with Maxwell's in Cooper's notebook. Something about Project For a New American Century. Apparently some sort of conservative think tank."

Jessie rejoined them.

"Hear anything?" Julian reminded Jessie.

"One thing. The Middle Easterner said something about Pearl Harbor."

Julian scooted up in his chair. "You sure? Pearl Harbor?" Julian thought back to Nidal, as he was dying. *New Yor Man Wash.*

"No doubt. Strange."

"Anything else. City names? New York. Washington."

"Nope."

"Building names?"

"Nope."

"See any architectural drawings?"

"Nope."

"Did Cooper confide in you? Away from the bar."

"Some."

Julian nodded then took a gulp of coffee. "Jessie, I have a question. You don't have to answer. But if the answer is yes, you might want to just smile."

"Shoot."

"Have you ever had the occasion to sneak into a mortuary…maybe sometime in the last ten days?"

Jessie smiled and stepped back. "Say what!"

"I guess that's a no?"

"Shit yes, that's a no."

Jessie looked down the bar and excused himself again and then disappeared into the back of the bar. Julian and Cam tended to their mugs.

"Question," said Julian. "If you had to bring down a building, how would you do it?"

Cam decided to play along. "Bomb." No hesitation.

"Second choice."

"Big building?"

Julian nodded. "Very. Steel beams."

Cam thought for a moment. Then for another moment. "Don't know."

Jessie approached in a hurry. "Sorry, have to get back to work." He placed a folded dollar bill on the counter and pushed it toward Julian. "Change."

Julian looked confused. "Haven't paid."

"Change," said Jessie again. He locked onto Julian's eyes, then raised his eyebrows.

A white piece of paper peeked from the fold. He cupped his hand over the bill and pocketed it. "Thank you."

"Cooper said someone might come by someday. Days, months, years—— he wasn't sure."

Julian nodded. "We're nearly family now. Let's stay in touch."

"I'd like that, Julian. One night. Conversation. An evening with Gentleman Jack."

Julian extended his fist. "Excellent choice."

"We play Thursday night, same place." He extended his fist to Julian then Cam. "Nice meeting you. Say, did anybody ever tell you, you look a whole lot like Maxwell's kid?"

Surprised, Cam bumped his fist, looked at Julian, and then back at Jessie. "I get that a lot."

CHAPTER THIRTY-EIGHT

Julian waited till they got back to the car to check the paper inside the fold of the dollar bill.

ABRAHAM RETI COCHRANE

He handed it to Cam. They searched each other for an answer.

"Coop's handwriting," said Julian. "He probably left it up to Jessie to decide who to give it to."

"I wonder if the cops paid him a visit."

"Someone famous?" asked Julian.

"Got me."

"Let's head back."

They made a quick stop at a McDonald's drive-thru for lunch, then went to Dunkin' Donuts across the street for dinner, and worked their way north to the church.

"You a good shot?" asked Julian. He reached for a fry.

"OK."

"How many times have you been to the range?" The smell of Big Macs watered down his thoughts.

"I don't know. A few." Cam skipped the fries and went for a cream-filled doughnut.

"You think you could kill someone? No hesitation."

Cam pondered the thought before ruining the pristine icing on the doughnut. They stopped at a light. "If it was anybody from Dexion, I could cut off their balls, gouge their eyes out, and then, after a sufficient amount of groveling, shoot 'em." He took a big bite of his doughnut. "Does that make me a bad person?"

"It makes you human. Could you shoot somebody in the head from twenty feet?"

Cam lowered his half-eaten pastry. "Don't know."

Julian turned right at the next light. They ended up in a random over-grown park off Columbus Drive. Julian grabbed a couple cans off the street and a few more as they worked their way through the dense foliage.

Julian held up both handguns. "Which one?"

Cam grabbed the Wilson Combat 1911.

"OK, this stump is the altar. These cans represent Dexion's head."

Cam nodded. Julian walked twenty feet, placed the cans on a hardy branch six feet off the ground, took two steps to the right, and then turned his back to his son.

"Shoot."

"After you move away." Cam lowered the gun and flipped on the safety.

Julian turned around. "I'm staying. Do it. Better me now, than your mom later. You'll be nervous. You'll have seconds to aim and fire."

"No way."

"If you can't do it, we stop looking and call the FBI. No reason to go on." Julian looked at his watch. "They have fourteen hours."

Cam sat down on a fallen tree trunk. "What happens after I shoot you?"

"Your mom would be worse…much worse. If you incapacitate me, or kill me, take everything we have to the FBI and let them finish up." Julian maintained eye contact to make sure Cam understood.

"This is absolutely insane."

"I assure you, I agree. But to have any chance at all, one of us has to be able to shoot one of these damn guns––bull's-eye––from twenty feet."

Cam held the gun two handed, arms extended, and sighted down the barrel.

"You can do it," said Julian. "It's all about attitude. Five in a row. Then, we move out before the cops show up."

Cam clicked the safety off then moved the gun hand to hand to get a feel for the handle. "Spegel cocobolo grips. Talked Max into dumping the issue grips last year. Put a narrow 0.09 front sight on it, deepened the 0.125 back notch. Also got rid of the standard mag funnel and put one of those tiny flat-sided fast-mag funnels on it. Fine weapon."

"A few times, huh?"

Cam held it at arm's length and stared down the sight again. After five seconds, he looked at Julian and then back at the gun.

"These guys are pros," said Julian. "We get one chance…if we're lucky."

Cam dropped to the ground, in a prone position, and sighted down the barrel for a third time.

"Back away. Give me a couple freebees."

Over the next minute, Julian learned more about his son than he had in the previous twenty-four hours. Cam surrendered everything into excellence with the firearm. Determination etched his face; intensity he had not previously shown glinted from his blue eyes.

Julian waited. Around him an insistent whisper hissed through the trees. He noticed an old stone-and-cement park bench, with angry graffiti branding the back. Beyond that, early evening sunlight stained the cobblestone walkway. And beyond that, a luscious green carpet lay before the towering skyscrapers, desolate like the Serengeti plains. He watched the sun dissolve into its afterglow. A big dome sky––a patchwork quilt of purple and magenta––filled the western horizon on the other side of the buildings. *My last sunset?*

"Five cans, two inches apart," said Cam.

Cam steadied himself twenty feet away. He was silent, inscrutable. He fired. The tall trees stifled the echo but did nothing to soften the sharp report of the gun. A flock of nearby mourning doves wheeled into the air. The last can on the right flipped and fell gently in the tall grass.

"Excellent," said Julian. "Fine shot."

"Was aiming for the one in the middle."

"Oh."

He fired again and missed. He offered no excuses. He took aim again and fired a third time. He grazed the second can from the left. It remained standing. Cam looked up.

"I'm good to go. I can do this." His eyes had lost their uncertainty.

"The cans cower before you." Julian smiled, walked over, and put his arm around his son.

Forty-five minutes later, they were holed up once again in the rector's office at Trinity.

"Abraham Reti Cochrane has yet to be born. I've been through a bazillion family trees, including the Cochrane clan from Ontario and the Cochranes of Shoreditch, England. Five generations. Nothing." Cam clicked the mouse. "There was a play entitled *Alexander Cochrane*, on Broadway, 1964--February 17, one night. Couldn't find a review."

"No recent funeral services for a Cochrane?" said Julian.

"Nope. Lots of Cochranes though. There was an Abraham Cochrane in England, died December 5, 1827. Several John Cochranes. One was a chess master, in the nineteenth century. He wrote a book on the subject and is credited with the Cochrane Gambit."

"There is a Reti opening--the King's Knight Opening--in chess. I used it on Cooper."

"Something only you would know." A statement.

"Nf3, c5, e4."

"What?"

"Nf3 is the opening move. He'd usually respond c5; then I'd move, e4." He paused and thought back to the games they had played. "You're right. One problem. No board."

"There is a John Cochrane, 1800s, bigwig politician from New York, vice presidential candidate on the Fremont ticket, 1864." Cam paused as a he clicked the mouse a few more times. "Here we go." A smile filled Cam's face. "There's an A.R. Cochrane listed as being buried in the Old Burial Ground."

Julian sat up, alert. "Our Old Burial Ground, Harvard?"

Cam nodded as he directed the mouse in a symphony of computer clicks. "One and the same. No dates."

Julian picked up the photo of Cooper's chest. "He wasn't hung was he?"

"No clue. Can't figure out what the A.R. stands for either."

They both reached for a doughnut––eating in tonight. Julian looked at his watch. Six thirty. "Two hours. Then we make a decision."

Cam studied Julian. "What?"

"I can't imagine we'll actually find anything," said Julian. "We need to decide whether to try to fake our way through it or call the FBI."

"With a fake *Amphilochus*?"

"Scout around for a book that looks really old."

"We won't see Mom until they see the goods."

The two men stared at each other without talking––a matrix of worry and apprehension outlined their faces.

"Keep looking for all things Abraham, Reti, and Cochrane." Julian retrieved his gun from the counter. "I'm going to wander the chapel, clear my mind. You said Forest Hills Cemetery, right? And the Old Burial Grounds?"

"Yep."

"Should be dark enough in thirty minutes. We can go to Old Burial Grounds first." Julian turned to leave.

"Hey."

Julian stopped and turned. "What?"

"Were you really going to stand there and let me shoot you?" Cam's lips moved halfway toward a smile.

Julian's face creased in return. "Whatever it takes."

Julian ambled up and down the church aisles. Several couples sought the sights or spiritual guidance. His attention was drawn to the stained-glass windows. He knew them all very well, both the upper and lower levels. The final rays of the setting sun gave unusual brilliance to *The Five Wise Virgins* on the south transept. In another pane, the crimson and green of Saint John's garments of glass dispersed a cornucopia of colors throughout the rafters. He quickly found pew, number twenty-three, his spot. As he sat down, the ritual kneeling and soft whispers came to mind. He settled back and appraised the moments of his life and realized how tired he was of dealing with events, one after another. He felt out of step, with life, with everything. He thought of the myth of Sisyphus––rolling the boulder up the hill over and over and over for eternity. His sense of faded hope had a particularly keen edge. Maybe it wasn't meant to be.

He peeked over his shoulder at the stained-glass rendition of Christ in *The Resurrection* in the north transept. Dressed in white, his hand was raised shoulder level, his face shaded white. *Christus pallidus*. He transposed Elvis's face onto the stained-glass figure.

Julian roused himself from his melancholy and wandered to the south transept to study more closely the magnificence of the windows. *The Sower and the Reaper. The Angel Troubling the Pool. The Evangelists. Luke and John.* Each one was a masterpiece in its own right. He finished one side, ended up at the front, and sat down on the altar step looking toward the rear. The church was empty now. For the hoi polloi, dinner trumped salvation. He looked out over the pews, row after row, neat and clean. Very linear. Very tidy. Like a vast venetian blind laid out over the floor of the church. In his mind, he divided the rectangles into squares. Two big squares in each transept and four big squares in the nave. Eight big squares. Sixty-four seats per square. Sixty-four times eight…five hundred and twelve little squares. He imagined a person in each spot, one exactly in front of the other. Perfect squares: like chess pieces on a massive chessboard.

Abraham Reti Cochrane.

Reti!

Julian jumped up and hurried over to the first stained glass in the south transept. At the bottom, written in petite glass chips, was a tribute to a Joseph Dillingham. *Joseph Dillingham, Born August 15, 1799. Died February 23, 1864.* He paused for just a moment to wonder what Mr. Dillingham might have done to warrant immortality on the church window. He quickly checked the seven windows in the south transept again. He looked for familiarity. He found nothing. Julian raced across the back of the church to the north transept and worked his way window to window. *Gambeson. Schiller. Johnson. Brooks.* The fifth one, as clear as the remnant sun light beaming through the pane––

MEMORY OF ALEXANDER COCHRANE BORN APRIL 27TH 1813 DIED AUGUST 11TH 1865.

Julian let his eyes drift up and take in the stained-glass mosaic. *Abraham and Eunice*!

CHAPTER THIRTY-NINE

TRINITY CHURCH
Monday, September 10, 2001, 7:00 p.m.

"Time to put down your mouse and come out and play," said Julian. He leaned through the rector's office door, feeling more affable than when he left.

"What?"

"Come."

Thirty seconds later, they stood in front of *Abraham and Eunice*. In tandem, they turned and looked at the pews in the transept.

"Your missing chessboard," said Cam. There was an animation is in voice that had not been heard for many days.

Julian pointed to the row of pews abutting the wall of the church. "White?"

"Have at it."

"Are those ladies still out in the lobby?" asked Julian.

Cam walked to the nave and peered around the corner. "If they are, they can't see us."

"They'll hear us. Got a hammer?"

"I noticed a rock paperweight in the office."

Julian mapped out his imaginary chessboard. For his virtual game, he imagined worshipers in the pews as the white pieces and the blacks. He moved the distinguished Englishman with the robust stomach and the neat plaid coat––his knight––Nf3, then marked the spot in his mind. Cam returned with a stone covered in shellac over a decorative napkin. It looked like a grade-school art project, a gift of some sort. Thoughts of Coop's kids breezed through his mind. Julian wondered how many lives Coop had changed and saved.

Julian tossed the stone a few inches into the air a couple times and worked his way to the pew two rows up.

"Nf3," he said to Cam. Then he whispered more to himself than Cam, "Let's do this for your mom."

The wood underneath the seat was definitely thinner. Julian checked one final time to assure the spot. On his knees, he thought back to his time with Sister Mary Beth and his bedtime prayer and then of all that had happened since. He couldn't recapture that feeling. He drew the rock back and brought it full force against the veneer. The stone dropped out of his hand as it glanced off the wood. He felt pain, then numbness.

"Damn!" He shook his hand, thankful he hadn't said anything worse. He rose up and scanned the church for the ladies.

"Want me to try?"

Julian first shook his head and then his hand a few more times. He picked up the paperweight. This time he rotated it, so the most protrusive portion of the stone pointed out. He lay on the floor, on his side, raised the stone overhead with both hands, and then yanked down with full force. A grunt escaped his mouth. A sharp crack echoed back and forth through the vaulted ceiling. The stone wedged into a lemon-sized hole. As he wiggled it free, he motioned for Cam to give him the flashlight. Peering in, he found one-hundred-year-old dust and disappointment. No case. No book. Nothing.

"Well?" said Cam.

"Vintage muff balls."

"Can you look down the row?"

"There are studded partitions every other seat."

Julian sat up, with his knees angled toward the rafters, forearms on his knees, and the rock in his hand. "Thought I was onto something."

Cam turned and looked at the *Abraham and Eunice* again. A man in the front row hadn't flinched. The church personnel stayed in hibernation, presumably not wanting to interrupt the spiritual affairs at hand.

"You're right; I know it," said Cam without equivocation. "Try his response--cf5."

"I can't bash in every seat."

"Heck of a lot easier than digging up coffins."

"He didn't always play cf5. Sometimes he'd respond d4, the Queen's Gambit. Nf3 is not an unusual opening move. Reverse it and you have the Latvian Gambit. It could be anything, anywhere."

"You said, Nf3, cf5, e4. That was your reflex response. That's the key."

Julian studied Cam then went to black's c5. He made the same-size opening as before, with the same result.

"There is only one person in the world who would know e4. This whole thing is for you."

Julian heaved himself off the ground. He checked his watch and then found his virtual pawn camped out on white's side--e4. This time he retrieved a 1934 Indian Head nickel in very good condition. Once again, silence took hold. The air slowly oozed out of Cam's optimism.

"What time is it?" asked Cam.

"Eight twenty."

Cam's shoulders slumped as his briefcase of enthusiasm leaked to empty. He eased himself to the ground and leaned up against the wall of the north transept. "We have to call the FBI."

"Maybe that's what we should have done." Julian's voice shared Cam's despondency.

Julian pulled Coop's note from his pocket and studied it. *Abraham Reti Cochrane. A.R. Cochrane.* "We need to call then head out to the Old Burial Grounds." He paused. "Maybe bash the wall in the basement down first. We still have twelve hours and a bag of doughnuts."

Julian got a quarter of a smile out of his son.

Cam rose to his feet. He was halfway down the north transept aisle before he turned around. "This has to be right! The Old Burial Ground is not something you two had in common, is it?"

Julian shook his head.

"Wall between every other seat. We make thirty-two holes. Now."

Julian didn't respond. He considered his options and looked at his watch.

"OK," said Cam. "Your response to his move was e4?"

Julian nodded.

"Cooper must have been tormented for years about this whole thing. Whether to tell you or not. He knew your spirituality got you through. You were family. He was dying. What to do? He decided to compromise. The tattoos and the horse buckle were the tantalizers. Something to tempt you, start you thinking. But he had to give you every reason to back away anytime you wanted." Cam paced the aisle. "Give you time to think about what was involved. His Bible was left behind by the police and Maxwell and found by you. That, along with his chest ink and the note––Abraham Reti Cochrane. It's all intended for you. And *e4*.. That's what your response would be, the one he remembered." Cam stopped talking; he paced toward the nave, then reversed pivoted and return to the back of the north transept. "What move would make it impossible for you to respond e4?"

Julian hesitated only a moment. "Nf6."

"Show me."

Julian walked to black's side of the board, then stopped at Nf6. Cam followed.

"The stone," said Cam.

He dropped to the floor; Julian backed away.

The stone easily penetrated the wood and made a *ping* sound as it continued through the void toward the back of the pew. It took both of them a moment to realize what they heard—a long moment to penetrate the fog of hopelessness that only moments before shrouded their minds.

"Metal!" Their response was simultaneous.

CHAPTER FORTY

Julian dropped to the ground and peered through the hole. The rock rested next to a black box, cobalt-blue glass rosettes sparkled from the side.

"Cam, my boy!"

They worked together to remove the board. Cooper's handiwork became obvious, although he had done an excellent job of covering his tracks. It would have easily escaped notice.

The black box was actually tarnished silver, molded, about the size of two big shoeboxes side by side, and probably weighed fifteen pounds. Julian handled it like a very large newborn, carefully placing it in the aisle of the north transept.

"The mother lode!" Julian's face radiated anticipation.

"What is it?"

"Money for any venture capital project you could imagine, then some." Julian took his eyes off the ancient artifact long enough to share the moment with his son. "This is a Macedonian ossuary chest. A smaller silver copy of the one made of solid gold found in burial tomb of Alexander the

239

Great's father. The embossed sixteen-point starburst is the Vergina Sun: the Macedonian royal emblem."

Julian gently rubbed his hands on the sides of the box then grasped it and slowly tilted the lid. No vellum codex. Joy turned to disappointment.

"Another chance to back away," said Cam.

Julian nodded. "Six things."

"What?"

"Reverend Toulukinopolis said there were six things. These are the rest."

"I see only two," said Cam.

"You see three. The Bucephalus horse buckle drew me into the search. *Amphilochus* and Alexander's copy of the *Iliad* are two and three. This ossuary chest is number four. I bet Alexander put some of Bucephalus's bones in it." Julian reached down and pulled out an ancient gold coin then handed it to Cam. "Do you know who that is?" He referred to the face on the coin.

Cam studied it, working his fingers over the bust. On the back was a naked jockey on a horse, with a palm branch. "Philip?"

"Excellent guess. Philip the Second, king of Macedon from 359 to 336 BC."

Julian picked up the remaining object at the bottom of the chest.

"This is six. A sardonyx cameo set in gold. See the snake wrapped around the lady's neck?" He pointed to the subtle markings. "Who is it?"

Julian handed it to Cam, who once again worked his fingers over the work of art. "Mom?"

"Two for two. Olympias. King Philip married her when she was twelve years old. They had only one child together. She apparently kept snakes in her bed. Some sort of religious thing. Not hard to imagine why Philip moved on to other wives."

Julian reached in and removed a piece of paper lying tight against the bottom. On the flip side was another message, again in Cooper's handwriting. Julian held it up so they both could read it.

Isle alone, the dandy,
A story he's writer of.

Made the Point a 'altar'
Did a foreigner, his labor of love.

Nearly a club brought his death,
Gutta-percha, they cackled.

The Irish, no such luck,
In the great soldier's debacle.

From poor boy to president,
To earth the rains fall.

To his family, crazy,
No locks for freedom's call.

All look south, but one
The leader of them all.

Neither spoke as they read and reread it.

"Notice how many paragraphs?" Julian asked.

Cam reached up and counted. "Seven." He looked at Julian, whose expression showed an attempt to knead a connection from his brain. After a moment, Cam's eyebrows rose, and his eyes brightened. "Letters! The seven letters on his chest."

Julian nodded and smiled then got up to pace the aisle. He ended up in front of *Abraham and Eunice*. He looked at Alexander Cochrane's memoriam in beautiful yellow-gold glass. Just above that, separated by the lead casting, on beautiful teal-green opalescent glass was written a verse from the New Testament.

"Cam?" Julian turned toward his son. "Did you notice this?"

Cam joined Julian at the window. He read, "Nothing is covered up that will not be revealed, or hidden that will not be known."

"Luke 12-2," said Julian. "Q."

"We've got some diggin' to do." Cam smiled again. "And we have eleven hours."

Minutes later, they were back in the rector's office.

"What do think?" asked Julian.

"Good thing he kept his day job."

They read the poem several more times.

"Grammatical error," said Cam. "'*A*' instead of 'an' in line three."

Julian made a quick check of line three then scanned the document again.

"Seven paragraphs," said Cam. "The last three…fall, call, all. Ruins the rhythm. Should be six paragraphs. One of them doesn't fit."

"Get on Google. Make sure this isn't some damn poem we should know about."

Cam jiggled the mouse and then hit a few keys with rapid-fire strokes. "Hard to imagine. Although I've never understood poetry. Whitman, Shelley—they all sound lame to me."

"At first I thought he was talking about one guy," said Julian. "But the key is this line here," He marked the second to last line with his thumb. "'*All look south, but one.*' 'They' is missing but assumed. More than one. Maybe seven."

"Graves, buildings, streets…something public," said Cam.

"If it's seven, not one, we do one at a time. Distinctive words?"

Cam typed as he spoke. "*G-U-T-T-A P-E-R-C-H-A.*" He clicked a few times. "OK. Gutta-percha. A tropical tree native to Southeast Asia."

"Road trip."

Cam smiled and continued. "Evergreen leaves. Produces gutta-percha latex. Good insulator. Uused to cover telegraph cable, especially underground and underwater." Cam looked up at Julian. No reaction. "Gutta-Percha Furniture Company. Guttie golf ball."

Cam read to himself. "Ka-ching! Here we go. The trivia section. Congressman Preston Brooks beat Senator Charles Sumner on the floor of the United States Senate with a cane made of…"

"Gutta-percha. Statues! Parks! Now we're cooking." Julian glanced at his watch. *9:20.* "Hell, there must be a million statues in this city. Too bad we don't live in Whatchatuchi."

Cam read the poem again. "'Nearly a club brought his death.'" He grabbed a piece of scrap paper and wrote down Charles Sumner, then circled the *S*. "Weird syntax."

"Don't bother." Julian's eyes brightened. "Go to some Boston website and look up the Public Garden. That's where he buried it. There's a Sumner statue there. Your mother and I had a picnic lunch at his feet twenty-seven years ago. Our first date." Julian's pause was noticeable, but not awkward. "There are six or seven statues there. Has to be the Public Garden. It's close. And nobody is ever going to dig it up."

After another flurry of clicks, Cam read off the screen. "Edward Everett Hale, Thaddeus Kosciuszko, Colonel Thomas Cass, Charles Sumner, George Washington, Wendall Phillips."

Julian waited a moment. "That's only six. We need seven."

"They only list six."

"Hell, we've probably both walked through that place a thousand times. We should be able to remember."

"Only the tourists," said Cam.

Julian sighed then looked at his watch. "Let's work backward. See what paragraph doesn't match up." His eyes zeroed in on the last two lines. 'All look south but one, the leader of them all.' That has to be Washington."

Cam's fingers plopped like jackhammers on the keys. "Colonel Thomas Cass. Irish Regiment, 9th Massachusetts Volunteers. Killed at Malvern Hills." Cam looked up. "Seven Days Battle. Lee's first command. Malvern was a disaster for Lee."

Julian read, "The Irish no such luck, In the great soldier's debacle." Then he put a check next to it and the gutta-percha paragraph.

Cam's mind and fingers continued their synchrony. "Thaddeus Kosciuszko, born in Poland." He read to himself. "Engineer. Chief engineer of West Point. His fortification there… the American Gibraltar."

"'Made the Point a altar.'" Another check.

"Wendell Phillips. A major abolitionist. Fanatical. His family tried to have him thrown in an insane asylum."

"'To his family, crazy, no locks freedom's call.'"

"Edward Everett Hale," said Cam. He looked up at Julian. "That's the old guy statue on the east side of the park. Born in Roxbury, Massachusetts. He was editor of the *Boston Daily Advertiser*, pastor of the Church of the Unity, an abolitionist, and a writer. He wrote sixty books. Here we go. *Man Without a Country*."

"'Isle alone, the dandy. A story he's writer of.' I don't think Cooper was planning on Google. Too easy."

"Which one is left?"

"'From poor boy to president, To earth the rains fall.' Mean anything to you?"

"Maybe that one is Washington," said Cam.

"Nope. The first statue you see is his. Faces west."

"Don't recall any other presidents in the park. There are presidents on dollar bills. Maybe he buried it with money."

"'Where the rain falls.' Big help." Julian's sarcasm was frustration aimed at himself.

"Time's a wastin'."

Julian checked his watch again. 8:50. "I think they close up shop at nine. Let's turn off the lights and lock the office door. We'll wait for them to leave. I found the alarm code in the drawer. We may need to get back in here."

CHAPTER FORTY-ONE

PARISH HOUSE, TRINITY CHURCH
Monday, September 10, 2001, 9:07 P.M.

Black hoodies covered their heads. The sun had fallen into night. A breeze kicked up sandwich wrappers and newspapers as it slipped down Clarendon Street, and tiny raindrops cut into Julian's face. The night had turned mean.

Julian and Cam crouched in the stairwell leading down to the thick, four-hinged door. Over the apse of the church the brassy glow of the city hung in the air. They listened for the breath of the metropolis, subtle but clear. All the parked cars in either direction were empty. All the shadows—vacant. There were no lingering pedestrians.

"On three," said Julian. He waited. Full-sized raindrops now splattered on his face in a sudden downpour. He looked right then left one last time. "Ready...three!"

One at a time, they eased out of their subterranean lair into the thickness of the night, pirouetted left, and headed north in front of the parish house. They joined up at the light, hesitated for a black Lexus, and then darted across the intersection. The Public Garden was only four blocks away. They figured Dexion watched the front of the church and their cars;

walking seemed the best option. Each carried a collapsible shovel, the kind that army surplus stores sell. They were hard to hide.

The dull thud of their heels on the damp sidewalk sounded loud to Julian, like the whop of an approaching Apache helicopter. He slowed. They passed under awnings and trees. Upper stories were anonymous red brick facades—rental apartments, law offices, small businesses—done a million times before. A wet manhole cover reflected a dimpled, black archetype in the streetlights, the snowflake pattern used by utility companies. They worked their way through one pod of light to the next, stopping in the shadowed recesses to check for lingering stares, oblique glances, and trench-coated dawdlers.

"Anything?" said Julian.

"I don't think they saw us leave."

Julian nodded and scanned the street, looking ahead and behind. The rain slowed. The street was misty and indifferent. It didn't look the same at night. An insistent hiss filtered out of nowhere, interrupting the white noise of the city. Julian stopped and held his arm out, halting Cam in his tracks. He listened, standing motionless. There it was again. Julian groped at his back pocket, fumbled, and then finally squeezed his cell phone out and bent it open. *Unknown caller.* He showed it to Cam as he twirled back into the shrouded recess. Cam nodded.

"Hello," said Julian, hesitantly.

"Very interesting. You are no longer in the church," said the mechanically rearranged voice. "Hot on the trail, I presume."

Julian hesitated and lowered the phone. He willed his eyes to make adjustments to the darkness. The syrupy night air painted the secrets of the street opaque. A black Mercedes C-240 passed by; Michelin radials slapped at the rain-soaked pavement. It slowed temporarily then sped off. He shrunk further into the shadow. Julian knew he needed to make the exchange on his own terms. If they were caught in the open with the vellum, they were goners. Julian brought the phone back to his ear.

"Reverend Philips, go fuck yourself."

He clapped the phone shut, picked up his shovel, and took a brisk step north toward Commonwealth Avenue. Cam, taken aback, was slow and had to double-time it to catch up.

"What was that all about?"

"He knows we're on the move." He stopped and looked at Cam. "Safety off. Don't think too hard about pulling the trigger. Aim for the gut—harder to miss."

Cam nodded. They moved on, making double time down the block. Julian's hand caressed the Sig P229 that was snug under his belt.

"Now he knows we're onto him." Cam said it as a statement when he meant it as a question.

"If things suck, go on the offensive. Like in chess. Confuse the opponent." Julian reset his jaw.

They reached the boulevard. The Public Garden was two long blocks east. The street represented old money, Kennedy-type money. Elegant, four-story-tall, three-window-wide early twentieth-century dwellings, one after the other, disappeared into the darkness. Stones of various types strained against the thick ivy––somber brick, limestone, brownstone. Windows of all types dotted the facades, with hood moldings and label moldings on top. Some were dark voids; others had lacy-white curtains highlighted by icicles of light. The roofs sprouted gabled dormers and arch dormers. At street level, there were wrought-iron fences and well-tended flowerbeds. It had all been grand once; now it was inundated with time. The dark and the rain took the fat out of the grandeur. Julian had always considered it pretentious and gloomy.

The two lanes were separated by a forty-foot median. Big trees, knotty maples and towering burr oaks, some lit, some saturated with darkness, dotted the island. A walkway bisected the greenery. A few statues stood tall, and raindrops winked faintly off heads and arms from the light of nearby halogen bulbs.

An old gent happened by with a lady. He wore a gray summer suit, cuffed. He carried an umbrella, a ready smile, and deep-set eyes that probably had seen many things. He looked like he came from a long lineage of somebodies; he was maybe a third or a fourth. Both sides of the street were lined with cars, anonymous and empty. There were low-end BMWs, Saabs, a Mercedes or two––gray. The rain slowed from big drops to a drizzle. An old yellow taxi with a blown muffler rumbled by with a low growl followed by the wet hiss of its tires. The noise died around the corner.

"Crocs watch you the first time, get you the next," said Cam.

"That's what I'm afraid of."

The night pressed in on them. They felt exposed, and they were carrying shovels.

"It's dark, but not dark enough," offered Cam.

Julian nodded. "Sidewalk or median?"

"Sidewalk is open and better lit. Median."

"So the sidewalk. Unexpected."

Julian took off in a low crouch, hugging the shadows at the edge of the walkway and ducking into an aperture between a maple and a downspout. He moved shadow to shadow. He flattened his back against the clinker brick wall; they waited. The irregularities bored through his wet sweatshirt. Then Cam started forward.

"Wait," said Julian, holding up his arm.

A stretch limo, the glass tinted dark like a beer bottle, drove west on the opposite side of the median. Not fast. Not slow. They waited for it to pass. Seinfeld quipped on the TV inside the house; muffled laughter followed.

"Let's go," Julian finally said.

At the intersection, four guys appeared out of the shadows. One short, messy guy carried a pint of Guinness. He wobbled a bit and wore rap fatigues, the crotch of his pants hanging to the ground. Another guy looked like a matzo ball, with sunglasses sucked into his jowls. Apparently, the sun never sets on thugs. A tall one's neck was branded with an angry tattoo––a jaguar with big teeth. He had hungry cheeks, scary looking like Snoop Dogg. Another guy with a thick neck acted like the leader, a legend in his own mind. His hands hung deep in his pockets like they were attached to weights, and his shoulders hunched forward. A nasty scar that reflected light off his left check matched his attitude. Previous street surgery. Julian and Cam nearly ran into the group. Julian mumbled an apology.

"What you say?" snapped Thick Guy.

Julian stopped and drew in a long breath. The rain felt cool against his face. He tried to sense what was going on. "Nothing." The laggard of the group––the tall, tattooed one––jumped out to block his way. Julian and Cam stopped and turned.

Thick Guy approached the curb and looked Julian eye to eye. He reeked of beer. "You disrespectin' me?"

Matzo Ball stepped out onto Commonwealth. They were surrounded.

Julian said nothing. He kept his eyes on the leader. Take care of the leader, and it's a done deal; the others will follow. A pair of gray halos circled a set of headlights fifty yards away, heading north to south on Berkeley Street. He waited. He noticed Thick Guy had bulging muscles in his temples. His right eye twitched. A big gap filled his grimace.

"Bad idea…getting somethin' started," said Julian.

The thug's lips curled. Another gap popped into view. He looked at his buddies. They laughed on cue. The short one on the right tipped his lager bottle. Thick Guy took one step forward onto the street.

"What are you going to do, beat us with your shovel?" said Tattoo. He followed with a nasty laugh.

The car turned west onto Commonwealth. The lone corner light left the street gray. Julian reached over, grabbed Cam's arm, turned east, and headed toward the park. He bumped shoulders with Tattoo behind him, sending him to the ground. A hidden Guinness sloshed on the punk's coat; then a count later, the clink of glass breaking interrupted the quiet.

Julian took three steps then another. He heard a shoe hitting against gravel behind them. He snatched the Sig out of his belt, dropped the shovel, and spun around with two hands on the gun, extended.

"Dude!" Thick Guy held his hands up and stepped back.

Julian gave no more than a glance at Tattoo cowering on the street. "Lots of gravity tonight." Then he turned to Thick Guy. "Not the shovel. Thought this might work a teensy bit better." He checked north and south on Berkeley and then backed his way to the next curb. "Although plastic surgery with my shovel on your uglier than crap face would be sweet." The four backed away, heading south on Commonwealth.

Julian stashed his piece, grabbed the shovel, and then spun around and took off for closest shadow. Ten seconds later, two sets of car lights swept over them and lit up the tunnel of trees ahead. Julian crouched down and then ran, ducking low, around a gargoyle-guarded walkway to a five-foot spruce fronting an oriel window on one of the townhouses. His face met a maze of cobwebs. The car lights halted at the corner. They looked like hazy cotton balls in the murk. The first car turned right, the second––a blue Mustang––continued on very slowly for twenty yards then went faster. Julian and Cam became the shadow. To the north, perhaps a hundred yards ahead, he could see the cross traffic on Arlington Street and the lights on George Washington and his steed in the Public Garden. The heavy air turned them yellow. He pulled up his left sleeve. *9:24.*

"That them?" Cam whispered nodding at the Mustang. Raucous music worked its way through an overhead window.

"Maybe."

They waited. The clock in Julian's head ticked. Cars appeared and disappeared in a totally random fashion for the next three minutes. Sirens in the distance echoed off the brownstones. The bulky buildings around them retreated in the dark mist. The streets were mirror black. The city dark returned.

Cam leaned back against the bricks. "We need to make a run for it." The frustration in his voice was clear.

"Can't let them see us enter the park." Julian shivered; the cold had finally made it to his skin. Water dripped into his eyes. Julian stood and leaned forward. He checked each doorway, each window, each immaculately kept garden and saw nothing. "Let's go."

They headed east. Twenty yards ahead, their pods of darkness gave way to the bustle and traffic of Arlington Street. Prickles of doubt probed Julian's mind. He slowed, trying to get a fix on the traffic light's rhythm. His stomach tightened. Yellow. Red. He counted to himself. At "ten," he doubled his pace to nearly a jog. They arrived at the crosswalk and continued without hesitation across four lanes into the Public Garden. A sharp right put them in a clump of maples out of sight from the passing traffic. He spied on the thoroughfare from his lair, looking for sudden stops, lane changes, and familiar cars. He waited six minutes. People usually moved from places of concealment––like parked cars––after five. In short order, they worked their way to Charles Sumner's statue, then hunkered down behind its base. The pink granite looked metallic gray in the misty dark. The ground was soaked.

"Now what?" asked Cam. He unfolded the blade of the shovel and secured it with a screw clamp.

Julian removed one of their two flashlights from the pocket of his sweatshirt. "Let's find the seventh statue. We've got eight hours."

CHAPTER FORTY-TWO

PUBLIC GARDEN
Monday, September 10, 2001, 9:43 p.m.

In a crouch and a jog, Julian and Cam zigged and zagged their way through the park, moving parallel to Boylston past General Kosciuszko, Colonel Cass, and finally Mr. Phillips. The Prophet of Liberty stood in front of a ten-foot-high marble slab. Chiseled into the wall were his words, "Whether in chains or in laurels, liberty knows nothing but victories." They crouched down behind the barricade, out of view from both Charles and Boylston Street. The precipitation waxed and waned, from spitting rain to drizzle. Luminous white tents of light spotted the park. Big hunks of darkness filled the spaces in between—lots of black, lots of trees, lots of hiding places. The normally tame park was a dark portrait of itself. Directly in front of them, several weeping willows cast long shadows over the walkway.

"Hangman's noose," said Julian, more to himself than to Cam.

"What?"

"They used this place for public hangings in the early 1700s."

Cam nodded. Julian's pupils widened; the blackness softened, shapes formed. Mud oozed over his shoes. Cold worked through to his toes. Julian pointed north toward a flagpole; his hand glistened with water.

"On the other side of the pole is Hale's statue. The seventh is at the corner." He pointed diagonally across the park. "The White memorial."

Cam's eyes brightened with recollection. "Hardly lacking in self-esteem."

"I'm surprised Trump hasn't bombed it and put up a Yankees cap-wearing statue of himself."

Julian scanned the streets, checking the cars. In a fast walk, they headed across the park. They stayed well away from the cement trails, skirting the lagoon, suspension bridge, and the famous duck statues. The pond smelled like a soldier's boot, which mixed well with the wet-sock smell of the park. The poorly lit statue funded by Robert White stood on the street side at the corner of Beacon and Arlington. Cars waited at the light. Traffic was heavy. Headlights bounced off the gray granite statue; watermarks, fungus, and city muck blemished the young lady. Julian attempted to slow the rise and fall of his chest. He drew in sustained breaths through his nostrils, squatted, and listened. An orchestra of voices and laughter bent through the mist from passing cars. Across the street, the Cambridge Trust Company sign lit up several stories of brick. He cast his vision down Beacon, checking for something, anything not right. He found the Bull and Finch Pub, its entrance made famous by the TV show *Cheers*. The thought of John Ratzenberger, George Wendt, and Kelsey Grammer sitting around the bar brought a transient smile to his face. Julian wondered what advice Ratzenberger's character, Cliff Clavin, would give him. The *Cheers* theme song barged into his head—not surprising since it was encoded into the DNA of every baby boomer. Certainly the lyrics were not as profound as say, Job of the Old Testament, but perhaps provided as much solace and possibly more relevance in the twentieth century. He suspected Gary Portnoy didn't know he was competing with God when he wrote it.

Julian lowered his body and remained motionless. He focused on the memorial. Green, tarnished horns of plenty occupied the three o'clock and nine o'clock positions of an eighteen-foot round pool. Embossed on its foot-high wall was the inscription, "In Memory of George Robert White 1847-1922." In the middle, where the dials would have been, stood a five-foot-tall statue on a pedestal of the same height. The statuette was of some anorexic winged goddess who appeared to have procured an early nineteenth-century boob job. The wings and the boobs just didn't work for Julian. Maybe it was just the wings.

Julian jabbed Cam in the ribs. "On the pedestal." He pointed.

Cam focused. He recalled the "Eccle" tattooed onto Cooper's mangled left shoulder. "Bingo." He flashed a smile. "Ecclesiastes 11:1. Cast thy bread upon the waters for thy shall find it after many days."

Neither spoke as they worked the scripture into the construct. A minute passed.

"So that's what we've been looking for?" Cam paused. His face showed disappointment. "What the hell does it mean?"

Julian surveyed the surrounding area. Twenty feet of mosaic pebble formed a semicircular terrace in front. In the back was a four-foot-high hedge juxtaposed to a wrought-iron fence, eight feet of sidewalk, and Arlington Street.

"All cement," said Julian. "There's nowhere to bury anything," His disappointment was obvious.

"Inside."

Shovels aside, they crawled commando style across the patio, up two steps, and peered into the pool. Pennies, dimes, and quarters littered the bottom, hardly worth a panhandler's time. Julian slinked over the edge. The water was only a few inches deep. He pushed and prodded the central pedestal. No hidden passageways opened. Julian felt embarrassed for even checking. He reminded himself that Indiana Jones was born of celluloid. They crawled the perimeter looking for marks, signs, anything that might indicate subterranean contraband. Finding nothing, they edged back to their shovels then headed for the cover of a nearby towering durmast oak—uphill the entire way.

"What now?" asked Cam.

Julian slumped his wet shoulders against the jagged bark. The wind swirled. The rain stammered over the lagoon's surface. "We're getting to the point of no return, as far as the FBI." Julian looked at his watch. A knot gathered in his stomach.

"Why in the hell didn't he just put it in a safe-deposit box?" said Cam, slamming his shovel to the ground.

"Because he didn't want anyone to find it. Period. He couldn't bring himself to destroy history. He absolutely couldn't malign the backbone of Christianity. He was running out of time, literally." He paused. "A bank keeps it dry and safe forever, with a paper trail. Something he didn't want."

"So he left a trail only you could follow."

The wind whistled through the trees. Neither of them said anything for a couple of minutes. They were stumped. They were also hungry, wet, and cold. A siren disrupted nature's sounds and altered the moment.

"Did you ever stop loving Mom?"

Julian jerked and looked at his son. He didn't answer.

"Mom told me everything. Karlie convinced me you were on the dark side of the Force." He paused. "For what it's worth, I think I'm a better person."

Julian reached over and patted Cam's knee. "That's the key: learn from living. Avoid the do-overs. That's all anyone can do." He reached into his innermost shirt and pulled out an envelope containing Cooper's poem and the photo of Cooper's tattoos. He paused and laughed. "I guess if I'm Darth Vader, you're Luke Skywalker." He handed the photo to Cam but kept the poem. He gave Cam one flashlight and kept the other. He turned his on and drew it over the poem. "There are nights…in my dreams…when I smell her perfume."

Julian's admission dealt an awkward moment but only for a moment.

"Ecclesiastes 11:1 has something to do with charity," said Julian, as he reread the poem. "The act of giving brings rewards later. Something like that. Not much help. At least for me." He performed a cerebral dissection of each line of the poem. "Maybe he wallpapered another verse on his left shoulder. Not 11:1. Wish I had a copy of Ecclesiastes."

Cam dropped the photo to his lap. "Maybe that's it. Charity. Something to do with charity. Words made by using the letters." He hesitated. "Cart hiy. Or chair ty. Or city rah."

Julian gave him a nice-try look and read the poem again. Then he flipped his flashlight off.

Cam continued. "Arch ity. Is there an arch in the park? How about archy ti? Archy is used as a suffix for leader; ti is the seventh note of the scale or a Chinese learning tree, or something. Can't remember. Tray chi. Chi is life force. Twenty-second letter of the Greek alphabet."

Julian remained silent, thinking.

"The Q is in the center of the pentagram, with one letter per statue surrounding it. What's in the center of the park?" asked Cam.

"The lagoon."

Cam pondered the thought. "And the suspension bridge!"

They worked their way forty yards to the figure-of-eight lagoon, spanned in the middle by what was supposed to be the world's smallest suspension bridge. Four six-foot square pylons anchored the structure with globe lights attached to posts which extended up from each pylon. The white span was lit brighter than a Broadway marquee. They didn't dare cross it.

"Arch!" said Cam. "Arch ity. Arch tiy. Arch yit." Cam gave Julian an I-told-you-so smile.

Julian raised his eyebrows and shook his head.

Steps led down to a sidewalk passing under the viaduct. Cement and brick fortified each bank, forty feet in each direction. They checked for loose bricks and irregularities in the infrastructure. Julian clicked on his flashlight and then paced slowly around the base of two of the masonry support towers. He scaled the cement incline underneath and checked for defects between the bricks, like missing grout. Then, he checked again. They jogged up the steps and ran around the short end of the pond and rummaged around at the opposite side. They made the same search with the same result. Stifled, they retreated to a tree larger than the first, a huge willow with long, spindly limbs bowing down over the water. Underneath it, they were nearly invisible from the other side of the pond and the street. Julian pulled out the poem and the photo again; this time he took the photo.

"The ducks!" said Cam, after a few minutes. "Mrs. Duckling. Center of the park."

"Mrs. Mallard," corrected Julian as he recalled his favorite childhood book. He gave Cam another nice-try look. They extracted themselves from their shelter and crept toward the north side of the water's edge. Mrs. Mallard and the eight ducklings glistened, gold and wet. They were set in timeworn bricks––odd, irregular, and scuffed––and surrounded by gravel and pavement.

"Is *Make Way For Ducklings* on the official Harvard reading list?" Julian posed the question as they made their way back to the tree.

"Probably, in some comparative lit course. One of those courses where they spend a week evaluating *Horton Hears a Who* for Orwellian influences."

"You're kidding, right?"

"Sadly, I'm not."

Julian passed out the hardcopy again. "It's eleven."

Neither spoke. Julian scanned the park. He saw no movement and no suspicious shadows. Several minutes passed. Through the branches, a ruffled mirage of the city reflected off the corrugated surface of the water. They thought and made small talk. Then, it was quiet once again. The night closed in tighter. Time ebbed, relentless. Details of their endgame blurred.

"Julian, what are we going…" Cam dropped the picture in his lap again and paused. "You knew Cooper better than anyone. Think. He's in the park maybe on a night like tonight. A dark, chilly spring night. He's holding a two-thousand-five–hundred-year-old vellum codex. He's alone. He can't tell anyone about one of the most important archeological finds of the twentieth century. He's dying of cancer. Desperate. What would he do?"

Julian dropped the poem. He leaned back against the tree, rested his hands behind his head, and closed his eyes. He tried to clear his mind. A cold chill aborted his attempt. The drizzle had finally gotten to his inner level. He kept his eyes closed. A minute passed, maybe more. Suddenly, he startled to attention, grabbed the poem, and read it for the umpteenth time. "Wrong question." He looked up at Cam, wide-eyed. "You asked the wrong question!" Julian shifted around. "It's not, 'what would he do.' It's, 'what would he *not* do.'"

Cam didn't follow.

"What would Cooper not do," said Julian, again. "He wouldn't make a grammatical error in an eighty-word poem. Remember '*a*' for '*an*.' Simple. Hell, he's probably published fifty articles. No way would he make that error."

"Why?"

"Why would he do that?" Julian repeated, reveling in the moment. "To get rid of a letter!" Julian laughed out loud. "Too many letters."

Cam gave him a blank expression. Julian waited for him to catch up. Ten seconds passed. "Fibonacci! Like Erasmus, Nietzsche."

"Exactly." Julian raised his knuckles toward Cam. "I'll give you the letters." Julian turned on his flashlight and scanned the poem. He dabbed each letter with his thumb as he counted out the Fibonacci sequence. "OK, one, *I*; two, *S*; three, *L*; five, *A*; eight, *N*…thirteen, *D*…twenty-one, *O*… thirty-four, *F*…fifty-five, *D*…eight-nine, *U*…one hundred forty-four, *C*…two hundred thirty-three, *K*." Julian looked up. He smiled. His shoulders melted into the trunk, as he relaxed. His chill disappeared.

Cam gave him another blank look.

"My God, son. Haven't you ever read *Make Way For Ducklings*? You live in Boston for God's sake." Julian was nearly giddy. "I'll have to talk to Livy about this major child-rearing faux pas. Has to be Dr. Seuss's fault."

Cam grinned then lowered his head so he could look out over the water. The city's light reflections were blurred by the wind and rain. "'ISLAND OF DUCK.' In the lagoon." He laughed again. "My bad."

Forty feet off the shore was a spit of land no more than twenty feet wide. Twenty or so weathered wooden posts erupted out of the water to protect the swan boats from shoreline decimation. Layered hunks of dark gray granite were jacked four high into the bank, which rose five feet over the water. A dense forest of seven or eight trees sprouted from the dot of land like a Chia Pet on a bad hair day. Apparently, a botanical zealot headed the planting committee. Two trees reflected red in the ambient light. The others looked olive. The tallest one was maybe forty feet high. A couple others arched out over the water.

"You sure?"

"It makes sense," said Julian, looking at Cam. "Cooper went to England in March to see what? Lady Di's island grave." He moved his gaze out over the lagoon. "That's the island McCloskey drew in 1941. It's on the last page of the book. I can still see it. Mr. Mallard is waiting on the island for the little misses and Jack, Kack, Lack, Mack, Nack, Ouack, Pack, and Quack. That's it. Nobody is ever going to dig up this park, let alone that island." He hesitated. "Buried forever."

"Disturbing. You remembered their names."

CHAPTER FORTY-THREE

PUBLIC GARDEN, BACK BAY
Monday, September 10, 2001, 11:10 p.m.

Julian's certainty helped dissipate his hunger and cold. He stripped off his sweatshirt and laid it on the ground. On top he piled two more shirts, his wallet, the envelope, his cell phone and both flashlights. He wrapped them up, tied the bundle to the shovel, and then headed for the lagoon. Cam followed. The end of his shovel also sported luggage.

They only had to go forty feet. The water was cold, not ice cold, but close. Julian wondered how Cooper would have done this during the spring thaw. The raindrops felt like acid-point darts hitting his back. His legs disappeared into the black water; his feet sunk into the caldron of thick goo. An occasional can or rock provided the only traction.

"It's colder than shit," whispered Cam.

"Just find your happy place." Julian considered what he said. "Between your ears."

Fifteen feet from shore, the water caressed Julian's chin. He held his shovel high over head. His legs felt numb; it felt like an ice-cold spur had been driven into his spine. *Coop must have used a raft.* Julian's right foot dipped into a hole and dropped his head into the murk. He found his footing and jerked above the surface. Nervous puffs of breath came in fits. His body was on fire.

"You OK?" asked Cam, who bobbed along five feet behind him.

"I'm good."

The huge boulders at the edge of the island were ice slick with algae. Julian worked his way to a clearing, threw the shovel on shore, and then grabbed an overhanging limb to pull himself up the incline. Involuntary shivers racked his arms and legs as he helped Cam ashore. They both found their shirts and rubbed their bodies dry. Julian pulled on his shirt then spent the next few minutes jumping up and down, trying to warm himself. The thick foliage provided protection from the rain.

A soft mat of leaves and mulch carpeted the island. There was very little ground cover under the canopy of tree limbs. Julian got on his hands and knees, flashlight in hand, to inspect the ground.

"Look for a place where the soil hasn't quite settled or a depression or pieces of dried roots. He probably had to chop through a bunch of them. Watch for mulch mixed with chucks of dirt."

Cam nodded as he got down on his knees and pounded over the ground. "It's a small island. Why don't we compare notes?"

They found eleven areas that afforded ample space for a three-foot-wide hole. They prodded and probed to narrow it down.

"What do you think?" Julian finally asked.

Cam didn't hesitate. He walked to an area several feet to the left of the biggest tree. He stooped over and picked up a stick. "Here." He made an *X* in the ground then held up the piece of wood. "I thought this was part of a dead limb. It's not. It's a piece of root. Look." He held the light beam on the end. "Chopped. With a shovel."

"I agree. The area felt raised to me."

Cam turned the end of his shovel to a right angle with the shaft then rotated the screw to secure it. He got on his knees and hacked at the mud. With a straight blade, Julian dug and cleared away the dirt. They started with a four-foot-diameter area. The ground was wet; the excavation was demanding. As expected, tree roots made their progress even more taxing. At one point, a two-inch root redirected their efforts. They worked in darkness. Their conversation was sparse. Julian's earlier chills turned to sweat. At the eighteen-inch-deep mark, they stopped to reconsider.

"Was this really your first choice?" asked Cam, winded, looking into their hole.

Julian nodded. "Where was your second?"

Cam snapped on his flashlight and directed his beam toward an area under a sapling eight feet to the north. "How far down would you go?"

"Don't know." He swiped the sweat off his brow with the back of his hand and angled his wrist so he could read his watch. "Midnight." He sat back on his feet to rest. "I would go down three feet, minimum. That's assuming Cooper waited for the ground to thaw."

"You still sure about the island?"

"It has to be. Just think." He reviewed in his mind the tattoos on Cooper's chest. Each letter on the pentagram represented a statue . The *Q* in the middle and the Ecclesiastes notation on Cooper's left shoulder further hinted at the Public Garden location. Finally there was the poem, one verse per statue, but really a guise for the real clue hidden in the text in the Fibonacci numbers. *Island of Duck.* Julian rubbed his hands on his sweatshirt. "It has to be."

Julian laid the handle of the shovel against the wall of the hole, flipped on the light, and walked toward the sapling.

"We changing spots?"

"Don't think so. Just want to check again." On his knees, he scraped away the leaves and stabbed at the soil a few times. He held the light at ground level to look for shadows and then glanced over at Cam. "Keep digging." He probed all the other potential sites then returned to the excavation. Cam had done another three inches. "No old roots. No loose dirt in the other spots." He grabbed his shovel.

"Maybe I could start digging by the sapling."

Julian put his shovel down again. "OK. Let's say you're going to plant a tree. A little tree. How deep is the hole?"

"No clue. Never planted a tree."

"If I'm burying something I don't want found…three feet," Julian said, reconfirming what he had decided several minutes before. He scanned the island. He looked at his watch. "I say we work together. One hole at a time. We might be able to do three holes before we collapse. We have to go to the deadline. No choice. Maybe a hole an hour. That would be six holes, maybe. Maybe a hole every forty-five minutes. That's seven holes." They looked at each other. In the ambient light, Julian could see genuine doubt in Cam's face. The creases by his eyes were drawn, the lids low. "Cam, we have to do this. We can eat and sleep later."

Julian extended his fist, knuckles first. Cam did the same. They went back to work. The rain picked up to nearly a downpour, but only a small fraction made it through the foliage. They made small talk, but not about Livy. Cam asked questions of Julian, about his earlier life. Julian's arms ached with the buildup of lactate. His heartbeat rang in his ears. Julian buried the shovel one last time and felt something solid—not like a root. It felt more like a rock. He probed six inches away, then twelve inches away, and then twelve inches the other way. He dropped the shovel handle nearly parallel to the bottom and carefully carved half-inch slices of dirt away. Cam realized they were onto something and directed his efforts in a similar fashion. After a couple more minutes, Cam dropped his shovel and aimed the flashlight into the hole. The dull, gray sheen of metal winked back.

"I can't believe it," said Cam, wiping his forehead with his sweatshirt. "Unbelievable."

Julian defined the edges of the case then used the shovel's edge to pop it free. He grabbed the handle and set it on the mulch next to the hole.

"It's heavy," said Julian. "Twenty pounds."

He reached into his pants and extracted two keys that he had found in Cooper's desk. He cleared away the dirt, looking for the keyhole. The four wheels of a combination lock scratched at his finger.

"Hell," said Julian. "A combination lock." He dropped the keys back in his pocket.

"We don't have to open it. Let Reverend Fuckface figure it out."

Julian looked around for a small twig to pick away the embedded dirt. He bent low a couple of times to blow away the fine grit. After twenty seconds, the wheels turned easily. He sat with his feet dangling into the hole, the case on his lap.

"Let me try a few numbers, then we can get out of here." He glanced at his watch. "It's 12:50." He turned the wheels again. "OK, this has to be easy. Something I would know."

"Birthdays, anniversary dates, that sort of thing. Just like at Karlie's."

"Zero, eight, one, seven," said Julian as he set each dial. "Birthday." Nothing. "His." Julian paused. "One, zero, zero, eight." Nothing.

"Yours."

Julian thought for a moment. Then, with surprising suddenness, he tipped his ear up and held his finger to his lips. After a moment, he turned and crouched down in the hole, squinted at the shoreline. He focused on the shadows.

"You hear that?" whispered Julian. He rotated around so he was facing the far bank. "Sounded like a voice."

Cam lowered himself onto the mulch carpet of the island.

Neither flinched. Their breathing slowed. "Scoot over, and get the guns," said Julian.

Over the next minute, Cam retrieved their weapons. The rain's rhythmic beat against the leaves and water went uninterrupted. They waited another minute. Satisfied, Julian turned his flashlight back on and aimed at the case.

"Let's go," said Cam. "We're in deep shit if we get trapped out here." There was a new sense of urgency in his voice.

"One more number. "Zero, two, zero, six."

Julian pushed on the clasps. One and then the other popped open. He looked up and smiled at Cam. "Trinity's address."

Julian opened the case and peered inside.

CHAPTER FORTY-FOUR

PUBLIC GARDEN, BACK BAY
Tuesday, September 11, 2001, 12:48 a.m.

It happened without warning: a bright ray. It was more than a flashlight; suddenly it was daylight. It came from the near shore, the one they had come from. Maybe a car headlight. Maybe a light used for nighttime highway construction. Lots of watts. Forty-feet away, Julian spied a faint profile and ducked into the hole. Cam rolled behind the hole, down the bank toward the water. Their confusion was interrupted by a deep voice.

"Very good, Julian. I didn't think you could do it. I'm genuinely impressed."

Julian recognized the voice immediately. The deep baritone was unmistakable, the one he remembered from South Church years ago. "Phillips."

"I underestimated your guile."

"This wasn't part of the deal. I was supposed to call you when I found something."

"Thought I'd save you a dime."

Julian shielded his eyes, probing the darkness. He could only see a shadowy silhouette and something glimmering, perhaps the muzzle of a gun. Then he saw another. There were two shadows, each with a gun. He assumed there were more.

"I haven't found anything yet."

Reverend Phillips laughed. "Oh, but I think you have. Night-vision goggles."

"What about Livy?"

"Oh, she's fine…for the time being."

Julian snatched a peek into the case again to confirm what he had only glimpsed at before. "So, we give you the case, and we get Livy. Live happily ever after."

"Something like that."

Julian secured his gun and released the safety. He got Cam's attention. "Scoot over behind the tree," he said under his breath.

"What?" said the preacher from the bank.

"Nothing. Just talking to Cam."

"Julian, there's no reason to stall. I know it's cliché, but you really are sur- rounded. If you don't come voluntarily, I'll send someone out to get it. My friends get very cranky when they have to get wet."

Julian fiddled with the case, then closed the latches and spun the dials. He placed it carefully into the bottom of the hole. "We'll kill you well before you reach the island."

"I doubt that. Nevertheless, you kill us, you kill Livy…and Jessie."

The image of his bartender friend from Bukowski's popped into Julian's mind. "You son of a bitch."

"That's what he said. Plus some other things. He's a big guy. Didn't go without a struggle."

"Alive?"

"Of course. I'm just doing God's work."

"Silly me. I forgot God was a gang leader."

"This is taking entirely too long," said the cleric. "I'm normally a patient man, but you really have no choice. You're between a rock and…actually you're between several armed men. Not a strong negotiating position."

"I'm sure Cooper and Maxwell and Agnes and the lady before Agnes and the little old lady in front of the tattoo shop all greatly appreciated your patience, being a preacher and all. Oh, and Reverend Toulukinopolis. One of your brethren."

"All unfortunate accidents, I can assure you. Acts of God, if you will."

Julian extracted himself from the hole and walked to his sweatshirt to retrieve his phone.

"You ready?" asked the cleric.

Julian walked back to the hole in no particular hurry, then squatted down at the edge.

"I just want to be clear about one thing," said Julian. "You will get the papyrus. I promise. But we're going back to the original plan. I'll call you when I'm ready to do the exchange. If you harm either Livy or Jessie, you will go to jail. I just can't shake the feeling that Cam and I will be victims of an unfortunate act of God if we deviate from the plan now."

"I'm not sure that's still an option."

"You said you were a patient man."

"It's late."

Julian clicked a picture and then flipped his phone open and dialed 911.

"What are you doing, Julian?"

Julian ignored the preacher. He spoke into the phone more loudly than needed. "Hurry, please! I just heard shots fired from the Public Garden. Somethin' bad goin' down." He pushed the disconnect button.

"Clever. Very clever. But I don't hear any gunshots." The reverend turned his head. "Lenny, Grover, either of you fire your weapons?" He smiled, turned his hands up, and shrugged. He paused a moment. "Get the damn case."

Julian hesitated a moment, then removed the Sig from his pocket, aimed it into the air, and fired three shots in rapid succession. "Oops."

Lenny and Grover heaved themselves out of the water and flattened onto the ground.

"You're making a big mistake," said Reverend Phillips.

"No, you son of a bitch, you're making a big mistake. You'll get want you want, my way. If you even touch Livy, you'll need God's help more than you know. I suspect at this point, God is not doling out grace easily when it comes to clerics named Phillips."

CHAPTER FORTY-FIVE

PUBLIC GARDEN, BACK BAY
|Tuesday, September 11, 2001, 1:00 a.m.

Julian caught glimpses of movement on the far side of the lagoon––at least two people. As soon as the spotlight faded to dark, the image of the preacher with two-and-a-half people coalesced on the near bank. Julian and Cam hunkered down in the hole and waited for the police. Two patrol cars responded. One stopped on Arlington in front of Washington's statue; the other stopped on Charles Street in front of Hale's statue. Cam and Julian had their stuff packed, ready for a forty-foot walk through the muck. Cam had tied all the gear to one shovel. Julian carried the case.

Julian checked his watch. 1:04. The rain had stopped. The night sky had cleared; clouds now scudded in front of the moon. He watched four flashlights bob up and down––little jagged J's––in random fashion over the park. One time was a cursory scan made of the lagoon and the island. As soon as the police finished their search on the east side, Julian and Cam crawled out of the crater. Julian grabbed the free shovel. Within three minutes, he had the hole filled and mulched. He stashed the shovel under the one shrub on the island, and then he lowered himself into the water. The trip to land took only a minute. They dried and dressed, then carried their guns ready. Julian knew they had no chance on the streets, but once they were in a vehicle: advantage St. Laurent. The cleric's resources would be thin.

Sixty seconds later, they blended into a dense shadow between the statue and the hedge. The winged anorectic looked worse from the back. Behind them the flashlights bobbed. Julian scrutinized Beacon Street. He checked the parked cars, timed the lights, and gazed behind the shadows. Finally, he handed the case to Cam, stashed his gun, stepped through the hedge, and, in one step, vaulted over the fence. He received the case back from Cam then headed diagonally across Beacon to his right, moving east. Cam stayed twenty feet behind by design. Julian reached the *Cheers* pub; his breaths came deep and steady. He ducked down into the stairwell, drew his gun, and waited. Cam was only seconds behind him. Julian yanked out his phone. The cab arrived four minutes later.

Their destination: Trinity. The most obvious place might be the least obvious. Julian discussed his plan as they raided the cupboard and refrigerator. He'd forgotten how good a peanut butter and jelly sandwich could taste. Cam tackled a hunk of cheese. Julian took a quick detour into the bathroom to get a picture of Agnes and then worked his way through the basement. They ended up sitting next to each other on the steps of the altar, guns resting on their laps.

"You remember those two homeless guys under the portico, left of the door as you're facing the church?" Julian handed Cam a couple twenties. "Don't scare 'em. They may be hungover or drunk. Or, maybe worse, sober. I'm sure they'll remember Livy. Stay in the shadows, under one of their wraps. Disgusting, I know. Push redial each time a guy enters the church. If my phone vibrates more than ten seconds, I'll answer."

Cam stood, and Julian followed. They faced each other for a moment, standing eye to eye. Then embraced; it was more than a guy hug.

"Just think about your mom. You shouldn't have any trouble pulling the trigger. Then…"

"Hey, I'm good. No need to rehash."

Julian gave Cam five minutes to disable the church alarm system and get settled and then made the call to Reverend Phillips.

"Hey, asshole," said Julian, "I'm ready. Livy and Jessie ready to go?"

"They're unharmed," said Reverend Phillips over the phone. "This is how it is going to work."

"No, this is how it's going to work." Julian paused but not long enough to let the reverend interrupt. "I'm at Trinity. The alarm is disabled. The left front door is open. Be here in fifteen minutes with Livy and Jessie. You can look for cops if you want. You won't find any."

There was a prolonged pause. Julian imagined Reverend Philips formulating his counter offer, moving the players in his head, and calculating the risk—considering then reconsidering. Julian could almost hear the wheels turning.

"Nonnegotiable," added Julian.

"Livy will die. Jessie, too."

"Hell, you're going to kill us all anyway." Julian paused. "Nonnegotiable. Or I go to the cops then the *Globe*. Suddenly, they're my best friends and your worst nightmare."

There was another pause, this time not so long. "Twenty-five minutes."

"Twenty. For some reason Agnes doesn't want to get out of the bathtub."

Julian sought higher ground and found a nifty little upper deck pew, just right of the altar. He suspected it was for dignitaries. It limited his escape options, but there was no way anyone would be able to sneak up behind him. Tonight he anointed himself a dignitary. He waited. Minutes later, his cell phone vibrated once, then again, then yet again, and then again. Then it was still. About the time of the last call, he saw the first of the preacher's lemmings leave a shadow and enter the chapel, his gun extended. The fake cop. The same thick neck. The same buzz cut.

"Up here, jerk off." He resisted the urge to fill the son of a bitch with bullets. "I sent my son away. Head start. I'll stay up here until you're convinced the church is empty. Then we'll conduct business."

Reverend Philips stepped into view. It was curious how the cleric looked out of place with his pasted-on piety. His face was sculpted with soulless intensity. A long, black trench coat hung from his thick shoulders; his hands rested deep in the pockets.

"Give my men a few minutes."

The devil had found a voice. In the cavernous hall, it sounded like a voice straight from hell. Julian and the ecclesiastic misfit traded stares for the next three minutes. Silence buzzed in his ears; the fundamental stillness was unsettling. Finally, a henchman approached and whispered into his chief's ear. The reverend nodded.

"What about the locked doors?"

"I don't have the keys. Shoot the locks if need be. I'm sure you found the rector's office open."

The preacher nodded but said nothing. Julian knew he had the upper hand until he handed over the case.

"What's your plan?" asked Reverend Phillips. Weariness tainted his voice.

Julian held up the case. "This is a tamper-proof case. Inside is another water-resistant case. The big case has a four-digit combination. The inside case has a keylock. You hand over Livy; I give you the case. Then Jessie, and I give you the combination and the key. We leave unharmed. Done deal."

The reverend nodded. He paused. "The combination, now… as an act of good will."

The ball was in Julian's court. He pondered the proposal. Finally he said, "Zero, two, zero, six."

The reverend hesitated, looked around, and then nodded to a shadowed profile standing in the narthex. The shadow disappeared.

Julian took it as a good sign. He made eye contact with the preacher. "I'm coming down. No sudden moves." He received a confirmatory nod.

In seconds, he was standing in the south transept under *The Resurrection*, the stained-glass production high on the south wall of the church. Julian held the case in his left hand; his cell phone was wedged between the case handle and his palm. His right hand gripped the Sig, which was buried in the bottom of his pocket. He worked his way toward the back of the church to maintain his view of the narthex, so he could keep tabs on the players. Julian startled when his phone vibrated, although he was expecting it. He counted to himself, one thousand one, all the way to ten. He waited a half-second more then dropped his phone. Its rattle echoed throughout the chamber.

A minute later, Julian caught sight of Livy edging reluctantly from the entrance into the nave. His heart sank. Her face was drawn. Still in her bathrobe, she looked scared and tired, overwhelmed by events not of her own making—a pawn in a game much bigger than any one person. She held her arms around herself, clutching her bathrobe close to her body. Julian labored to maintain his look of wary caution. The henchman escorted her halfway down the middle aisle to the crossing where the reverend grabbed her by the arm and yanked her close. The henchman backed his way to the north transept, his pistol ready. The other gunman stationed himself on the south side of the narthex, near the entrance. He searched for the dwarf and couldn't find him. *Standing guard at the church entrance.* He checked the back of the nave again. *Jessie?*

Julian entered one of the pews, with the case extended in his left hand and his right hand angled from his side. He took one measured step at a time and then reassessed after each. His head swiveled right and left. Livy maintained a brave front; fear held her tight. The henchman in the back roved toward the altar, positioning himself diagonally behind Julian. The foe in the north transept––the bogus cop––had yet to move. The cleric stood like a statue, twenty-five feet away. Julian stopped after fifteen feet and waited. For ten seconds, nothing was said, and no one moved. The knot in his gut returned—same with the bile in his throat. The preacher drew a gun out of his coat pocket and let it dangle at his side.

"You disappoint me, Julian. You didn't really think I could let you go, did you?"

Julian smiled. "Damn, you spoiled the ending."

Game time. Julian focused on the preacher's pistol. It moved a fraction. Maybe it was just a gesture. Maybe not. Julian's muscles responded in the first nanosecond. It had to be coincidence, not subsequence.

"Here you go," said Julian, much louder than needed. His left arm moved back, bringing the case horizontal. He heaved it in a high, looping arc toward the altar. Before it crashed on the floor, a volley of two shots echoed from behind the altar that sounded suspiciously like a Wilson Combat 1911. The henchman in the north transept grabbed his stomach; his eyes yanked open in total surprise. The gun he held clunked impotently on the ground, then his body followed, first falling to his knees and then to his side in the fetal position. His shirt turned a dreadful shade of crimson. Reverend Phillips's head followed the case for a fraction of a second and then rotated another ninety degrees to his rear at the sound of the gunfire. Julian had already advanced two giant steps when he heard the pistol held by the foe in the south transept engage and fire. He felt a jolt in his left shoulder. It took his breath away but pushed him toward the minister. Livy wrenched her arm free and headed for the altar. A scream chased the echo of another gunshot as she fell, hands forward, near the fifth row of pews. The cleric nearly had his revolver to ninety degrees when Julian launched himself across the man's body, moving toward his right hand and the gun.

The reverend's mouth opened. His face flinched, and he pulled the trigger. The bullet sailed low and right. It smashed full force into the back of pew 133, splintering the deeply polished walnut and sending wood fragments over a ten-foot section of the row and then continued into that pew's hymnal to page 221 and stopped. Julian instinctively turned his right shoulder toward the floor. His 190 pounds landed full force in the minister's solar plexus. The preacher and Julian continued into and over the edge of the pew directly behind them. A huge exhalation escaped from the minister's mouth, like the sound of a lonesome moose, and preceded his head crashing into the rock-solid bench. A dazed look filled the eyes of the cleric. Julian seized the moment and delivered his right elbow to the top of the man's pious collar. The preacher dropped his firearm and grabbed at his neck, and then he slumped back on the wood bench, out cold.

Julian pushed off the charlatan, grabbed the gun off the floor, then did a nifty pirouette down behind the pew edges lining the middle aisle. By this time, Cam had shuffled across the back of the altar, north to south, and directed a volley of shots at the gunman huddled behind the last row of pews in the south transept. He missed, badly shattering the corner of the *The Storm and the Lake.* The fourth henchman, the dwarf, appeared in the main entrance, stopped, and fired three times at Julian, who was kneeling in the aisle. All went high. The chancel organ took a direct hit from one of the strays and groaned an odd tune. One of the five stained-glass windows in the chancel––a mosaic portrayal of the Trinity––took another. The third ripped at a seat and spewed a shower of splintered walnut over Julian's head. In a low crouch, Julian reached Livy, who was huddled in the third row. He looked back at the preacher, who reclined in the ninth, feet extended into the aisle––still out. Julian yanked the Sig from his pocket and drove the dwarf to take cover in the narthex with three rapid shots. Keeping low, he led Livy toward the altar. He grabbed the gray case and then worked his way left. They followed the cover of the first row of pews, then ducked under the rope. They reached the trapdoor about the same time Cam offered a final shot. Julian yanked the marble slab up and hopped on the ladder. Livy was close behind. Cam was on the ladder and shut the door as Livy stepped onto the dirt floor of the cellar. Julian steadied the ladder. Cam jumped the last three steps, and then Julian shoved the wood structure toward the horizontal.

Without a flashlight, the subterranean lair was as dark as coal. Julian couldn't tell if his eyes were open or closed. Little phosphorescent bubbles danced all around. Before he proceeded forward, he swung Livy around and hugged her, and she hugged him back.

"Did they hurt you?" he asked.

Julian heard her sniffle. He felt tears on her face. "I thought I was going to die."

At the sound of the altar hatch opening, Julian spun around and fired two bullets at the cone of light.

CHAPTER FORTY-SIX

The door leading to the cobblestone floor of the parish house basement was easy to find once they worked their way around the bend in the tunnel. Only thirty minutes earlier, Cam had been in the subterranean lair. Julian barred the access then ran over and helped Cam push a filing cabinet behind it as a stop.

"You locked the front door, right?" said Julian.

Cam stopped. His face turned the color of the puke colored walls. "Shit!"

He bolted up the stairs, gun drawn; Julian followed, step for step. They raced down the hall. The dwarf stampeded through the four-hinged door as they lunged into the kitchen. Cam dove under the table and peeled off three shots. The felon ducked behind the doorframe of the utility room, waited, and then returned fire. Bob's tank shattered along with one of the pictures over the sink. Julian fired into the wall where he suspected the gunman was standing. The height-challenged criminal peeked around the partition and fired two more times, his aim no better than the first time. Bob fell off the counter, landed six feet away, and slithered for freedom toward the pantry. Julian grabbed Cam's arm and yanked him back into the basement where Livy huddled.

Cam and Julian moved the two remaining filing cabinets to the foot of the stairs. They hunkered down in the portion of the basement tucked under the kitchen. Overhead, another pair of feet showed up, muffled voices followed. Julian looked at his watch, then reached for his phone and pried it open. A "No Service" label branded the screen.

"Hell."

"What?" said Livy, a resigned look on her face. She sat with her knees drawn to her chest.

"No service. Cam, check your phone."

Cam, reeling from his faux pas, was slow to react but got the same result. Voices drifted in from the rat-infested part of the cellar under the chancel. Cam raised his gun and dealt two shots through the wall. Several expletives returned.

"Save your bullets," said Julian. He walked over and sat down next to Cam and put his hand on his son's knee. "You did well today. I'm proud of you."

Cam glanced up and then returned his gaze to the floor. "I screwed up."

"You saved our lives. We had no chance with four guys shootin' at us. That fake cop––the guy in the north transept––was probably their best shot." Cam continued to look away. "Hey, you were worried about leaving me hanging. I would've done the same thing. We'll be fine." Julian looked at his watch. "It's 2:30. In four hours, the cops will be all over this place."

Julian bumped Cam's knee with his fist then moved over to Livy. He knelt down in front of her and raised her chin. Her right earlobe was painted with a patch of dried blood; an amethyst-drop earring was missing. He caressed her shoulder with his left hand. "You OK?"

She reached up and took his hand in hers. With concerted effort, she managed to put a smile on her face. "Hey, you know me, just tired." She kissed him then leaned away. "Thank you for saving my life." Livy moved her eyes in the direction of the case. "Where was it?"

"Public Garden. Duck Island, in the lagoon."

She nodded and smiled.

Julian parked himself against the wall. He scanned the room and noticed again what a truly dismal place it was. A moldy odor permeated the dank air. The recent rain had made it more oppressive than before. Water oozed through the brick walls, which were painted yellow in some areas and crumbling in others. The cobblestone reflected a sickly gray color in the pale light.

The thick overhead planks looked like old bones, cracked and corrugated with age. They heard the sound of feet pacing above them. Voices were unintelligible mumbles. Julian took inventory. On hooks secured in a ceiling beam were two fly rods with lures attached. In the corner were an old pair of boots next to a hoe and a sundry of garden tools. There was a bag of grass seed, Kentucky bluegrass, and a bag of fertilizer, Scotts. Keeping them company were the wise men, Mary, Joseph, and the baby Jesus himself—plaster Nativity facsimiles of age-old questions that would never be answered.

Julian figured a brief respite was the best that they could hope for; Phillips wouldn't give up. He doubted they would make an assault, although enough men coming simultaneously from both sides would do the trick. But Dexion's work was clandestine, not brute force. Julian knew what the alternatives were. He scrutinized the dreariness and considered the possibilities. Four hours. If they could just hold out. He checked his phone again then snapped it closed. Livy startled from her fugue.

"Home free?" she said.

Julian didn't respond. He needed to continue the we're-OK ruse a little longer.

Livy stood and analyzed the room, like she was assessing it for a home makeover, deciding where to put the queen bed and the matching armoires.

"They could put anything down here, couldn't they?" Her expression indicated the query was rhetorical, a statement.

Julian remained silent.

"Like what they did to Maxwell."

Julian established eye contact and maintained it. Often words weren't necessary. Since Maxwell's death, they had been on a collision course to finish the business started twenty-seven years earlier. Before tonight, the consideration had been dramatically inappropriate. Suddenly, it wasn't.

"Maxwell's death was immediate," said Julian. "No time to think." He considered their circumstance. "No time to plan."

Livy nodded; her eyes continued to skim the cell.

"Cam, how many bullets do you have left?" asked Julian.

Cam answered without looking. "None."

Julian stood up and took off his shirt. Underneath was a Kevlar vest, the one he had found in Livy's garage. He removed it and handed it to Cam.

"Put this on."

Cam didn't move.

"Put this on," said Julian again, firmer this time. "It was Maxwell's. Put it on."

Livy walked over to her son. "Please, Cam. For me. Do it for me."

Cam looked at his mom then Julian. He took the vest and slipped it over his shoulders. Julian yanked the Sig and the extra magazine out of his pocket and handed it to Cam. Again, Cam declined.

"Please, Cam," said Livy. She waited. "It's the way things work."

Cam took the gun and magazine and put them in his pocket.

Julian looked at Livy then Cam. "Wait or make a dash for it?"

Cam hesitated then raised his eyebrows. "One five gallon can of gas, and we're history."

"Which way?" asked Julian.

"I'd go upstairs," said Cam. "There's no way we could get up the ladder and through the hatch. Twenty-foot climb. No way."

"Livy?" said Julian.

Livy nodded a whatever then wandered over to the workbench. She bent down to pick through supplies on the shelves next to it.

"When?" asked Julian.

"Soon," said Cam. "Before they have time to regroup. I'd say five minutes."

"Five minutes?"

"Soon."

Julian nodded, then walked to the workbench to scavenge a weapon. He happened upon a new Stanley screwdriver and tucked it into a back belt loop. A two-foot section of steel pipe lay in a distressingly rusted box among a nest of rusted nails. He secured the pipe then got down on his knees next to Livy to rummage on the lower shelf. Two voices drifted in from the dirt-floor cellar.

"Julian," said Cam.

He turned to find Cam holding a flashlight in one hand, the Sig in the other.

"Only two guys." He looked at the wall. "Two shots. I have a vest. We could be out of the church in a minute."

"I thought you said upstairs."

"I did."

"What if someone is standing at the altar, shooting down?" He paused before he added, "Maybe more than two."

Cam's head gave a nervous twitch. Indecision painted his face. "Agnes's bedroom." Cam moved his gaze to the ceiling. "We could barricade ourselves. It's one level closer to the street. The cell phones might work." His face carried a hint of desperation, his voice, the same. "Anything is better than this."

Julian nodded then returned his attention to the shelves.

"What's behind the brick wall?" asked Livy. She stood a few feet away with her hands on her hips. The robe opened at her waist, revealing the bottom of a T-shirt and the entire length of her left leg. "It looks new."

"A tunnel," said Julian. "Old. According to Agnes, they used the church for crimping, in the late nineteenth century."

"What-ing?"

"Crimping. Shanghaiing. They would get unwary travelers drunk at the tavern across the street. Slip 'em some opium, take them through the tunnels to the Charles River, then to the big sailing ships to who knows where."

"Wake up in Tahiti?"

"Something like that."

"What if I could get us through the wall?" said Livy.

"Lots of luck," said Julian. "I checked it. Rock solid."

"What if?' said Livy, again.

"Don't know? Agnes's bedroom is a known."

Livy nodded then hitched her robe together and pulled up her sleeves. "Cam, come here."

Livy ripped off the top layer of the fertilizer bag and placed it on the floor. On it, she dumped all the rusty nails. She rummaged around and collected everything with rust she could find and added it to the stack. Then she handed Cam a brush, wiry and stiff.

"OK, guys, we're going to blow the shit out of that wall. Cam, get the rust off this stuff and onto the paper." She turned to Julian.

Julian smiled. He was taken aback by Livy's surge of energy. "I don't know where the tunnel goes."

"Beats the hell out of anything at the top of the stairs."

Julian hesitated. "Even if it's a dead end…blocked?"

"We could hide out." Livy reached up for a tarnished hacksaw then handed it to him. "Saw the frame of the bike into three two-foot-long pieces."

Julian didn't ask and didn't hesitate. He hoisted the nearly new two-thousand-dollar Paketa off its hooks. It was surprisingly light.

Livy went to the corner to get an old car battery. She carried it over and placed it in the now-empty metal container. She blew the grit off the top and removed the caps. Around the battery, she poured the fertilizer. There was enough to fill the metal tub to the top.

"I need the saw," she said to Julian. She cut one of the two-foot tubes in half then secured one piece in the vise and, with a rasp, whittled away at the end of it. She made strong, angled strokes. Seconds went to minutes. Perspiration dotted her forehead. No one spoke.

They all smelled it at the same time—the stiff odor of gasoline. It wasn't subtle. There was no need to acknowledge it.

"From your survival books?" asked Julian, trying to maintain the group's focus.

"No, *MacGyver*."

"You're shittin' me," said Julian. He stopped what he was doing.

"Who's MacGyver?" asked Cam.

"What," said Julian. "A TV show from the eighties. Richard Dean Anderson. Right?"

"Yep." Livy didn't stop to look up, but the corners of her mouth turned up. "He was really cute."

"Hell," said Julian. "We're banking on a guy with a damn mullet?"

"Yep." Livy kept bashing at the end of the pipe. She didn't elaborate any further.

They continued to work for several minutes more.

Cam stopped and looked at his mom. He had a smirk on his face, curiously inappropriate considering the circumstances. "'Like a women scorned.'"

Livy stopped, a blank look on her face. Then it brightened; she smiled and nodded.

Julian watched the interaction. "What?"

Cam turned his gaze to Julian. "'Hell hath no fury,'" he said, quoting the first part of the line. He paused and looked around. "This is overkill. You're trying to kill 'em, aren't you?"

Livy nodded.

"Still not following," said Julian.

"Remember Oklahoma City?" said Cam. "McVeigh used fertilizer––ammonium nitrate––with fuel oil, to give himself more bang for the buck. Nitrogen gas is what's produced––what explodes. Like the stuff used to make airbags deploy. The passenger-side airbag packs enough power to kill a person." Cam stopped and angled the fertilizer bag so he could read the ingredient label. "With this stuff, the battery, and the ether in the engine cleaner, she'll generate a blast sixty times that. Not much fire. That'll give us a hole in the wall. Done deal."

"But…" said Julian.

"Mix magnesium with oxygen,you get a very hot, bright flame. You blow up ammonium nitrate at a thousand degrees instead of two hundred degrees and you'll get maybe five times the bang. Like McVeigh. Plus fire. Mixed with the shit the reverend is dumping on the floor upstairs…" Cam looked at his mom. "Like I said, watch out for a women scorned."

Julian held up the pipe. "Magnesium?"

"Alloy," said Livy. "Best I could do on short notice."

"No matches," said Julian.

Cam pulled the Sig out of his pocket.

"That'll do," said Julian, smiling.

"Think you can get a bullet close to the end of that pipe from thirty feet?" asked Livy.

"We'll see, won't we?"

"What about us?" said Julian.

Livy peered up from her work without expression. Then she gazed at Cam with a look only a mother could give her child.

"She's not suicidal," said Cam. "She'll try to aim the blast with the filing cabinets."

They looked at one another. Julian nodded. Cam nodded. Sometimes words weren't necessary.

Creases appeared on Livy's forehead and around her mouth. "Julian, take over for me."

She scraped the little bits of metal into a cup then grabbed a hammer and an awl, plus a couple of screwdrivers. About two inches from the top of the metal box, she used the awl to poke a hole. She made it bigger with the screwdrivers, until the one-inch-wide bike-frame tube fit through it. Then Livy pulled it out and stood it upright in the vise. From a faded plastic spackling container, she drew out some white glop on her right index finger and plugged up one end of the tube. She turned it over and retightened the vise.

"Julian, fillings." Livy extended her hand, not taking her eyes off the pipe.

He scooped them in his hand and dumped them in the cup. She halved Cam's rust pile and poured half in with the bike scrapings, mixed them, then poured the mixture into the pipe. She worked with impressive dexterity, like she had done it thousands of times. Julian made a mental note not to upset her before her next period.

The smell of gasoline permeated the crypt. The cleric's intent was clear––to create fear in the enemy. The upstairs door opened; the baritone cleared his throat.

"Julian."

Julian remained silent. Livy continued to work. She poured the rest of the rust into the battery then replaced the caps. She shoved the filing-filled pipe snuggly against the carburetor cleaner, which was nested in the fertilizer, tight against the battery. The end of the pipe protruded two inches out of the hole in the bucket.

"Julian, it's three o'clock in the morning. I'm tired. I'd like to see the case."

Livy indicated to Cam that she needed help carrying the bomb. Moments later, they had it nudged up against the brick wall.

"What are my choices?" Julian yelled back to the preacher.

"Very few."

Livy and Cam were back at his side. He whispered. "What's the plan?"

Livy held up one finger. "One minute."

"You sure this will work?"

"Hell, no."

Julian shook his head and offered a nervous half smile. "Why should I give it to you?" he yelled back at the cleric.

"Slow death or fast death––your choice."

Julian looked at Cam and pointed to the filing cabinets. "Give me a minute to think." Ten seconds later, he announced, "We're coming up. I'm putting the gun on the stairs." He laid the empty Wilson Combat on the fifth step from the bottom then grabbed the flashlight off the worktable and gave a chin nod to Cam. "Cabinets are in the way."

Julian and Livy squeezed behind the remaining filing cabinet. Cam lay on the ground and snaked through their legs. He emptied the first two bullets out of the magazine and then popped them back in and replaced it in the handle of the Sig. Cam draped his arm around the far corner of the cabinet, partially under the workbench. He rested the barrel of the gun on a staple box. With his hand steady, he took aim.

"Julian, I'm waiting." There was a pause. "You have no place to go," said the preacher.

"OK, OK," said Julian. "We're coming. Let me get the case."

CHAPTER FORTY-SEVEN

C am pulled the trigger. The firing pin rammed home. The explosion, magnified horrifically in the cavern, reverberated through Julian's head. He looked up at gray metal and noxious smoke; to his side lay bricks and mortar. The ceiling beams creaked a worrisome sigh. Julian felt a hot blast of air on his neck; he tipped his chin and stared straight ahead. Surreal was the conflagration. Scattering bursts of crimson filled the far end of the basement. Fiery streamers shot across the span, and smoke coiled up through a flaming breach in the ceiling. A section of Cooper's desk sputtered with flames next to the stairs. A gasoline-fed holocaust roared above them. His eyes fastened onto a jagged hole where the brick wall used to be.

"Livy?"

"I'm OK."

"Cam?"

The pressure on his chest lessened. The cabinet levitated over him then crashed down on the refuse-strewn floor. Julian looked up at his son.

"Nice shot."

Cam coughed and waved away the smoke with his right hand; he held a hammer in the other. "Old wood. Ceiling's ready to go."

He extended a hand and helped Julian to his feet, who, in turn, pulled up Livy. Julian grabbed the case and a flashlight and then steered through the carnage. The haze changed to thick, deadly smoke, and tendrils of flame shot down the stairs. A pile of stones partially filled a ragged portal in the brick wall. On the other side, an inky black void. A horrible odor spewed from the murk. Julian dodged the flames and squatted over the bricks, tossing them aside, one after another. Cam and Livy joined in the frantic dig. Their eyes watered; their breathing was labored. The blaze feasted on the ceiling, which creaked louder and hinted at collapse.

Julian went through the gap, flashlight first. Livy, then Cam, followed. Julian panned the room—something the size of a walk-in closet. A wood-frame door filled the opposite wall and was pitted with divots and embedded stone. On the floor, human remains lay bloated, eviscerated, and partially covered with brick and concrete. A pool of putrefaction surrounded the carcass. The smell was overwhelming and easily seeped through the thin cotton of the shirts covering their faces.

"The real Agnes," yelled Julian.

He spun around and tried the door. It was locked. Cam stepped in with the hammer. They were through the rotted wood in seconds. Fifteen narrow wooden steps led down to a landing. Then, they came to the same thing again, with more stairs and another door. Cam bashed the thick timber door and then made two strikes against the lock. It popped open to a large cavern, which was black and soggy. Julian hesitated then stepped onto a wooden platform. The first plank, frayed by time and eaten by decay, gave way. He lunged forward, twirled, and then made a desperate wave at the doorframe. Cam blindly reached out, clutched onto Julian's arm, and worked him back to the doorway. The case landed with a thud somewhere below; the light shattered and died. The entirety of the rotted structure crumbled down around the case.

Then, there was absolute blackness. It was spooky dark––are-my-eyes-open dark––like in the rat cellar. A hodgepodge of smells––the putrid odor of death and the pernicious smoke––slowly melded with the dank stench of rotted wood. The conflagration above them made an odious racket. This wasn't a crackling fire that a person might cozy up to on a snowy January day. It sounded mechanical, like a brutal machine. Julian reclined, his body taut, his breathing heavy, and his brow cool with sweat.

Nobody spoke for the first minute.

"How far down are we?" Cam finally asked.

"No clue," said Julian, sitting up, his voice steady with manufactured calm.

"Which way?" said Livy. Her labored voice echoed in the cavern. She pulled her robe tighter.

"Not much choice," said Julian. "The parish house will end up in the cellar. It'll probably be months before they clear all the bricks away."

"Did you see what was down there?" asked Livy.

"A glimpse. Bedrock. Wooden beam supports. Stone."

"How far down?" asked Cam.

"Not short. Ankle-breaking height. Ten feet. Fifteen feet."

They all knew fifteen feet would make their decision irrevocable. Ten feet, maybe not.

"We're talking about a hundred-and-thirty-year-old tunnel under a hundred years of Back Bay development," said Livy. "Utilities. The *T*."

The hum of the inferno toyed with their minds.

"Don't know," said Julian. "What do you think, Cam?'

"Any rats?"

Julian turned in the direction of his son's voice. "You afraid of rats too?"

"Come on. Hardly. Rats wouldn't crawl into a pit. This is supposed to go to the Charles, right?"

"No rats. But I was trying not to die, so I didn't notice."

"I say we go forward," said Cam. "The smoke is getting stronger, but it shouldn't be—heat rises. There's a draft. The tunnel has to go somewhere."

Very disorienting and frightening was absolute darkness. Fear of the wrong decision kept them from making any decision. Millions of tons of earth loomed above them. No one would know they were missing for months, maybe ever. Julian held his cell phone up as a light source and then reached over the deck. A hunk of the plank remained attached; it was rough, worn by time, and covered with a thin layer of dew or algae. He found a dime-sized pebble embedded at its edge, where it abutted against the doorframe. He tossed it over. Any noise the pebble might have made died immediately in a throaty boom from above—something they both felt and heard. A few moments later, a gush of smoky air rushed by.

"We're buried alive," said Livy.

CHAPTER FORTY-EIGHT

TUNNEL UNDERNEATH BACK BAY
Tuesday, September 11, 2001, 3:30 a.m.

The echo from the collapse of the parish house faded. The smoke, unseen, burned their eyes and offered a tangible hint of their circumstance. No one moved for fear that the slightest motion would initiate the decisive event.

"How far do you think it is…the Charles?" said Cam.

"Can't be too far. They carried drunks," said Julian.

"Probably in wheelbarrows," said Livy.

"Did you ever see any openings on the river?" asked Cam.

"No," said Julian. "Rowed it a million times. I remember seeing metal grates. No idea what they cover."

They stayed quiet another minute. The air cleared slightly, but the din, despite the collapse, persisted and even seemed louder. Perhaps the darkness made their hearing more acute.

Julian spoke. "Livy, I'll toss my shoes up here for you. Cam, you come last."

Decision made.

Julian rolled over onto his stomach. The wood felt cool and slimy He slinked back a few inches at a time until he hung by his fingers. He waited a beat then let go; with his feet wide, he relaxed and let gravity be gravity. The landing was abrupt, teeth chattering. The littered ground was packed mud, cold and wet. His head slammed against rotted lumber.

"Julian? Julian?" said Livy.

He did a quick assessment. "I'm OK. It's about fifteen feet." He stood up and brushed himself off. "Give me a sec."

Julian clicked open his phone and then turned and felt his way through the void. Inch-long steps brought him to a tunnel entrance. It was five feet high and surprisingly wide, maybe seven feet. All brick and stone, old and irregular. A labor of love crafted by someone a long time ago. An effort had been made to maintain it, at least for a while. Cement was layered over more cement, old over older. Every age had its defining contraband, whether it was sailors, slaves, immigrants, weapons, alcohol, or drugs. He turned and worked his way back to the ledge.

Five minutes later, they were together. Julian got down on his hands and knees to probe the pile of rotted wood for the case and the flashlight. He found both. The flashlight would not be a factor. Julian insisted Livy keep the shoes; he took her bright red, silly socks in return. Single file and stooped, they inched forward through the tunnel; people were shorter back then. The tunnel angled down slightly. The walls were slick with oozing water and smothered in years of debris. Initially the water was sole high. It quickly became ankle high over an equally thick layer of sloppy goop. Julian's legs felt like lead in the quagmire; each step was taken with deliberation. At the end of their first hundred yards, tired and winded, he stooped down to feel the water.

"What?" asked Cam.

"Want the good news or bad news?" Julian stood up.

"The good news," said Cam.

"The water is moving, not stagnant."

They continued forward. Within another fifty yards, the water was to their knees.

"My battery is about to die. Cam, your phone."

Cam handed it to him. "How about the bad news?"

"It's getting deeper," said Julian, stating the obvious.

"We aren't going down anymore," said Cam.

"The tunnel has to be blocked."

"It rained last night," said Cam. "Hard."

They trudged on. The condition of the walls deteriorated. Evidence of the previous night's rain arched out from cracks in the cement. The water tugged at Julian's legs. A chill coursed through his body. The dark made it difficult not to think about being buried alive—his childhood nightmare. How many tons of earth and buildings were layered over him? There was no way out. No way to be rescued. No one would ever miss him. He'd be gone forever. He tried to banish the thought. The water was now chest high; two feet separated the surface of the water and the top of the tunnel.

"The current, it's so strong," said Livy.

Julian could hear her teeth chattering and his own.

"How far do you think we've gone?" asked Julian. He stopped and planted his legs to keep steady.

"Maybe a half mile," said Cam.

"Head back?" said Julian.

"To what?"

Julian paused. "Maybe life. There may be some way to scale a sheer fifteen-foot wall. Old boards. Rocks."

Neither Livy nor Cam said anything.

"I'm getting really cold," said Julian. "And tired. To get back we'll be going against the current. The tunnel has to be collapsed ahead. Something we may not be able get through."

"There has to be holes," said Cam.

Julian elected not to pose the next question. They kept going. The buoyancy of the water made the case lighter. He kept the phone near the apex of the tunnel. He let the current carry him along; his feet merely skimmed over the refuse and mud. Twenty seconds later, the cacophony of rushing water jacked up around them. Julian turned and righted himself. The water was three inches over his nipples—only twelve inches of clearance now. He jammed his leg into the side of the tunnel then spun around backward, off balance and under the water. After one life-altering second, his head exploded above the surface and into the ceiling.

"Cam! Livy!"

"Here," said Cam.

Julian coiled around. The undercurrent reached with frosted fingers and yanked him forward. His left thumb happened into a crack; he slowed. Cam slammed into his back, and then Livy slammed into Cam. The phone, perched in Julian's tenuous hold, burst out into the pitch-dark air like a slippery bar of soap and disappeared into the pitch-black water.

The darkness was once again total. The sarcophagus offered twelve inches of air. Water swirled at his chin. Julian's breath, in terror-shortened gasps, was muted by the crushing sound of water reverberating though the subterranean channel. Julian jammed his legs into the wall for a third time. His fingers clawed at the slimy vertical. The water torqued and twisted at his legs with a corkscrewing surge of power. At what seemed like the last moment, he stopped himself. A wall of water slammed into his back, then Cam, then Livy. Panicked breaths came in fits and starts from all three.

"Cam!" Julian yelled, even though his son was smashed up against him. "You secure?"

"I'm…good." Cam struggled for air.

Julian angled his head up to talk as angry foam churned at his neck. His body burned with cold. "I'm goin'…forward. Stay here."

The current's fists wrapped around his legs and assaulted his back. He couldn't feel his feet or fingers or find the notches in the wall; desperation etched the stone. There was only six inches of clearance. His ears slipped into the watery tumult, and the nearly total silence throttled his fear to an even higher level. The torrent rested away any semblance of control he thought he had. He put his right arm in front to brace for the blow he knew would come. Seconds later, a rock dodged under his arm and careened into his chest; pain exploded through a million nerve tendrils. His last breath gushed from his throat as his body melted into stone. A waterwall lanced against his back and crushed his chest up against the rocks. Chimerical blobs bounced in the dark: death would be next.

A random surge of underwater turbulence lifted his foot onto a brick perpendicular to the wall. He pushed up and angled his body off the flange. With his body sideways to the torrent, his chest moved out in the vacuum. His lips kissed the ceiling. The apparitions cleared, and he steadied himself and got a foothold. Julian willed himself to gain control. His panic dissipated.

"Cam!" This time he yelled all out.

"Here."

"You OK?"

"We're good."

"There's a wall of rocks. Twenty yards." Julian paused. "Sticks…maybe… from…the river. We must be close."

The unremitting torrents pummeled his body. With feeble strokes, he probed the earthen works. The tiny aquatic vacuums sucked his hands into the defects of the wall like a drain in a bathtub. The ceiling was solid. The collapse had to come from the side. With his body anesthetized by the cold, he couldn't perceive changes in the surge. After one long minute, his back hit the side of the tunnel. The angle at the ceiling gave him only four inches of breathing room. *Water's rising.* A fresh wave of panic layered over Julian's fear. He sucked in three deep breaths. With his left arm at maximum stretch toward the middle, he drew it down, back and forth, groping for openings. Nothing. He did the same with his feet. The socks were shredded, numb skin against brick. Nothing. He reached behind him. Nothing. Wrong side. An inch at a time, he started back toward the middle. He had to move six feet; his torso and legs were flogged with every step. His ears broke above the surface.

"Julian?" Cam sounded panicked.

"What?"

"I've been calling."

"Deeper water…looking for a hole."

Just left of midline, he found the spot––a high-flow gap, maybe eighteen inches top to bottom and side to side. Angled stone and sticks bridged the top; debris was smashed tightly into the ceiling. After a couple deep breaths, he lowered his shoulder and reached in; the jet stream nearly sucked his arm off. The water inched higher, forcing precious seconds out of the tunnel.

"Cam!"

"What."

"Found… a…hole. Not sure how…how…long. Send Livy…angle left… then wait."

"Got it…left…wait."

Julian reached down and pulled a single brick up out of the swirl and then pitched it to the other side.

"Ready," called Cam. "Here comes Mom."

"Go."

Julian held out his left arm and angled his left leg from his body. Blinded, he waited.

"Livy, talk to me."

"Here…here…here."

She slammed into him, arms extended. Julian slowed her with his legs then cupped her in his free arm. They bumped heads. Her breathing came in labored gasps. Her robe swirled in the churn. Goose bumps covered her thin frame. She shook in his arm, so he held her close.

"Got her…ready…left…talk to me.

There was a pause.

"Here…here…here," echoed Cam, as he charged toward them.

Cam banged into two outstretched arms then racked into the wall. His head dipped below the surface. He jerked up, coughing, and banged his head into stone. Julian wrapped his arm around Cam's chest. The coughing lasted for thirty seconds.

"You good?" asked Julian.

"Let's do it…my ass is about…to freeze…off," said Cam.

"Livy, you'll have to take off…your robe. Give me…the tie." He paused and took a couple breaths. "The water…still rising. We've gotta go now. Need…shoes."

While he waited, he reached back into the hole found another loose brick and yanked it out. Livy passed him a shoe. Julian turned sideways and wedged himself into a steady position. He worked the laces out then slipped the shoe on, then repeated the same with the other. He tied the shoestrings together, then to the robe's tie. He handed the makeshift rope to Cam who secured it to his wrist.

"Hold on…to…my neck," said Julian. "If I…bang your arm, let go. If I pull on the string…pull me back. If the string goes…limp, wait ten seconds… you come. Got it?"

"Got it," Cam said.

Julian grabbed Cam's hand one last time. He held it tight then let go and prepared. The water was higher still––only a two-inch clearance. It swirled around them like an amped-up Jacuzzi; their lips caressed the ceiling. They'd be dead in minutes. He edged to the hole and readied himself. He sucked in three good breaths then counted to five and went feet first into the shoot.

The vise clamped down immediately; the churn crushed his legs. He was in hell. Thrashed and battered and disoriented, he couldn't tell up from down. His feet were solid against something. The surge folded him over a log inside the opening––an impossible position. With his leverage lost, he couldn't push. He had seconds. He felt Cam dip down next to him and plant his feet solidly on the blockade next to his chest. Cam's hands moved from his neck and into his armpits then tightened. Julian's body straightened, and he unleashed an absolutely brutal flurry of kicks against the rocks and sticks. Something in the tunnel gave and then broke away. This moved him a few inches deeper into the subterranean rapids. The pain in his chest and legs was now beyond anything he had ever known. More kicks came with reckless abandon. His lungs shuttered from the pressure as his life force ebbed into oblivion. The chimerical blobs reappeared. His kicks petered out to pathetic impersonations of the first. He felt more sticks give way. More bricks moved. The water stampeded faster through the hole, further compressing his body into the lethal vortex. Cam's hold was tenuous, nearly lost. Julian wanted to scream. Thoughts of his own suffocation nipped at his brain and grabbed at his throat. He knew it was now or never, so he banged Cam's arm. Julian's knees flexed and, like an air hammer, exploded out against the debris. He kicked once then twice. Apparitions reappeared and took form. A cold, white horizon crept in from the edge of his vision, pushing the ghosts away. He couldn't do it. His legs crumpled further into the abyss. His last recollection was a huge weight on his back compressing him even further. Then there was nothing.

CHAPTER FORTY-NINE

TUNNEL UNDERNEATH BACK BAY
Tuesday, September 11, 2001, 4:10 a.m.

A critical mass was reached. The balance tipped.

With the extra weight, the remaining bricks and glop and goo flushed out into a one-foot-deep stream on the other side of the impasse. Julian followed, with Cam riding his back. Cam bolted up, immediately gasping for air, nearly striking his head on the ceiling for a third time. He yanked Julian, whose head was slumped forward, to a sitting position. Cam adjusted his grip around Julian's chest then yanked up once and then twice, with enough force to break a rib.

Julian coughed and then took a huge inhalation. After another, his head was even with the horizontal, sucking in the soggy air. He stood up, bent over, trying to obliterate the air hunger and scatter the ghosts. Livy fired down the rapids and clipped him full force. He let out a yelp as he slammed back onto her; they skidded to a halt ten feet away.

"Mom?" yelled Cam.

"Here, up here."

Cam inched forward like a blind man until he stumbled and fell onto the heap. The water was a foot deep, but rising. Bricks and cement smashed into their backs, one then another, then three or four at a time. Small pieces and larger chunks. They scooted out of the way.

"I think the dam's going to blow," said Julian, finally gaining his bearing.

With the darkness absolute, instinct took over. They headed in the direction of the icy current, moving in double time, wildly swinging their arms. The force of the water accelerated, along with the debris. After twenty yards, a ripping sound echoed from behind them. Twenty seconds later, a surge of water and debris knocked them off their feet and swept them forward like leaves in a storm. They righted themselves then attempted a sprint. The water was at knee level, and their bodies were spent; they ran in a syrupy quagmire. Fifty yards later, Julian thought he saw something and stopped. He jammed his arm out and halted Livy and Cam. All three bent over with their hands on their knees, sucking in the dank air. A chorus of gasps echoed through the chamber.

"Light!" said Cam.

Confirmed.

Ninety feet later, they darted head-on into a solid cement wall. They looked up through a chimney-like, four-foot-by-five-foot passage. Fresh air and fingers of moonlight filtered through the steel bars above. Julian could see Cam and Livy's faces illuminate with smiles, but he focused on the wall. Ten feet up, rungs of K-bar poked out of the side every eighteen inches.

The water bunched up around their legs. Within moments, it was nipping at their waists. Another crash echoed from the blackness.

"Dam's crumbling!" Julian leaned up against the wall, hands forward, feet spread apart---C-shaped. "Cam! On my back. Now."

Cam hopped up, placing his hands on Julian's shoulders and his knees into Julian's back. In one continuous motion, he flexed the bulk of his right thigh muscle and launched himself upward toward the first rung: it was all or nothing. At maximum reach, his left hand banged into the mottled steel, and he clamped down; his body swung forward, and his knees came full force into the cement. He cringed, waited for the pain to melt away, and then crawled up the wall. Cam readied himself on the rung and reached down. Julian cupped his hand. Livy rammed her foot onto the spot. She was light. Julian heaved, and Cam pulled. She grabbed onto the rung then mounted the wall around Cam to the second step. Before Julian could make an attempt to mount the vertical, a rock slammed into his leg, and he collapsed into the churn.

"Go," yelled Julian. "The grate. You need to get through the grate."

"After we get you."

Julian worked himself to the upright; the new slash on his leg felt like fire in the grunge. "I'll ride the swell. It's coming."

Cam reached down. "Grab my arm."

"I can't. Go."

"No chance. They're missiles."

Just then a tidal wave of water slammed Julian against the wall.

It wasn't meant to be.

One final thunderous *whoop* echoed through the tunnel. He had seconds before the surge exploded out of the opening with a final salvo of lethal stones.

Julian thought of what could have been. *So close.* He angled sideways to make himself smaller or maybe to find that thin line to the other side––if there was another side. He thought of the lost papyrus. *This is it.* The moonlight slicing through the grate drew his attention to Cam and Livy. *They won't make it either.* The noise grew louder.

Just then the shoestrings attached to Cam's wrist brushed across Julian's arm.

"The rope!" yelled Julian.

Cam's hands were polished slick with a mix of dirty water and grit. Seconds passed. The deadly slurry rumbled toward Julian. He squinted into the void and then at Cam and then back into the void. His feet danced an edgy jive. He sensed the subtle ebbing of the water away from his body, so he drew his arms up around his head.

"Now!"

Julian jerked around and squared himself to the wall, grabbed the makeshift lifeline, and leaned back. It took all his strength to overcome gravity's force and creep one step at a time up the cement vertical. He only had to go ten feet; it might as well have been a mile. Water lashed at his back. The rush of tumbling water and bricks reverberated out of the tunnel. He took another step then another. He felt a knot slip, so he stopped and steadied himself. The burn in his hands sent shocks of pain to his head. His arms felt like dead slugs. Cam's hand brushed against him then fixed onto his hand. One heave and Julian reached the step. Another heave and his foot was planted next to Cam's. The final surge struck. A seismic tremor reverberated through the wall. Julian reached around to the back of his belt and found the thick screwdriver still woven into his pant loop.

"Go."

Cam worked his way past Livy and shot up the steps. The cement chimney ballooned out to form a eight-foot-by-six-foot nest for the grate. The bars were rusted with age, maybe fifty or sixty years worth. Or, possibly the steel was a child of Roosevelt's Federal Works Agency, seventy years worth of rust. A padlock secured the outside. Julian climbed around Livy and reached the steel bars about the time Cam finished rattling them.

"Solid," said Cam.

Julian peered down at the rising water. He grabbed the bars tight and shook. Nothing moved. "Damn." His eyes strained against the dark. "The bolt, buried in the cement. The one by your shoulder."

Cam offered a few wild jabs with the screwdriver. It glanced off the wall with hardly a scratch.

"Try another one." The urgency in Julian's voice ratcheted to a new level.

Cam stretched toward the other corner. Same result. The water churned at Livy's knees; she stood one rung below.

Over the next ten seconds, Julian scanned the grate for corrosion, bubbled paint, and cracks. The sound of swirling water grew louder and broke his concentration. He looked down. An eddy of water spun near Livy's waist. His eyes jerked up and scanned the steel bars yet again. Back and forth, double time. *Slow down. Think.*

His gaze finally settled on the door in the middle of the grate––small, maybe eighteen inches on a side. A single rusted bolt that ran parallel to the steel bars secured each hinge.

"Let me up."

Cam started down.

"Stay here," said Julian. They shared the same rung. Julian planted his left hand in the back of Cam's pants and clamped down.

"With both hands," yelled Julian, "lean out and wedge the screwdriver between the bolt and the grate. Then give it all you've got."

Cam secured the tool tight against the steel then wrenched down. It didn't budge. He backed up and adjusted the screwdriver. "Hang on."

Cam stretched out over the swirling caldron of black water. He lifted his feet; his body swung out, mechanically positioned directly under the bolt.

Two hundred pounds versus seventy-year-old oxidized steel. He waited. Still, nothing happened.

Julian followed Cam's eyes down. Livy angled her mouth up toward the grate; eddies ruffled her ears He couldn't see her eyes. She said nothing.

Cam moved his legs and hinted at a bounce. Still nothing. On the third bob, the bolt finally snapped. Cam dropped into the water and jetted feet first into the wall below. He regained his spot on the ladder then positioned the screwdriver as before.

Frantic hands scratched at Julian's belt––Livy's. He searched for Cam's eyes. "Now!"

Again, Cam swung out beneath the aged steel. He drew his knees up then fired them into the swirl. The whirlpool seized his legs; his body torqued to one side. His pants sunk low on his hips. Cam drew in a huge breath, yanked his knees up, and then fired a second thrust into the boil. The bolt securing the second hinge snapped. He pushed Julian's hands away from his belt, cut two perfect butterfly kicks through the black slurry, and at full extension, grabbed onto the steel grate.

Julian and Livy crowded onto the final step, jaws angled skyward.

Cam pulled himself up, his lips firm against the steel, then blasted the steel door with his right palm to jar it free. He forced the gate up and out of the way with his right arm as he hung by his left. A clang announced the collision of steel against the cement outside. He grabbed the edge of the orifice, swung out underneath, and then did an adrenalin-amped pull-up out of the death trap.

Julian grabbed the back of Livy's T-shirt and pushed her toward the opening. Cam straddled the hole, reached in, and pulled her straight up. Summoning every ounce of his strength, Julian used the grate like playground monkey bars and inched his way toward the opening. He was totally spent, and with the water bubbling around his mouth, Livy and Cam reached down and hauled him from the watery mausoleum.

Together they staggered ten feet up a shallow incline, a grassy area nestled on the bank of the Charles River. It was still dark. In the east, the horizon glowed with the first hint of the sunrise—a new dawn he'd thought he'd never see. The skyscrapers, outlined by a thin rim of ochre, pushed up against a sky that was layered more dark blue than black. A rope of gray smoke rose from a fire no more than a mile away, and a fading white moon hung in the western sky. The air was chilly. Julian took in two huge gulps of air. The sound of water rising through the steel grate and dropping off the cement edge produced a white noise that nearly lulled him to sleep. A repetitive clang, clang, clang woke him a few minutes later. He staggered to his feet and stumbled forward to the pit.

"What is it?" asked Cam, looking at him from his supine position.

Julian knelt down over the hole, stuck his arm full length into the pit, and pulled out the burnished gray case.

CHAPTER FIFTY

J ulian stood in front of Livy and Cam, who were sprawled on bank of the Charles River. The gray case bent the green grass at his feet. A streetlamp from Storrow Drive provided only faint light.

"Do I get a good-morning kiss?" asked Julian.

"Not on the lips," said Cam.

Sleepy-eyed, Livy looked up. She shivered in the penetrating night air. "Brush your teeth yet?"

Her smile hadn't changed in twenty-five years.

"Been busy."

"I'll let it slide this time."

Julian looked over at Cam. "You mind?"

"Damn. You've earned a hell of a lot more than that. Just don't make a lot of noise."

Julian sat down next to Livy then leaned over inches from her face until they were eye to eye. He had no quips, no jokes. He kissed her gently. There was no urgency. Her lips were a connection to emotions he hadn't felt in two decades. They shared the morning air in their single breath. After the kiss, he laid back and then reached for her hand, as he had done so many years ago.

Their fatigue was total. They lay for fifteen minutes, sleeping or thinking. No one spoke. Julian finally racked his body into the upright position and wandered to the edge of the Charles. Across the way, the golden dome of MIT appeared black in the dark sky. He looked east, then west, up and down the river. The waves lapped at his feet, tiny cousins to those in the tunnel. One thought nipped at his mind: *the cleric thinks I'm dead.*

Julian roused his family. Hungry, tired, and cold, they headed east. After a hundred yards, Julian found what he was searching for, the Charles River Boating Club shell rack. Using the screwdriver, he yanked the hinges out of the painted wood.

"Let's bust out one of these bad boys."

They were on the river heading west minutes later. Julian and Cam maneuvered the sleek craft close to the Storrow Drive shore, under the Harvard Bridge, then further. It was peaceful. He had spent many hours gliding up and down the river, sometimes on dark mornings. He loved watching the knife-like bow cut through the black mirror of the water's surface. Over the years, it had become his private place, a time to ponder life and purge the bad parts from his mind. He realized in the end, however, they never really left but just hid out behind an obscure gyrus in his brain, only to surface at a later period of vulnerability.

The three of them spoke very little. Livy sat low and braced herself against the cool air. They rounded Magazine Beach Park at a good clip. Julian and Cam worked well together. Julian aimed toward the River Street Bridge then went ashore near Riverside Press Park. He made a mental note to return the boat. They worked their way, on foot, east to Putnam Street. Halfway down the street, Julian removed the red socks, now rags, and handed them to Livy.

"Any way you can return 'em? One has a hole."

Livy managed a sleepy laugh as she eyed the shredded material. "No problem."

They passed Allston Street then Prince Street. The apartment was as they had left it. Cam held up the empty mayonnaise jar and flipped it to Julian. They shared a smile.

"Livy, you take the first shower. Cam and I will wrangle up some grub. Clothes are in the far bedroom. Karlie won't mind. They're your style, maybe twenty years ago."

Livy walked over and kissed Cam on the cheek and then gave a quick peck to Julian on the lips. Minutes later, she returned, rubbing her hair with a towel. She looked great. The long-sleeve T-shirt and the jeans stretched over every curve.

"A little tight, but not bad," she said. "Shower felt like a million dollars." She sniffed. "Smells great."

She helped herself to the scrambled eggs, toast, and cereal.

Twenty minutes later, they sat, quiet and content, around a circle of empty bowls and crumb-covered plates.

"Can anyone tell me why we're still alive?" asked Livy.

"Hard to know," said Julian. He paused. "Two weeks ago, I would've found an answer at Cooper's place."

Quiet settled over the table.

Julian grabbed the case and laid it on his lap. "I didn't think I'd ever get to this point. Not sure what to do."

He looked at Cam then Livy.

"What's the plan?" asked Cam.

"We've got some wiggle room. The reverend thinks we're dead," said Julian.

Livy put her arms on the adjacent chairs and leaned back. Her hair fluffed out, half-dry. She had no makeup on, the fine lines at the corners of her eyes were barely visible. She looked as fresh and beautiful as the first day he met her.

"We can't forget Jessie." Julian took his eyes off Livy and looked at Cam. "We could…but we can't."

"Did you see him?" Cam asked Livy. "Midforties. Solid. Think linebacker in high school and then add twenty years worth of beers. Looks a little like Nick Nolte."

"I didn't see anybody."

"Any idea where they stashed you?" asked Julian.

"No," said Livy. "They chloroformed me at the house. I woke up in a basement." Livy rose from the kitchen chair then moved over to the couch. She had to reposition the cushions that were strewn over the floor. In the process, she picked up the movie poster, *Big Problems*, but didn't comment. "That must be where Jessie is."

Julian thought for a moment. "How long was the car ride to the church?"

"Ten minutes, maybe less. No more."

"We can end this, now," said Julian. "Go to the *Globe*. Call the police. Done deal. We should end this now." He paused. "But if we do, Jessie dies."

Fatigue clouded their brains. Ideas were sparse.

"You aren't going to let Jessie die," Cam finally said. It was a statement, not a question.

Julian said nothing. He rose from the table and headed into the kitchen. "Coffee?"

"I'm spent," said Cam. "We're luckier than shit to be alive. We'd be crazy not to go to the *Globe*."

Julian returned with a pot, three cups, and some sugar. He sat down slowly, in no particular hurry. Cam noticed.

"You already have a plan, don't you?" said Cam.

"Cam, if we can save Jessie——"

"What if Phillips is dead?" asked Cam.

Julian considered Cam's question then continued. "You guys wouldn't even have to come, but we remain together until this is a done deal. We can't stay dead forever." Julian got only sleep-deprived stares back. "I think it could be a win-win at no risk."

"That sounds worrisome," said Cam.

Julian looked at Livy. "You think you could rally for a couple more hours, now? After that, we can sleep all we want." He took a huge gulp of coffee then stood. He looked at his watch. Tuesday, September 11, 2001, was six hours old

CHAPTER FIFTY-ONE

C
am and Julian showered and changed into spares that Julian had stored in Karlie's closet. They took Karlie's car. Forty minutes later, they pulled into the Logan International short-term parking.

"Which airline?" asked Julian. He looked at Cam in the backseat of the Honda.

"Your plan."

"Your airport."

"United. Concourse C. That's where I've been hanging out with Google's people. Gate twenty-seven."

Julian nodded. Minutes later, they stood at the United kiosk.

"We going somewhere?" asked Cam.

Julian reached for his still-wet wallet. He stopped midway and looked at Cam. "Our paraglider."

"Damn fancy paraglider," said Cam.

"Backup. We've got one shot," said Julian.

Julian handled the transaction for three tickets. They worked their way toward gate number twenty-six. They walked past Samuel Adams Boston

309

Brewhouse, and Dunkin' Donuts. They passed The Grove, which sold specialty nuts, and Bijoux Terner, which advertised quality accessories, then parked their weary bodies in a connected row of seats near the gate. Blue vinyl chairs, with burnished chrome, were connected to a square, Formica-topped table. Julian adjourned to a pay phone within eyeshot of Livy and Cam. He dialed the number included on the original ransom memo then waited two rings.

"Hey dickhead, this is your worst nightmare," said Julian. "I can't believe you're still alive."

There was silence at the other end, and then Reverend Philips spoke. "And you."

"Actually I'm not. I'm sitting here next to God. He tells me you are totally screwed." Julian laughed to himself.

"How did you––"

"I'm Harry Houdini. Shut up and listen; it's my quarter." Julian paused. "OK, you get one more try to get this right. But only if Jessie is alive and well."

There was another pause. Julian listened for the sound of wheels turning. Instead, he thought he heard the echo of urine striking the floor.

"He's still alive. Unharmed."

"Good for you. Listen. I have the papyrus, safe and sound. Maybe not so sound. I haven't looked. You can have it. All you have to do is bring Jessie to the airport. No one else. No rent-a-thugs. No half-thugs. No guns. Nothing. Just you and Jessie. I'm here until eight o'clock. Then I disappear. I'm really tired. I'm not in a good mood. If you don't show up, or you get caught in traffic, you're shit out of luck."

The preacher didn't respond immediately.

"You really have no choice," continued Julian. "You lost when we didn't die. By the way, did we kill any of your thugs with our little firecracker?"

"One."

"So sad. Anyway, if you decide you need to get your hair done or get your butt waxed, just look for me in the *Globe*."

"Which gate?"

"Concourse C. Gate twenty-six."

Julian hung up and wandered back to Livy and Cam. Livy was nearly asleep; Cam was wide-awake. Julian plopped down next to his son.

"He comin'?" asked Cam.

Julian nodded. "I think so." He looked straight ahead and clutched the case with his left hand.

"So, if he doesn't show, do we fly somewhere?"

"Maybe LA. I have connections. Protection."

They waited. Julian checked his watch several times. Livy dozed next to him.

"Curious," said Cam.

"What?" said Julian.

"See that guy over there with the gray sports coat, white shirt, and dark hair. Middle Easterner."

Julian nodded.

"And that guy, looks like his brother. White long-sleeve shirt."

Julian nodded again.

"I've seen them both. Here. Several times. Since June. Always sitting. Always watching. Never flying."

"So," said Julian, looking at his watch again. His foot bounced up and down.

In the background, the first boarding call for United Flight 175 echoed through the concourse. The guys Cam was observing stood up.

"Today they're flying," said Cam.

Julian turned toward Livy to roust her from her nap. Thirty yards down the concourse, he spied the preacher and Jessie. Julian scanned the area. Passengers gathered their belongings and headed for the gate. There were not many. No security was in sight, only bored airport personnel. He took his gaze outside. The tarmac basked in the sun; there was not a cloud in the sky. Evidence of the previous night's rain was all but gone. It was a beautiful day. Julian stood up. Cam followed.

The reverend stopped fifteen feet away. His tired eyes surveyed the area. Julian made eye contact with Jessie and got a nod and an upturn of the right side of his mouth.

"You OK, Jessie?" asked Julian. He didn't have to talk loudly.

"Threatened my granddaughter if I made trouble."

Julian walked halfway toward him and put the case upright on the marble floor. He reached into his pocket, removed a three-quarter-sized brass key and placed it on the case. He took a couple steps back and waited.

311

The reverend spoke, "That's it?"

"That's it."

The cleric pushed Jessie toward Julian. The preacher followed. When he got to the case, he grabbed the key then picked up the case. He sat down on the closest seat and worked the combination.

"I haven't checked it," said Julian. "Suspect it's in a million pieces. We had one hell of a night. You can't imagine. Well, maybe you can." Julian watched the cleric's arms work behind the case lid. "There should be pieces big enough to get authentication. But then again, I suspect ancient Greek documents aren't something you can get from Barnes and Noble."

Satisfied, the preacher closed the case's top and looked up. Relief registered through his fatigue. He rose then spun around to leave.

Julian spoke up. "Reverend, you really didn't think it would be that easy, did you?"

The reverend stopped and turned—a quarter turn. The kind of turn that says, "I'm not really stopping." He asked, "What else is there?"

"Our lives. You leave. We leave. Then there's an act of God, and we're dead." Julian shook his head.

The reverend returned a stony glare.

"You know, it's interesting to me how you get God to act every time you need some really nasty shit done."

"So."

"Just a little more information for you to chew on. I have enough evidence against you and your little short-shit helper to put you both away for a couple hundred years. But you would probably like that. Unfettered access to the guys. I can put your associate at the scene of Cooper's murder and Maxwell's murder. I can put you and your little prick friend at the parish house the night of Agnes's death. I have forensic evidence coming out the wazoo. The little guy will cop a plea the first chance he gets; he won't have a chance in hell when he gets to prison. That leaves you hanging. These are heinous crimes. Two old ladies. Two preachers. A cop. You're totally screwed. If you walk out of here, I make a call. Cops hate cop killers."

Julian looked around. "Here your thugs are as worthless as a limp dick on a wedding night. I really don't give a damn about what's in the case. It probably won't change anybody's mind anyway. I do give a damn about the fact you killed my very best friend and my brother. That bothers me a lot. A whole lot."

The reverend turned all the way around. He stood ten feet away, wearing the same black trench coat. His expression had lost its flavor. "You have my complete attention."

"You're asking yourself, is this guy bullshitting me? Like in that Clint Eastwood movie. Did he fire six shots or only five shots?" Julian held up his right hand, like a gun. "You can take your chances. Roll the dice." The intercom interrupted with the second boarding call for United Flight 175. Ten more people headed for the gate. "There is no statute of limitations for murder. But we're screwed too. An hour ago, we were sitting pretty. You thought we were dead. We had the artifact––our prime bargaining chip–– and a chance to put Dexion to a well-deserved death, forever. But, it's hard to keep up that charade. And you had Jessie. Couldn't let my buddy die."

"I'm still listening."

Julian reached in his pocket and pulled out a plane ticket.

The cleric looked at the ticket then at Julian. A blank expression layered over his fatigue. "What's that?"

"It admits one person, you, to that plane right there." Julian turned and pointed out the window. "All you have to do is walk over to that lady…" Julian turned and pointed again. "…give her the ticket, walk down the Jetway, and join the friendly skies. That gives us each a four-hour head start; time to get our respective shit together and decide on what's next. Hell, you could fake some illness…get them to stop in Denver." Julian paused and looked out at the plane. "We each have something hanging over the other––threat of mutual destruction. Anything happens to me or Livy or Cam or Jessie or Jessie's granddaughter or anybody I've ever known in my life––even Ms. Young, my second-grade teacher––then you go down. And vice versa. Win-win. All you have to do is get on the plane."

Julian looked at his watch. "Final boarding call is coming up."

The preacher glanced at the ticket, then the airline attendant, and then the case. His face was creased with indecision. Julian sat down in the chair and crossed his legs. A passenger, late for the flight, ran by.

"Not sure you have a whole lot to think about," said Julian. "We took your best shot and lived. Now you're screwed. This way, at least you save the many billions-of-dollars church empire. Isn't that what King Constantine had in mind when he had his little chitchat with Hosius of Cordova?" Julian put his hands together and clapped two times. "The conquering hero."

"Fair enough. I may be falling prey to your bluff. But I doubt it. You have proven to be astonishingly resourceful." Reverend Philips nodded, grabbed the ticket, and then headed for the Jetway.

"Your cell phone, too."

The cleric retrieved his phone and handed it to Julian then said, "Don't get too comfortable."

Julian, Cam, and Livy waited patiently by the window until the plane pulled away fourteen minutes later. United Airlines Flight 175, nonstop to Los Angeles, took off at exactly 8:14 a.m..

Minutes after that, Reverend Philips emerged from his area of concealment on the Jetway.

Julian, Cam, and Livy entered Fox Sports Skybox and Grill on the B Concourse for their second breakfast. Julian figured they had four hours of wiggle room, plenty of time. They found a spot in front of one the ten TV's, most showing football, golf, tennis, or soccer events. No bowling. No fishing.

"I can't believe he bought it," said Julian, after they sat down.

Thirty minutes later, as Julian readied to pay the check, he glanced up at a TV. The sports venues had vanished. Instead, the camera showed a wide shot of the Hudson River, with the twin towers of the World Trade Center in the background. Smoke poured from the upper stories of the one of the towers. In red, at the bottom of the screen, was indication that the Dow Jones futures were trading down 120 points. Julian walked over and asked the waitress to turn up the volume.

A crowd gathered. People eventually spilled out into the concourse. Everyone watched in silence. The announcer had no clue what was happening or if it was a small plane or a big plane. Flights were unaccounted for. Over the next eighteen minutes, confusion reigned. At 9:03, when a second plane plowed into tower number two, the South Tower, one thing became perfectly clear: everyone's life had forever changed. The silence in Concourse C was interrupted by sobs of anguish and groans of disbelief. The X-generation had their own I-remember-where-I-was-moment; the rest of the country had another.

Julian was drawn into the heartache. Then it dawned on him. He looked at Cam then Jessie. "Steel melts at fifteen hundred degrees centigrade." Julian said it in a sober, matter-of-fact way, with no segue. "Did you know that?"

Cam understood. He now knew the answer to the question. "With a Boeing 767 topped off with ten-thousand gallons of aviation fuel." He paused. "That's how you take down a building." Cam's face was a shade whiter than the beige tabletop. "Or two really big buildings."

Jessie also put two and two together. He remembered Nidal's agitation at the bar. "'It will be your Pearl Harbor.' That's what that guy said to the others. At Bukowski's. I remember."

Later the TV commentators suggested that United Flight 175 was feared to be one of the flights involved.

"I guess the world will never know now," said Cam.

"What?" said Julian, his attention affixed to the TV.

"*Q. Amphilochus.* The case. Gone forever."

"Yeah, gone."

Cam studied his father. "The world will never know."

"Yeah, never know."

By nine-thirty, Julian noticed National Guardsmen and local police patrolling the area. Concourse C choked with stranded passengers. They wandered like lost sheep, unsure what to do or where to go, each dragging their clumsy luggage at their sides.

The whole experience was unique to the twenty-first century: watching a major tragedy unfold on TV in real time. Everybody waited for the next shoe to drop––another building to explode, another plane to crash––while at the same time hoping for the cavalry to show up. The good guys couldn't lose, could they? Julian watched from a different perspective. He remembered the calculations in the margins of the Nidal's schematics—someone's attempt to figure out if the buildings would fall down and go boom. Sometime before ten, the South Tower seemed to disappear in a haze. It would be several minutes before the announcer stated the obvious––that the tower was no more. Julian realized it immediately. He looked at his watch. It was 9:58 a.m..

CHAPTER FIFTY-TWO

LOGAN INTERNATIONAL AIRPORT
EMBASSY SUITES
September 11, 2001, 12:00 p.m.

They continued their vigil at the nearby Embassy Suites. The TV announcer confirmed earlier speculation. United Flight 175 out of Boston's Logan International was the second jet to strike in New York City and was now melted into the flames that consumed the South Tower of the World Trade Center.

The rest of that day melted into the next. There were meals, restless sleep, muted conversations, and then more eating and more sleep. Julian and Livy stayed in the back part of the suite; Cam and Jessie stayed in the front.

Whether it was uncertainty over the fate of the country or themselves, the need for human contact finally overwhelmed Julian and Livy—sometime after the second meal. Perhaps they were simply trying to chase away their nightmares. It started as an innocent bump in the night. Accidental. First him then her. Julian noticed the return volley; it nudged him from the edge of sleep. He wrestled with indecision. He decided to put the ball back in her court with another touch, less subtle, but not egregious by any means. Nothing happened. He wrote off the first as a triviality and settled in to extend his siesta. A minute later, she nestled her back against him, fitting perfectly into the *C* he mapped out on his side of the bed. Awake enough by this time, he knew he was treading in dangerous waters. He considered the entire systolic and the diastolic of their relationship, from their engagement of twenty years ago to their most recent kiss. Her deceased husband, his brother. On the surface, the situation was nearly adulterous. *To hell with it.*

He reached around and placed his arm on her waist. And waited. She snuggled her pelvis into his. *Preliminary confirmation.* His hand floated to her breast and traced a pattern. She snuggled closer. *Final approval.* Julian rose up on his elbow to clear a spot on her neck then drew close with his lips. He draped his bare leg over hers: the fit, perfect. He felt a shiver.

In Julian's mind, the events of the day were as far away as could be. The events of twenty years earlier were at hand. Livy turned, openmouthed, and kissed Julian full on the lips, at first with a tremendous sense of urgency then slowly, deeply. Her passion was contagious, as it had been before; this he had forgotten and now remembered. Her body was tense. Then she relaxed and shared his breath and his body. She rose up and tugged off her T-shirt. Julian did the same, and then he melted in the softness of her breasts. He held her tight, savoring their intimacy. Neither spoke. Then he moved his mouth down to explore her body, here and there. There was no urgency. He explored further. A few minutes later, Livy cried out. But they didn't stop. On and on, back and forth. Then, they made love and ended in an exhausted tangle.

Sometime later, closer to morning, he was poked out of a solid sleep. Whispers led to tickles then to more. Afterward, she cried for all that had happened twenty years ago and recently—Maxwell's death and everything else. Julian didn't let go. He understood that sometimes there was an infinitesimal line that separated ecstasy and sorrow.

They slept again until the sound of the shower woke them. Julian looked at the clock; the small hand hung on the ten. He snuggled close. A few nips on her neck liberated more passion. When it was over, Livy straddled Julian. Her breast fell onto his chest. She played with the curls on his head. They joked. He caressed. She looked wonderful but tasted better.

"I love you," said Livy. "I don't think I ever stopped."

Then, she rose from the bed, wrapped herself in a towel, and scampered into the bathroom.

Wednesday's weather was as beautiful as Tuesday's. But the mood was foul as the nation tried to make sense of the previous day. While Livy, Cam, and Jessie ate breakfast, Julian toured the city, gathering remnants of evidence he and Cam had left scattered here and there, in their cars, the rector's office, and Livy's house. Unfortunately, his phone and the pictures he had taken were somewhere, probably with Jimmy Hoffa.

He secured an immediate audience with Detective Fred Ellis, an old friend of Maxwell's. Julian began his narrative at Cooper's crime scene. He led the detective every step of the way. He gave a detailed description of the dwarf, with the goober on his neck and a skanky tattoo, maybe a snake or a rope, on his left bicep. He gave the detective the reverend's cell phone. Julian assured the detective that the good reverend was dead and suggested that the dwarf might be the best bet to cop a plea and flush out the rest of the players, although he admitted it was only a hunch. Julian intimated that Detective Ellis might find the bodies of two old ladies, a young thug, and a gopher snake in the rubble that used to be the parish house. Detective Ellis informed Julian of FBI speculation that a terrorist group calling themselves al-Qaeda might be responsible for the World Trade Center attack and might have set the explosion at the church as a diversionary measure. Apparently, both jets that hit the World Trade Center had taken off from Logan International. Julian assured him that was not the case. The detective was appreciative to get the police evidence back. Julian apologized for the delay. There was a question about a dried pool of blood in the north transept of Trinity Church. Julian feigned ignorance. He elected not to mention Cam's excellence at marksmanship, nor Livy's keen talents in bomb construction. Regarding the second issue, Julian figured Fred could get together with MacGyver and compare notes. Julian signed the affidavit and was on his way.

Amazingly enough, the Sig hadn't fallen out of Cam's pocket during the tumultuous journey through the tunnel. Julian had it stashed underneath the front seat of Karlie's Honda. He took fifteen minutes to score a new cell phone at a Cingular shop in a strip mall then called Detective Ellis to give him the number. By one thirty, he was back at the Embassy Suites. Livy and Cam waited. Jessie was gone; he had departed in a cab to his brother's house in Charlestown. Cam reported Jessie would be back in touch about Julian filling in at shortstop the following weekend.

By two thirty, Cam and his girlfriend, Bailey, Julian, and Livy were stretched out by the lagoon at the Public Garden. The sun fell from its apex.

The buzz of yellow jackets surrounded a nearby trash bin. Bailey asked why their legs looked like bruised tomatoes, although she didn't use those exact words. With this prompt, it was impossible for Cam to resist a chronicle of his deeds of valor. The two most important women in his life seemed to enjoy the tale and probably suspected aggrandizement through hyperbole. Julian could have given testimony that in fact there was none. But he didn't. They enjoyed the warmth of the sun and each other's company and joked with no limits on bad taste. At three fifteen, Julian received a call from Detective Ellis, who confirmed Julian's suspicion that the dwarf was indeed a squealer. And that he, the dwarf, had received a local call from the Reverend Philips only thirty minutes earlier. He assured Julian that all known suspects, including the good reverend, would most likely be in custody within the hour. A sting operation had been formulated; apparently the reverend sounded very interested in meeting with the dwarf in a secluded spot. He added that a squad car would be dispatched to the park until then.

As soon as he hung up, Julian checked his Sig again and then walked to the edge of the lagoon. Cam looked at Livy and mouthed, "What." She mouthed back, "Let him be." After several minutes, Cam excused himself and walked over to his dad.

"Hey," said Cam, startling Julian.

"Hey."

A moment of awkwardness settled between the two.

"What's up?" asked Cam.

"Just chillin'."

"Want to talk?"

Julian sat down at the water's edge, picked up some small pebbles, and then pitched them one at a time into the water. Cam joined him on the grass. They watched the ripples move out in concentric circles. Cam pitched a bigger stone. His ripples moved out and collided with Julian's.

"What's it all mean?" asked Julian.

"What?"

"Everything. Reverend Philips. What happened in New York."

"Religious wackos, all."

Julian stood and skipped a stone across the water. A quintuple. He turned to look at his son. "Tell me, what motivates a person to fly a jet full of people into a goddamn building? Or electrocute an innocent little old lady?"

Cam had no answer and indicated so with his eyes.

Julian craned around, shoved his hand in his pockets, and stood peering into the water, for solace or answers. Cam glanced back at Livy, concern on his face.

"Maybe Macbeth had the answer," said Cam to break the unnerving silence.

Julian shared an empty gaze. "The Scottish king or Shakespeare's version?"

"Shakespeare's. 'Life is a tale told by an idiot, full of sound and fury––'"

"…and 'signifying nothing,'" finished Julian.

After a few moments of silence, without warning, Julian slipped off his shirt and handed it to Cam. Startled, Cam jerked around and looked at Livy again. Her forehead furrowed with concern. She rose to her feet.

Julian reached into his pockets and pulled out his wallet and gave it to Cam. He did the same with his keys and the Sig. He sat down and picked off his right shoe and sock.

"What's going on?" Livy approached him from behind. She put her hands on his shoulders.

Julian brought his left foot up and repeated the task.

"Julian," said Livy. "Talk to me."

"Just need to take care of some business," said Julian. "Cam, keep the gun handy." Julian let them know that the Reverend Phillips had apparently missed his flight and, consequently, was still alive.

Julian headed into the lagoon. The water seemed warmer than before, but not by much.

Cam reached out to stop him. Livy grabbed her son's arm and pulled it back. "He's fine," she mouthed.

Julian continued, one tentative step at a time. Soon he climbed onto the island using the same branch as before. It was easier during the day. He stooped down for a moment to see if anyone was paying attention. The squirrel feeders hadn't noticed. The shovel was in plain sight. He grabbed it and rifled through the loose dirt.

He was back on shore ten minutes later.

"It makes sense now," said Cam. He reached out to grab a rectangular twelve-inch plastic container from his dad.

"What?" Julian dried his chest and arms; Livy dried his back.

"Your plan at the airport didn't make sense before. Too many holes." Cam paused. "And…"

Julian looked up expectantly while he put his socks and shoes on.

"You never once opened the case while we had it," said Cam. "Curious was your lack of curiosity."

"Remember I told you Reverend Toulukinopolis said there were six things." Julian broke into a grin then reached up and gave Cam a high five. "That night on the island I saw two separate containers inside the case; I was certain the preacher didn't know about Alexander the Great's copy of the *Iliad*. All Greek to him." Julian chuckled to himself.

Dressed, he carried the opaque case over to the tree.

Livy put her arms around his neck and kissed him. Not casual. Not serious. "Nice."

CHAPTER FIFTY-THREE

PUBLIC GARDEN, BACK BAY
Wednesday, September 12, 2001, 3:50 p.m.

Julian eased down next to a tree. A minute later, he had *Amphilochus* out of the plastic case and on his lap. The leather was stiff with time; its surface was friable in his hands. It was dirty beige or maybe a tad darker. Various shades of black, amorphous globs corrupted the cover.

"Give me a moment," said Julian.

Julian's focus became one. He smelled it and then caressed it before, with the softest touch, he opened the cover and turned the first page. Then he turned another page and then many after that. A minute became an hour then longer. Livy, Bailey, and Cam moved aside, to stand guard and allow him to savor the relic. Julian studied each page with a keen eye. He referred back to previous pages, back and forth, until he was done. He looked around, disoriented, forgetful of where he was or whom he was with. The sun flirted with the treetops. He spied Livy under the willow tree that he and Cam had hidden under just two nights before. Carefully, he placed the document back in the case then walked to the willow.

With reticence, he stepped into the sheltered area, like he was arriving late to a meeting. "Sorry."

Cam looked up. "Well?"

"It is wonderful." He sounded different; without knowing it, he had morphed into *Professor* St. Laurent. "A truly magnificent work. A Greek tragedy in the finest tradition. It's short, only eight or nine thousand words I suspect. Amphilochus and Alcmaeon are twins…one lives…one dies and then comes back to enlighten." He looked at Cam. "If only…" He reconsidered. "Two thousand years has added resonance to the work. It's a crucial document, which most certainly represents *Q*. And it was written four hundred and fifty years before the birth of Christ." Julian stopped to replay it in his mind. "The beatitudes, the Sermon on the Mount, they are all there."

He stopped talking and caressed the top of the case.

"So, what now?" said Cam.

The creases on Julian's face deepened; the luster in his eyes diminished. "Dexion or religious extremists, in the name of the almighty dollar or Allah…it's all the same!" Then, in a disquieting whisper, he repeated, "It's all the same." He paused. "Different agendas, but the same result: innocent people murdered by zealots in the name of religion." He looked at Livy and Cam then at Bailey. "Stop for a moment and think how absolutely loathsome and absurd all this is, humans killing other humans because of books written two thousand years ago." He shook his head and gazed out over the serene water; the tall buildings of the Boston skyline reflected brightly off the now mirror-like surface. "They're just books for God's sake."

Everyone was quiet as they considered his words.

"Buried for more than two thousand years. Now it's your choice," said Cam.

Julian picked up a yellowed willow leaf and studied it. He traced the veins with his finger.

"Cam, we sat under this very tree less than thirty-six hours ago, thinking about Cooper––what he would do. Remember, we asked ourselves the wrong question." He looked at Cam for an inkling of recollection. Cam nodded. "Again, we are asking ourselves the wrong question. This is about more than Christianity. What happened yesterday forces us to look at a bigger picture––all religions." He held the leaf up to Cam. "They all depend on scripture––books, very old books. They're absolutely mandatory, like these veins are to this leaf." Julian held the leaf for a moment longer and then let go and watched it weave its way to the ground. "What if all the books are wrong? "

"You're being generous in even wondering," said Cam. "The books are flawed, no doubt. *Amphilochus* is just another instance to add to the list. Genesis has unequivocally been debunked. And the Immaculate Conception? More like immaculate deception. Matthew simply mistranslated the Hebrew word 'almah,' from Isaiah 7:14. You substitute the word, 'virgin,' which Matthew used, with the phrase, 'young woman,' which is closer to its true meaning, and that changes things a lot. Pretty much takes away the basic tenet of a whole religion. I could go on, but there is no need. All scripture is predicated on the existence of some sort of deity, an extraordinarily unlikely notion. Since God is most certainly man-made, then scripture simply represents some sort of multivolume historical novel in which an Orwellian-like Big Brother barks out maxims along with his homicidal edicts while watching our every move. Unfortunately for us, some of the loonies have taken the Orwellian concepts of doublethink and a dystopian future far too seriously."

Julian's shoulder slumped back against the tree. Lines of angst weighed heavily on his cheeks. Breezes whispered through the trees around them. Distant voices from a nearby softball game blew into their lair; argumentative tones rose regarding a play at first. Julian looked up, initially perturbed, then shook his head in amazement.

Unsettled by the quiet, and thinking aloud, Cam said, "So what happens if you punch little holes into a hot air balloon? Not much, at first. The holes are small. But if you make enough holes or a big enough hole, then the hot air really starts to leak out, and the balloon collapses completely. Maybe that's what Cooper and Reverend T. were worried about. That *Amphilochus* is a game-changing hole in the hot air balloon of organized religion."

Julian pondered Cam's thoughts as he studied the codex. "Points well-taken, but the authority of scripture is unquestioned by the multitude. That is what we are dealing with. We have to give the polis new eyes. Get them to look at their Bibles or Korans differently, maybe as maxim-filled self-help books, instead of *manifestos*." He offered Cam a nod of the head and a half smile.

"But the human mind is an absolute belief machine," said Cam. "Humans are wired to believe. And billions of people have invested vast amounts of time and effort to make religions work––validate that belief. Anything that indicates that scripture is bogus will be dismissed, at least subconsciously, simply to justify the previous commitment––the cerebral equivalent of putting good money after bad. So ultimately, it's a brain-wiring issue. A very tough nut to crack." He paused. "Reverend Phillips and those crazies flying the jets yesterday, they're all religious psychopaths. Do you really think that *Amphilochus* will even make a dent in the belief-hard-wiring encoded into their screwed-up brains?"

Julian considered the question. "Maybe. Maybe not. All I know is that there's a hell of a lot of religious intolerance in this world. Maybe if we plant a large sliver of doubt we'll get people––even religious psychopaths––to ask questions, examine their text, and ultimately understand that their way is not the only way."

"You're sure?"

Julian didn't answer.

"It's a zero-sum game," said Cam.

Julian jaws tensed then relaxed. His shoulders drooped.

"Zero-sum. Game theory. One side wins. One side loses. Zero-sum. Not good."

There was no change in Julian's expression.

Cam continued. "It started out non-zero-sum. Way back. The Muslims, Jews, and Christians all worshiped the same God. Muhammad had hopes of bringing the Christians and Jews into a single Muslim religion. He offered olive branches. Incorporated a twenty-four-hour fast into the ritual. He even called it Yom Kippur and had Muslims pray facing Jerusalem. He even had a ban on pork and called Jesus a messenger of God. Something for everyone. Non-zero-sum. Win-win. Then, it all changed. One God became better than the others. All but one text, heretical. All intolerant of the others. Inquisitions. Jihad. A big, fat mess. Zero-sum."

Julian nodded in understanding. "Then, if we let it out of the bag that everything in the Bible may not be kosher, the gulf grows. A bigger zero-sum, if that's possible."

"You got it. You take away the circumstance of a special conception, jettison all the silly miracles, and put words into Jesus's mouth by way of *Amphilochus,* that leaves you with a pretty ordinary guy. That's lots of ammo for the Muslims and Jews."

Julian shifted his gaze, but focused on nothing. He sighed then dropped his hands deep into his pockets.

"Maybe you should sleep on it. No need to make a decision now."

Incredulous certainty returned to Julian's face. "Have you forgotten already? All the deaths. Nearly two thousand years of Dexion. It all ends now!"

"Even if it's the wrong decision?"

Livy took one tentative step forward, reached out, and grasped Julian's hand. She half-turned and took Cam's hand in her other hand. "There is no way to know what the right answer is," she said to no one in particular. Then, looking at Cam, she said, "The only way to end it is to expose it. Like Reverend T. said."

"We have to change the paradigm," said Julian. "In my mind, it can't get much worse. If we do nothing, nothing changes. If by exposing *Amphilochus* we can distance ourselves––and I mean people of the world––from religious bigotry and turn it in the direction of non-zero-sum game, then I say we do it. I truly believe exposing it outweighs the downside, whatever that might be. And if Coop or Reverend T. were still alive today and could bear witness on how the events of yesterday have altered the landscape, I'd like to think they might agree. I hope they might agree."

Cam reached down and picked up what he thought was the willow leaf Julian had dropped, opened his wallet, and carefully placed it between two plastic flaps of the picture sleeve.

Julian and Livy shared a glance and then got an approving nod from Cam.

Julian scanned the park. Night hid in the recesses, slinking out as the sun dipped further in the west. Bashful fireflies clamored in the black pockets, waiting to follow the night. Just for an instant, Julian was back in Harvard Yard reaching for the chapel door. He thought about what had been, and what was, and all that he had to be thankful for, whether it was from twists of fate or God or random events occurring for no particular reason, affecting all those that followed in totally unpredictable ways. Inches from his face, a firefly blinked, illuminating no more than a cubic centimeter of space. *Such is life.*

He discarded the thought and reached for the case.

"Now let's get together with some fine reporter at the *Globe* and give him or her a Pulitzer Prize winning story. After that, let's get something to eat."

He secured Livy's hand in his, wove his way through the nest of willow branches, and ambled over the bridge.

THE END

AUTHOR'S NOTE: The reader may obtain a copy of *Amphilochus* as translated by Julian St. Laurent. via e-mail or snail-mail at Bhughes011@gmail.com. The original document is on display at the Smithsonian Institute in Washington, DC.

Made in United States
North Haven, CT
13 July 2023

38993634R00183